Praise for *After the Fall*

Peter David mixes wry humor . . . with tense drama. . . . [His] narrative is populated by a vast array of previously minor characters from the screen incarnations of *Star Trek*, all vividly fleshed out into well-rounded personalities. . . . This is a whole new *New Frontier*, but no less welcome."
—Sci-Fi Online

"Peter David takes the series in a daring new direction. . . . [Plenty of] audacious surprises. . . . A whole lot of fun."
—Treknation.com

Praise for Peter David and *Star Trek: New Frontier*®

"Peter David is the best *Star Trek* novelist around."
—Starburst

"A new *Star Trek* novel by Peter David is always a good bet. . . . David has made good use of minor characters from the *Star Trek* universe."
—SF Site

"He effortlessly makes the most of his own characters while developing some from small-screen *Trek*."
—Dreamwatch

STAR TREK
NEW FRONTIER®

After the Fall

Peter David

Based upon
STAR TREK: THE NEXT GENERATION®
created by Gene Roddenberry

POCKET BOOKS
New York London Toronto Sydney

POCKET BOOKS, a division of Simon & Schuster, Inc.
1230 Avenue of the Americas, New York, NY 10020

This book is a work of fiction. Names, characters, places, and incidents are products of the author's imagination or are used fictitiously. Any resemblance to actual events or locales or persons, living or dead, is entirely coincidental.

Copyright © 2004 by Paramount Pictures. All Rights Reserved.

Originally published in hardcover in 2004 by Pocket Books

 STAR TREK is a Registered Trademark of Paramount Pictures

This book is published by Pocket Books, a division of Simon & Schuster, Inc., under exclusive license from Paramount Pictures.

ISBN-13: 978-0-7434-9185-3
ISBN-10:   0-7434-9185-8

This Pocket Books paperback printing December 2005

10 9 8 7 6 5 4 3 2 1

POCKET and colophon are registered trademarks of Simon & Schuster, Inc.

Manufactured in the United States of America

For information regarding special discounts for bulk purchases, please contact Simon & Schuster Special Sales at 1-800-456-6798 or business@simonandschuster.com.

A Note to Our Readers

Everything must move forward. Everything must progress. Without progress, there is boredom and even backsliding. The *New Frontier* is no exception to that.

With the exception of the first chapter, *After the Fall* is set three years after the end of the previous *New Frontier* novel, *Stone and Anvil* (and mere days before the events seen in *Star Trek: Nemesis*). As is the case with the real world, a lot has happened in three years. The *New Frontier* cast is not a collection of toys remaining exactly where you left them until you're ready to play with them again. Many members of the *Excalibur* and *Trident* crews have gone down unexpected paths, and you'll be very surprised to see where they've wound up.

We here at *New Frontier* C&C (Command and Control) wanted to make this clear to you so that you won't go through the book waiting for the reset button. There will be no one time traveling to a key point in the past in order to restore the status quo. There will be no shocking revelation that we're in a parallel universe. It is not a hoax, nor a dream, nor an imaginary tale (well, no more imaginary than any of them). What you hold in your hands is the "current" reality of the *New Frontier*. We suspect if our heroes can deal with it, so can you.

So come along and see who's broken up, who's still together, who's where and who's who in the *New Frontier*.

—The Management

BEFORE . . .

i.

On the day Soleta was reasonably sure she was going to die, she found herself both surprised and not surprised to see Ambassador Spock standing at the far end of her cell.

Every joint, every muscle, every synapse in her body seemed inflamed with pain, and yet she still managed to sit up. She wanted to stand, to look properly formal as the occasion might call for. Try as she might, however, she was unable to gather the strength to do so. So she settled for sitting on the dank floor and simply staring at the tall, lean Vulcan. He, in turn, stared at her. No words passed between them for a good long time.

It was Soleta who finally broke the silence. "Well?" she inquired. "Aren't you going to say it?"

He cocked an eyebrow as she knew he would. "What am I expected to say?"

"I believe the appropriate phrase would be, 'How the mighty have fallen.'"

He pondered that for a moment, and then informed her, "That would not be logical."

"Why not?"

"You were never particularly mighty."

"No," and she slumped her head back against the cell wall. "No, I guess I wasn't."

They remained that way for a time, and then Soleta allowed a small smile.

"Do you find your present situation amusing?" asked Spock.

"Not especially. I'm simply considering the fact that, when we first met, I was in a cell. On Thallon. Do you remember?"

"Of course," Spock said in a tone that indicated it was absurd to think he would forget—not the incident itself, but anything at all that had ever happened to him in his entire life.

"It is ironic, the way in which life wraps back upon itself," she said. "You and I, trapped in a dungeon on Thallon, prisoners of the royal family. Then we escape, and in later years members of that same royal family wind up on the Federation ship I'm serving on after their family loses power. And now they are no longer a part of my life, nor I of theirs, and I'm back in a dungeon . . . while from what I hear . . ."

"They are climbing back into power," said Spock. "Yes. That is true. A new Thallonian regime is apparently on the rise. I estimate that in another two point three years, they will be fully in charge. There will, however, likely be marked differences between the former monarchy and the new paradigm. I believe the most likely structure will consist of a—"

"Mr. Spock."

Although naturally any emotion perceivable on his face was minimal, it was still obvious that he was surprised at the interruption.

Soleta sighed. "I don't really care."

"Ah. Because, as matters stand, you will not be alive to see it."

"That's very much how the day is shaping up, yes." She gazed up at him through unfocused eyes. "You're not going to help me, are you."

"Pardon?"

"I said you're not going to help me. Not try to find a way to get me out of here."

"I regret that it is beyond my power to do so."

She snorted disdainfully. "I don't believe that for a moment."

"That something is beyond my power?"

"No. That you would regret anything." She leaned her head back, the cold metal of the cell proving oddly comforting against the back of her head. "Not you. You never regret anything. Ever."

"What would draw you to that conclusion?"

"Well," she almost stammered, as if the reply should be obvious, "because everything you do, you do because it's the logical thing to do."

"So?"

"So?!" Soleta couldn't follow what he was talking about. "So if you always take the logical path, how can you ever have any regrets over it?"

He considered it a moment. "Apparently," he said at last, "you are confusing the logical path with the right path."

"Aren't they the same?"

"No, Soleta. Not at all." Slowly he circled the cell, his hands draped behind his back, his long robes sweeping around his feet. " 'Right' and 'wrong' are purely subjective terms, to be left to theologians and lawmakers. There have been any number of occasions in my life—indeed, I would venture to say, in every-one's lives—where I have been faced not with a right and wrong path, but instead with a variety of paths that are all undesirable. Where one person or group of persons was made to suffer, for instance, instead of another person or persons. In such instances, I made the logical choices, did what had to be done. Given the exact same circumstances, I would make the exact same choice."

"So where do the regrets come from?"

"The regrets, Soleta," he said wistfully, "come from my inability to conceive of a different path that would solve all problems in such a way that none be made to suffer."

She chuckled low in her throat. "That, Mr. Spock, is illogical."

"That, Soleta," he replied, "is precisely my point."

Before she could say anything else, there was the sound of a heavy-duty security lock being disengaged from the door nearby.

Several Romulans entered, dressed in full armor, as was customary for guards. It seemed ludicrous to Soleta; she was hardly in shape to pose a threat.

"Who were you talking to?" demanded the foremost guard. He was looking around the cell suspiciously.

"No one." She realized, upon opening her mouth, that her voice was far more strained and parched than she would have thought. It sounded totally different than it had when she'd been talking with Spock.

She further realized that she was in far more pain than she'd thought she was. There were marks on her from all manner of physical brutality that she had undergone. Strange. Strange that she hadn't felt that earlier or noticed it. It was as if her mind had bifurcated for some strange reason. . . .

Well, not so strange at that.

"Remarkable, isn't it," she said thickly. Her lips were swollen as well; she hadn't noticed that before either. "What the mind will do to protect itself from dealing with what the body's going through."

"What are you talking about?" he demanded.

"Biology. You?"

The guard who'd entered behind the first one was scouring the cell with his scowl. "Who was she talking to?"

"She hasn't answered," said the first. *"Who were you talking to?"*

"That's a very large weapon," she observed. "Do you use it in order to make up for shortcomings in other areas?"

"I'll use it on you, you murdering half-breed!" His hand hovered near the hilt.

"Now there's a threat."

"It's no threat."

"And yet," Soleta said, "I don't see you doing it."

He started to pull his disruptor, the prospect of which didn't bother Soleta one bit, but then the second guard put a hand on his fellow's arm, preventing the precipitous move. The first guard took his hand away from the weapon, but then abruptly brought his foot up and around. He slammed it into Soleta's face.

She didn't even feel it. The impact was sufficient to

knock her backward, but other than that, it didn't register. She was that numb.

Thudding onto the floor, she lay there, her arms out to either side, her legs splayed. Her mouth moved for a moment and then spat out a glob of green blood to the side.

"Who," repeated the guard, "were you talk—?"

"Myself," she said.

"You were talking to yourself."

"Do you see anyone else here?" she inquired, sounding remarkably calm considering her clothes were in tatters and her body was covered with bruises and open wounds.

Clearly they did not. They'd already looked several times.

With mutual looks of exasperation, they strode forward and grabbed Soleta each by one arm. There were several other guards in view as well, and they already had their weapons out.

For one joyous moment, Soleta considered the notion of dropping both of the guards with a nerve pinch. As their bodies sagged to the ground, she would use them as shields for the few seconds it would take to yank their weapons out of their holsters and fire upon the other guards. Once she'd taken all of them down, she would use all her Starfleet training and stealth techniques to make her way to an airfield where she would find a vessel of some sort and get the hell off the Romulan homeworld.

"What are you thinking?" demanded one of the guards.

She rolled her head around to fix her gaze upon him. "What an odd question."

"Answer it."

"I was thinking," she said, "about a cunning escape plan."

"Oh really. And are you planning to put it into effect?"

"No."

"Why not?"

"Too tired . . ."

They were the last words she was able to get out before her head slumped forward.

ii.

Hiren, the Romulan Praetor, had heard much about the female half-breed who had been apprehended, without incident, upon arrival on the homeworld. He had not encountered her himself. An interaction at such an early stage in the interrogation would have been most unseemly. He had people whose job it was to attend to her, and he had every confidence they would do so with their customary efficiency.

So it was with growing surprise that he heard the continued reports, which were telling him far less than he'd been expecting to hear. So much so that he had decided it was time to intervene and see this creature for himself.

He was less than impressed when she was first

dragged in. Two of his guards were hauling her forward. The Praetor was seated in his great chair at the far end of the council room. None of his counselors were present at the moment. He had instead opted for a private conference. There was a large circular table with a partition at one end that allowed people to be brought through so they could stand in the middle of the large O shape, and that was what was done with the female. The guards didn't even have to throw her to the floor. They simply stepped in opposite directions and she slumped down without so much as a murmur of protest. They then moved back out of the table ring, leaving her lying on the floor in a heap.

"Stand up," the Praetor said.

At first she didn't appear to hear him. But then, slowly, she arched her back and then braced herself with her hands and feet. Her chin was outthrust, her back now straight. She was wavering slightly, as if having difficulty remaining standing, but she didn't seem inclined to fall. Her eyes were swollen, her nose broken several times. She was clearly not in good shape.

Hiren's gaze shifted from the female to the guards. "I do not recall," he said slowly, "authorizing physical brutality in attempting to pry information from her." When he spoke, it was with a low rumble in his broad chest. He was wearing a helmet, but his hair was gray under it, and his black-and-gray eyebrows were overgrown and thick. There was not much in the way of mercy in his eyes.

"The physical injuries were not as a result of the interrogation, sir," one of the guards said. "Over the past few days, she has been disrespectful in all that she has done and said. She sustained her injuries during our endeavors to teach her proper respect."

"I see." He considered that, then nodded. "All right. Yes, very well. And you," and he shifted his attention back to the female. "Soleta. Is that not the name you bear?"

She looked as if she wanted to speak, but then winced in pain and instead settled for nodding.

"I have heard much about you."

Still no answer. She just stared at him.

"I thought," he said after some thought, "that you would be taller."

"I am," she told him, "when I stand on ceremony."

This drew an angry growl from one of the guards, who started toward her with the clear intention of punishing her for her insolence. The Praetor, however, chuckled, and put a hand out. This stopped the guard in his tracks, and he reluctantly stepped back.

"Was that," Hiren asked more politely than he needed to, "supposed to be a joke?"

"That was the plan."

"I can see why my guards beat you."

"And where, as well."

He studied her for a long moment then, trying to take the measure of her. It was difficult for him to decide whether she was remarkably brave, or simply so disconnected from what was happening that she didn't know enough to be frightened. It was always difficult to determine such things when dealing with Vulcans.

"But you're not precisely a Vulcan, are you," he said, completing the train of thought aloud.

She said nothing.

One of the guards growled, "The Praetor asked you a question, female."

"The Praetor asked me a question to which he already knows the answer," Soleta replied. "He doesn't need me to tell him that which he already knows."

"You are correct," said the Praetor, leaning forward with marked curiosity. "You have Romulan blood in you. But your Starfleet did not know it."

"No. They didn't."

"Fools," he said dismissively. "I can smell it upon you. It seeps from every pore. How could they not know?"

She shrugged. "It was not something that revealed itself in routine physicals."

"But they finally found out."

"Yes."

"Because something happened to you that was more traumatic than a routine physical."

"I was very badly wounded," she said. "During a ground battle in the war."

"The war. The war with the Selelvians and Tholians on one side, and your precious Federation on the other."

"I'm sorry if we made a lot of noise and woke you," said Soleta.

Outraged at her tone, one of the guards came up behind her and this time the Praetor made no effort to stop him. He brought a fist around to cuff her in the back of the head.

Soleta whirled, faster than Hiren would have thought possible, and her hand clamped on the front of the guard's face. It stopped him cold, and her fingers squeezed, tighter and tighter. His hands dropped to his sides, his mouth opened in a voiceless scream, and even as the other guards advanced quickly to get to them, Soleta shoved him away. He tumbled backward and hit the floor, staring up blankly at the ceiling.

Without pause, Soleta turned back to face the Praetor, and guards were bringing up their weapons and aiming from every direction. She was the merest pull of a finger away from enough firepower to kill her ten times over.

Hiren was on his feet, and he raised a hand and said, *"No one move!"* His voice thundered across the room, demanding complete and immediate obedience. He was not disappointed.

Soleta was carved from ice. She literally did not look as if she cared whether she lived or died in the next few moments.

"What did you do to him?" demanded Hiren.

"I used the Vulcan death grip."

"There's no such thing as a Vulcan death grip."

She looked at the Praetor, looked at the guard whose face was a series of green blotches, and then looked back at the Praetor. "There is now," she said calmly.

"The Romulan blood in you no doubt inspired you."

"No doubt."

"Praetor!" one of the guards called out. His disruptor was still leveled upon Soleta, as were the weapons of all the other guards. Clearly he was looking for permission to annihilate the upstart half-breed.

"Lower your weapons, Centurion," said the Praetor mildly.

"But Praetor—!"

Hiren's brow darkened. " 'But' and 'Praetor' are two words joined at the speaker's peril, Centurion."

Slowly the guard lowered his weapon, as did the others. For her part, Soleta didn't react at all. Her death could have been a second away and she wouldn't have acted any differently. The casual viciousness she had displayed boiled in her Romulan blood, but her pure inscrutability certainly came from her Vulcan aspect.

"You were badly wounded." He spoke as if nothing had happened in the intervening moments between when he'd last been speaking to her and now.

"Yes."

"In the ground battle."

"Yes."

"And while they were putting you back together, the detailed tests they performed upon you revealed your Romulan heritage."

"Yes."

"A heritage you inherited through the fact that a Romulan became involved with your Vulcan mother."

"No," and her lips thinned. "When a Romulan named Rajari raped my Vulcan mother."

"You have only your mother's word that she was raped."

" 'Only' and 'your mother's word' are four words joined at the speaker's peril, Praetor."

There were collective, barely stifled gasps from all around, and it seemed for a moment that the guards were once more about to open fire on her. A severe glance from Hiren was enough to keep them in place, albeit barely. "You, female, do not seem to have much regard for what could happen to you, due to that mouth of yours."

"You can only kill me once, Praetor."

"Don't be so certain," he told her. "We're very inventive."

She inclined her head slightly in acknowledgment of that possibility, but otherwise was silent.

"So Starfleet confronted you about your background. And you admitted you knew of it and deliberately kept the information from them." When she nodded, he continued, "And their response was . . . ?"

"The office of the Starfleet senior counselor decided I would be reduced in rank and reassigned to a job requiring lower-level security clearance."

"And your response was . . . ?"

"I left."

"I see." He paused. "Your commanding officer. Did he have an opinion on this?"

"He fought the Starfleet decision. He was prepared to resign over it. He did not do so only out of deference to my wishes."

"So he did nothing."

"No, he did something."

"What did he do?"

"Put the Starfleet senior counselor in the hospital."

The response caught Hiren so off guard that he blurted out a laugh. Soleta, as always, remained impassive. The Praetor calmed himself and noted that the guards kept casting uneasy glances at the corpse of the fallen guard upon the floor. He did nothing about it. It pleased him on some level that they were discomfited.

"Your commanding officer sounds like quite an individual."

"He was."

"How did you become so badly injured in the firefight?"

"Saving the life of my commanding officer's wife."

"I see. Very well. And you decided, after all that, that the best thing for you was to come here, the home of your mother's rapist."

"Yes."

"Why?"

"Because," she said evenly, "I am someone who needs to feel a part of something. Once, it had been Starfleet. It no longer is. I cannot be part of the Vulcan race, for I am not one of them. So I reasoned that it would be the best course of action to endeavor to try and be part of the Romulan race."

"And you thought we would accept you, just like that."

"I did not know how you would react. I presented myself to your officials."

"You presented yourself," said Hiren, allowing an edge of anger in his voice, "as partly responsible for a bombing that resulted in the deaths of many Romulan nobles."

"That is correct."

"A bombing you claim . . ." He glanced at the report in front of him. He had been looking at it from time to time surreptitiously, but now he made a great show of consulting it. ". . . was masterminded by your father, Rajari . . . even though he was dead at the time."

"I was his cat's-paw, yes. I had no idea of the true nature of the mechanism I was setting into motion until I had already done so."

"Well," said the Praetor levelly, "such gullibility on your part doesn't do much to recommend you, does it."

"No, Praetor."

"And how would you react, I wonder, upon learning that my brother was in that building when it exploded."

"I would extend my condolences."

"Your condolences," Hiren informed her, "will not bring him back."

"No, Praetor. A time machine or magic spell would be the only things that could do that, and I have access to neither. My condolences are all I have to offer."

"You could offer up your life."

Soleta's gaze never flickered from his.

"You could offer up your life," he repeated, "as a sign of penance."

"I cannot do that, Praetor."

"Because you are afraid," he said triumphantly.

"No. Because I am surrounded by armed guards who are ready to annihilate me the moment you give permission. My life, and the disposition thereof, is not in my control, and has not been since the moment I set foot on this planet. I can't offer up something that is not mine to give . . . although, obviously, it is yours to take."

"So you admit I can take your life."

"If I make any sort of threatening move, Praetor, your people will turn me into a small pile of gelatin. To deny that you can take my life would be insanity."

Slowly he began to walk around the table, his arms folded across his barrel chest. "You knew that you would be given a skeptical reaction, and to exacerbate your situation, you admitted involvement in the bombing. Why in the stars would you do such a thing?"

"Because I lived for years with a secret that I was worried would eventually come out . . . and it did, to my detriment. If I am to start over again, as I'm seeking to do, I do not wish to repeat the same mistake. I want to live with my conscience clear, not fear what will happen if the truth of a secret suddenly becomes common knowledge. Accept me for my mistakes, or . . ."

"Or kill you?"

"I have nowhere else to go, Praetor," she said. "If I am rejected here . . . I may well decide simply to end matters myself, rather than have to cope with the reality of being alone in the galaxy."

"How maudlin."

"Perhaps. It is, however, how I feel."

"All right," he said after a moment's consideration, "I admit you present certain . . . possibilities. However, we have grave doubts about your loyalty to the Romulan Empire."

"Doubts."

"Grave ones," he said, nodding. "Our interrogators asked you questions about Starfleet. You refused to answer. Questions about assignment of Starfleet forces. Crew complements in both your ships and your deep-space stations. Possible weaknesses in planetary defense grids . . ."

"I refused to answer those, yes."

"So then we began interrogating you with escalating degrees of severity. And still you refused to cooperate."

"Yes."

"Are you, in fact, a Federation spy?"

"No, I am not."

"If you were," Hiren demanded challengingly, "would you admit to it?"

"Of course not."

"Then why should I believe you?"

"You shouldn't. If you do, you're a fool. You know nothing of me."

"I know this much," said the Praetor. "My very efficient gatherers of information have subjected you to all manner of incentive in order to learn what you know of the Starfleet matters I just asked you about."

"Yes."

"And you told them nothing."

"I know. I was there."

"I don't understand," he said, leaning forward, his hands resting on the edge of the table. "You were forced out of Starfleet. You owe them nothing. It is the height of absurdity to allow yourself to be treated this way in order to protect an organization that tossed you aside."

"They didn't toss me aside," she told him. "I was . . ."

For the first time she appeared to hesitate. Her attitude of almost infinite self-confidence and glibness failed her for the moment. She looked down, licked her swollen lips, then faced the Praetor's stare once more. "I was not candid with them when I first learned of my . . . my nature. For every moment that I served with the knowledge locked within me, I was false to them. They deserved better than that, and I was not . . . strong enough to give it to them. Their actions were entirely appropriate."

"Yet you were not so sanguine about their actions that you opted to stay."

"I had known the freedom of the galaxy on a starship, Praetor. To be bound behind a desk, to never walk the decks of a . . . to never serve . . ."

She started to choke. Hiren was certain she was about to burst into sobs. He would not have blamed her. He had seen far stronger individuals become slobbering wrecks after far shorter periods of interrogation than she'd endured. But then she took a deep breath and composed herself once more. "I . . . couldn't stay," she said simply. "But I can't betray them now."

"If we continue to interrogate you as we have, you will eventually die if you don't cooperate," he told her.

"Your mind, your body, will not be able to withstand it. One or the other will give up. If it is your mind, then your body will be a husk, and of no use, so we will destroy it. If it is your body, then obviously the mind is moot. Why subject yourself to that? Tell us what we want to know."

"No."

"You dare say 'no' to me?"

"I have no choice in the matter."

"You do."

"Would that I did," she said with obvious sadness.

"Then I have no choice either."

He pulled a disruptor from his side. It was larger than the weaponry of his guards. His master-at-arms swore that it was capable of putting a hole in a starship while firing from the planet's surface. Hiren had never had the opportunity to test the veracity of this claim, but there was no denying the power the disruptor generated. If he fired it at Soleta, what was left of her would wind up in the next room.

"A harsh solution," she sighed.

"Or merciful, depending upon your point of view."

"Since my point of view is your weapon's muzzle . . ."

"Yes," agreed the Praetor, "and it will be your last point of view. Tell my people what they wish to know. Tell us everything you can about Starfleet, and I will be merciful."

"I can't do that."

"Then you will die."

"That I can do."

He held the weapon steady, pointed at her face. Any

guard who was remotely within range of the blast area backed out of the way.

"Cooperate," he urged her.

"No."

"*Dammit, female!*" he thundered, and the air of affability he'd displayed so well dissolved. "Enough games! Enough banter! You may tell me all you wish that you care not whether you live or die, but know you now that your death is imminent! Imminent and woefully unnecessary! Cooperate with my interrogators and you will be permitted to live. Not only live, but live well." His tone altered slightly to a blend of cajoling and threatening. "You desire to take up residence on this world? That can be arranged. You will live, not like a lord, but well. Quite well. And comfortably. An honored guest, if you wish, for the rest of your long life." Then his voice hardened and there was clearly no bargaining with it. "But this is your only opportunity to take advantage of that offer. It has a life span of exactly twenty seconds. After that, I will save both my interrogators and you much wasted time. Twenty seconds, female. Nineteen . . . eight—"

She raised a hand. "You don't need to do that."

A thin smile appeared on his face. "So you submit?"

"No. It's just that I have a fairly accurate time sense, and so know when twenty seconds are up. If you would like, I can simply inform you when the time's elapsed."

He stared at her, incredulous. This slip of a female, unblinking, uncaring, retaining loyalty to an organization that had displayed no loyalty to her. In the face of certain death, her attitude was madness . . . suicide . . .

"That's twenty," she said matter-of-factly. Her gaze never wavered. It wasn't as if she were daring him to shoot her. She wasn't that crazy. She had simply made up her mind and was willing to live, or die, with the consequences.

"You're a fool."

"Then I will die as I have lived."

For a long moment, so long that it seemed as if time itself had slowed to a crawl, nothing happened.

And then the Praetor slowly lowered his weapon. If the guards looked surprised, or disgusted, or if they disapproved, they were wise enough not to show it.

"In addition to being a fool, Soleta . . . you are also very loyal."

"Yes."

"Had you told me all you knew of Starfleet, once you were done, I would have killed you since you would have been of no further use to me."

"I suspected that might be the case," she admitted. "But either way, my suspicions had no bearing on my actions."

"I did not think so. So tell me, Soleta . . . if I were to find a use for you . . . would I warrant that same brand of loyalty?"

"No matter how long I were in your employ, I would still never answer the sort of questions you demanded about Starfleet. . . ."

"To hell with Starfleet," he said contemptuously. "Do you seriously believe Starfleet has any true secrets from us? We know what they are up to, they know what we are up to. There's no knowledge that a former

Starfleet lieutenant would have possessed that we do not already have. I am asking if the situation were reversed, could you be trusted to sustain the same degree of discretion for any . . . assignments . . . that I might dispense to you."

"Yes, Praetor."

"Even if those assignments ran contrary to Starfleet interests?"

That brought her up short. As unlikely as it seemed, apparently she had not considered that. She gave it some thought. Hiren waited. Finally she said, "My loyalty to Starfleet, Praetor, extends to all that has gone before . . . but not all that is to come. If I am to be part of something else . . . then I cannot do it in half-measures. I won't betray my old life . . . but my new life would start now, if you would have me."

"Is that the Romulan within you talking? Or the Vulcan?"

"The Vulcan, most definitely."

"How do you know?"

"Because," she said, "I do not know the rightness or the wrongness of it . . . but it is most definitely the logical thing to do."

AFTER . . .

New Thallon

i.

Prime Minister Si Cwan could feel it in his bones: This was going to be a good day.

At that moment he was busy stretching not only his bones, but his muscles. It was the first thing he always did when he awoke each morning. He was very much the creature of habit, most methodical. First he would simply lie there a moment, staring up at the ceiling. At that point he was already fully awake; if someone were coming at him with a knife, he would be up and out of bed in a heartbeat, ready to take on and destroy his assailant. Barring such an extraordinary need for alacrity, however, he was content to allow the reality of a new day to creep upon him rather than reaching out, seizing it, and strangling it.

After lying there silently for a time, he would work his muscles. He began with his feet, turning them at the ankles, then drew his legs up and down, flexing his knees. Eventually he worked his way up to his arms, where he would bring his palms together and push them against each other, working the muscles until he was satisfied they were good and loose. Then he would rotate his head, freeing up his neck.

After that, he would make love to his wife.

Not always. But more often than not.

Making love to her was always the first confirmation for him that the day was going to be as good a day as he hoped.

Thoroughly relaxed, his muscles tingling as the blood flowed through them, he reached over to his wife's naked back. He never failed to be impressed by how clearly delineated her spine was; he could see practically every bone. It was probably because she was so slender. His red hand was a stark contrast to the paleness of her own skin. He rested one finger at the top of her spine, just below her hair, and started to run it down her back. She trembled slightly at the touch, indicating her first signs of wakefulness, and his hand made its way toward the top of her bare buttocks.

At which point, to Si Cwan's surprise, she reached back and batted his hand away.

He looked at his own hand in surprise, as if it had let him down somehow. His wife, meantime, was fighting her way toward wakefulness. She gazed at him through bleary eyes, as if trying to remember who she was, who he was, and what the hell they were doing in bed together.

"Oh," she said finally. "Right. Of course not."

He stared at her. "What?"

"I'm . . . sorry." She blinked owlishly, then brought up her arm to shield it from the rays of the morning sun filtering in through the large window nearby. "Just . . . finishing a conversation . . ."

"What conversation?"

"Having it . . . in a dream."

"That makes sense," said Si Cwan. He looked at her a bit accusingly. "You slapped my hand away."

"Did I?" She glanced at his hand. "Sorry. I just . . . you startled me awake, that's all."

"You usually like it when I—"

"I know, I know. I just . . ." She reached over and patted his shoulder consolingly. "I didn't sleep well. Had a lot of bad dreams."

"About what?"

"It doesn't matter."

"It does to me, Robin," and he propped himself up on one elbow. "Among my people, dreams can be indicators of prescience. They should be studied for the slightest hint of what they may reveal about the future."

"Cwan . . ." Robin Lefler was shaking her head. "You're overreacting. . . ."

"I am reacting just precisely as much as is required. Now tell me your dream."

"All right," she said. "You were explaining to me how you were going to far prefer being a woman from now on, and then Mackenzie Calhoun—nattily attired in a black tuxedo which nicely complemented your chiffon evening gown—swept you away across a ballroom while his late son, Xyon, led the orchestra in a rousing polka."

Si Cwan briefly considered this, and then said,

"Then again, there are times when dreams should simply be dismissed as the mute ravings of a demented mind."

"That's probably for the best," she agreed.

Once more he reached over toward her, clearly intending to cup her breasts, and yet again she pulled away. "Robin—!"

"I have a headache, Cwan! I know it sounds cliché, but I do. That happens when I don't get much sleep. I'm just . . . I'm not in the mood right now. Okay? It's not that I don't love you, or that I'm not attracted to you. You know I'm still attracted, right?"

"Of course I do. What woman in her right mind wouldn't be?" he asked matter-of-factly.

"Right. Okay. So just . . . ease off, all right?"

"All right," he agreed. He paused and then said, "You know . . . you might just want to take the day off."

"Oh, really. And what would I do on my 'day off'?"

"I had that holosuite built for you. You could do whatever you wanted. Go wherever you wanted."

"I know, I know," she sighed. "Maybe I will. I don't know. Just . . . look, don't hate me just because I'm in a bad mood. . . ."

"Of course I don't hate you," he said, sounding surprised. "What an absurd thing to say."

"Thanks. I appreciate it."

He watched her slide out of the bed and admired her naked body for as long as it took her to slip a robe on. He began to ask her if she would be joining him for breakfast, but all too quickly she made her way across their large bedroom chamber and into the bathroom.

Moments later he heard the hydro shower come on.

Si Cwan flopped back onto the bed, allowing his head to sink into the pillow.

It appeared this day, for which he had such high hopes, was already off to a less promising start than he'd anticipated.

ii.

The news that the Priatians had arrived was initially brought to Robin Lefler. It was brought to her because none of the aides on Si Cwan's staff wanted to deal with the prospect of bringing it directly to Si Cwan himself.

This quickly became evident to Robin as she looked up from her work when Ankar delivered the news. Ankar was one of the senior aides, and he was very careful not to simply barge into Robin's small but efficiently organized office. As Si Cwan's wife, she could have had the largest office in the Protectorate manor. But her position as Starfleet liaison entitled her to something far more modest, and she had opted for conservative appearances over ostentation.

"Come," she had called upon hearing the door chime, and the door slid aside to reveal a clearly agitated Ankar. From his face, one would never have known he was concerned about anything, for his inscrutability was legendary. But Robin had learned to read him well, and could tell there was something up from the aimless way in which his hands moved about.

"What's the problem, Ankar?" she asked, turning aside the computer screen upon which she had been studying recent updates from Starfleet on known hostile races.

"It was felt you should know," said Ankar, "that a group of Priatians have arrived."

She stared blankly at him. "Have they?"

"Yes."

"And you felt it necessary to tell me."

"Yes."

"Should I know who the Priatians are?" she inquired.

"There is no reason for you to, ma'am," Ankar assured her. "They have had no interaction with either you or the Prime Minister since you and he were intimately bonded over a year ago. . . ."

She rubbed the bridge of her nose. "I cannot emphasize to you how much I prefer the term 'married.' "

" 'Married'?"

" 'Wedded' would suffice. 'Joined in bonds of holy matrimony' even works. But 'intimately bonded' . . . I mean, God, it sounds like something out of a romance novel."

" 'Married.' " He rolled the word around on his tongue experimentally, then nodded in apparent satisfaction and continued, "The Priatians have not really been heard from since you and Si Cwan were . . . married. With so much going on, between the wars, the rebuilding of the empire into the Protectorate . . . it is easy to understand how they may have escaped your notice. That you wouldn't know who they are."

"Okay," she said uneasily. "I appreciate your letting me off the hook in that respect. But that still leaves the question on the table as to why you'd tell me that a delegation . . . I assume it's a delegation?" He nodded. "A delegation," she continued, "of Priatians has arrived. I mean, are they here to see me?"

"Not as such, no," Ankar admitted.

"Meaning they want to see Si Cwan."

"Yes."

"And not me."

"That's correct."

"But you—meaning you and the other aides—are trying to fob them off on me."

"I would not use the term 'fob off,' " he corrected her cautiously.

"Well, I sure hope you're not gonna be going with 'intimately bonded,' because . . ." Her voice trailed off and her lips thinned. Understanding began to dawn. "I may not be familiar with these Priatians . . . but Si Cwan is."

"Yes," said Ankar. His shoulders sagged in what appeared to be relief.

"And for whatever reason, he's not going to be happy to see them."

"Yes."

"And you didn't want to have to deal with his reaction, so you figured that if I brought them to Si Cwan, his reaction would be far more restrained."

He crisscrossed his arms and bowed to her. "Madam is wise beyond her gender and station."

"And you are gutless beyond your years."

"Thank you, madam," and he bowed again. "Shall I . . . ?"

"Bring them in?" Robin leaned back in her chair and gestured expansively. "Why the hell not?"

For a third time he bowed as he backed out of the room. Minutes later there was another chime at her door, and it slid open to reveal what she immediately took to be the Priatian delegation.

There were three of them. They did not, at first glance, seem particularly impressive. Subsequent glances did little to improve the initial impression.

Actually, they reminded her a bit of squids.

Their heads were soft, fleshy and elongated, with two silvery black eyes fixed upon her unblinkingly. Two tentacles were protruding from either side of their copious robes, somewhere right around the middle, about where their waist would have been had they been human. When they moved forward, it was with a soft sound that was a combination of popping and sucking, very faint but constant. It made her wonder just exactly what their means of locomotion was, and then she decided that she'd really prefer not to find out.

The lead Priatian spoke, and he didn't seem to be opening anything resembling a mouth. She quickly realized that the angles of his head served to hide a remarkably narrow jawline and that there was indeed a mouth hidden somewhere beneath there. She made no endeavor to try and figure out where their organs for smelling and hearing were, suspecting she might not be too thrilled with the answer.

"Greetings, Ambassador Cwan Mate," said the Priatian in a warbling voice. "I am Keesala. These are my associates, Pembark and Marzan."

"Actually, I'm not technically an ambassador, since I'm still attached to the Office of Interplanetary Affairs, a division of Starfleet. Due to the specific circumstances of my situation and the volatile history of the region, I'm here in more of an advisory capacity and guarding Starfleet's interests. So the best way to address me would be as Lieutenant Commander Lefler."

"Oh," said Keesala. "Very well. Lieutenant Commander Lefler, I bring you greetings from—"

Just to satisfy her curiosity, and sensing that the introduction might last some moments, she mumbled a unique code word, which shut off, for four seconds, the universal translator embedded in her ear. Just as she thought, the result was a series of clicks and what sounded like slurps coming from the Priatian's mouth. Seconds later, the universal translator kicked back in.

"—and our ancestors going back six generations," finished Keesala. His face was hardly the most expressive thing she'd ever seen, but he seemed pleased that he had accomplished the introduction. She gestured for him to take a seat. Not surprisingly, he and the others remained standing. "We have come here seeking an audience with Prime Minister Cwan and the advisory council of the Thallonian Protectorate."

"I see." Even though nothing had been discussed, Robin had the strangest feeling that she was seriously about to put her foot into a hornets' nest. Certainly if Ankar had been so determined to avoid Si Cwan's reaction, it wasn't going to be anything good. "And would they know what this is in regards to?"

"I suspect they will, yes," Keesala said gravely.

"Would you care to tell me?" she asked.

"Would it benefit us?"

She gave that a moment's consideration. "I don't see how it could hurt," she said. "I mean, I'm getting the distinct feeling—just a hunch, mind you—that you think you're not going to get a fair hearing."

"Your hunch," said Pembark, speaking up for the first time, "is most canny." Marzan glanced at Pembark but remained silent.

"So, that being the case," Robin said, "it's all to your advantage to garner my alliance. I can get you heard where ordinarily you might not be."

"Very well," said Keesala, who, when one came right down to it, hadn't been all that difficult to convince. "We have come here over a matter of some territory."

"I see. Whose?"

"Ours."

"All right." Lefler was with them so far. "So where is this territory?"

"It is beneath your feet."

Robin's eyebrows knit as she stared downward. "You mean it's subterranean?"

"No. It is the planet upon which you are currently dwelling."

She leaned back in her chair, steepling her fingers. "You're saying this world that's now called 'New Thallon' was once your world."

"That is not correct."

"It's not?"

"We are saying," Pembark spoke up, "that all the planets are ours. All of them."

"In the Milky Way galaxy?" As claims went, she was having a good deal of trouble buying into it.

"Of course not," said Keesala.

"Well, that's a re—"

"Merely all the planets in Thallonian space."

"—lief," finished Robin, feeling suddenly a lot older. She shifted uneasily in her chair. "So you're saying . . . what? That you're planning to conquer Thallonian space? Is that what this is? A threat?"

"Not at all," Keesala assured her. Pembark and the still mute Marzan made some odd gesture that appeared to be nodding in agreement, although Robin couldn't be one hundred percent certain.

"So you're not threatening us."

"No."

"Then I don't understand."

Although Keesala's face continued to convey little in terms of expression, she was positive he was regarding her pityingly. "How tragic that an appeal to compassion, to justice, to rightness . . . these things are incomprehensible to you. That all you understand are threats."

"That is not fair!" Robin protested. "No one's said anything about compassion or rightness. I have a very highly defined sense of justice, thank you very much, and the United Federation of Planets, which I represent, shares that sense. The problem is that you still haven't made clear to me exactly what the nature of your cause or complaint is."

"We have told you. We desire the return of our planets."

"Okay, here's the thing," Robin said, getting to her feet and deciding that now might not be a bad time to usher them out of her office.

And suddenly Marzan spoke up.

As opposed to the higher-register, quavering sound of the other Priatians' voices, Marzan's voice was deep and powerful. Robin almost felt as if the walls around her were vibrating slightly in response. Marzan glided forward a few feet. When he orated, it was with such authority that Robin sat back down without even realizing she had done so.

"In the days of our ancestors," Marzan intoned, "we were as many in number as the stars in the night sky. The Many Worlds were ours, for they had always been ours. Other races, other species developed on them as well, with their own societies and beliefs. But all of them acknowledged that we were first among equals, and deferred to us in all things. We were the children of the founders of life, and all these worlds had been bequeathed us. Our population stretched from one end of this stellar territory to the other. And the founders of life, whom we called 'the Wanderers,' looked upon the population that they had placed upon the Many Worlds, and found it good. At which point, they opted to continue their Wanderings, so as to place more of their seed in other realms. 'Wait for us here, our children,' they said unto us, 'for eventually, we shall return from our wanderings when our work is done, and we will settle here and reside with our children on the Many Worlds. We will bring with us the final great peace and the final great prosperity.' "

Robin started to ask a question, but Marzan kept right on talking. Quickly she closed her mouth, not wanting to appear rude . . . and at the same time dreading the prospect of having to provide a report of this incident to Starfleet. The other Priatians, in the meantime, barely seemed aware of their surroundings. They had been caught up in Marzan's narrative, bowing back and forth slightly and continually murmuring under their breath what could only be described as prayers.

"And then," continued Marzan, "long after the departure of the Wanderers, the New Ones arrived. They came to the Many Worlds seeking refuge, claiming their own environment had become inhospitable to them. We allowed the New Ones sanctuary in the Many Worlds. We did not understand that these New Ones were not the last. Not remotely. They were the vanguard, and more New Ones arrived, and more. We, the children of the Wanderers, were a peaceful folk. We did not realize the threat the New Ones presented until they had so insinuated themselves into our society that it was too late. We gave them entire worlds, for we felt it would be selfish for us to deny them residence in the Many Worlds. That the Wanderers had left us such a bounty, it would be sinful to prevent others from sharing in it. We were wrong. Wrong and foolish, for however much we gave the New Ones, they demanded more. And more."

"And more," intoned the others.

"And more," said Marzan.

"And—"

"*I get it!*" Robin blurted out. They looked most surprised at the interruption, and for a moment Robin felt badly, but only for a moment. Then she took a breath, let it out slowly, and repeated more softly, "I get it. The point is made. They kept wanting more. The situation isn't incomprehensible to me. Believe it or not, it's not even unprecedented in human history. So . . . what you're saying is that these New Ones, these are the ancestors of what we would now refer to as the Thallonians?"

"That is correct," said Keesala. Marzan, as if responding to an unspoken cue, stepped back so that he was in line with Pembark. "Over many years, they kept at us, wearing us down in many ways. First we met them with compromise, and then we eventually met them with force. But they had many ways to undermine us, and were far craftier than we."

"Some believe," Pembark spoke up, "that the Wanderers sent them as a test . . . a test that we failed."

Keesala fired him what appeared to be, even with his fairly inscrutable mien, a warning glance. "Others, such as myself, do not believe that," Keesala said cautiously. "In fact, most of us do not. We believe we treated the New Ones as the Wanderers would have wanted us to—with trust and compassion. And that we were betrayed as a people. And that the Wanderers will avenge this inequity upon their return."

Abruptly they lapsed into silence, and Robin felt

the need to try and fill that silence. "Look," she said, rapping her fingers on the desk, "there's no doubt your people got something of a raw deal. But by your own admission, it was a long time ago. History is not like a starship. You can't change the course of it simply through willpower."

"With respect, madam," replied Keesala, "that is the *only* way one can change it."

"All right, fair enough," she allowed with a small smile. "But what I'm saying is that, even if it all played out exactly the way you describe it . . . there are people on those worlds now. Whereas all of you are on . . . what? One?"

"One," confirmed Keesala.

"Right, exactly. That's what I thought. Let's say, just for laughs—"

The Priatians promptly emitted a high-pitched noise so annoying that she clapped her hands to her ears. *"What the hell are you doing?"*

"We are laughing," Keesala explained. "We thought it was what you desired."

She moaned inwardly. "Let us just say," she began again, cautious to avoid any flippant idioms, "that everyone living on those worlds cleared out tomorrow. Which won't happen, but let's say it did. It's not as if your people would be able to turn around and make use of all those worlds. Your population is too small."

"That," Keesala said, "would be our concern, not yours."

"Yes, I suppose it would be. But, let's face it . . . either way, it's not going to happen."

"Then we cannot be held responsible for what will occur."

"What will occur . . . when?" she asked cautiously.

"When the Wanderers return and cause all those residing in what is now called Thallonian space to depart."

"I see," she said, once more tapping her fingers. "And when, uh . . . do you perceive this happenstance will, uh . . . happen?"

"Soon," Keesala said, and Pembark added, "Very soon."

"You know what?" sighed Robin Lefler. "I had a feeling you were going to say exactly that."

iii.

The only thing that could make this day worse would be if the Priatians showed up.

The Grand Chamber of the New Thallonian Protectorate was designed in a series of concentric circles of tables arranged in stadium-seating style. There had been much debate about exactly how to set up who would be sitting at what level. Ultimately they had settled on the simplest, most nondiscriminatory way possible: geography. The worlds whose orbits brought them closest to the world of New Thallon were the closest to the twin tables of the prime minister and prime arbiter, the facing tables at which sat Si Cwan and his opposite number, the prime arbiter, Fhermus of the House of

Fhermus (as was customary in that House, the head of the House changed his name from whatever it had been to the House name upon his ascension).

Fhermus was a Nelkarite, hairless and gold-skinned like the rest of his race, although tall and powerfully built. The Nelkarites had had their share of political uprisings in the past. Partly because of that, and partly in spite of it, the Nelkarites had been among the first to embrace the notion of the New Thallonian Protectorate. Furthermore, Fhermus himself had been a major supporter of the notion that such a protectorate simply would not work unless Si Cwan himself were a part of it in a major way.

It was not a concept that Si Cwan had readily embraced, since he'd been rather badly burned during a similar endeavor undertaken by another race several years earlier. Indeed, Si Cwan had come to the conclusion that he simply could not work within any sort of governmental system. What he knew, what he understood, was the way of the monarchy. He was no politician. He was a member of the ruling class. It had been his family and those who had come before who had built up the Thallonian Empire into a mighty body of worlds. Who had kept peace through tyranny in the section of space the Federation bloodlessly referred to as Sector 221-G. And when the Thallonian Empire had collapsed, the entire sector had dissolved into chaos as old rivalries, long repressed, broke out anew.

The Federation had dispatched the *U.S.S. Excalibur*, under the command of Mackenzie Calhoun . . . supplemented later on by the *Trident*, captained by Calhoun's wife, Elizabeth Shelby . . . to help maintain order in the escalating disarray. Si Cwan had signed on (although "stowed away" was the more accurate term) to serve as a sort of roving guide and ambassador, since there were still many who had the greatest respect for him and what his family represented. He had even managed to find and rescue his younger sister, Kalinda, long feared to be dead.

During his time of service, he had cherished the notion of a new Thallonian Empire that would bring unity and glory back to Sector 221-G. A neighboring race, the Danteri, had offered him just that opportunity, but it had gone horribly awry. So when a coalition of worlds in the former Thallonian Empire sought him out, he'd been understandably hesitant.

As he worked with Fhermus, however, and representatives from other worlds as well, a workable government model had evolved. Si Cwan, as the elected prime minister, was effectively the ruling head of the Protectorate. Fhermus, as prime arbiter, was the elected Voice of the People. What typically frustrated Si Cwan the most was the notion of having to deal with dozens of different voices and trying to accommodate all of them, when he'd much rather just hack off their heads and be done with them. Fhermus was the go-between, dealing with the representatives of the fifty-seven different races in Thallonian space, sifting through their concerns, establishing priorities, smoothing over difficulties when it was possible. He was also their advocate when it came to convincing Si Cwan of actions to be authorized and taken.

All discussions between Fhermus and Si Cwan were open and public, held right there on the floor of the Grand Chamber. Some of the arguments and debates between Si Cwan and Fhermus bordered on the epic, with nuanced disagreements giving way to heated shouting matches. The bottom line, however, was that Si Cwan and Fhermus shared a deep and abiding respect for each other's character and intellect. One or the other could give in and neither would ultimately feel threatened by it.

It was a delicate balance, but one that the two men had successfully transformed into—if not the perfect form of government—certainly something far superior to the borderline anarchy that had previously characterized the region.

Unfortunately, it now seemed as if that balance was being threatened, and for possibly the most ludicrous reason of all . . . at least insofar as Si Cwan was concerned.

As opposed to the usual situation where Si Cwan and Fhermus were arguing with each other, a special session had been called and the two regular adversaries were both being grilled by the other representatives.

It was predictable that the most vocal voice of protest was the representative from Boragi III. The Boragi were notorious for stirring things up until a conflict arose, manipulating all sides while staying carefully neutral, and then coming in and picking up the pieces. Knowing their history as a race, Si Cwan had kept a wary eye on their reps, certain it was only a matter of time before they tried one of their typical maneuvers.

All things considered, they'd actually waited longer than Si Cwan would have credited them with being willing to wait.

The Boragi's delegate, Tusari Gyn, was on his feet. His skin was sallow, the bone ridge of his forehead protruding, as he spoke with that faintly unctuous air so typical of his race. His eyes were in constant motion, which was one of the most disconcerting Boragi traits.

"Certainly the esteemed adversaries must see," said Tusari Gyn, "that it is that very adversarial nature to which our government owes so much."

"That is not in dispute here, delegate," Fhermus informed him. "However, what irritates me is your insinuation that this turn of events is somehow going to impact on the ability of either me or my counterpart here," and he indicated Si Cwan, "to carry out our designated duty."

"Oh, but we have insinuated no such thing," Tusari Gyn assured him, employing the imperial prefix of "we," as he usually did. It was a common Boragi tendency. It implied that the entirety of the race thought with one mind and was therefore unanimous in its views. Strength in numbers and all that.

"*Flark!*" snapped back Si Cwan, earning an annoyed glance from Fhermus for the language. He could not have cared less. "That happens to be exactly what you are insinuating, and I for one could not be more offended."

"We intended to give no offense. . . ."

"And yet you've given it anyway." Si Cwan rose from his seat and circled the floor of the Great Chamber.

"We cannot help it if you have taken that which was not intended . . ."

"And we cannot help it if you do not stand behind your clear intent."

Fhermus put up his hands as if trying to ward off more hostility. "This is getting us nowhere," he said, making no attempt to keep the annoyance from his voice.

"The Boragi bring up a fair point," commented the representative from Mandylor V. "This situation represents a clear conflict of interest. Call this whatever you wish, but these developments are nothing less than an alliance between the House of Fhermus and the line of Cwan."

"Our point exactly," said the Boragi, before sitting down to let the Mandylor representative carry the argument. *This*, Si Cwan mused, *is typical. Be at the forefront of the protest and then fade back and let others carry the ball.*

"This is not an alliance," Fhermus protested. "This is . . . is happenstance! Nothing more!"

"How can you say that?" It was the delegate from Respler IV-A. Si Cwan wasn't all that surprised that the Mandylor and Respler delegates were among the first to cry foul. Both worlds had had revolts against the royal family suppressed with rather violent means, back in the day. If anyone was going to be quick to criticize, it was they. "This is as classic an alliance scenario as it gets! Marriage is the traditional means of joining two powerful groups. . . ."

"And I suppose," Si Cwan said, "that my marriage

represented a joining of my family to the Federation? Is that how that works?"

"Well, your spouse's priorities are a matter of some concer—"

The Resplerian's voice trailed off as a chill wafted through the air of the council. Si Cwan stood there for a long moment and then, step by slow step, walked up the stairway of the chamber until he was standing less than five feet away from the representative, who was visibly shaking.

"Were you," Si Cwan asked with exaggerated calm, "casting aspersions upon my wife?"

"In all fairness, Prime Minister," he said, rallying for strength, "you brought her up."

"I am not interested in 'all fairness.'" Si Cwan's voice was flat and even. His expression could have been carved from stone. "I am interested only in what you are saying about my wife."

The Mandylor ambassador chose that moment to step in, doubtless to preserve the alliance his people had with the Resplerians. "Prime Minister," he said, "my colleague is no doubt referring to the expressed concerns that your wife is acting as the eyes and ears of the Federation . . ."

"The activities of this council are broadcast on the ether!" Si Cwan pointed out to him. "There are no secrets here! That was part of the point of conducting our business in this manner. The eyes and ears of the Federation? Let the Federation look and let the Federation listen! Is there anyone here who has something he feels needs to be hidden? Some business that cannot be subjected to Federation scrutiny? Unless, of course, the implication goes deeper than that. Unless someone here desires to imply that my wife is some sort of security threat. A traitor, perhaps, who will stab me in my bed or find a way to sell us out to a hostile race. Is anyone saying that?" His gaze swept the chamber like a phaser beam. "Anyone at all? Anyone challenging my wife's honor?"

A silence fell, shroudlike, upon the proceedings. Si Cwan was pleased. He had a sense that no one believed he was actually going to fall upon anyone who did challenge his wife's honor. On the other hand, clearly, no one was ruling out the possibility either, and so were keeping civil tongues in their heads. That suited Si Cwan just fine. He might be the new and improved people's Si Cwan, but there was certainly no harm at all in keeping some small bit of fear instilled within them.

Fhermus inserted himself into the silence of the chamber. This was exactly the sort of situation that Fhermus thrived upon: an instance where, through force of personality and implied threat, Si Cwan had thrust himself into a delicate predicament. Fhermus, with his melodic vocal tones and mellifluous manner, was going to endeavor to quell it. Si Cwan, when he had walked around the base of the Grand Chamber, had done so in a clockwise manner. Naturally Fhermus moved counterclockwise, which Si Cwan could only note with quiet amusement. The sleeves of Fhermus's garment were wide at the ends, and he inserted one hand into each opposite end. He had once told Si Cwan he did that deliberately so that no one would be watching his hands or any other part of his body language, but instead attend only to the seductive singsong of his voice.

"My colleagues," said Fhermus, "I am perfectly aware that the very nature of this discussion—the fact that the Prime Minister and I are acting as allies to address this matter, rather than in our typical adversarial relationship—would almost, by definition, seem to lend credence to your concerns. But we have been going back and forth about this, both publicly and privately, for nearly a week now and I have yet to hear a single one of you offer an opinion as to what we should have done differently." Someone started to speak up, but Fhermus spoke right over him. "We are, after all, discussing affairs of the heart here. In those matters, the concerns of elders rarely have a say."

"They do on our world," the Mandylor representative spoke up. He slapped the back of one hand into the open palm of the other. "Marriages are arranged! They are the province of the parents! The youth have no say in such matters, none. If they tried to pick their own mates, it would be an outrage!"

"If that works for you," Si Cwan spoke up, "then so much the better for you. But we Thallonians, although we have been known to employ similar practices, do not do so exclusively. And it is, to my understanding, unknown in the Nelkarite society," and he glanced at Fhermus for confirmation. Fhermus inclined his head slightly, indicating the correctness of Si Cwan's words. Cwan continued, "So tell me, delegate: If two of your young people told you in no uncertain terms that you should be compelled to conduct your business in the way, not of your race, but of ours . . . how would you react to that, eh? Enlighten me."

The Mandylorian looked uncomfortable. Pursing his lips a moment, he then admitted, "I would be less than enthused."

" 'Less than enthused,' yes, precisely," said Si Cwan. "And our young people would be no less so 'less than enthused,' don't you think?"

"But we are not speaking of just any young people," the Resplerian now said. Si Cwan felt as if they were double-teaming him. At least he had to deal only with the two for the moment, although he did keep hearing mumbles and murmurs of assent from the others. Let them mutter all they wished. It was those who actually had the nerve to address him directly that concerned him. "We are speaking," continued the Resplerian, "of your sister, Prime Minister, and your son, Prime Arbiter. Certainly they must understand that they are held to a different, higher standard than other young people."

"In point of fact," said Fhermus, "no. Not only do they not understand it, but they would be the first to say that such a double standard would be completely unfair. And anyone here who has youngsters of their own knows how readily the cries of 'But that's unfair!' can come to their lips."

This actually seemed to prompt acknowledging smiles from some delegates. It was the first ray of hope that Si Cwan had encountered since the whole miserable affair began.

The truth was, he could have strangled his sister, Kally, for putting him in this position. But one would never have been able to tell that from the conviction with which he spoke. "The grim fact, my friends," he said, "is that whatever powers of persuasion you might think that my respected adversary and I bring to these chambers in our deliberations . . . they are of absolutely no relevance when it comes to governing the impulses and directions of our own youthful relatives. My sister, Kalinda, met Tiraud, the son of Fhermus. They took to each other instantly. He courted her, although I would have to say that her courting of him was equally as aggressive. Time passed, the relationship flowered, and now Kalinda and Tiraud desire to be lifemates. What would you have us say to them? Seriously? Would you have us say, 'Your feelings are all well and good, but we have to elevate the sensibilities of the fifty-seven delegates above yours?' How many of you are holding us to a standard that you would never think of applying to yourselves? How many of you would truly be willing to make the best interests of your family secondary to political considerations?"

He saw one or two hands hesitantly begin to raise, but just as quickly lowered again. "I thought as much," he said.

"The prime minister's point," said Fhermus, "although a bit more belligerent than I would have liked, is well taken. He and I have willingly placed ourselves into positions that require us to prioritize others above ourselves in almost all things. Our families have not.

Cwan's sister, my son, they came by their relationship honestly. They are in love. But I assure you, the prime minister and I are most definitely not in love." This drew a genuine laugh from almost the entirety of the chamber. "And simply because family members are joined as mates will not prevent us from conducting business as usual."

"And if the union falls apart?" demanded the Mandylorian. "Have you given thought to that? Excessive hostility can be just as much a hindrance as excessive cronyism."

"Considering how the two young ones dote on one another," said Si Cwan, "that is not a major concern for me. But I feel comfortable in saying that, were negative circumstances to arise, they would have no more impact on our ability to fulfill our responsibilities than the positive circumstances."

"And now," Fhermus said, "I believe I speak for the prime minister as well in saying that this subject has been a focus of this chamber for entirely too long, and I think our time and our constituents would be far better served if we moved on to another topic . . . indeed, virtually any other topic."

This sentiment seemed to generate nods of approval. Si Cwan cast a glance at the Boragi. Tusari Gyn's face was inscrutable. Si Cwan had no clue whether Gyn was happy with the outcome or disappointed. Or perhaps he didn't really give a damn either way, and considered this nothing more than a mental exercise.

"Excuse me."

It was Robin's voice. *Uh-oh*, thought Si Cwan, and he had no idea why he thought that up until he saw her standing on the outer rim of the chamber with three members of what were clearly the Priatian race standing behind her.

How did I know? Si Cwan sighed inwardly. He seemed to have some vague recollection that today was supposed to be a good day. But that notion seemed very, very far in the past.

Deep Space

"Do you ever think about her, Xyon?"

Xyon was lying naked on his bed, his arm tucked behind his head, the sheets scattered around. Lyla was next to him, idly fingering the long blond hair that was cascading around his shoulders. When he didn't immediately reply, her hand wandered to his smooth chest, rubbing it in slow circles, which she knew he liked. She didn't say anything immediately, letting the quiet continue. Indeed, it was very quiet in Xyon's ship, a small one-man cruiser that was, at that moment, going nowhere. It simply hung in space, and since space was not exactly the noisiest of places, naturally the ship was deathly silent. It was almost like being in a floating coffin, although Xyon rarely chose to think of it that way.

Her head was resting on his right shoulder. Idly he stroked the top of her head, cupping the bald skin. "What 'her' would that be, Lyla?" Actually, he more or less knew who she was referring to, but was hoping against hope that he was wrong so he wouldn't have to deal with it.

His hope turned out to be futile. "Kalinda. That is who I am referring to, Xyon."

"Yes, I kind of figured that," he admitted. "Why are you asking?"

"Well . . . because, for one thing, I look just like her."

"Okay, fine," he said. He sat up so abruptly that her head almost thudded to the floor, but she corrected her position instantly so that she remained level. Naked, he walked across to the control console of his ship, which was also called the *Lyla*, and demanded, "Do you want me to change your holobody? I can do that for you."

"That won't be necessary, Xyon," she assured him.

But he shook his head. "No, no, you're right. Looking at you now," and his eyes drank in her red skin, her smooth head, the familiar curves of her face, "I can see that maybe I made you look a bit too much like her."

"I'm identical, Xyon."

"All right, then, exactly like her. Designing a holobody . . . it's like writing. You know what they say about writing?"

" 'Reading maketh a full man, conference a ready man, and writing an exact man'?"

He stared at her blankly. "Uhm . . . okay . . . but that wasn't what I was . . ."

" 'Of all those arts in which the wise excel, Nature's chief masterpiece is writing well'?"

"That's not exactly what I had in mind eith—"

" 'Writing is like getting married. One should never . . .' "

"Write what you know!" he blurted out in exasperation.

That brought her up short and she stared at him blankly. "I'm sorry?"

Xyon calmed himself, reminding himself that Lyla was only an artificial intelligence. Perhaps one of the most advanced forms of artificial intelligence in the known galaxy, granted, with roots in what had once been a genuine living brain. But what was powering the ship now was a manufactured creature, and she had her limits. All she was trying to do was understand, and it was fruitless and ridiculous to get upset about her.

"When you write something—a book, a story, whatever," he said, with far more calm in his tone than he'd displayed earlier, "you're supposed to base it in that which you have a degree of familiarity. That way you know what you're talking about. It has a feeling of . . . of . . ."

"Authenticity?"

"Yes!" he said, pointing at her. "Exactly right. Authenticity. If it rings true for you yourself, it will likewise ring true for your audience. So when I acquired the holotechnology that would enable me to provide you a body of physical substance, I designed a form for you that was the female with which I was the most familiar. That helped make you more 'real' to me. In this case, I selected Kalinda's form."

"I would have thought you would be the most familiar with the form of your mother," she pointed out.

Xyon stared at her. "You can't even begin to understand why that would present a problem, can you."

Lyla paused and considered that. As was always the case when she was thinking, her face became expressionless. That was because her mind, part of the ship, was working. So her face, rather than becoming "thoughtful," simply went blank as if she were in a holding pattern. Usually a question would get less than a second's hesitation, nothing even really noticeable. Then her expression cleared and she fixed her gaze upon him once more. "Does it have something to do with that which is referred to as the Oedipal complex?"

Xyon stared at her blankly. "The what?"

"The Oedipal complex. An ancient Earth psychoanalytic term, derived from a tale involving the slaying of one's father and having intercourse with one's mother."

For a long moment, Xyon didn't react. Then the edges of his mouth twitched, his eyes crinkled, and he let out a long and sustained laugh. Lyla tilted her head slightly, watching him with rapt curiosity. "Is that amusing to you, Xyon?"

"A little," he admitted, wiping the tears from his eyes. "I mean . . . I'm not my father's biggest fan, but even I wouldn't go so far as to kill him just so I could try to have sex with my mother . . . even if she were still alive." He shook his head. "Humans. Trust them to come up with some of the most demented notions."

"So your point," said Lyla, returning with machine-like precision to the original subject of the discussion, "was that you patterned me on Kalinda because she was the female whom you knew the best and most desired to engage in intercourse with."

"Something like that," he said.

"When you are with me, do you pretend I am her?"

He didn't answer immediately. Sensing his hesitation, Lyla said gently, "I will not be disturbed if you answer in the affirmative. I can't actually take offense at such things. If what I am—my form, my design— pleases you for whatever reason, that is sufficient for me. If it did not, then I would desire to possess that which does. It is just that simple."

"Lyla," he sighed, "you would be amazed at the number of things in this galaxy that are 'just that simple,' except they aren't."

"Really?" She sounded intrigued. "What would that number be?"

Before he could think of a response, the ship's proximity alarm went off.

Lyla immediately vanished. The ship's power cells, while efficient, were not infinite. If there was any sort of emergency situation that might require either fight or flight, it was imperative that energy be conserved. The drain Lyla's hologram manifestation required was simply not a necessary one in a potential emergency.

Xyon lunged for his pants, which were draped over his control chair, missed them, staggered and regained his footing, then grabbed them and yanked them on as fast as he could. Too fast, as it turned out, for he toppled backward and landed hard on the floor. Lyla's voice came from all around him. "Are you injured, Xyon?"

"My pride, mostly," he grunted as he scrambled to his feet, snatched up his shirt from the floor, and yanked it on over his head. He was at his console, checking his readings, and glanced at the monitor to confirm visually what his instruments were already telling him.

Space itself was wavering before him and then, barely a hundred thousand kilometers away, a Romulan vessel shimmered into existence.

It was many times larger than his own ship, and he knew it instantly as a new type of ship called the Spectre class. Naturally it had a cloaking device, but there was an additional modification to the engines that was a brilliant throwback to technology long abandoned.

Even with a cloaking device, the typical Romulan ship left a minuscule particle trail that Federation starships could lock on to with a bit of patience and luck. The Spectre class, however, wasn't typical. Romulan scientists had hit upon the notion of installing an ion glide, which was a delicately crafted foil that ran between the winglike nacelles of the ship. The ion glide served as what ancient star voyagers referred to as a "solar sail," allowing the ship to be pushed along on the ions of solar winds. It wasn't effective for system-to-system travel, since it was too slow to be practical. But in passing through heavily populated regions of space, or entering an area where a battle was anticipated, the ion glide was ideal, because it left no trail of particles—ion, tachyon, or otherwise—but instead was simply buffeted along. Any trace ions were indistinguishable from standard background radiation. In effect, the ship was silent and completely undetectable. A ghost. A spectre. There were only five like it in the fleet.

The only reason the *Lyla*'s alarms had gone off was

because the ship was decloaking near them. Had the Spectre not done so, it could have rammed Xyon's ship if it was so inclined, and Xyon wouldn't have realized it until he was floating in space surrounded by fragments of his vessel.

"Weapons systems online," he snapped. Immediately his onboard weaponry came on, his pulse cannons targeting the starboard engines of the Spectre.

This prompted an instant hail from the Romulan ship. "Let them hang a few seconds," Xyon instructed, and for long moments the insistent beeping of the hail was the only sound in his ship. "All right," he said at last, "put them on."

A sharp female voice came through his com system. "Stand down your weapons right now," she said without preamble.

"Are you going to make me?" he demanded.

There was a pause, and then the Romulan—sounding extremely peeved—said, "What are you, twelve years old? What the hell do you think you're playing at?"

"Just being sure to send a message that I'm not a pushover," he replied.

"Xyon, knock it off. Honestly. I have better things to do than listen to you engage in the kind of macho posturing that, frankly, your father did far more convincingly and with much more style."

His face flushed red at that, which she undoubtedly would have figured it would. "You know, I have half a mind to—"

"Yes, you've made that abundantly clear," she interrupted. "Now stand down your weapons. If you do, I'll come over there and we'll do business. If you don't, I'll beam you directly into our brig."

Xyon sighed in frustration and then said, "Lyla, stand down weapons systems."

"Yes, Xyon." The targeting systems switched off and the pulse cannons powered down. Xyon told himself that he really hadn't lost anything. Even if he'd fired on the Romulan ship with its shields down, the cannons wouldn't have managed to inflict any incapacitating damage before the Romulan disruptors turned him into space debris anyway. It was all for show. But it assuaged his ego, which was considerable.

Moments later, he heard the telltale hum of a transporter beam resonate through his bridge. He leaned back against his control console in a carefully manufactured casual posture. A slender figure appeared in outline a few feet away from him and then fully coalesced in a shower of sparkles.

She stood there, attired in Romulan armor that suited her rank, and glowered at him. "Don't screw around with me, Xyon," she admonished him. "I'm not in the mood."

"You take life too seriously, Soleta."

"I take it just seriously enough. I certainly take it seriously when some idiot points weapons at my ship during an agreed-upon rendezvous."

"Your ship snuck up on mine."

"It's a stealth vessel, Xyon," Soleta pointed out with a world-weary sigh. "Sneaking is what it does. Do you have it?"

"It?"

"It."

"Do I have it," he echoed. "You know," and he strolled in a circle around her, his hands draped behind his back, "you could be polite. Sociable. Make small talk. Ask how I am, discuss current events, exchange gossip."

"Yes, I could," Soleta agreed, her immobility a stark contrast to Xyon's casual air. "On the other hand, I could beam back to my ship, we could turn around and leave, and we could take the gold-pressed latinum we brought along as payment for you and instead buy ourselves a damned good time at Wrigley's Pleasure Planet. You have five seconds to deci . . . You know, wait, on second thought, I'll decide for you." Pulling her com unit off her belt, she barked into it, "One to beam—"

"All right, all right!" He put up his hands in a surrendering fashion. "Fine. I've got it right here."

"Stand by," she said into the com unit as Xyon walked into the back room that served as his private chamber. She watched him go through narrowed eyes. "You must really be starved for attention, to have to resort to such idiotic tricks as this."

"I find my amusements where I can," Xyon replied from the next room. He reemerged holding a data chip. Soleta unslung a data reader from around her shoulder and extended an expectant hand to him, palm up. He made a great show of hesitating before placing the chip into her hand. She shook her head in mute disapproval of his antics as she inserted the chip and studied the details that came up.

"This is it," she said finally. "Detailed plans for the new weapons system the Orions are developing."

"Yes, I know. It's what you wanted."

"It presents a threat to Federation security."

He put up his hands. "Oh, *grozit*, spare me. The Romulans don't give a damn about Federation security. The Romulans care about their own security. You have no intention of sharing this information with the Federation at all."

"The Praetor assures me that he intends to be forthcoming with the Federation in such matters."

"You need a little work on that one, Soleta, if you're going to sound remotely convincing." She scowled at Xyon, but he didn't especially care. "I'm sure that when and if the Praetor is forthcoming, it's going to be very much on his timetable, not the Federation's. A timetable that includes not only finding the weaknesses in the weapons system, but developing an equivalent system for the Romulans. A system to use against . . . who? The Orions? The Federation? What's going on in the minds of the Romulans, Soleta?"

"Things that do not concern you, Xyon."

"I'm not concerned. I'm just curious."

"Yes, as was the cat. And we know what curiosity did for him."

Xyon stared at her blankly for a moment, and then looked annoyed. "All right, is this another Earth thing I'm supposed to know about? Because if it is, it's the second one today, and I'm getting tired of it."

"Second one today?" She made no effort to hide her bewilderment.

"Yeah. First there was something about some mythic figure named 'Oedipus' and his mother . . ."

"I will add two bars of gold-pressed latinum to your payment," she said, "if you drop this entire line of conversation and promise me you will never bring it up again."

"Deal," he said.

She nodded and spoke once more into the comlink. "Subcommander," she said, "beam seven bars of gold-pressed latinum to these coordinates immediately."

"Yes, Commander."

Seconds later, the bars of latinum, packed in individual containers, appeared on the floor. As Xyon knelt to inspect them, Soleta said, "Were there any difficulties involved in obtaining this information?"

"Nothing worth mentioning."

"Did you have to kill anyone?"

His gaze flickered up to her and his eyes were hard as diamonds. "No one worth mentioning," he said.

"I see."

"Do you?" Xyon was still kneeling down, his voice low and annoyed. "You sent me on this assignment because you knew I'd get it done, and that I wouldn't care what was involved, and you didn't care to know. Are you now condemning my methods for accomplishing it?"

"No," she said quietly. "I've said nothing of the sort. But I find it interesting that you react as if I had."

"Stay out of my head, Soleta."

"I am."

"Someone with the level of issues that you have

with the Romulans, with the Vulcans, with Starfleet, with the entirety of your life until now, doesn't get to lecture me."

"I wasn't intending to lecture you, Xyon," she said with a touch of annoyance. "However, for what it's worth, I am strongly considering beating the crap out of you."

"You can try," he said challengingly.

"Not today."

"Why? Too much effort?"

"No. Too much crap."

At that moment, Lyla's holographic form appeared. "Xyon," she said, "since energy systems have been routed away from the weapons, do you wish me to resume my physical form?"

Soleta gaped at her and then at Xyon. He shifted uncomfortably, suddenly feeling very exposed. "That won't be necessary right now, Lyla. . . ."

"Oh, that's funny," said Soleta, clearly trying to avoid snickering.

"What is?" Lyla inquired, wide-eyed.

"You can go now, Lyla, and Soleta, it's not funny and it's none of your business."

"None of my business, perhaps, but if you don't see the humor, you're just not looking," she snorted.

"*Stop laughing at me!*" he said angrily, and took a step toward her to get right in her face about it.

Her hands were lightning quick, and before he knew what was happening, he was on the floor, looking up in surprise. Soleta had a disruptor in her hand and it was pointed squarely at him.

"Twitch and you're dead," she told him.

Xyon didn't twitch. Lyla, either not having heard Xyon or—more likely—judiciously choosing to ignore him, continued to remain where she was and look with interest from Xyon to Soleta and back to Xyon.

"You're pathetic," continued Soleta. "With your posturing and boastful words and meticulously manufactured insouciance. And all the time, you're still pining after a romance from years ago that you're so weak-kneed about, you manufacture holographic playtoys while remaining too afraid to let the actual girl know that you're even alive."

"We've been over this," he retorted. "If people think I'm dead, it makes it that much easier for me to operate."

"If people think you're dead, it makes it that much easier for you never to have to confront the way you feel about them, or they about you."

He said nothing for a moment and then, with a glower, demanded, "Are you going to kill me or are you just going to stand there?"

"Killing you would almost be doing you a favor," she told him. "Better no life than a half-life."

"Interesting. You were never so contemptuous of me all the times you've hired me to do your dirty work."

"Actually," Soleta corrected him, "I was. I just never let it show. I may not be quite as inscrutable as a Vulcan . . . but I'm no slouch, either."

She stepped back, holstered her disruptor, and then said, "I suppose she's moot anyway."

"What are you talking about?" He slowly got to his feet but made no sudden moves toward Soleta, although he did rub the small of his back to ease out the pain he was feeling.

"She. Kalinda."

He tried to comprehend what she was saying, and then a slow dread grew in the pit of his stomach. "She . . . she's dying? Dead?"

"Just as good: She's engaged. To the son of some high muck-a-muck in the Thallonian Empire . . . I'm sorry. The New Thallonian Protectorate." She said the words with barely masked derision.

"Kalinda's engaged."

"That's right. So you might as well enjoy yourself with your imaginary friend," and she nodded toward Lyla, "because that's the best you're going to get." She touched a finger to her forehead and tossed off an ironic salute. "A pleasure as always, Xyon. Enjoy the latinum. Don't spend it all in one place. Subcommander," she spoke into the link, "beam me aboard."

She blurred out of existence, leaving Xyon alone in the cabin. Alone except for the holograph of Lyla, who was gazing at him with limpid eyes. She waited for him to speak, but he said nothing. Finally she asked, "Xyon? Is there something I can . . . ?"

"Find another form," he said brusquely.

"What other form would be pleasing to you, Xyon?"

He thought about it and then said, "It doesn't matter. An Orion slave girl."

"Like the one you killed while getting the disk?"

"She tried to kill me first, Lyla."

"All right," she said, her calm voice never wavering. A moment later she was a scantily clad, green-skinned female with blazing eyes and thick, lustrous hair. "How's this?"

"Fine," he assured her without looking as he watched the Romulan ship vanish from sight, and speculated about other things in the universe that could just disappear no matter how closely you kept an eye on them.

Space Station Bravo

Captain Kat Mueller strode into the office of Bravo's chief administrator and snapped off a highly military salute. The chief administrator looked up at the blond, somewhat glacial Starfleet captain from behind the desk and shook her head, an amused smile on her lips. "What the hell are you doing? This isn't the twenty-first-century army. Since when do we salute in Starfleet?"

"I'm actually mounting a one-woman campaign to restore it," Kat informed her, her chin outthrust defiantly. "I think it displays an old-world sense of respect for the chain of command."

"See, whereas I think that the term 'Yes, sir' or 'Yes, ma'am' pretty much accomplishes the same thing." The administrator was standing now, and she came around her desk, her arms open wide. Kat hesitated only a moment, since she wasn't really all that much for hugging, but then sighed and gave in to the inevitable. She accepted the embrace, and the two women patted each other's backs for a moment. "It's good to see you, Kat. Command agrees with you."

Mueller stepped back and replied, "I didn't actually think it would, Admiral. Your confidence in me was an inspiration."

"Kat, it's just the two of us here. You can call me 'Elizabeth.' "

"If you say so, Admiral Shelby."

Elizabeth Paula Shelby shook her head as she leaned back against her desk, half-sitting on the edge. She gestured for Mueller to take a seat, and Mueller did so. "How is the *Trident* crew?" she asked.

"The usual. Mutiny. Chaos. We've had to court-martial forty-seven officers and crewmen. It's an all-time Starfleet high, so naturally we're all very proud."

Shelby gazed at Mueller's impassive face. "Is your sense of humor characteristic to your elevated rank, or to you in specific?"

"Me in specific. I am wholly original."

"You are wholly strange."

"And yet I make it work."

"That's still open to debate," Shelby informed her, shaking her head with an exaggerated air of tolerance. "I mean, how many Starfleet officers insist on walking around with a Heidelberg fencing scar on their face?"

Mueller reflexively touched the mark on her cheek and smiled grimly. "Anyone who acquired one would. That's another trend I'm hoping to spark."

"Kat," Shelby said, "let me assure you that, all things being equal, I could sit around all day and listen to you explain how your trend-setting is going to revolutionize the look and conduct of Starfleet for generations to come."

"And yet . . . ?"

"And yet, as always, all things aren't equal. I have things to do and, tragically, so do you." Dropping all trace of banter, she said—all business—"How badly banged up is the *Trident?* Will the facilities here at Bravo be sufficient for repairs?"

"I believe so, yes."

"Because I could order you back to drydock for a full refit . . ."

Mueller firmly shook her head. "Absolutely not necessary, Admiral. We took some hits, yes. But the Selelvian renegade took far worse."

"Your report said you destroyed her."

"Yes, that would fall under the category of 'far worse,' " Mueller deadpanned. "My people assure me that the damage we sustained is under control. In fact, they told me we could likely have handled it completely on our own. It was my decision to put in here at Bravo to make it easier on them, and to avail ourselves of your diagnostic facilities on the off chance there was something we missed that could become a danger later."

"Take care of the big problems when they're small problems." Shelby nodded in approval. "You made the right decision, Kat. Whatever you need in terms of station personnel, it's yours."

"Thank you, Captain."

Shelby sighed and she rapped her knuckles on the desk as she stood up and walked around it. She didn't sit but instead continued to pace. "It's like the Selelvians don't realize the war is over and they lost."

"There's only scattered resistance, Admiral," Mueller assured her. "Being offered by independent terrorist cells who refuse to acknowledge their government's surrender. It's nothing that Starfleet can't handle."

"I know. Still . . . I mean, we had a Selelvian officer on our ship, Kat. Lieutenant Commander Gleau." Her voice was tinged with regret. It was hardly the first time she'd pondered the lost opportunities, doubted herself insofar as how she'd handled the entire ugly business with Gleau. "If we had realized the threat his people represented . . . if somehow he could have wound up serving as a go-between representing Federation interests, instead of . . ."

"Instead of being murdered?" Mueller shrugged. "Second-guessing is pointless, Admiral, especially when it comes to matters over which you had no control."

"You're right, of course. Still . . ." Shelby seemed about to pursue the train of thought, but then she let it drop. Instead she tapped her computer screen and said, "Since you're here, there's something I need to discuss with you."

"All right." Mueller, seated with her back stiff, crossed her legs in a careful, precise manner and waited.

Shelby studied the computer screen for a long moment, clearly wanting to make sure what she said was accurate. Finally she turned back to Mueller.

"Sector 221-G," she began.

Mueller promptly laughed. It was an unusual sound, almost startling since she did it so rarely. Sort of a smug grunting noise more than anything else. "Don't you mean the Thallonian Protectorate?"

"I suppose I do, yes."

"Somehow," said Mueller, as if reexperiencing a tale of woe that she reflected upon with great regret, "it always comes back to Sector 221-G. So what's happening there now? Has Si Cwan's great experiment finally collapsed upon itself?"

"Kat," Shelby said scoldingly, "I have no patience with that sort of negative attitude."

"Admiral, there's a pool going as to the exact stardate the entire Protectorate will come unraveled."

"Yes, I know, but . . ."

"A pool, I might add, that was your idea."

"To be fair," Shelby said, raising a finger, "there were mitigating circumstances as I may have been . . . quite inebriated at the time. . . ."

"And you're still running the pool."

"These things take on a life of their own. . . ."

"And you're holding all the credits in a secure account."

"All right!"

Mueller lapsed into amused silence while Shelby impatiently blew air between her teeth. "The point is that the business in 221-G has nothing to do with anything that Si Cwan is up to."

"Oh." Kat sounded faintly disappointed.

Shelby indicated the computer screen and Mueller leaned forward to see what she was pointing at. "We picked up something during a routine unmanned scientific probe a week ago."

" 'Unmanned scientific probe'?" Mueller said, one tapered eyebrow arching ever so slightly. "Once upon a time, that was a euphemism for 'spy probe.' "

"That may very well be, Kat, but nowadays it's a euphemism for nothing and an accurate label for a routine unmanned scientific probe."

"Really. And tell me, Admiral . . . were that not the case, would you tell me?"

Shelby stared at her levelly for a long moment, and then said in a voice devoid of tone, "If you'll permit me to continue, Captain."

Mueller, who knew an unspoken answer when she didn't hear one, nodded and kept her gaze fixed on the monitor screen.

"Now then . . . the probe picked up some rather disturbing emissions emanating from within the sector. We weren't able to localize them or determine the point of origin since they were free-floating. However, given the drift time and amount of decay, and after running some estimates, we were able to nail it down to a general area spanning subsectors 18-J through 27-L."

"Quite a bit of area to cover."

"Yes," agreed Shelby, "but it's the best our people could do, given the circumstances."

"And just exactly what are these emissions that have our scientific-probe folks so worried?"

"Funny you should ask," Shelby said in a manner that indicated it wasn't actually funny at all. "They are emissions strikingly similar to those generated by a transwarp conduit . . . the means of transportation generally favored by the Borg."

"How strikingly similar?"

"A ninety-eight percent match."

Mueller leaned back in the chair, her fingers interlaced. "Hunh" was all she muttered at first, and then she continued after a few moments, "And that two percent could be chalked up to either scientific error, or an improvement or change in the technology by the Borg themselves."

"Or," Shelby pointed out, "it could also indicate that we're dealing with some other race entirely. Something that's popping into and out of 221-G without wanting to be noticed."

"Which could mean a potential threat."

Shelby looked a bit saddened. "I loathe thinking of it that way. The mission of Starfleet is exploration. To seek out new life and new civilizations. Not to be paranoid that the aforementioned new civilizations are going to make attacking us their top priority."

"An open hand can disguise a dangerous mind," Mueller said. "My father always said that. Very little that I've encountered in my life has done anything to make me think he was even the slightest bit incorrect."

"Be that as it may," Shelby said firmly, "if nothing else, we should be working to cover Si Cwan's back. If someone is sneaking into the Thallonian Protectorate for the purpose of an attack . . ."

"Or as a potential ally for Si Cwan so he could attack us."

Shelby looked at her askance. "I don't see him doing that."

"What better reason *to* do something besides it being something that others don't see coming."

"I'm sorry, no. After everything we went through, after all the Federation has done for him, I don't see him conspiring to attack us simply because we're not expecting him to."

Mueller shrugged. "Expect nothing. Anticipate everything."

Shelby blinked a moment and then smiled. "So you quote Mac too, do you?"

"Did Mackenzie Calhoun say that?" Mueller frowned a moment, trying to remember, and then nodded. "Oh. Yes, he did. Funny. I thought I'd always believed that on my own, but you're right. I got it from him."

"That'll happen," said Shelby, and there was a wistfulness in her voice that she couldn't quite hide. Then quickly, loudly, she cleared her throat and told Mueller, "Starfleet wants you to take the *Trident* into 221-G, see if you can discover the exact nature and origin of the emissions, and determine the precise nature of what it is we can look forward to."

"And once we've determined it?"

"Report back to me. Oh . . . also, keep Robin Lefler in the loop. She's still connected to Starfleet, however tangentially, and 221-G is her backyard. If there's something going on there that she should know about . . ."

"You think she can be trusted?" asked Mueller.

Shelby's eyes narrowed. "Are you saying her marriage to Si Cwan renders her untrustworthy somehow?"

"I'm saying if it turns out that Si Cwan is indeed up to something or allying himself with someone who presents a danger, Robin Lefler could find herself with a severe case of divided loyalties. And I couldn't say for sure exactly on which side she'll fall. Then again," she shrugged once more, "you know her better than I."

"Robin Lefler," Shelby assured her, "is a Starfleet officer."

"So was Soleta."

A pall fell upon the office at that moment. Kat Mueller had always been someone who was very confident in her opinions and never doubted the inherent rightness of what she had to say. Yet for the first time in a very long time, she wished she could have taken back what she had just said.

"My apologies, Admiral," Mueller began.

But, surprisingly, Shelby waved it off. "No. No, you're right. You should never apologize for being right. I walked right into that one. Caught me fair and square."

"I wasn't trying to 'catch' you at anything, Admiral."

"I know that, Kat. I really do. Soleta was . . ." She tried to find the words and only partly succeeded. "Soleta was . . . an accident waiting to happen, I suppose. And then it happened, and there was nothing any of us could do but pick up the pieces. She made her decisions, we made ours, and that's how it goes. Still . . . Soleta notwithstanding . . . I don't think we need to worry about Robin Lefler abandoning us or turning against us unexpectedly. Robin is a bit more . . . stable than that. Besides," and she almost laughed at the notion, "if Robin went at all off track, you just know her mother would be all over her about it."

"Her mother's a holograph."

"Her mother's a machine identity," Shelby reminded her. "At this point, she can link up with just about any AI in the entirety of the Federation. Thank God she's benign, since I keep having the uneasy feeling that—if she were so inclined—she could find a way to blow all of us up just by thinking really hard."

"Yes, well . . . that's another situation that I continue to 'anticipate,' " admitted Mueller.

"You're hopeless, Kat."

"Yes, but it's a constructive sort of hopelessness. Am I dismissed, Admiral?"

"Absolutely."

Kat got up to go, headed for the door, and then stopped at the doorframe. She turned to see Shelby sitting there, staring and grinning, her hand propping up her chin. "May I inquire as to what might be so amusing?" Mueller demanded.

"You always do this," said Shelby, gesturing toward the door. "You're always about to walk out and then, at the last moment, stand in the doorway and make some pithy observation that seems ridiculous on the face of it, but often turns out to be true. Sometimes I think you haven't made up your mind between being a Starfleet captain or a drama queen."

"Truthfully," said Mueller, "I think the dividing line has been narrowing for decades now, if not centuries."

"All right, then, out with it. What's on your perpetually suspicious mind now?"

"I'm not being suspicious about anything. I was just wondering if . . ."

"If what?"

"How you're doing. Without him, I mean."

"Him?" She looked blank for a moment, and then sheepish that she'd had to wonder even for an instant what it was that Mueller was talking about. "Oh. Him. Mac."

"Yes, of course him."

"Are you insinuating, Kat," she asked with a hint of challenge, "that I'm somehow incapable of surviving without him? That I can't manage?"

"Not at all," Mueller assured her. "But on the one hand, the two of you are married, and on the other hand, you see each other . . . what? Once a month? Less?"

"I haven't been keeping track," said Shelby, "because I really have better things to do with my time than count the number of days until I see my husband. And . . ."

Her voice trailed off and her shoulders slumped a bit. "And . . . if I focus on the time apart . . . that just makes it harder. So I . . . don't. Focus on that." Then, in a surprisingly informal move, she laid her hands flat on her desk and settled her chin on them, like a child peering up from a grade-school desk. "Besides . . . I'm never without him. Not really. We stay in touch via subspace radio, and even when that's not possible, he's never far from my thoughts. At least two, three times a

day, I find myself wondering what Mac would do in a
particular set of circumstances. And then I use that
knowledge to guide myself through . . ."

"By doing the opposite of what he would have
done?" deadpanned Kat.

Shelby laughed at that. "Sometimes," she admitted.
"But more often than not, thinking what he would do
and then emulating him helps me. So in a way . . . it's
like having him here."

"In a spiritual, philosophical way."

"Yes."

"And as far as sex goes . . . ?"

Shelby moaned softly, pulled her fingers apart, and
thumped her chin on the desk several times. "Torture. I
have dreams that melt my brain cells."

"Well, you know, Elizabeth," Kat said slyly, "we're
all modern thinkers. Adults. Even married couples have
the option of taking 'companions' during times of
lengthy separation. For release. It's just good sense
from a health point of view. Hell, worse comes to
worst, there are very convincing holodeck programs
that . . ."

"*Ohhhh* no," Shelby said immediately and shaking
her head with as much vehemence as she could muster.
"Programming holos for sexual entertainment? It's
barely one step above self-gratification."

"Spoken like someone who hasn't tried it."

"Why, have you?" She fixed her stare upon Mueller,
who—to her shock—looked away with a half-smile.
"You *have?*"

"I didn't think it appropriate for a captain to become involved with a subordinate," Mueller told her. "So I found myself some . . . creative outlets. All very discreet."

"Well—not intending to sound judgmental—but I couldn't do that. Neither could Mac. Nor do either of us expect more from the other than we can provide."

"Meaning?"

"Meaning," Shelby told her patiently, "that if Mac engages in some recreational . . . encounters . . ."

"He knows that you would still be his wife at the end of the day."

"Exactly."

"And likewise," continued Mueller, "if you should feel the need for—oh, let's call it 'release'—with, say, some appropriate, attractive fellow who is ideally just passing through and not looking for any sort of long-term attachment, why, Mac would likewise not carry any resentment over your actions."

"You've described the situation perfectly," said Shelby, nodding in approval.

"I see." Mueller considered that and then asked, "So . . . have you been involved with some appropriate, attractive fellow?"

"Oh God, no."

"And do you intend to be?"

"Oh God, no."

"And if Mac became involved with some woman . . . ?"

"I'll kill him. And her. Maybe together, maybe separately."

"So when you were speaking just now about being

understanding and a modern thinker and all that? That was . . . ?"

"A lie. Complete and total."

"I appreciate your candor in regards to your lack of candor, Admiral," said Kat Mueller. "It's very refreshing."

"Thank you. I've worked hard to refine it."

"It shows."

She turned and headed out the door. Shelby called after her, just before the doors shut, "Oh, if you run into Mac and try to have an affair with him, I wouldn't hesitate to kill you, too."

"Understood," Mueller called as the doors slid shut. Shelby, for her part, leaned back in her chair, thought about Mac for a good long while, and then prepared to send him a communiqué just for the purpose of letting him know she was thinking of him. The fortunate thing was that she'd just gotten a similar communiqué from him saying much the same. So a response would seem the most natural thing in the world, which was good.

She wouldn't want to come across as being too possessive.

New Thallon

i.

"I cannot *believe* you put me into that situation!"

Si Cwan was stalking the inside of Robin Lefler's office, the edges of his robes whisking about the floor. Robin, for her part, was making a point of paying him no mind. She was reading over recent dispatches from Starfleet, wanting to keep up on the latest regulations. Even when she spoke, she didn't glance up at him. "I didn't put you into any situation."

"You brought a half-dozen Priatians into the middle of the council!"

"It was three Priatians, they came looking for me, and I chose to escort them in and make certain they received a fair hearing," she said patiently. "In my position as liaison for the Office of Interplanetary Affairs . . ."

"In that position," he interrupted her fiercely, "you are entitled to listen to what is transpiring and perhaps maybe, just maybe, do what you're told to on occasion."

That drew her attention away from the computer as

she looked up at him. "Well, excuse the hell out of me for not playing the good and dutiful wife, rather than the Starfleet officer who has her own concerns."

He threw up his arms in exasperation. "That is not what I was saying at all! You're twisting it . . . !"

"That is exactly what you were saying, and I'm getting it perfectly accurate," she retorted.

"When I . . ." He took a deep breath, and Robin could see him mentally counting to seven, a habit she had drilled into him in order to make encounters such as this more palatable. She'd actually wanted him to count to ten; he'd preferred five. As with so many things in their life, the result had been a compromise. "When I asked you to escort them out of the chamber, I was doing so not as husband to wife, but as prime minister to a representative of the Federation."

"And yet you looked so damned much like my husband, I couldn't help but confuse the two."

"Robin—!"

Robin slapped the desk with her palm. "Why did you refuse to listen to them, Cwan? Do you have *any* idea how humiliating that was for me? You just dismissing them like that? Them and me?"

"Yes, I have some idea of how humiliating it was," he shot back. "Almost as humiliating as having one's wife show up with—"

"You said it wasn't about my being your wife. That it was all about you as prime minister and me as the Federation representative."

He balled his hands into fists and shook them impotently. "I didn't say that!"

"Yes, you did! Barely thirty seconds ago!"

"You're twisting it again!"

"Which me is twisting it? The wife me or the rep me?"

"Robin!"

"Cwan!"

He turned and slammed a fist into the wall. Fortunately the wall was reasonably solid. Otherwise she had no doubt that he could've punched right through it.

"Feel better now?" she asked, batting her eyes at him.

"No," he growled.

She leaned back in her chair and sighed deeply. "Cwan, what would have been the harm of hearing them out?"

"Because I've heard it all before!" he told her, shaking out his fist to restore some feeling to it. "They weren't going to say anything new. The Priatians have been lobbying for redress for as far back as I can remember. They came to me when I was head of the ruling house, they came to my father before me and his before him. They keep saying the same damned thing: Restore to us the worlds you took."

"Did you take them?"

"Yes, but that's not the point."

She blinked. "Actually, I'm kind of thinking that is the point."

He dropped down into the chair opposite her. "First, it's not as if there's just one race of Priatians. The representatives you saw are from the group that refers to itself as the True Bloods. The ones who believe themselves direct descendants of their so-called founders."

"The Wanderers."

"Yes, exactly. But on other worlds in the area that you call Sector 221-G, there were offshoots of the True Bloods, many developed through inbreeding and such. Offshoot races that, by this day and age, have as much in common with the so-called True Bloods as you would have in common with . . ."

"My husband?"

He made a grimacing face. "The comedy of Robin Lefler, my friends," he said to an imaginary audience. "Look, Robin . . . yes, it's true that my ancestors drove the True Bloods off many worlds in which they were in residence. But only because they resisted and refused Thallonian rule, something that others on those self-same worlds had no problem with."

"No problem once they were conquered, you mean."

"Well . . . yes," he admitted. "But we cannot turn back the hands of time, cannot undo what's been done. Let us say—just for the sake of argument—"

"Good, because I just never get tired of argument."

"—that I acceded to their request. Even if I could do so unilaterally. Let us say I waved my hand and said, 'All former Priatian worlds are restored to you.' What then? The worlds which the Priatians demand we 'return' to them are populated by races that have little knowledge or concern about who was there before they were. They are their own peoples now. Most of them have representatives sitting in council.

Do you think they're about to hand control over their worlds to a people who haven't set foot on the respective planets for centuries? Realistically, Robin, do you believe that?"

She looked down. "I suppose not," she admitted.

"You suppose correctly. It's a dead-end discussion, Robin, and one I chose not to get into yet again. We have far too many things to worry about that actually can come to some sort of successful resolution, and the Priatian demands are simply not one of them. I didn't want to waste my time, the council's time. All it would have done is make the Priatian representatives feel foolish."

"They felt foolish when they were turned away."

"Perhaps, but at least it was quick," he told her. "If I'd given them what they wanted, they would have been verbally abused for half an hour by the council and then sent on their way, no closer to accomplishing their mission than before. This way, I saved them that half hour of humiliation."

"My husband, the humanitarian."

"Thank you," he said archly, "but truthfully, I aspire to more greatness than most of humanity can reach."

Her eyes narrowed. "Am I sadly mistaken, or did you just insult my entire race?"

"Not entire, no. I said 'most of.' It goes without saying that you were not included in that grouping."

"Well that's very generous of you," she said sarcastically.

He extended a hand toward her, but she pulled

away. "Dammit, Robin!" he snapped. "Now you're just being stubborn."

"You'd be the expert on that."

"Stubborn and petulant as well, because you fully know that I'm right about this. I'm right and you're wrong and that's what galls you."

"You're what galls me, Cwan."

He waved off her response dismissively. "No. You know as well as I that the glory days of the Priatians belong to the past. You feel badly for them because you're a compassionate woman—which is one of the many reasons that I love you—and because you perceive the Priatians to be poor, downtrodden-but-noble individuals who have suffered over the centuries and deserve some sort of recompense. And perhaps they have and perhaps they do. But it's not going to happen because it's impossible, and you know it. You know it. Thallonian space has simply moved on without them, moved away from them."

"Is that a fact," she said humorlessly. "I seem to recall . . ."

"Oh, gods, here we go," he moaned.

". . . that Thallonian space had moved on without you," continued Lefler without relenting. "Moved away from you and your whole royal family, so much so that your homeworld was reduced to floating bits of rock. I even seem to recall saying you couldn't turn the clock back at a time when you were on the *Excalibur* hoping that somehow, in some way, you could restore the Thallonian Empire. And now look where you are."

"Yes, look. Look at the Prime Minister overseeing a

ruling council that is a mere shadow of the efficiency and glory that characterized the Thallonian Empire."

"But it's a start."

"Yes," he agreed reluctantly, "it's a start." He leaned forward, running his fingers across his bald pate. "Blood and thunder, woman, what do you want from me?"

"Give the Priatians a start. Offer them a seat on the council."

"I did. Ages ago. They refused."

"Do it again."

"They'll refuse again."

"Then let *me* offer it," she insisted.

"*Fine!* And when they turn you down, will that put an end to this discussion?"

"Yes."

"Thank the—"

"At least for the time being."

She said it with a teasing smile. Nevertheless, his fingers moved down to the bridge of his nose and rubbed it with evident pain. "You know, Robin," he said, "once upon a time, the job of a woman in Thallonian society was very straightforward. Would you like to know what it was?"

"Not especially."

"It was to make the lives of men as simple and unperturbed as possible. Any woman who failed in that task was taken out into the town square, stripped, and made to run around the square five hundred times while chanting, 'I apologize for my ineptitude.' "

"I would call that barbaric."

"See, whereas my ancestors would have called that the 'good old days.' And between you inserting yourself into interplanetary affairs, and my beloved sister Kalinda forming a romantic relationship that's giving me no end of grief in the council, I'm starting to think there's something to be said for those 'good old days.' "

"You would, my love," she sighed. "You would."

ii.

Tiraud of the House of Fhermus was lying on his back, one arm outstretched, enjoying the gentle breeze that fluttered across the grassland. What made the moment particularly attractive to him was that his fiancée was lying next to him, her head tucked in the crook of his elbow. She was holding strands of grass in her hand and blowing upon them idly.

His bronze skin glittering in the broad sunlight of the afternoon, Tiraud bore something of a resemblance to his father. His face was rounder, though, his eyes set closer together, his lips thin but twitching at the edges as if he were perpetually on the verge of a smile, but never quite finding life amusing enough to fully provoke it.

"What are you thinking about, Lind?" he asked his fiancée. These were the first words he'd spoken in close to half an hour.

"About how pleased I am to be here with you," Kalinda replied. To her, smiles came easily. That hadn't always been the case, but ever since she'd met Tiraud, she was just too happy *not* to smile. It almost frightened her, the effect he had upon her. She didn't know how anyone could know quite this much joy. In the back of her mind she was always concerned she'd discover that no one could, or should, be quite this content. "About how happy you make me. About our wedding."

"No regrets?"

She sat partly upright. "Why should I have regrets?" asked Kalinda. "Why? Are you having regrets?"

"No."

"Hesitations?"

"Absolutely not," he said firmly.

"Then why ask?" She eyed him suspiciously. "Usually when people ask questions that seem out of the blue, it's because they themselves have concerns they're reluctant to bring up. Is that what's happening here?"

He laughed at that. "Lind, it's nothing like that at all."

"Then what . . . ?"

"It's just that . . . I'm almost afraid of my good fortune. I feel as if I'm so lucky that a capricious god or gods will look down and say, 'Hey! You! You're not supposed to know this degree of bliss. We're going to take it away from you, right now.' "

"Oh, Tiraud," she moaned, and lay down next to him, cuddling up against him. "You're being ridiculous. No one is going to take me away from you. Honestly, I have to wonder what you could possibly have done to the gods to make you think they'd . . . they'd . . ."

Her voice trailed off. At first it didn't dawn on

Tiraud that there was a problem, but then he realized she'd stopped talking altogether. He sat up, staring at her in bewilderment. "Lind? Is something wrong? What's wrong . . . ?"

Finally it occurred to him that the best course of action would be to look not at Kalinda herself, but in the direction she was staring. He followed her gaze and saw what appeared to be a humanoid male approaching. Tiraud wasn't entirely sure how old the newcomer was because, truthfully, most humanoids looked alike to him.

Nevertheless, there was something about this new arrival that Tiraud found deeply troubling, and it wasn't just because of Kalinda's response to him. There was air of menace about him. His flinty eyes were focused on Kalinda in such a way as to suggest that the rest of the world didn't matter to him. That, indeed, if the rest of the world tried to get between him and her, it would not go well for the rest of the world.

"Who is that?" Tiraud asked Kalinda softly.

Kalinda jumped slightly, as if she hadn't expected Tiraud to speak. Her gaze darted back and forth nervously as she whispered, "You . . . you see him?"

"What?"

"You see him?" Her voice was a bit louder.

"Of course I do. I'm not blind. Why would you see him and I wouldn't . . . ?"

"Because . . ." She licked her lips as if they'd suddenly gone bone dry. "Dead people. Sometimes they're visible to me. Haunt me. I told you about it."

"Well, yes," said Tiraud with uncertainty. "But I

simply assumed you were speaking metaphorically.
And I'm not sure what that has to do with this fellow,
because he's clearly not dead. . . ."

"Gods almighty. . . ." She rose to her feet, seemingly not of her own volition, but rather as if a pup-
peteer had grabbed hold of strings trailing from her
body and hauled her up. "You . . . it's . . . it's you . . ."

Tiraud was on his feet now as well. He was disliking
the situation more and more. He was suddenly wishing
that he had some heavy armament upon him, because
the closer this man drew, the less he liked it. Fortunately enough, one of his rank always carried a dagger.
It was more ceremonial than anything, harkening to a
more savage, fearsome time in the history of his family.
But antique or not, it cut just as efficiently as if it had
been forged yesterday, and he was now grateful for the
weight of it hanging from the back of his belt.

"It's me," agreed the newcomer. His eyes flickered
toward Tiraud, looked him up and down, then turned
back to Kalinda as if Tiraud's presence was a nuisance
at best. "This him?"

"Him?"

"Your betrothed. I was told you were engaged."

"Yes . . . yes I . . ."

Then she moved quickly toward him, Tiraud apparently forgotten. Reflexively Tiraud reached for her
to hold her back, but she was already away from him.
And she was crying out, *"Xyon! Gods, Xyon!,"* which led
Tiraud to conclude, unsurprisingly, that the intruder's
name was Xyon.

She threw her arms around him, clutching him

eagerly, desperately, continuing to call out his name. He embraced her as well, holding her so tightly that Tiraud thought she might break in half. Obviously she did not, but Tiraud's brow furrowed and he felt a distant thudding in the base of his skull. Some fundamental, primal, inner sense of warning told him that this "Xyon" was not someone he wanted to confront capriciously, but the more his anger was growing, the more he considered just how handy his dagger was.

"You were dead!" Kalinda was crying out, although her voice was partly muffled by the fact that her face was buried in Xyon's chest. "You were dead! Your ship . . . they said you used it to lure the Black Mass . . ."

"Black Mass?" Tiraud was unable to keep silent any longer. "That . . . that mythological creature they tell children about to scare them into submission?"

Xyon stared at him pityingly as Kalinda said, "It's no myth, Tiraud. The *Excalibur* faced it down. I was there. I saw it, this huge mass, it was so . . . so . . ."

"Black," offered Xyon. "Hence the name."

Xyon's voice appeared to startle her back to reality. Like an absentminded party hostess, Kalinda said, "Tiraud . . . this is Xyon. The son of Mackenzie Calhoun. Xyon, this is Tiraud . . . the son of Fhermus, of the House of Fhermus."

Tiraud forced a brief smile. Xyon didn't even bother, which irked Tiraud all the more.

"And there was this black hole in space, and the *Excalibur* was trying to lure the Black Mass into it," Kalinda was continuing, even though Tiraud would happily have forgone the rest of Xyon's riveting tale if it meant getting rid of him that much sooner. "And at the last moment, Xyon and his ship swept in, and decoyed the Black Mass to its death, except Xyon was lost, too . . . except," and she regarded him incredulously, "except he wasn't. You weren't."

"No."

"You weren't pulled into the black hole."

"No. It was a near thing, but I managed to shake loose from the gravity field before it was too late."

"But the area was scanned. We scanned it. There was no sign of you."

"The *Lyla* has cloaking technology. A little antiquated by today's standards. About half the ships nowadays can pick us up if they know what to look for. I was planning to update it . . ."

"Wait. So you . . ." Still trying to comprehend all the facts that were being presented to her, Kalinda paused. "So you . . . are you saying the cloak . . . malfunctioned?"

"No." He looked perplexed. "Why would you think it . . . ?"

"You weren't stuck being cloaked."

"Stuck? Why would I have been stuck?"

"Because . . . if you weren't stuck," Kalinda said slowly, "then . . . you were hiding."

He sighed. "Yes."

"Deliberately."

"Yes."

"You went out of your way to let me . . . and your father . . . believe you dead."

"That's . . . yes, I suppose that's one way to look at—"

She slugged him.

Kalinda was not huge, but she was wiry and strong and worked out regularly, and when her fist slammed into Xyon's solar plexus, it caught him off guard. He let out a stunned gasp of air and staggered back, almost losing his balance but rallying at the last moment.

Tiraud, who had been about to insert himself forcibly into the proceedings out of growing jealousy, suddenly decided that things were proceeding apace just fine. He stepped back, leaned against a tree, and folded his arms, grinning.

"What did you hit me for . . . ?" demanded Xyon, rubbing his chest where she'd struck it.

"What did I hit you for?" Her face was purpling . . . which, considering her face was normally red, didn't require that much shift in coloration. "What do you think I hit you for, you great lummox!"

"Be . . . cause I let you and my father think I was dead?"

"You have to *guess* at that?" she fairly bellowed. "That's something that you're *not* one hundred percent *sure* of? You think there's some *latitude?* A vague chance that I might be angry about something else?!"

"I had my reasons, Kally."

"Your reasons?!" She was getting angrier and angrier. "Oh, this ought to be good! Impress me, Xyon! Dazzle me with whatever the hell was going through your mind at the time, if anything. Explain to me why

you decided to let your father and your lover believe that you were dead!"

"*Lover!*" snarled Tiraud, who suddenly was back to not liking the situation at all. "You were his lover?!"

"She was referring to someone else," Xyon said quickly. "Weren't you, Kally."

"No, I was referring to you, and I can be honest in front of Tiraud because that's what people in love are! Honest!" she said in a defiant voice, and turned to Tiraud for confirmation. "*He* won't be upset! He knew I'd been with others when we got together!"

"Actually, I kind of thought you hadn't," Tiraud admitted.

Fortunately enough for Tiraud, Kalinda didn't hear him. "And he would never run out on me!"

"I didn't run out on you!" Xyon protested. "I just . . . I knew you'd be better off without me than with me."

"Oh, you got to make that decision entirely on your own? My opinions didn't factor in at all?"

"*No, they didn't!*" He put his hands to the side of his head as if dealing with a pounding headache. "You know, I had a mental picture of how this was going to go, and it's amazing how little resemblance to that this bears."

"Well, that's just too bad, Xyon. Not everything goes the way you imagined it would. And do you know why?" She advanced on him, continuing to thump him with her pointing finger. "Because the universe exists of people possessed of free will. We think what we'll think, do what we'll do. And most of the time, we get to utilize that precious free will in order to decide the nature of our future."

"That's what I did," Xyon said defensively.

"That's not what you did! You decided not only your future, but mine and your father's, without giving us a voice." She reached over and shook him, snapping his head back and forth as if he were a rag doll. "You decided, all on your own, what was best for our futures without giving us the slightest consideration."

"Consideration?"

"Yes, consideration! About how we felt! About our mourning for you! You should have returned to the *Excalibur* . . . !"

"Right, right. That would be the ship that blew up not all that long after I departed. Is that the ship to which you're referring?"

Kalinda was thrown for a moment by that observation, but then rallied. "Yes, that's right. And who knows? If you'd been there, with your ship, able to take on passengers . . . you might have made things better! All of us thought that Captain Calhoun had been killed when the ship blew up. If you'd just returned to the *Excalibur* and been there for the emergency, then . . . then maybe you could have saved him and we all would have known he was all right!"

"Well, that's just terrific, Kally," snapped Xyon. "Is there any other blame you'd care to heap upon me? The grief I caused you, the inconvenience of my father's apparent death. Perhaps you'd like to assign me the responsibility for the Selelvian War as well. Come on!" and he spread his arms. "My shoulders are wide enough.

I can support whatever you care to heap upon them."

"You're being ridiculous."

"*I'm* being ridiculous?!"

"Well, at least we agree on something!" she said with mounting frustration.

Xyon pivoted in place, looking as if he wanted to walk in three directions at once. As if he had so much energy combined with so much frustration that he literally didn't know what to do with it all. "I have to say, Kalinda, this has been a thrill for me. A genuine thrill. I am so damned glad I came back . . ."

"Why *did* you come back?" She folded her arms across her chest. "I mean, if you'd already decided that our lives were going to be so much better with you not in them, then what possible purpose was to be served by showing up now, out of the blue?"

"I told you! I heard you'd gotten engaged."

"Right. To Tiraud."

Feeling as if he'd been silent for long enough, Tiraud said, "No doubt you came to offer us your heartiest congratulations?"

Xyon looked him up and down with an air of such insufferable superiority that it made Tiraud want to wipe the look off his face. He restrained himself only because he knew that women's sensibilities were not like men's. As angry as Kalinda was at Xyon, Tiraud knew full well that—like any woman's—her sentiments could turn 180 degrees on a moment's notice. If Tiraud attacked and killed Xyon, as would undoubtedly be the case during any such altercation (because, ultimately, whatever fierce characteristics Xyon might possess,

Tiraud was still nobility while Xyon was some . . . some brigand, as near as Tiraud could tell), then the martyring of Xyon could turn Kalinda completely against Tiraud.

"No, *milord*," Xyon said, his use of the honorific dripping with sarcasm. "To be perfectly honest, no. Not congratulations. I thought I'd come and try to stop Kalinda from making a mistake."

"A *mistake?*" Kalinda gasped it out, and then her mouth moved speechlessly for a few moments as she tried to regain her breath. "Xyon . . . you've been gone! For years! Hiding!"

"I wasn't hiding!" Xyon informed her. "I was doing things. Important things."

"Oh? Like what?" she said with challenge in her voice, but then shook her head. "No, on second thought, don't even tell me. Don't tell me because I don't want to know, because it doesn't matter. I've changed, Xyon. I'm not the same girl I was when you knew me."

"You look much the same."

"Looks can be deceiving," Kalinda pointed out. "For the last few years, for instance, it looked like you were dead. Not only that, but hasn't it occurred to you that I might actually be in love with Tiraud?"

This time Xyon didn't even bother to glance at him. "No." He shrugged. "Never crossed my mind."

"*All right, that's it!*" shouted Tiraud. "I've had all I'm going to take—!"

He started to advance on Xyon, and Xyon stepped back with a grim smile of amusement. "Oh, but I have so much more to give."

Tiraud's hand started to move back toward the dagger, but suddenly Kalinda was between the two of them, facing Tiraud, her back to Xyon. "Step back, Tiraud," she said. "I mean it."

"He has insulted me!"

"And what do you think of him?"

"He's an idiot! A lowborn idiot!"

"Then why should you care what he says? What matter the words of a lowborn idiot?" she demanded.

Xyon's smile spread. "Seems she has you there, milord."

"Stop calling me that!"

"My humblest apologies," said Xyon, apparently having come to the conclusion that the best thing he could do would be to treat Tiraud with heaps of mock respect. "Would you mind telling me what is the proper title with which you should be addressed?"

"Well, it's . . ." He shifted uncomfortably. "It . . . *is* 'milord,' but . . . that's not the point!"

"It's not?" asked Xyon with polite confusion. "Then what is?"

The point is in my blade, thought Tiraud, but before he could put action to words, Kalinda came between them once more. When she spoke, however, it was not with the anger and hurt that had pervaded her tone only moments earlier. Instead it was with sadness and even a sense of regret.

"The point is, Xyon . . . you're too late," she told him.

He tried to laugh. "Too late?" he said. But it was a

pathetic attempt at joviality and not at all convincing.

"Xyon . . . you have to understand." She took his hand in hers, which boiled Tiraud's blood, but he kept his peace. "The fact that you're here . . . now . . . everything we've been saying over the past few minutes, all my reactions, the arguments . . . has completely obscured the fact that I'm thrilled to see you. You were . . . *are*, I mean, I guess I'll have to get used to referring to you in the present tense again . . . are a daring, courageous individual. I owe you my life. He saved my life, Tiraud." She tossed the comment to her fiancé.

"Much obliged," said Tiraud, who could not recall a time in his existence when he was less interested in how someone had saved someone else's life.

"But the thing is, Xyon," she continued, "I think I've outgrown you."

"Out*grown?*" There was incredulity on his face.

"Yes. It's as if you're . . . you're frozen in time from another part of my life. I loved you, I mourned your loss, and then I moved on. And you're standing here in front of me now, absolutely unchanged, and expecting me to move backward to be with you."

"No, I don't . . ."

"Yes, you do! You don't even really, fully comprehend why what you did was wrong. How it was selfish and self-centered. That's unfortunate and limiting, but I realize that it's . . . well, that's just the way you are. You haven't grown up. But I have."

There was a frostiness in his entire manner as he said, "This is the first time you've seen me in years,

Kalinda. There is absolutely no way you can just . . . just judge me like that."

"What else did you expect me to do? Xyon . . . I couldn't keep my life, and myself, in deep freeze, until you were ready to deal with it. The universe doesn't conform to your schedule. Can you really be so selfish as not to see that? Then again, you're the one who refused to let any of us know you were alive for years, so I guess the answer to that is, yes, you can be just that selfish."

"I . . ."

He seemed to want to say something, but he didn't. Instead he straightened his shoulders, standing upright in such a way that Tiraud realized for the first time just how tall Xyon was. Or perhaps he was just trying to make himself look bigger.

"This was a mistake," he said finally. "I should never have come back to you. I should never have expected you to understand."

"Oh, it's my fault now, is it?" There was no anger in the way she said it. Just regret. "And what was I supposed to understand?"

"What it took for me to come here."

"Xyon . . ."

He paid her no mind. Instead he turned his back to her and walked away. Kalinda started after him and Tiraud reached out to her to try and prevent her from following Xyon. But it wasn't necessary, because she stopped on her own.

"Tell your father!" she called after him. "Let him know, at least! It's cruel to leave a hole in his heart just because it suits you to skulk around the galaxy pretending you're dead. He still mourns you!"

"Oh yes," Xyon shouted back without bothering to turn around. "I'm sure I'm uppermost in his thoughts."

She started to say something else to him, but her voice was drowned out by a roar of engines. A small space vessel had risen from behind a hillock, and it was angling down toward Xyon. For a heartbeat, Tiraud hoped that it was an enemy vessel or, even better, that it would simply land atop Xyon and squash him flat. Instead it descended until it came to rest a few feet away from Xyon, and a hatch irised open. Without a backward glance, Xyon stepped in. Then the door shut and the ship lifted off.

Kalinda watched it go, dry-eyed, stoic.

"He was your lover?" Tiraud demanded as the ship receded into the sky.

"Tiraud," she sighed, "do we really have to discuss this now . . . ?"

"Yes, we really do."

She turned to face him and there was mild surprise on her face. "Actually, no. We really don't. I get a vote in this and I say we don't."

"Lind . . ."

"And I hate that you call me 'Lind.' It's Kalinda. Or Kally. Not 'Lind.' Got it?"

She walked away from him, leaving an irritated Tiraud saying, "Right. Got it."

Tiraud had never hated an individual so quickly and thoroughly as he hated Xyon of . . . of whatever damned planet he came from. As for Mackenzie Calhoun, who was apparently Xyon's father . . . he'd never met Calhoun, but already he wasn't too wild about him, either. Then again, from the things his father had told him about the Federation in general, he didn't think he'd be especially thrilled about any UFP starship captain right about then.

U.S.S. Trident

Kat Mueller still wasn't entirely certain what to make of Commander Desma.

That much had apparently become clear to Desma as well, for she was standing in the doorway of Mueller's ready room with a look of concern. Outside, on the bridge, Mueller could hear the brisk conversation between her crew members as they continued their mind-numbingly boring assignment to search for particles characteristic of transwarp conduits. Science officer M'Ress was overseeing the operation, working closely with Mick Gold at conn and Romeo Takahashi at ops. If there was anything out there, Mueller was confident they would find it.

"Problem, Commander?" asked Kat.

Desma took a deep breath and then entered. She appeared a bit flustered, which was odd, since Desma in and of herself represented two things that Mueller rarely saw flustered: first officers and Andorians.

She had the blue skin, plain white hair, and antennae that were typical of her race. Her face was rounder, though, far less angular than the typical Andorian's, and her eyes were unusually intense, giving the impression that she was mentally dissecting you even if she was just staring at you.

"I believe we need to clear the air, Captain."

"Oh." Mueller stared at her uncomprehendingly. "Well . . . all right. Talk to Hash at ops, have him coordinate with engineering, and they can run a diagnostic on the atmospheric filters."

If Mueller looked bewildered, Desma was no less so. "No . . . Captain . . . I mean . . ." She shook her head. "I mean the air between us."

"Oh," Mueller said again, and then understanding dawned. "Oh! Clear the air between us!" But then she was once more bogged down in a deep layer of confusion. "Is the air between us cluttered? That is to say, do you have a problem with me, Commander?"

"Do I?"

Now Mueller was beginning to feel a bit impatient. "Commander, I'm strongly suspecting I'm going to have enough trouble supplying my own answers for this conversation. I'll be damned if I have to supply yours as well."

Desma drew herself up stiffly. "I'm not asking you to speak on my behalf, Captain. I am quite capable of speaking for myself."

"Well, thank God one of us is," said Mueller with an amiability she didn't feel. "Commander, what are you going on about?"

"Permission to speak freely, Captain?"

"I don't see that I could possibly avoid it."

"I feel," Desma said, pacing back and forth in a

small, very precise line, as if she were a one-female parade, "that you consider me an intruder."

"You're my second-in-command, Desma," Mueller reminded her. "You're part of my crew. My good right arm. In what way would I possibly be considering you an intruder?"

"It's nothing I can readily put into words, Captain."

"Well, I hate to point this out," Mueller said with rising impatience, "but words are pretty much all we've got at our disposal. So find the words or find the door."

"Captain, I'm not stupid."

"Imagine my relief."

"I know," Desma continued gamely, "that I was not your first choice for executive officer. Or any choice, really. I know that you were practically ordered to by Starfleet."

"First of all, let's get a few things straight," Mueller said, leaning back in her chair and affecting an air of casual detachment. "In Starfleet, no one gives out orders that are 'practically.' Either orders are issued or they aren't. There's no ambiguity, no middle ground. So in answer to your question—and although it wasn't actually a question, I'm choosing to regard it as such— no, I was not ordered to bring you on as my executive officer, practically or otherwise."

"But there was some arm twisting going on," Desma insisted.

Mueller shrugged. "I think it safe and accurate to say that you came highly recommended."

"Perhaps even vigorously recommended?"

"I wouldn't dispute that characterization," admitted Mueller. "Yes, Starfleet brass at the highest levels repeatedly recommended you for the post. But it was a recommendation *only*, vigorous or no. A recommendation that, as a Starfleet officer and captain of the *Trident*, I was fully empowered to attend to or ignore, at my discretion."

"May I ask, Captain, why you chose to accede to Starfleet's request to give me this assignment?"

"None of your damned business."

"Captain!"

"It's really not, Commander," Mueller told her, rising and stepping around from behind her desk. "In case you've lost track of the number of pips each of us has on her uniform, I don't have to answer to you."

"I didn't mean to infer you were . . ."

"No, you didn't mean to *imply* I was, but the inference which I drew was, I think, a fairly accurate one."

"Captain, seriously . . ."

"I'm being serious, Commander," Mueller said, and the coldness in her eyes made it quite clear that she was. "If someone above me in rank asks me for my rationale over a decision, then I will give it. When a subordinate asks, the *inference* I draw is that she lacks confidence in my ability to make decisions."

"No, Captain," Desma fervently assured her. "I have no lack of confidence at all in your decision-making ability."

"None?"

"None at all."

Mueller considered that a moment, then leaned

against the desk. "If that were the case," she pointed out, "if that were really, truly the case . . . you'd have no need to ask me in the first place, would you? Your confidence in the decisions I make would be all you'd need. You wouldn't doubt me. You wouldn't doubt yourself. You would instead simply take it on faith, which is how the chain of command is supposed to work. Tell me, Desma . . . do you think you're unqualified in some way?"

"No, Captain, I do not."

"Incompetent, perhaps?"

"No!"

"Of lesser ability than other potential candidates?"

"No, Captain."

"That's impressive," Mueller said, raising a single arched blond eyebrow and sounding caustic. "So you're saying that you were the single most qualified candidate out of the entirety of Starfleet. Best educated, most experienced, better than anybody."

"Now wait, Captain . . ."

Mueller made a *tsk-tsk* noise. "Sounds to me like your ego has run wild, Desma."

"Captain, it's nothing like that at all. I'm not saying I'm the best-qualified person in all of Starfleet . . ."

"Why aren't you?"

Desma blinked in confusion and her antennae responsively twitched. "Why aren't I what?"

"Saying you're the best-qualified person in all of Starfleet," Mueller said to her readily.

"Be . . . because I don't know if it's true . . ."

Mueller slammed her open hand so hard on her

desk that Desma jumped slightly. *"You never admit it. Not ever."*

"But . . ."

"Not. *Ever.*" Mueller felt as if she and Desma were connected by a thin strand of energy, gut to gut. "Desma, I know what you're thinking. You're thinking that because your people, the Andorians, were such a help to the Federation during the Selelvian War . . . and because so many of your people suffered casualties during the attacks on the Andorian embassies . . . that Starfleet somehow felt it 'owed' you this assignment. That the Andorian membership in the Federation has always been shaky at best, and your presence here would contribute to a smoothing over of possible lingering resentments. Am I right?"

"Well . . . something like that . . ."

"Stop thinking it. It's pointless, you're only hurting yourself with it, and it's of no relevance. It's causing you to perceive slights on my part that aren't there, and there's no way in all the levels of hell that I'll allow myself to be dragged into any sort of dispute that has even the faintest evocative whiff of the difficulties M'Ress had with Gleau."

"The . . . what that who had, Captain?" she asked, puzzled.

"It doesn't matter," said Mueller, brushing aside the question. "The only thing that matters is this: As a second-in-command and executive officer, your career path is angling you toward command. It's the direction you're heading whether or not you want it, and you can take that as true from someone who definitely didn't want it. Presuming you reach that exalted rank, you don't need to be carrying doubts along with you as to how you got there or whether you deserve to be there. None of that is going to matter worth a damn. Instead the only thing that's important—the only thing that the people who have staked their lives to your abilities are going to care about—is your getting the job done with conviction and confidence. That's all. Doubts, uncertainties, and confusions are to be shared with the ship's counselor, and your spouse . . . but only if your spouse outranks you. Otherwise keep your damned mouth shut. So don't come in here and start telling me about all the doubts or issues you have with your having assumed the post of executive officer here. They're of no relevance to me, and they shouldn't be to you. I'm not your mother, and those people out there aren't your children. Do the job or step aside for someone else who can. Are you intending to step aside, Commander?"

Desma squared her shoulders. "No, Captain, I have no intention of doing that."

"Then do your job and stop second-guessing yourself and me."

"Aye, Captain."

With that, her head held high, Desma turned on her heel and walked out the door, leaving Mueller to marvel at the spectacular amount of crap she had just laid upon her first officer.

"Captain's personal log, supplemental," she said softly. "I've been letting my animosity toward Commander Desma show in my attitude toward her. I have to restrain myself in that regard, because it undercuts my main reason for taking her on.

"Desma is under the impression that I gave in to pressure from Starfleet to accept her as my second-in-command. The fact is that there was a good deal of pressure, most of it coming from the Office of Interplanetary Affairs. Although I've no proof, I suspect a deal was cut behind closed doors that an Andorian would be given a high-profile position aboard a Starfleet vessel at the earliest opportunity. There is concern that Andorians are underrepresented in Starfleet, and a perception of bias. It is my belief that there is no bias. Most Andorians are screened out by the requisite psychological profiles for entering the Academy. And they're screened out not because they are Andorians per se, but because they are by nature a fairly violent race.

"Commander Desma is one of the rare exceptions, possibly because of the unique circumstances of her upbringing. For that reason, she was a prime candidate for this opportunity.

"Nevertheless, I found myself repulsed by the notion of taking her on as first officer, despite the pressure from the OIA. I could not understand why I felt such personal revulsion at the notion, but after some meditation, I realized: The only Andorian I'd ever known was Lieutenant Commander Cray, and he turned out to be a traitor. Because of that negative experience, I was concerned that I was developing a racial bias against Andorians. To categorize them as a violent race is simply to observe a continuing characteristic of the species, in the same way that one would think of

Klingons as warlike and Vulcans as logical. But to actively distrust them on the basis of the actions of an individual . . . that is not an attitude in keeping with a Starfleet captain.

"So I accepted Desma's application as first officer, really, out of self-interest. To try and cure myself of a potential bias that could affect my performance by forcing myself to face something—someone—against whom I was unreasonably prejudiced. She is, to all intents and purposes, a guinea pig through which I'm working out issues I have with her species.

"Her presence here is one of the most selfish acts I've ever performed. I cannot let her know this, however, as it will further aggravate a situation that is already delicate. So I must make greater effort not only to hide, but to overcome, my fundamental antipathy for her. It is the only way to erase this potentially fatal weakness from my personality."

She took a deep breath then and let it out. "I just wish to God," she said, "that there was someone on this damned ship I could talk to about it other than myself. End log entry."

For long moments after that, she sat and stared out the window at the passing stars. It was odd. Mueller had always been someone who sought solitude. It was one of the reasons she'd been so comfortable being in charge of the nightside, until circumstances had propelled her front and center and, eventually, into captaincy. Yet she'd always thought of captaincy as the ultimate solitary position, so one would have thought she'd be happy there.

It was only upon taking on the assignment and sitting in the big chair that she'd realized captaincy wasn't about solitude. It was about loneliness. That was a very different thing. Even when she was sitting on the bridge, surrounded by her crew . . . she was still lonely.

"Ah well," she said to no one as she stood and smoothed her uniform jacket, "too late to complain now."

She headed for the door of the ready room and, as it slid open, almost collided with Lieutenant M'Ress.

The Caitian science officer rocked back slightly on her paws, but her perfect sense of balance prevented her from tumbling back. Instead she provided enough leeway that Mueller was able to stop herself from actually banging into M'Ress.

"Sorry, Captain," said M'Ress, the catlike officer recovering with her typical grace. "Just coming to get you. We've found something."

That was typical M'Ress: getting so excited about something that she had to go and get Mueller instead of just summoning her via the com unit. "Let's see it," said Mueller, stepping out onto the bridge.

Desma smoothly stepped up and out of the command chair, calling, "Slow us to one-half impulse."

"One-half impulse, aye," Mick Gold snapped back from the conn. The *Trident* obediently slowed as Mueller stood in the center of the bridge, studying the screen.

"All right," said Mueller, "what am I looking at?"

"Bringing it up on the screen now, Captain," said

M'Ress. Mueller noticed that M'Ress's tail was switching. Typical behavior when she was enthused about having discovered something. "We've been tracking random particles of highly energized tachyons that have no natural explanation. We find them occurring in greater and greater concentration, and we now have localized what we believe to be the point of origin. I designed a schematic to visualize it."

The screen shifted to display the course that the *Trident* had been following. A series of glowing red spots were superimposed. M'Ress began, "The spots represent the—"

"Trail of tachyon emissions, yes, I understand that, Lieutenant," said Mueller. "Am I seeing what I think I'm seeing?" She pointed to the left-hand side of the screen, which coincided with their own position.

"Yes, Captain," said M'Ress with clear satisfaction. "I believe we've found a sinkhole."

Mueller had never actually seen such a thing, but she had certainly read about it in various briefing papers that outlined what to do if the Borg happened to show up in your vicinity. (Papers which, for all their variety, nevertheless managed to boil down to pretty much the same thing: "Get the hell out of there.")

"Sinkhole" was the nickname given the origin point of a transwarp conduit. It more or less looked like a whirlpool in space, at least from an emissions point of view. That was what Mueller was looking at now. The tachyon particles, glowing red on the screen, were scattered about on the right-hand side of the screen, but began to draw tighter and tighter in as her eye tracked them across. Then, finally, there it was: The tachyon particles converging into a great, glowing whirlpool effect. A sinkhole. It was no longer there; they were staring at a ghostly image of what had been there earlier, but wasn't anymore.

Still, it was daunting to see it, even in the form of trace records. One would never have been able to tell by Mueller's demeanor, because it remained as detached and frosty as ever. But inside, a faint chill was gripping the base of her spine as she imagined what it would be like to see one of those damned things opening up in front of you, knowing that it was about to spit out something great and terrible: a Borg cube, nigh invincible, looking to assimilate whatever it encountered that was of the slightest use, and dispose of whatever wasn't.

"Captain?"

Mueller realized to her chagrin that M'Ress had been talking and she, Mueller, hadn't been paying attention. She drew herself up, shaking off the distraction, and said, "Sorry, Lieutenant. Just . . . weighing options. Give me that again . . . ?"

"I was saying," M'Ress said carefully, as if wanting to make sure that Mueller was fully attuned to her this time, "that we don't know for certain if, unlike other transwarp conduits of record, this one was being utilized by the Borg."

"My guess," Romeo Takahashi drawled from ops, "is that it wasn't."

"Explain," said Mueller.

"See that planet?" He indicated a small orb hanging

not far from the point of origin of the conduit. "That nice, blue and green, still-in-one-piece world?"

"Of course. It's still there," Mueller realized. "If the Borg had come through here . . ."

Lieutenant Arex, the three-armed, three-legged Triexian security chief, spoke up from his station at tactical. "Then there'd be nothing left. From all that I've read and studied about the Borg, even if the planet had nothing that was of interest to them, they'd chew it up just for the minerals to help power their vessel."

"Plus Borg ships leave an identifiable ion trail," M'Ress spoke up, studying her science scanners. "I'm not picking up anything like that."

"All right, people, you've sold me. This isn't the Borg we're dealing with." She folded her arms. "M'Ress, can you give me an idea of how long ago that thing was in existence? When did a transwarp conduit last open here?"

"Hard to know for sure, Captain," admitted M'Ress. "Based upon standard deterioration of the particles, I'd say seventy-nine hours . . . but that's as much guesswork as anything."

Desma spoke up, standing at Mueller's right elbow. "So what vessel readings are we getting? What's come out of that thing within the last seventy-nine hours?"

"That's the problem. Near as I can tell: Nothing."

"*Nothing?*" Desma sounded surprised and confused, and Mueller's reaction was pretty close to that, although she didn't indicate it. "How can that be?"

"There have been reports," Arex said slowly, "that the Romulans have improved their cloaking devices to such a degree that they now have vessels that move without leaving any sort of energy signature."

"Ghost ships, they call them. Something like that?" Desma asked. Arex nodded. "But that doesn't entirely make sense."

"No, it doesn't," agreed Mueller. "At least we know the Romulans have cloaking devices. I hadn't heard of them developing transwarp conduit technology, however."

"Nor have I," M'Ress said. "And considering the vast amounts of energy a transwarp conduit requires to be produced, I don't believe they have any vessels either in their fleet, or even on the drawing board, that would be capable of it."

"Do we?" asked Mueller.

M'Ress shook her head, her long mane waving around her. "Not to my knowledge."

"Nor mine," said Mueller, "and I have higher security clearance than you."

"So when ya boil it down," Hash observed, "we're talking about a level of technological development that's beyond anything that anyone in our little section of the galaxy currently has available to them. And maybe even beyond what the Borg have available."

"We don't know that for sure," said Mueller. "It's possible the Borg possess the capability for some sort of stealth technology. But stealth isn't a huge priority for the Borg."

"No, they *want* you to know they're coming," Gold said ruefully from conn.

"I wouldn't say that," countered Arex. "I'd say the

Borg simply don't care if you know they're coming or not."

"There's another possibility," M'Ress pointed out. "Maybe it's a naturally occurring transwarp conduit."

"Is there a record of such a thing?" asked Mueller.

"No, Captain. Then again, there was no record of a wormhole that developed through anything other than natural means . . . until it was discovered that the Bajoran wormhole was created by an alien intelligence. So there's no reason to think that the reverse couldn't be true: that we've discovered a naturally occurring space phenomenon that was previously thought to be only manufactured."

Mueller stared at the screen for a long moment, and then said, "Wait a minute. We may be overlooking something that's staring us right in the face. The planet."

"Which one, Captain?" asked Desma.

"The one that's in one piece, so we know the Borg didn't plow through here. Whose is it? Is it anyone's? Is it a race even remotely capable of creating a transwarp conduit?"

"Already brought up the specs, Captain," said M'Ress.

Mueller had to admire the efficiency and thoroughly professional demeanor that M'Ress displayed. It had been only a few years ago that Mueller had been highly suspicious of M'Ress, brought aboard as a junior science officer after being time-displaced from her own environment . . . as Arex, her former shipmate, had been. Except M'Ress had seemed to have been handling the transition with far less equanimity, and had wound up having some spectacular head-to-head blowouts with Lieutenant Commander Gleau. Mueller had dismissed many of M'Ress's complaints out of hand, pigeonholing her as an ungrateful whiner. But she had come to realize that she had badly misjudged M'Ress's concerns, and after the business with Gleau went down, she'd sworn to herself she would never underestimate M'Ress again.

And M'Ress had thrived with the new opportunities and challenges presented to her. Her installation as science officer had put some noses seriously out of joint, as other officers who'd been around longer felt slighted. Mueller had gathered them all together and told them to get over it or get out. A couple had gotten out. Most had stayed, and M'Ress had remained as science officer.

"Planet's name is Priatia," M'Ress continued. "Class-M world, with a spacefaring population. The Priatians," and she was reading off the write-up in the Federation data banks, "are the oldest race in Sector 221-G. Once the most dominant, but the combination of war and disease decimated their race."

"Decimated," Hash spoke up lazily, "means reduced by one-tenth. I suspect you mean they lost far more folks than that."

M'Ress fired him an annoyed look, her eyes narrowing. Mueller could have sworn she heard a low growl, and smiled slightly at that. "All right. It nine-tenthed them," said M'Ress. "The point is, the Priatians are not known to have anything approaching the level of technological sophistication that a transwarp conduit would require. If they had, they certainly could have fared far better in their struggles to survive."

"Who were they struggling with?" asked Desma.

"The Thallonians. More accurately, the ancestors of the modern-day Thallonians who colonized this area of space and took it from the Priatians who were already residing here."

"All right," Mueller said, after considering the matter. "All right . . . M'Ress. Take as detailed readings as you can from this. I want a complete report, A to Z, soup to nuts, got it? Once you're done, I want . . ."

"A course laid in for Space Station Bravo? Already in, Captain," Gold said in that annoyingly anticipatory way he had.

"Well, good," said Mueller. "Considering it's where we just came from, it's comforting to know we can find our way back."

"Why not just report back to Admiral Shelby using subspace radio, Captain?" asked Desma.

"Because, Commander," Mueller told her, "I'm still not sure what it is we're dealing with, and whether or not someone whom we can see, hear, or detect is involved with it. That means I don't know who's listening in. Until I do, I'm going to try and keep things as quiet as possible."

Even as she spoke, she watched the world of Priatia with vague suspicion. She could simply have mounted an away team to go check out the world, but that was beyond the mandate of her orders. Not that that would have stopped her if she had a concrete reason presented to her to go down there. There was no proof, however, of anything. Not even a reason for suspicion beyond the proximity of the world to the transwarp conduit, and that alone wasn't enough for Mueller to risk any sort of incident. Besides, small though it was, it was still an entire world, and when one didn't have the faintest idea of what one was looking for or where to look for it, even the smallest world could seem very big indeed.

"They're watching us."

Keesala, in his observation bay, observed the Federation starship hanging there, not far away at all. The fact that it was there made his legs shake, and he leaned against a console to make certain his knees didn't buckle. "They're watching us," he said again. "They know. They know."

"They know nothing," said the creature standing next to him. It reached over and laid a tentacle upon his shoulder. It was oddly comforting. "They know nothing, suspect nothing, and . . . most importantly . . . can do nothing. You understand that, do you not?"

"Yes," said Keesala.

"We have not come back after all these millennia simply to be deterred by such as they." Another tentacle flicked disdainfully in the direction of the viewscreen.

"Of course you have not."

"Then ignore them, as I have," said the creature. It turned and slithered away from him, bumping its head several times on the ceiling as it went and muttering to itself about the annoying small confines of the world the Priatians had constructed for themselves.

And Keesala watched the Trident, *uncertain whether to be nervous about the ship's presence . . . or hopeful that the ship might indeed notice something untoward and come to Priatia to investigate. Nor did his uncertainty ease as he watched the ship eventually turn away from Priatia and head back the way it had come.*

New Thallon

i.

"You've been thinking about him, haven't you."

Kalinda moaned, very, very loudly.

She was seated in front of a mirror, making some last-minute adjustments to the crown of flowers she was supposed to wear around her head. Personally she hated the thing; she thought it made her look like shrubbery. But it was traditionally worn by all females of the royal house, which meant that Si Cwan had insisted upon it, and she just didn't feel strongly enough about it to fight with him over it. Still, she tried to do something decorative with it. She tilted it back, and then to the side, giving her an almost jaunty air. Then she sighed, gave up, and just put it squarely on top of her head. It wasn't remotely fashionable, but at least it was symmetrical.

In focusing on that mundane activity, she pretty much ignored Tiraud, who was seated across the room from her. The room was her private chamber, and she knew that if Si Cwan was aware that Tiraud was there, he'd have a fit. Her brother had many admirable traits, but full cognizance of what century they were living in and what a young woman had the right to do in that century were not, unfortunately, among them. Fortunately enough, Si Cwan—along with Tiraud's father, assorted family members, and the Avower, whose job it was to administer wedding vows—were all out at the summit where the wedding rehearsal was to be held. It wasn't far off, but if Tiraud was going to be going on and on about the same subject, it would seem like miles.

"Tiraud," Kalinda said with greatly pained patience. "You can't keep obsessing like this. Especially when you consider that it's been more than a week since Xyon showed up here . . ."

"*Aha!*" said Tiraud, jumping to his feet and coming toward her shaking a finger. "You mentioned his name."

"*You* brought him up!"

"Yes, but I didn't mention him by name. You knew who I was referring to without my having to say it, thus proving my point."

"If your point is to prove that you're going insane, then consider it proven." She made one final adjustment to the crown, then rose and smoothed her full green dress. "Tiraud, can't you get it through your head? You *won.*"

"Won?"

"Me. My affections. Xyon came here, made his appeal, and I sent him away. What more could you possibly want from a rival—or at least the man you perceive as a rival," she said quickly, anticipating what he was going to say and cutting him off before he could say it, "than for him to depart?"

"Except I don't feel he's departed. I feel his presence here."

"You're being ridiculous."

She headed for the door, but he came up behind her, took her by the shoulders, and turned her around to face him. She let out a little sharp breath of exasperation.

"*Am* I being ridiculous?" he demanded. "I don't think so. You've seemed distant for the past days, Kalinda. As if your thoughts are a million light-years away. As if they're upon him, wherever he is. I see you look to the sky, and I know you're wondering, 'Where is he? Is he out there? Will he come back for me?' "

She pushed his hands away from her shoulders. "Tiraud, how many times am I going to have to tell you you're wrong before you finally, finally get the message? Do I have to break off the engagement with you? Is that what will be required? Is that where we're going with this? That you've become so obsessed with Xyon that you'll actually create a self-fulfilling prophecy by causing our relationship to crack?"

"It would be Xyon who—"

"No! No, it would be you, Tiraud," and she thumped him hard on the chest. "Only you. Not Xyon, not me, not Si Cwan or your father or anyone else. Just you, so consumed with jealousy that it caused you to throw away our chance for happiness together. Right here and now, at this moment in time, Xyon lost and you won. You're on the verge of completely reversing that. Is that what you want? Well? Is it?"

"No," he said. He spoke very softly, and actually sounded contrite.

"Then stop acting like an idiot!"

"You're right."

"And stop disagreeing with everything I . . ." She paused. " 'You're right'? I mean, I'm right? You said I'm right?"

"Yes, I said you're right," he admitted. "I'm being a fool about this. You made your choice, and Xyon—who was the loser, and whom I hold in such low regard—was able to accept it. Not gracefully, mind you, but he accepted it nonetheless. And here am I, the 'winner,' squawking and making a fuss. It's absurd."

"Well . . . good," she said cautiously, but clearly relieved. "I mean, you know . . . it's about time you came around."

"We're going to our wedding rehearsal. We shouldn't be fighting. We should be rejoicing."

"Yes, exactly."

He eyed her bed and then her. "Do you think we would keep them waiting too long if we were to—"

"Yes, they'd be waiting too long," she said firmly but with clear amusement. "We can do the full rejoicing later. Let's attend to our priorities."

"I was trying to, but you want to go to the rehearsal," he teased her. She swatted at him affectionately, and just like that, all the hostility was gone.

He extended an arm to her, and she brought her own arm through it, linking them at the elbows. They emerged from her room and walked through the great halls of the residence wherein she and Si Cwan dwelt. Various politicians, lords, and servants acknowledged them or bowed to them. Once upon a time, Kalinda was bothered by such deference. Now she'd gotten used to it. Part of her wondered whether that was unfortunate or not, but she didn't dwell on it.

They passed through the gardens outside, a dazzling array of well-tended, beautifully sculpted bushes, and they were laughing and teasing each other and having a great old time, all of which came crashing to a halt the instant an all-too-familiar voice sounded from behind them.

"I hate to interrupt you," Xyon called, "but I have something to say. Tragically, Tiraud, I don't think you're going to be thrilled to hear it."

There was nothing nearby Xyon, no covering of any sort. Tiraud and Kalinda gaped at him. "Where the hell did he come from?" demanded Tiraud.

"Xenex," Xyon replied, sounding quite cheerful about it. "A lovely place, you should swing by and see it sometime. Now . . . to business," and he pointed at Tiraud with a magisterial air. "By the laws and traditions of Xenex," he called out, "I challenge you for the woman."

Tiraud just stared at him. Kalinda moaned softly. "This isn't happening," she murmured. "This is just some sort of insanely twisted joke that Si Cwan is playing."

"You challenge me?" demanded Tiraud. "*You* challenge *me?* Where the hell do you think you are, coming here and throwing down such a disrespectful provocation?"

"I have no need to respect you," Xyon informed him. "Because I intend to defeat you and claim the woman."

" 'Claim the woman'?" Kalinda felt as if she were living through some sort of waking dream. "Xyon, I'm not a piece of stray luggage!"

"This has nothing to do with you, Kalinda, and everything to do with him," Xyon said, and pointed once more at Tiraud. "I have issued a challenge. A challenge in keeping with the laws and traditions of my people. What say you, coward?"

"Oh, that's it," Tiraud snapped, and just like that, his dagger was in his hand.

Kalinda's eyes went wide when she saw it. She'd gotten so used to him wearing the ceremonial object in its jewel-encrusted scabbard that she'd stopped thinking about the thing as being an actual weapon. But now she saw him holding it, whipping it through the air with what was clearly practiced expertise.

Xyon's hands remained at his sides. A grim smile played across his lips. She had seen it before . . . on the face of his father, when confronted with situations of life and death. In such instances, Mackenzie Calhoun had never lost.

Despite Tiraud's training in self-defense, despite his claims of physical ability and his undeniable athleticism, Kalinda was suddenly afraid for him.

"Tiraud, stop!" she cried out. "Xyon, this is insane! You can't just—"

"Save it, Lind," snapped Tiraud, approaching Xyon on the balls of his feet, flipping the knife from one hand to the other so that Xyon wouldn't know from which direction the attack would come. "I'll endure his insults and attitude no longer!"

"Where did this 'Lind' come from?" Xyon asked, sounding very casual. He was standing exactly in the same place, making not the slightest move. It was as if Tiraud's attack was of no interest to him . . . or, at the very least, represented no threat. "Her name's 'Kalinda.' Or 'Kally' to some. But 'Lind'?"

"Xyon, this isn't a joke!" Kalinda ran forward, grabbing at Tiraud's shoulder. "He's going to kill you!"

"That's his right. I challenged him."

"No! You don't have the right to challenge him! The two of you don't get to decide my fate!"

Tiraud, not ten feet away from Xyon, whirled and faced Kalinda. "Dammit, Kalinda!" he practically shouted at her. "I have restrained myself because of you! I have bitten back the response I would have given this villain from the beginning because of you!"

"Spoken like someone who's never had to deal with a true villain," said Xyon.

Ignoring him, Tiraud continued, "I have done this out of my love for you! Out of my desire to be with you! And if you have any love for me, you will not ask me to ignore this challenge! You will not ask me to unman myself in that way!"

"I'm asking you to show restraint and not give someone taunting you the satisfaction of obtaining what they want."

He stared at her for a long moment and then said sharply, "You could not possibly understand."

And with that, he pulled abruptly away from her and charged straight at Xyon.

Xyon remained where he was, but his feet were

now spread wide and his hands were in front of him in a defensive position. He still held no weapon. If Tiraud was at all concerned with the dubious morality of carving up an unarmed opponent, he wasn't letting it show or slow him down.

He flipped the knife back and forward twice more and then gripped it with his right hand and drove it straight at Xyon's chest.

At the last possible instant, Xyon pivoted, allowing the knife hand to sail past him.

Tiraud's right hand vanished. So did his arm up to the elbow.

Kalinda gasped, at first unable to grasp what it was she was seeing. Xyon stood there, arms folded, looking quite smug and pleased with himself.

"Stuck?" he asked, sounding as concerned as someone could when they clearly didn't actually give a damn.

"*What have you done?!*" howled Tiraud. He wasn't afraid, but his fury was palpable. He yanked with futility on his arm.

"I saved your life, you idiot," Xyon informed him. "When it comes to matters of self-defense, I operate on instinct and reflex. If that knife had really gotten anywhere near me, I'd have had it out of your hand in a second and across your throat the following second. You'd be dying as your life's blood pumped out of you in—"

"I get the idea, Xyon!" Kalinda called out, still keeping several feet back, uncertain of what was happening. "But what have you done to him?!"

"Oh, well that should be obvious. He—"

Suddenly, despite the fact that his arm was anchored in the middle of thin air, Tiraud lunged at Xyon. The abrupt move nearly caught Xyon unaware, and Tiraud was so enraged that—had he gotten his hand on Xyon's throat—the Xenexian might well have been in serious trouble. But Xyon recovered with lightning speed and stepped back and out of Tiraud's way, whipping his hand around and striking Tiraud on the back of the head for good measure. Tiraud stumbled forward . . . and slammed into something that might well have been an invisible wall. He sagged, and the only thing that prevented him from slumping to the ground was his still entrapped arm, which caused him to dangle there as he blinked and tried to reorient himself.

"Your ship!" Kalinda cried out. "It's the *Lyla*! With her cloaking device!"

Xyon applauded appreciatively. "Never could fool you, Kally. Thing is, I left the hatch open." He walked toward her with a confident swagger. "The moment he shoved his arm into it, Lyla irised it shut. He's lucky I instructed her ahead of time simply to immobilize it, rather than just cut right through. I could have done that as well. But I didn't because of you, Kally. I figured you'd be upset."

"You figured I'd be *upset?!*" She strode toward him angrily.

"Kalinda . . . stay away from him," Tiraud managed to get out.

She ignored him, instead focusing on Xyon. "Xyon, I don't know what you're thinking! I don't believe even you know what you're thinking! Okay, no, I take that back. I think you've been on your own for so long that you've totally lost touch with reality!"

"No, I haven't. And the reality is that I issued a challenge in the traditional way of my people. He lost," he said, chucking a thumb at Tiraud, "and now you belong to me."

"You can't just do that!"

"Hey, it's your fiancé's fault."

"How do you figure that?"

"He didn't have to accept the challenge," replied Xyon. "If he'd refused it, I'd have had no grounds to proceed. Instead, by attacking me, he accepted it. In doing that, he gave up all claim to you."

"But don't you understand? He never had a 'claim' to me! I'm with him voluntarily! I want to be with him! I love him!"

"Only," said Xyon tightly, "because I was stupid enough to stay away. But I'm making up for that right now."

"You got the 'stupid' part of that right. As for the—"

Suddenly there were shouts, angry cries of "What's going on there?!"

Kalinda didn't even have to look; she knew what she was going to see.

Over the crest of a nearby hill, Si Cwan was looking down. Standing next to him were Robin Lefler, and Fhermus of the House of Fhermus, and the Avower, and any number of other guests and notables who were to witness the rehearsal. The fact that

Kalinda and Tiraud were running so late had been enough to prompt the others to head back and see what was keeping them.

Si Cwan had not been thrilled upon hearing the news of Xyon's being alive. He'd never liked Xyon, and had even come to blows with him. In death, he had chosen to think charitably of him; in life, less so. His return to life had been extremely off-putting for Cwan. As for Robin, when she learned of Xyon's survival her first instinct had been to inform Mackenzie Calhoun. But she had refrained from doing so at Kalinda's urging, since Kalinda was hoping and praying that Xyon would see the folly of his actions and choose to tell his father himself. Robin had promised herself she'd wait a month at most, and then she was going to take matters into her own hands.

It was all on the verge of being moot, though, for Kalinda was certain that if Si Cwan got hold of Xyon at that moment, Xyon's death would no longer be a falsehood.

Apparently Xyon thought the same thing. Si Cwan and company were still half a mile off as he said to Kalinda, "We'll have to discuss this later. Come on."

"Come on? Where do you think I'm going to—"

"I'm sorry, Kally, but it should be clear I've no time for this."

And with that, Xyon stooped and—before she realized what was happening—grabbed her around the legs and slung her over his shoulder. Kalinda let out an alarmed shriek as he crossed quickly to the invisible ship. "Lyla! Open up!"

The unseen door irised open and Tiraud yanked out his hand so quickly that he almost fell. Xyon completed the job by sweeping a leg and knocking Tiraud's feet out from under him.

"Xyon! Stop it! You can't do this! You're being an idiot!" howled Kalinda as she thudded on his back with her fists.

"And you're supposed to be with me! And I'll make you realize that!" Xyon shot back as he vaulted through the door. "Lyla, get us out of here!"

The ship didn't respond orally, but it didn't need to. Its reply instead came in the form of its powerful engines as the vessel lifted off, gaining altitude second by second. As if to boast, Xyon dropped the invisibility cloak and the ship shimmered into existence.

"Kalinda!" Tiraud shouted, but his voice was drowned out by the ship's engines. The ship turned gracefully, angled its nose skyward, and began to accelerate. The vessel wouldn't go to warp within a planet's atmosphere: the results would be catastrophic both for the planet and for the ship. In any event, the *Lyla* didn't need to resort to that. In no time at all, the ship was a mere blip on the horizon, and then not even that as it vanished into the afternoon sky.

ii.

Fhermus was stalking back and forth in Si Cwan's private meeting chamber. Robin was there, as was Tiraud.

As for Si Cwan, he thought his head was going to unscrew from his neck as he watched Fhermus's pacing.

News was out, of course, as to what had happened. Every member race of the New Thallonian Protectorate had been informed. There'd been no trouble getting the word out: Everyone seemed simply to have found out about it, almost spontaneously. First they didn't know; then they did. There was a collective sense of outrage, combined with the smirking undertone of condolences that were typically delivered to political rivals. It wasn't as if people had wished hardship or embarrassment on the houses of Cwan or Fhermus, but there were no laws against taking great amusement in that same hardship or embarrassment when it was inflicted upon them.

"What about planetary defenses?" Fhermus demanded. "Why the devil didn't we alert planetary defenses?"

"Brilliant idea, Fhermus," Cwan said, trying and failing to keep the sarcasm out of his voice. "There's every chance that, had I alerted planetary defenses, we could have shot Xyon down before he got out of range. And having done that, I'm sure we would have had no trouble reassembling my sister from the five or six square miles over which her remains would have been scattered. She would have made a lovely bride . . . or should I say 'brides.' "

"Perhaps a shattered condition on her part would have been preferable," sniffed Fhermus.

Si Cwan rose from his chair. "What is that supposed to mean?" he demanded.

"Father," Tiraud tried to interrupt, "it's pointless to get into all that . . ."

But Fhermus clearly didn't consider it so. He went straight up to Si Cwan, and they would have been nose-to-nose if he'd only been a head taller. "My son informs me this . . . this Xyon person . . . was your sister's lover. Is that true?"

"To the best of my knowledge," Si Cwan admitted.

"*Outrage!*" Fhermus stammered. "Outrage, I say! Her slattern past has brought ruin upon us!"

Si Cwan was about to put his fist through Fhermus's face and, as a result, risk the entire collapse of the New Thallonian Protectorate. But before he could do so, Robin Lefler had come between them. "Don't even think about it," she said to Cwan and, before Cwan could reply, turned toward Fhermus. "And you! That comment was completely out of line, and if you have an ounce of class, you'll apologize immediately."

"How dare you," snapped Fhermus. "To tell me what to do! You—"

But now Tiraud stepped forward, and there was both fury and supplication on his face. "Father, please!" he begged. "I still love her, and must ask you not to speak poorly of her!"

"Out of my way, Robin," Si Cwan said angrily. "He insulted my sister!"

"Your sister isn't here, and if she were, she'd have laughed in his face. The fact is that he insulted your pride. And you don't have time to get bogged down in things like this!"

Si Cwan's jaw twitched in obvious irritation. "He must apologize."

Fhermus started to reply in anger, but then saw the look on Tiraud's face. "Consider the comment apologized for," he said, and then his voice roughened, "for the sake of my son's wishes, if nothing else. We must work together at this time of crisis, rather than in our customary opposition."

"What are you going to do?" asked Tiraud.

"Obviously, we're going to find him and bring him back," Si Cwan informed her.

"His ship is cloaked. . . ."

Si Cwan waved the comment off as if it were nothing. "He's not piloting a starship with its nigh-infinite energy sources. A cloak is a substantial drain. He can't run silent forever. I've already alerted every Thallonian vessel out there, whether it's on routine border patrol, science expedition, or cargo run. None of it matters. They are being pressed into service as a whole with one mission: Find Xyon and return Kalinda here safely."

"I, obviously, will do no less," said Fhermus, drawing himself up. "All vessels at the disposal of the House of Fhermus plus, I suspect, all our allies, will be given similar dictates."

"It won't be enough," Tiraud said. "All members of the Protectorate should pledge all their available vessels. This is more than an insult against our house or the House of Cwan. This is an insult against the entirety of the New Thallonian Protectorate."

"My son is right!" Fhermus announced.

"No, your son isn't!" Robin said, and when she saw

the surprised and annoyed looks from everyone else in the room, she didn't back down. "I'm sorry, but he isn't. These were not the actions of someone who was out to insult the entirety of anything. This is a confused young man who has never been sure of anything that he ever really, truly wanted in his entire life, with one exception . . . that exception being Kalinda."

"It doesn't matter whether he intended insult or not, Lieutenant Commander," said Si Cwan in a coldly formal tone. "Insult is what he gave nonetheless, and insult is what has been taken."

"Still, there's no need to overreact. It's not as if Kalinda is in any danger."

"We don't know that," said Tiraud sullenly.

"I think we do."

"Prime Minister," Fhermus said, "would you kindly inform your wife that I am getting a bit tired of her consistently gainsaying my son."

"Excuse me, I'm standing right here," Robin noted. "You can talk directly to me."

"What would you have us do, Robin?" asked Si Cwan. He did not sound angry, but Robin suspected it was not without effort. "Just let him go until he decides, of his own free will and in his own good time, to return Kalinda? Do you have any idea how impotent that would make us look?"

"Since you asked," she said, considering every word before she spoke it, "I would say that Mackenzie Calhoun should be brought in. Have the rest of the ships stand down, let me inform Calhoun of the situation, and have him attend to it. He knows Xyon, he knows Kalinda, he certainly knows his way around the spaceways. He's the man most suited to handling this situation delicately."

"I know all too well of this Calhoun," Fhermus said with a sneer, "and very little of what I know centers around his being able to delicately handle anything. He storms into a situation, completely takes it over, and to hell with anyone else's concerns."

"That's . . . not entirely inaccurate," she admitted, "but still . . ."

"Lieutenant Commander," Si Cwan said, maintaining that same formal tone, "you, in your capacity as liaison, are naturally welcome to respond to this matter however you wish. Inform Starfleet, don't inform Starfleet. It is entirely up to you. If you do bring Calhoun into this and he finds Xyon and Kalinda, and restores her to me while turning Xyon over for punishment for his crimes . . . so much the better. If one of our people finds him first, then . . . so much the worse. For Xyon. If you understand my meaning."

"Don't get snarky with me, Prime Minister," she warned him. "You laughed at my dream. The one that Xyon was in. If I were you, I'd be having myself measured for a chiffon gown about now."

Fhermus stared at her. "Prime Minister, what is she talking about?"

"Nothing of consequence," said Si Cwan with obvious annoyance. "And I trust the lieutenant commander will not lose sight of what's important, especially in regards to my sister's abductor."

"Don't worry, Prime Minister. It's solidly in my sights."

What he was referring to, naturally, was what he'd omitted in his description of the "capture" scenarios.

If any of Si Cwan's people found Xyon and Kalinda first, then Kalinda would be returned safe and sound . . . but Xyon wouldn't be making the trip back to New Thallon. He, instead, would be executed right there and then. He had only two chances for survival: if he managed to avoid the reach of the angry New Thallonian Protectorate, or if his father found him first. And even with the second instance, his chances of survival were iffy at best, once Mackenzie Calhoun got through with him.

U.S.S. Excalibur

i.

"Captain Calhoun."

Mackenzie Calhoun snapped awake in his quarters, rolled off his bed, and hit the floor in a crouch. His head whipped back and forth automatically as he shoved his hair out of his eyes.

"It's good to see those catlike reflexes are still functional," came a softly sarcastic female voice.

Calhoun blinked but didn't demand that the cabin's lights be brought up, partly because of his state of undress, and partly because he was able to make out who was in his cabin . . . mostly because she was glowing.

"Morgan," he moaned, and flopped back onto the bed, arms splayed to either side as if he'd been crucified. "What time is it? And could you turn yourself down, please?"

Morgan Lefler, aka Morgan Primus, stood three feet away from him and promptly diminished by half the glow emanating from her holographic body that made her easy to see in the dark. Once upon a time, she had been a flesh-and-blood woman, the mother of Robin Lefler. Through a freak accident, her body had died . . . but her mind had been transferred in total to the computer core of the *Excalibur*. They'd tried to get her out, but the attempts had proven fruitless. So instead they'd decided to make the best of it by placing holographic circuitry throughout a number of key points in the vessel . . . including, in a decision that Calhoun had come to regret, his quarters.

"It's 0330 hours, Captain."

"It's the middle of the night."

"Technically, it's not."

"This for your technically," he said, tossing off a two-fingered Xenexian gesture that had unmistakable meaning if it was being thrown at another Xenexian . . . or, as was the case here, a computer entity that had full access to every recorded insult in the entirety of the Federation archives.

She put her hands on her hips and looked at him sourly. "That's nice, coming from a starship captain."

"I wasn't trying to be nice."

"Then you succeeded beyond your wildest hopes."

Calhoun rubbed his eyes and forced himself to sit up. "Can I assume," he said, "due to the lack of alarm bells or the fact that you're taking up my time with what you no doubt think is witty repartee, that we don't have an emergency at this particular moment?"

"That is a safe assumption," Morgan said.

"Then what the hell do you want?"

"We're having a rendezvous in half an hour. I thought you'd want to be awake for that."

"A rendezvous?"

"Yes, Captain."

"Was it planned? Was there a memo sent around that I missed?"

"No, Captain."

"Then what the hell . . . ?"

"We're to meet up with Starfleet ETV *Lynx*. We were informed of it eighty-seven seconds ago. Eighty-eight seconds ago. Eighty-nine seconds ago. Nin—"

"Knock it off." When Calhoun was so inclined, he was capable of shaking off sleep in an instant. Upon hearing this, he became exactly that inclined. He sat up straight, the last vestiges of fatigue gone from his face. "An emergency transport vehicle?"

"Yes, Captain. A high-speed vessel that is utilized by senior Starfleet personnel when a starship is not available—"

"I know what an ETV is, Morgan." He scratched his chin thoughtfully. "What's so blasted important that someone would commandeer an ETV when they could just use subspace communication? Who's heading out here, anyway?"

"Admiral Jellico, sir."

"Jellico?" He shook his head. "*Jellico?* Well, that explains that aspect, I guess."

"How so, Captain?"

"Because ever since the war, when our enemies managed to tap into the most secure of communications and garner critical information, he's been extremely paranoid about communiqués of any sort of delicate nature. He's been urging research into new technologies for developing secure channels and an alternative to subspace."

"There is no alternative to subspace communication at the present time."

"Yes, there is," said Calhoun grimly.

"There is?"

"Yes: commandeering an ETV and going places in person."

He rose from the bed, wrapping the sheet around himself, giving him the air of a Roman senator. "Morgan . . ."

"Yes, Captain?"

"Take a hike."

"Yes, Captain," she said. "Shall I inform your senior staff . . . ?"

"You shall not," he told her flatly. "You are to let them sleep until they're scheduled for duty. *Grozit*, with any luck, whatever Jellico has to tell me will be brief enough that he'll be gone before anyone wakes up."

"Very well. Captain, one more thing . . . ?"

"Yes?" he said with an annoyed sigh that indicated his rising impatience.

Morgan smiled insouciantly. "I dare you to meet him dressed the way you are right now."

"Go away, Morgan."

"Aye, Captain," she smirked, and vanished.

Calhoun showered and dressed quickly. His mind was racing, trying to conceive what it was that Jellico was going out of his way to convey to him. Calhoun intensely disliked the notion of going into any situation without a clear idea of what to expect. It was a habit that he'd had ever since the days of his youth on

Xenex when—as his people's warlord—he had staged a lengthy guerrilla war against the oppressive race that had stood for so many years with its boot upon the collective throat of his people. Eventually he and his people had triumphed, driving their oppressors off their world and restoring a free Xenex to its natives.

Those perilous days, when the lives of his men depended upon his seeing all sides and possibilities for any circumstance, had hammered into him the necessity of always being prepared. To consider surprise as anathema, even potentially fatal. That applied to all things for Calhoun, even something as non–life-threatening as a meeting with Jellico.

So what was up? Some sort of top-secret mission? Were the Selelvians massing for some resurgence of hostilities? Another threat, perhaps? The Tholians renewing their alliance with the Selelvians, or perhaps finding other, even more formidable allies . . . ?

Or was it something that was unique to Calhoun that . . .

Elizabeth.

For a moment, as Calhoun stood there in the hydroshower, he leaned against the wall to steady himself. That had to be it. Something had happened to Elizabeth, to his wife, and Jellico was coming to tell him in person because, really, how do you drop news like that in a standard Starfleet subspace message?

Natural causes? She was human, after all, and the human body could shut down at any time with no notice at all. . . .

No. No, it had to be some enemy. Calhoun

growled low in his throat, and imagined himself taking the *Excalibur* and using it like its historic namesake: as a great and terrible sword that would cleave through to wherever his wife's murderer or murderers were hiding and smite them down. And he would take great fistfuls of their blood, rub it on his face in the tradition of the barbaric Xenex he'd left behind, and howl his wife's name that, in the great beyond, she might hear of this triumph against her killers and smile in newly acquired peace. . . .

"Oh, this is ridiculous," he said as he stepped out of the shower. Throwing on a robe, he called, *"Morgan!"*

She immediately appeared. "Yes, Captain."

"You still on speaking terms with the computer at Bravo Station?"

"Of course."

"Interface with it, please."

She blinked several times. "Okay."

"Okay you're going to do it, or . . . ?"

"Okay, I'm interfacing with it right now. What do you wish to—?"

"What's Shelby doing right now?"

Morgan blinked once more. "Captain, she's sleeping. Biorhythms are normal. She's in her quarters. She's alone. Brain-wave scans indicate she's in REM sleep. She's doubtless dreaming of you. So what is . . ." Then Morgan's expression changed to one of sympathy. "Oh. You were afraid Jellico was coming here to tell you she was—"

"It was stupid," he said as he turned away. "Foolish

worries that come to you in the middle of the night, that's all."

"Mac," Morgan said softly, "before I wound up in this . . . condition . . . I lived a long time. Longer than you. Longer than pretty much most any other human. From what I've learned in that time, and from what I've learned of you . . . I think if, heaven forbid, anything happened to Elizabeth Shelby . . ."

"I'd know?"

She nodded. "Yes."

He laughed softly to himself. "You're probably right. Thank you, Morgan."

"Rendezvous in eighteen minutes."

"I'll be ready."

ii.

Standing in the transporter room, hands draped behind his back, Calhoun didn't feel ready. He was, however, convinced he had some inkling of what this was all about.

Soleta.

The guilt over her departure from Starfleet and her joining the Romulans still burned in his belly. Barely a week went by when something didn't remind him of her, and he would mentally berate himself yet again that somehow, in some way, he should have been able to prevent matters from reaching that point.

Ensign Penelope Halliwell was at the transporter

console, rubbing the last traces of sleep from her eyes. She'd been hauled out of bed specifically to cover Jellico's unexpected arrival. Mostly she was there just in case something should go dramatically wrong. Calhoun wasn't expecting that to happen but, as always, expected nothing but anticipated everything.

"You awake, Ensign?" he asked.

"Yes, sir," she said, "hiccuping" in a slight yawn.

"You sure? Wouldn't want the admiral's molecules to be scattered all over space."

"I'm on it, sir. . . ."

"Bridge to transporter room," came the voice of Morgan Lefler. Morgan oversaw the nightside since, naturally, she didn't require sleep. There were no holocircuits installed in the transporter room, however, so she remained at her station on the bridge rather than simply materializing herself down there to report.

"Transporter room, Halliwell here."

"We are being hailed by ETV vessel *Lynx*. Requesting permission to beam passenger aboard."

Such requests always had to be authorized. Under ordinary circumstances, it was the bridge officer on watch who tendered authorizations. But Halliwell glanced at Calhoun, who simply nodded. "Bridge, we have authorization for transportation, and . . ." She looked over at a blinking light on her console. ". . . we have coordinate lock. Prepared to beam passenger aboard."

"So ordered," said Morgan. "Keep me apprised if there's any problem. Bridge out."

Calhoun stood there, arms folded, as the transporter hummed to life. Moments later, Admiral Edward Jellico appeared.

It had been six months since Calhoun had last seen him. His once-blond hair had turned almost completely gray, and Calhoun was sure a few more wrinkles had taken up residence on his face.

"Welcome aboard the *Excalibur*, Admiral."

A wide grin split Jellico's face. "Good to see you, Mac," he said as he stepped off the transporter deck and strode over to Calhoun.

"You too, Eddie," said Calhoun with sincerity. The two men shook hands for an instant, and then patted each other on the respective shoulders. "You're looking good."

"I look like crap on two legs. You seem well, though. Are you?"

"Well, some of that may depend on what you felt was so important to tell me that you sped out here yourself to do it."

Whatever jauntiness there might have been in Jellico's expression quickly faded. "Can we talk somewhere private?"

"My cabin's right down the hall. Less distance to cover, less pointless chitchat to make."

"I've missed your blunt manner, Mac."

"Really?"

"Not so much, no," admitted Jellico, but then he smiled again, although Calhoun noticed that the smile wasn't reflected in his eyes. "Your cabin then."

Two minutes later they had taken up residence in Calhoun's quarters, and Calhoun was pouring Jellico a glass of Romulan ale. Jellico eyed the blue liquid steadily. Calhoun was holding the bottle a good two feet above the glass, but the ale was flowing in with pinpoint precision. Not so much as a drop was being spilled.

"Now you're just showing off," said Jellico.

"Best way to allow it to breathe," Calhoun told him as he handed the glass over and poured another glass for himself, this time from three feet above. Jellico snorted at the display and stared thoughtfully at his glass.

"Interesting choice of beverage."

"It's what I had on hand."

"Wouldn't be to remind me of absent company?"

"Admiral . . ."

"Mac," he sighed, "are you going to start beating yourself up over Soleta again? Or is the plan to beat me up this time about her? I mean, considering you already beat up the Starfleet Council—"

"I did not beat him up."

"You practically smashed his face in!"

"True, but 'beating up' implies a lengthy fight. Repeated blows. It's hardly my fault he was flattened with one punch."

"What if he hadn't been? What if he'd fought back?"

"Then I'd have beat him up," said Calhoun matter-of-factly. "Obviously."

Jellico snickered and shook his head. "Wow, Mac. Hard to believe you've pissed off as many people as you have."

"You used to be one of them. The *most* pissed off, as I recall."

"Things change, as we both know." He held up the glass and Calhoun clinked his own against it.

They drank in silence for a long moment, and then Calhoun lowered his glass. "So what's happened? What's she done?"

Jellico blinked in confusion. "She? She who?"

Calhoun was clearly surprised. "Soleta," he said, holding up the bottle of Romulan ale as if she were somehow inside it. "Isn't that why you're here?"

"Good lord, no. What made you think . . . ? Strike that. I can guess what made you think it. But no, it doesn't involve Soleta. Nor your wife, in case you were concerned about Shelby."

"Hmm? Oh . . . no. No." He shook his head. "No, it never even crossed my mind. I know Elizabeth can take care of herself just fine. But if it's not Soleta, then . . . ?"

"It's . . . a fairly personal matter, Mac, which is why I wanted to tell you in person." He was sitting on the edge of a chair facing Calhoun, and was leaning forward, rubbing his glass between his hands, sloshing the liquid within. "I mean, yes, I have security concerns regarding subspace these days, but I also felt this was the type of thing you should really be able to hear in a genuine face-to-face situation rather than a virtual one."

"All right, fair enough," Calhoun agreed, although he was dubious about it. What did Jellico think? That he was going to break down upon hearing whatever news this was and start sobbing on Jellico's shoulder? "So what's happened?"

"It's . . ." Jellico took a deep breath, in promise of something portentous. "It's . . . Xyon."

Calhoun stared. "What about him?"

"He's alive."

Calhoun continued to stare. "Yes."

Jellico was clearly taken aback. "You . . . don't seem surprised."

"Should I be? Ed," Calhoun leaned forward, "has Selar been talking to you? Is that what this is about? Because, if so, then I apologize for your being dragged into this. She's become obsessed about Xyon. I suppose I can't entirely blame her . . ."

"You're telling me you know that Xyon is alive?"

"Of course I know it. He lives two decks down."

"He's here?!" Jellico had been sitting, but now he put his drink down on the nightstand and stood, his manner one of great gravity. "Are you serious?"

"Of course I'm serious."

"And is the girl here, too? Kalinda? Because if she is, Mac," and Jellico was shaking his head, "and you're offering him aid and comfort, then you've stuck your head into a hornets' nest of . . ."

"Kalinda? Si Cwan's sister? Why the hell would she be here?" Now Calhoun was standing as well.

"Because your idiot son kidnapped her, that's why! What are you playing at here, Cal—"

And then Jellico stopped as Calhoun gaped at him. Calhoun felt a distant throbbing in the scar that adorned the right side of his face, the sensation he always experienced when he was under the greatest of stress. "My . . . son . . . ?"

"Yes! And if you're telling me that he's taken refuge here on—"

"No," Calhoun said slowly, and he leaned against the wall to help provide him support, for suddenly he couldn't feel his legs anymore. "No . . . he's not here . . ."

"Calhoun," Jellico said angrily, coming toward him, and no longer did he have the genial, almost avuncular air that he'd sported since coming aboard. Now he was sounding like the belligerent, judgmental Jellico of old. "I'm not stupid."

"No. I am. How could I have misunderstood what you—" The throbbing was extending to a pounding that threatened to envelop his entire head.

"Then don't misunderstand this. If Xyon is aboard this vessel, then you must turn him over to—"

"Selar's son, Ed. His name is Xyon, in memory of my . . . dead . . . son. Although these days, he usually goes simply by 'Xy.' "

Jellico blinked in confusion for a moment, and then his face softened. "Oh . . . my God. Of course. I should have understood immed—"

"It's not you. It's me," said Calhoun. "I just . . . I came to terms with it so long ago, I never . . . it never occurred to me . . ."

"There's no reason it should have."

"My . . . *son?*" Calhoun was still having trouble wrapping his mind around it. In some respects, he felt as if he were still sleeping. That this was all some sort of insanely skewed dream and he'd be waking up at any moment. "Are you sure? Perhaps it's some crazy mistake. Or an impostor . . ."

"Is it possible he's an impostor? I suppose," said Jellico with a shrug. "But if so, he's gone to a lot of work for no discernible reason."

As briskly and efficiently as he could, Jellico outlined for Calhoun all that he'd learned. Calhoun was seated, and he had set aside the glass into which he'd poured the Romulan ale. Instead he was knocking back the contents straight out of the bottle. Jellico wisely chose to make no comment on that.

Jellico's description of the events leading up to the kidnapping were fairly detailed. Calhoun didn't have to ask him the source of his information, since it was obviously Robin Lefler, and what she'd been told by the participants. He interrupted Jellico only once, to say, "A challenge? He issued a Xenexian challenge for a woman?"

"You've heard of the practice?"

"Heard of it? I did it myself once."

"Really. For anyone I know?" Jellico said with grim humor, and then abruptly a serious answer to his joke occurred to him. "Wait . . . not . . . ?"

Calhoun nodded.

"Shelby?"

"I was young and stupid," said Calhoun. "Back in my Academy days. You remember."

"Of course I do, considering the messes of yours I

had to clean up. You threw down some sort of chauvin-
istic challenge for Elizabeth Shelby and she wasn't totally *repulsed* by it?"

"Well . . . I did it with a great deal of charm."

"I can only imagine," said Jellico, who obviously
couldn't. "And did you ever relate this marvelous incident to Xyon?"

"I . . . might have, one evening. During a rare
bonding moment."

"Terrific." Jellico massaged the bridge of his nose
and Calhoun suspected his own headache was conta-
gious. "Just . . . terrific."

He then continued with his summary of all that had
occurred on New Thallon. When he concluded, the
two men sat there for a long moment in silence that
was broken only by the soft *glug* of the Romulan ale
being finished off by Calhoun.

Calhoun finally broke the quiet. "If they find him,
he's dead . . . again."

"That's what I hear."

"Then I'm going in after him."

"His actions have threatened to destabilize the region, Mac. Tempers are running hot."

"Yes, which is why they'll kill him. I understand,
Ed."

"No, I don't think you do, Mac. The sins of the son
are reflecting on the father."

Calhoun considered that a moment. "You're saying
I may not receive a particularly warm welcome myself."

"That's exactly what I'm saying, yes. They'll be
concerned that you're going to try and . . ."

"And what? Stop them from killing him?"

"Yes," Jellico said grimly.

"Imagine their surprise when they turn out to be right."

"Mac, you can't go barreling into Thallonian space with phasers blasting . . ."

Calhoun looked at Jellico incredulously. "Ed, what did you *think* I was going to do when you dropped this little bombshell on me? Nod my head, say 'Thanks for the tip,' and go back to business as usual? If it was your son, what would you do? Or are you telling me that I can't bring the *Excalibur* in there, that it'll run contrary to Starfleet regulations. Fine." He reached up for the pips on his collar and started to unfasten them. "I'll resign my commission. My personal ship is down in the shuttlebay, and that'll be all I need to—"

Jellico pulled Calhoun's hand away from his uniform shirt. "I think what this situation calls for, Mac, is for you to overreact even more than you already are."

"I don't need sarcasm right now, Ed."

"And I don't need you flying off half-cocked."

"Not to worry, Ed," Calhoun assured him. He circled the interior of his quarters while waggling an accusatory finger in the air, giving him the look of a caged professor. "For years now I've lived with the knowledge that my son is dead. Now you show up here, tell me he's alive. You can't possibly expect me not to do anything about it."

"At what point in any of this have I told you I didn't expect you to? Of course I expect you to."

Calhoun looked suspiciously at Jellico. "You do."

"Naturally. All I was trying to do was emphasize some of the difficulties you may be facing, so you'd be better prepared. You're the one who's flying off in all directions, and that's not the mind-set you need right now. Frankly, I'm a bit surprised at you. That's not the way I generally expect to see you reacting in a crisis."

"Fair enough," Calhoun allowed. He took a deep breath, let it out slowly. "I feel like . . ." His fingers fluttered around the top of his head. "I feel like my brain is splintering in all directions. Like I'm having trouble focusing. There's a dozen reactions all warring, one with the other, and I don't know which one to give emphasis to."

"You don't know whether to laugh or cry," Jellico said understandingly. "Whether—if and when you find Xyon—you'll embrace him or hit him."

Calhoun contemplated that and then said, "Probably both."

"You'll take the *Excalibur* into Thallonian space?"

"Of course."

"You should know that you'll have backup."

"Will I?" Calhoun raised an eyebrow questioningly. "Suddenly doubting my ability to get the job done?"

"Not at all. It's pure coincidence, Mac. The *Trident* is in and out of that region, doing a scientific survey that's unrelated to what's going on with Xyon."

"Are we sure it's unrelated?" Calhoun asked.

"I'm not sure what connection there could be," Jellico said, stroking his chin thoughtfully as he considered the matter. "They're investigating the possible generation of a transwarp conduit. I somehow doubt that Xyon's making use of a conduit."

"Yes, that's more the signature of the Borg, isn't it."

"Or possibly another, even more formidable race."

"Thank you, Ed. You've just given me something else to be worried about." Despite the seriousness of the situation, Calhoun allowed a smile. "Working with the *Trident* again. It'll be just like old times."

"All right, well . . . you know the situation now." He thrust out a hand and Calhoun shook it firmly. "You're walking into a powder keg and you might just be what lights the fuse, Calhoun. For God's sake, be careful."

"Aren't I always?"

"Almost never," said Jellico.

Calhoun shrugged. "Then I might as well stay with what works."

The Lyla

"It's not going to work, Kalinda."

From the moment that she'd been hauled onto the *Lyla* until Xyon had finally chosen to breach the silence between them, which had grown like a glacial wall, Kalinda had said nothing. Done nothing. Touched nothing. Not even looked in his direction. She had sat in a far corner of the main cabin, as far from Xyon as she could physically manage.

The silent treatment? Xyon found it amusing. He had never been able to understand why in the world women thought that lack of talking was some sort of punishment. Xyon wasn't necessarily the chattiest of individuals. Most males he knew considered the task of keeping conversation going with females to be the most onerous aspect of any involvement. So if, rather than haranguing him and complaining about her ill treatment, Kalinda was just going to sit there with her mouth tightly shut . . . okay. Fine. So be it.

Hours rolled one over into the other as Xyon put as much distance as he could between himself and New Thallon. All things being equal, he simply would have tried to warp out of the area at high speed.

That, however, was not possible, for the net that Si Cwan had drawn around the sector had been a very thorough one. There were ships everywhere. It seemed as if, no matter which of the infinite directions he traveled the spaceways, there were vessels on stakeout, waiting to snag him.

He had several advantages. One was the cloaking device, of course. But that wasn't an all-purpose cure-all for his difficulties. He had to be judicious about energy use, lest constant employment of the cloak leave him dry at a point where he truly needed the cloak to hide or his engines at full power to get away. Second, *Lyla's* long-distance sensors were extremely efficient . . . more so than just about any other ship he was likely to encounter. So he always knew when someone was coming his way before they knew he was there.

His main disadvantage was that his vessel simply didn't have the pure speed that larger ships possessed. Outrunning pursuers wasn't an option. He had to outthink them.

So began the cat-and-mouse pursuit that marked Xyon's endeavors to stay one step ahead of his hunters.

He kept mixing up his strategies so as not to become predictable and, thus, catchable. He would run under the cloak. He would stop dead still under the cloak. He would hide within asteroid fields. He would brazenly sit right atop nacelles of ships that were looking for him so their own ion emissions masked his presence. He would pretend that he himself was a search vessel on the lookout for that miscreant Xyon (a strategy that he employed only once, since the ship he tried to pull it on saw through his prevarication and came after him; if it weren't for his cloaking device used to run for cover and then giving the pursuing vessel the slip through a convenient nebula, he'd never have escaped).

All during his many trials, Kalinda continued to say nothing.

Nothing.

Not.

A damned.

Word.

Xyon completely lost track of time. Finding that the silent treatment wasn't as charming in the long term as it was in the short, he kept trying to engage Kalinda in conversation. She didn't move. She just sat there, watching, glaring. Her legs were pulled up so that her knees were just under her chin, her arms draped across them.

Well, at least she's not getting in your way, Xyon told himself, trying to find some degree of pleasure from that.

As much as he desired her, as much as he lusted for her, at absolutely no time did Xyon's thoughts turn to the notion of acting upon those desires. Of forcing himself upon her. He was certain he wouldn't need to. Sooner or later, she would relent. And not from torture, for he could never hurt her. Instead, inevitably, her genuine personality would reassert itself. She would come to realize that this Tiraud fool was not the one for her. That there was no one but Xyon who was suitable. Granted, the business of letting her believe he was dead for all this time presented a stumbling block as far as creating a trusting relationship was concerned. But he was certain they could work their way past it, as soon as she was willing to allow a genuine exchange of ideas to begin flowing.

Unfortunately, she continued to be sullen and withdrawn, and neither attitude showed the slightest hint of lessening.

"I said it's not going to work. If you're trying to put an evil eye on me, it's not going to work," he told her. Naturally she didn't respond.

Fatigue overwhelmed Xyon, so much so that he could not keep his head upright. His eyelids felt like slabs of lead. "Lyla," he said when he'd been awake for thirty-seven straight hours and couldn't take watching Kalinda for another minute, "I need you to stand guard on Kalinda."

"All right, Xyon," Lyla said as she materialized near him.

He'd neglected to change the default programming. Lyla was a dead ringer for Kalinda.

Kalinda looked her up and down without comment, except for what sounded like a single, derisive snicker. Xyon growled low in his throat and said, "A different appearance, Lyla, *please.*"

Her form wavered slightly and she rematerialized as a gorgeous blonde in a billowy white dress. "Will this do?"

"Fine, fine," Xyon said quickly, feeling rather embarrassed by the incident. "If she tries to do anything—

get to a control panel, alert someone as to our where-abouts—you stop her. Got that?"

"Yes, Xyon."

"Power down all unnecessary systems. If it gets a little cold in here, I can live with that. I need you work-ing, and the cloak, and right now, that's it. Don't even bother to hold our position. Just let us drift."

"Yes, Xyon. Whatever you say."

"How sweet. The perfect female. Compliant and willing." It was the first utterance to come out of Kalinda's mouth since he'd taken her. Her voice sounded cracked and hoarse, which only made sense, since she had taken neither drink nor food in all her time on the ship.

"Hah," Xyon said. "Finally talking to me, are you?"

"Kindly let Xyon know I was talking to you, not him," she told Lyla.

Obediently, Lyla turned to Xyon. "She was talking to m—"

"I heard her," growled Xyon, and he was about to say something else but thought the better of it. Instead he stomped into his sleeping chamber. As he flopped forward onto his bed, he was dimly aware that Lyla wasn't necessarily reliable in perceiving some sort of es-cape attempt on Kalinda's part. For all he knew, he'd wake up back on New Thallon with Si Cwan scowling down at him and a smug Tiraud preparing to carve him to bits. But he was so exhausted that he was asleep an instant after his head hit the pillow, so he wasn't able to do anything about his last-second concerns.

He jolted himself awake some hours later, doing so

with a kind of internal urgency as he realized that he had no idea what his situation was going to be like when he opened his eyes and looked around. But all was quiet.

Still, he was concerned. Something seemed . . . not right.

The ship was moving. That was it. There was a sense of direction, even propulsion. But he'd told Lyla to allow the ship to drift.

He walked quickly out to the forward cabin, running his fingers through his tousled hair. "Lyla," he called, "I specifically told you to—" Then his eyes widened from what he saw on the viewscreen. "*Grozit!*"

The surface of a planet was coming toward them at high speed. Which was, of course, an optical illusion. The fact was that they were plunging toward the planet. The atmosphere was apparently thin, since the ship wasn't superheating from the reentry, but the damned thing had enough gravity to pull the small ship straight down toward its extremely inhospitable— to say nothing of very hard—surface.

Lyla was standing there with a benign expression. Kalinda, for her part, was exactly where Xyon had left her. Her eyes looked bleary, her smile was ragged, but there was grim amusement on her face. She barked out a laugh upon seeing Xyon's reaction to impending doom.

"All engines, emergency fire-up! Full power to reverse thrusters! Now! *Now!*" He was at the helm, frantically redirecting the ship's course.

The *Lyla* lurched violently, the engines roaring to life. In a starship, such sounds would never have been heard anywhere outside of the engine room. In the much smaller vessel, it was deafening. He felt as if he were surrounded by a wall of solid sound.

The hull groaned under the abrupt exertion of g forces upon the ship's structure, and for one horrific moment, Xyon thought the ship wasn't going to hold together. That it would be torn apart, front and back, dumping Xyon and Kalinda out, miles above the planet. If the notion likewise occurred to Kalinda, she made no sign of it other than to emit another one of those weird laughs.

And then the *Lyla* responded to the urging of its pilot, and the ship skipped across the upper reaches of the planet's atmosphere, bumping wildly. Xyon was slammed back in his chair. Kalinda was sent tumbling, rolling across the floor. *At least she's not giving me that damned creepy laugh*, Xyon thought grimly.

The *Lyla* angled upward then, fighting against and overcoming the g pull of the unknown planet beneath them. Xyon held his breath as the field of stars loomed ahead of him, calling to him, and then the ship was clear. He continued not breathing until the planet was long behind them, at which point he exhaled deeply. He felt his heart pounding furiously against his rib cage, and tried to ignore it. "*Lyla!*"

"Yes, Xyon?" She was standing right next to him, smiling that same beatific smile.

"We could have crashed into that planet!"

"Yes, Xyon."

"Why the hell didn't you do anything to prevent it!?"

"Because you gave me explicit orders to allow the ship to drift, Xyon. You were very clear on the subject."

"But didn't it occur to you that having the ship crash was something I wouldn't want to see happen?"

"It did occur to me, yes," she said reasonably. "But I thought you might have had some sort of reason for it."

He moaned softly and thumped the back of his head against his chair. "You know . . . I thought I got all the glitches out of the virus that wormed its way into you six months ago. Now I'm thinking maybe not. You're not just a computer, Lyla. You're an artificial intelligence. I expected more out of you than just blindly following the exact wording of what I said without any thought beyond that."

"I'm sorry for failing you, Xyon," she said sadly, her head slumping and her lower lip protruding ever so slightly.

He rubbed his hand across his face, and then fired an infuriated glare at Kalinda. Having been tossed around fairly severely, she had managed to regain her position back in a corner of the cabin. She pulled her legs back up into that same defensive, almost fetal position. "And *you!*"

Her eyes widened in mock innocence.

"I don't know if you were paying attention," he continued, "but if the ship had crashed, you'd have died right along with me! So you have something at stake as well!"

"No, I don't," she said.

He pivoted so that the chair he was in was facing her fully. "Oh, so now you're talking to me, are you."

"Yes, I'm talking to you," she told him with an exasperated sigh. "Because it's the only way to get you to understand that you're not taking me alive."

"What are you talking about . . . ?"

"Haven't you noticed that I haven't eaten?"

That gave him pause. "I . . . figured you'd had something while I was asleep. Lyla . . . ?"

"No, Xyon." Lyla shook her head. "She has consumed nothing."

He looked into her face, took a good long look for the first time in hours. Her color was off, a much more pale red than he was used to seeing. Her lips were parched, and her eyes had lost a good deal of their luster. Her cheekbones were beginning to stand out in stark contrast to the rest of her face. He realized that her breathing was becoming labored.

All of his anger, all his swagger and bravado, evaporated. He rose from his chair, walked over to her, and crouched in front of her. He reached for one of her hands and she pulled it away from him. The movement was clearly an effort for her.

"What are you doing?" he asked her.

"I'm starving myself to death."

"You're not serious."

Her eye sockets were starting to look hollowed out. "Do I *look* not serious?"

"Kalinda . . ."

"You might have me, Xyon, but you're not going to

keep me. And I'm not going to waste my breath telling you what an idiot you are, or why you should release me, because that simply wouldn't be dignified."

"And this is dignified?" He started to touch her face and yet again she slapped his hand away. "Forcing yourself to waste away? Throwing away your life?"

"Better to throw it away than to beg for it."

"You don't have to beg for your life!" he told her in exasperation. "What are you talking about? Your life isn't threatened! You must know that!"

"Life," she said, "is about more than living it. It's how you live it. With free will. Where I want to be. My life is on New Thallon, Xyon. My life is with Tiraud. It's not with you. Not anymore. But you don't want to hear that," she continued before he could interrupt her. "So when the prospect of terminating my existence early presented itself in the shape of that planet, I opted for it. Thwarted in that," and she shrugged her shoulders. The gesture seemed painful. "I return to allowing nature to take its course."

"Starving yourself to death isn't natural!"

"Really? Funny," she said, and allowed her head to slump back against the wall. "To me . . . it seems the most natural thing in the world."

In mounting frustration, Xyon curled his fist and slammed it against the wall behind her head. She didn't react in the slightest. "And do you think I'm going to just stand by and let you die?"

"I don't know, Xyon," replied Kalinda in a whispery voice that sounded more like a sigh. "I don't know you, any more than you know me. I don't know what's compelled you to do this. I don't know why you're no longer the dashing hero I fell in love with. But you're not. And I'm in love with someone else. And that's all there is to that."

"But you'll die!"

"You keep saying that." She forced a smile even though it took her some effort. "You think I'm afraid of death? I, who converse with the dead when the mood and spirit seizes me? No, Xyon. Once you've seen through the curtain, the prospect of stepping around it isn't that daunting."

For a long time they sat there then, Xyon staring at her, Kalinda looking off into empty air.

Finally he said, "You'd really rather die than be with me?"

"No."

"Then—"

"But I would really rather die than be forced to be with you."

He had been crouching all during this time, but now he lowered himself to sitting so that he was on the floor opposite her. "I thought . . ."

She stared at him, saying nothing.

"I thought," he continued, "that once I had you away from the rest of them . . . from their influence . . . that you would know where you were meant to be."

"And you were right," she said. There was no harshness in her voice. Merely sadness. "It just wasn't where you expected, that's all."

"Apparently not." He leaned forward, and there was something about his manner that prompted

Kalinda not to pull her hand away when he took it. "Kalinda . . . I'm going to give you food and drink. Eat it and drink it please."

"Xyon, haven't you heard anything I've said?"

"Yes. All of it." He stood, brushing off the knees of his pants. "Lyla."

Her voice sounded in the cabin. "I'm here, Xyon. I've been keeping myself incorporeal. I thought it might lend to the air of privacy I thought your discussion required."

"That's the AI I'm used to seeing." He sighed heavily. "Chart us a course to New Thallon. Take us back."

"Really?" Kalinda tried to stand, but her legs weren't working properly and she slid back down to the floor.

"Really," he said.

"Xyon, I—"

"No." He raised a hand, stilling her. His jaw was tight, and although he was trying to make his tone sound light, he wasn't entirely succeeding. "You win. Okay? You win. I just . . . I think it'd be better if we didn't belabor it. I understand you. I heard you. I'm doing what you wanted. Right now . . . let that be enough, all right?"

She nodded.

A few minutes later, she was drinking water as if she were holding the last bit of it left in the galaxy, and was in the process of devouring the simple foodstuffs that Xyon had provided her.

For his part, Xyon stared out at the stars. He'd always loved them, felt attracted to them.

It was a harsh reality to realize that, no matter how much you think that something burns for you and only you, it actually doesn't care about you at all. That the siren song one is hearing is entirely in one's own head. He could lust after the stars and reach out to touch them all he wanted . . . but ultimately, he would just wind up getting burned.

U.S.S. Excalibur

i.

Xy, the Hermat/Vulcan half-breed who had once more commonly gone by the name of "Xyon," lowered his rocketball paddle and looked at his father. "My namesake is alive? Is that what you're telling me?"

The break in the action gave Burgoyne 172 a much-needed breather. S/he was lightly clad in black shorts and a black T-shirt, and s/he sagged against the wall gulping in lungsful of air. S/he started to say "Yes" but the word didn't come easily, so s/he settled for nodding.

Hir son took in this information in a stoic manner that Burgoyne knew he'd gotten from his mother. "That's interesting," he said finally. "Is he coming here? Is the captain planning to try and hook up with him?"

"Actually," said Burgoyne, having retrieved hir breath, "we're going to look for him. He's in Thallonian space, hiding out after having kidnapped Si Cwan's sister, Kalinda."

Xy regarded hir with those luminous eyes of his. "You named me after a kidnapper?"

"He wasn't a kidnapper at the time. He was a hero."

"Yes, a hero who sacrificed his life to save the *Excalibur.*"

"Right . . . except . . ."

"Except he didn't." Xy smiled.

"Not as such, no. Apparently he just allowed all of us to think he was dead, but he really wasn't."

"Well, this is just looking better and better, Father, I have to say. A kidnapper *and* a liar. What, wasn't there a mass murderer whose name you could have attached to me?"

"I'm starting to reconsider it, actually." S/he thumped the surface of hir paddle. "Your serve. Let's go."

The glowing ball ricocheted off the walls of the rocketball court with a speed that mere human eyes would have had the devil's own time being able to track.

There was nothing slow in Burgoyne's movements. Three years had not taken the slightest edge off hir agility or catlike speed. Whatever way Xy returned the ball, Burgoyne was able to be there to intercept it and send it howling back ninety-nine times out of a hundred.

Xy, however, didn't miss even that one time in a hundred. Also, Xy's reach was longer than his father's, since he was a good six inches taller. It was those few inches that made all the difference.

The youthful mixed breed, at a biological age of approximately twenty-six, had all of the best physical aspects of both his parents. His limbs were sinewy, his coordination sure and precise. His skin glowed with health; he possessed a dark tan that seemed to hark back to his Vulcan ancestors and their days of desert dwelling under a broiling hot sun. His ears were long and elegant, his chin tapered, and his hair was rust-colored and a bit shaggy.

For someone who was, as measured by the calendar, four and a half years old, it was quite impressive.

Burgoyne made one final lunge at a ball that was almost out of reach, caught it, and sent it back at high speed against the wall. The ricochet brought it back to Xy, who, in a fiendish cross-up, barely tapped it. It bounded lightly back, and Burgoyne, who'd been anticipating yet another powerful slam, completely overshot it. Burgoyne slammed into the wall, absorbing most of the impact with hir shoulder, while the ball rolled away across the floor.

"Father! You okay?" called Xy. He was next to Burgoyne in a heartbeat, his expert fingers checking over the impact area on his father's body for any sign of breakage.

Burgoyne laughed at Xy's display of concern. "I'm fine, Xy, really! I'm fine." S/he forced hirself to stand, wavering slightly before regaining hir balance.

"That's a relief," sighed Xy. "I'd hate to have to tell Mother that I'd damaged you."

"Yes, well," and Burgoyne laughed again, but this time with much less genuine amusement, "I doubt she would have been all that upset about it."

"Uh-oh."

"Xy, the situation between your mother and me . . .

it's nothing new." S/he stretched hirself, catlike, shaking out the shoulders to make sure there was no serious injury. "It's not as if you weren't aware . . ."

"I know, I know. It's just that . . ."

"Just that what?"

Xy shook his head. "I didn't want to burden you."

"I'm your father. I'm here to be burdened. Come on, out with it."

"I was . . . well, Mother's at it again, and I was hoping . . ."

The Hermat moaned softly. "Why are you burdening me with this?"

"Father!"

Burgoyne made hir way to a shielded seating area at the far end of the rocketball court, and Xy followed hir. "We're not playing anymore?" asked Xy.

"Shoulder feels iffy," said Burgoyne, whose shoulder was actually feeling fine. S/he just didn't want to continue getting trounced by hir son. "So what's your mother been saying?" s/he asked as s/he sat.

Xy kept the rocketball balanced on the flat of his paddle. "She wants me to undergo a series of genetic reconstructive treatments based upon the work of a scientist named Randisi, except Randisi's work has already been discredited by both the Krellner Institute and the Starfleet Surgeon General's office."

"Still," said Burgoyne, "genetic reconstruction might be the key . . ."

"I've gone that route, Father," Xy said in frustration. "Don't you think I have? Don't you think I made genetic research the top priority while I was getting my degree? I mean, it's not as if I don't have a lot at stake personally. The fact is, there's nothing in any sort of legitimate field of study that applies to my personal situation. There's been no research on Vulcan/Hermat hybrids because there haven't *been* any before me. The most I can possibly be is a test case to guide researchers who may come after me and are intrigued by my condition. Which is why I keep a daily journal of my activities, development, everything. I just don't understand."

"What, Xy? What is it you don't understand?"

"I don't understand," he said in frustration, "why Mother can't accept the realities of my condition. I have. You have."

"I haven't."

Xy looked at his father in surprise. "You . . . you haven't?"

"No," Burgoyne said firmly. "I've learned to live with it. I've learned to be grateful for the years we'll have together, however unfairly few they'll be. But I can't accept it. I can't say, 'I'm all right with this.' " S/he paused and then said, "I've had a lot of late-night talks with the gods. A lot. And I've found them to be so decidedly one-sided that I've come to the realization they're probably not listening . . . or even there."

"Father . . ."

"So don't tell me," Burgoyne said with unexpected heat, as s/he worked to push back the moistening in hir eyes, "that I've learned to 'accept' it. Your . . . situation . . . is not acceptable to me, and even long after you're gone, I still won't accept it. What I *have* learned to accept, however, is my utter inability to do anything about it. That's the difference between your mother and me. She won't accept even that."

"But it's poisoning us, Father. Don't you see that?" he asked, desperation tinging his voice. "It's getting so that every time Mother looks at me, I feel as if she's not seeing me. She's just seeing this . . . this failed project. And because she never lets her anger out, it's just getting worse and worse and—"

"I'll talk to her."

"Would you?"

"I said I would."

Xy reached over and put his arms around his father, holding hir tightly. "Thanks, Father. I mean it. Thanks."

And Burgoyne, who lately had been demanding of hir gods what the hell kind of purpose s/he could possibly serve in a world where s/he was so helpless to aid hir own son, sunk hir small fangs into hir lower lip and said, "That's what I'm here for."

ii.

Dr. Selar looked up in surprise when Burgoyne entered sickbay. Of course, for Selar, surprise meant that her left eyebrow was slightly raised. Astonishment was her left eyebrow completely raised, and total, mind-numbing shock warranted both eyebrows raised . . . but for no longer than a second. Two seconds at the outside.

Two other medical technicians were on duty. One was running systems checks, while the other was giving a routine physical to Ensign Sigerson. Selar, for her part, was standing in the lab section, taking notes on the development of a culture she was growing. "Are you ill?" she asked without preamble.

"Hello to you, too," replied Burgoyne. "No, I'm not ill. I feel fine."

"Then you may leave."

"I . . . appreciate your giving me permission to do so, but there's some things we need to talk about."

"You may feel completely free to send me a memo in regards to whatever those might be," Selar told hir.

S/he looked her up and down. "You seem more tired than you used to."

She stared at him blankly. "What?"

"More tired. Around the eyes."

"That is none of your concern, Commander."

"Are you getting enough sleep?" s/he asked.

"That is none of your concern, Commander."

"Did anyone ever tell you you're like a broken record?"

This was enough to prompt Selar—who had gone back to what she was doing—to look at him once more. "No. No one has. What is a 'broken record'?"

"I'm not sure," Burgoyne admitted, "but it's a phrase Shelby used once or twice when Captain Calhoun was being particularly stubborn about something."

"It is most likely some sort of reference to a corrupted computer file," Selar said, "and of no interest. Good day, Commander."

"Selar, I love a good brush-off as much as the next dual-sexed individual, but we really need to—"

"Good day, Commander," she said again in as clear and blunt a manner as she could.

Burgoyne seemed to consider the situation for a time. Selar, having said all she needed to say on the matter, was back at work.

Suddenly Burgoyne turned and called out, "Excuse me. Everyone. Dr. Selar and I need the sickbay for a few minutes. Everyone else, please clear out."

There were confused stares from the other medics. If Burgoyne had been trying to get Selar's full attention, s/he had more than succeeded. "What do you think you are doing?"

Burgoyne ignored her and instead clapped hir hands briskly. "That was not a request, people."

"You cannot simply come into sickbay and order my personnel out. Everyone," Selar said in a commanding voice, "stay where you are."

"Oh dear," Burgoyne said dryly. "It appears I'm thwarted. If only I outranked you . . . oh! Wait! I do! In fact," and s/he looked around in a manner that was clearly not enduring any backtalk, "I outrank everyone here. There's a word for refusing to obey a direct order from a superior officer on a Starfleet vessel . . . now, what's that word . . . it's right on the tip of my tongue . . ."

"Commander," Selar tried to interrupt hir.

Burgoyne snapped hir fingers, apparently "remembering." "*Mutiny!* That's the word. And there's this thing we do when mutiny is involved . . . some sort of trial . . ."

"*Commander!*"

"I've got it! Court-martial! That's it!" There was no hint of joviality in hir manner. "We court-martial people who are in mutiny! So . . . anyone who's interested in being court-martialed, stay right where you are so I can get all your names for the official record."

That was more than enough for the staff of sickbay. Within seconds the place had emptied out, leaving Burgoyne and Selar staring at each other.

"May I assume you believe that you are amusing?" Selar asked him.

"I like to think I have my moments."

"And you may go right on thinking that," she told him. If she were any race other than Vulcan, her annoyance would have been radiating from her. As it was, she simply stood stock-still, her arms folded tightly as if she were physically restraining herself. "Very well. You have your much-desired privacy. What do you want?"

"I need to talk to you about Xy."

"What about him?"

"He says you've been giving him a difficult time."

"Define."

"He says you won't leave him alone about some sort of genetic thing . . ."

"If you wish to discuss such matters with me," she said icily, "you might at least take the time to familiarize yourself with them so that you may speak with au-

thority rather than ineptitude. He is no doubt referring to the Randisi studies . . ."

"Which he said have been discredited."

"Randisi made some errors, but there is
potential . . ."

"He feels as if you're . . . you're shutting yourself
off from him. That . . ."

"I cannot be responsible for his feelings," Selar told
him flatly. "I am too busy trying to be responsible for
his life, particularly since he appears to have abrogated
all responsibility in that department."

"That's not true . . . !"

"It is an accurate summation," said Selar, sounding
like an automaton, "of his current state of mind. Since
he is making no effort to save himself, the responsibility has fallen upon me. I am the chief medical officer of
this vessel. The health of all crew members is my obligation. I will not set aside that obligation simply because my son feels put out over it."

"Selar . . . !" Burgoyne was clearly trying to find
some different way to approach what was, to Selar, a
very simple matter. "He feels like he doesn't have a
mother!"

This struck Selar as very curious. "Did he say that,
in exactly those words?"

"Not exactly, but the general meaning . . ."

"I do not deal in generalities, Commander, except
in the aspect of general health of—"

"He said that he feels as if, every time you look at
him, you see a failed project. And that it's poisoning
your relationship . . . or whatever tattered shreds are

left of your relationship. That's what he said. Exactly."

Selar had picked up a medical padd. She was holding it in front of her, her arms crisscrossed. It might as well have been shielding her heart. "I see."

"Well?"

"Well what?"

"Selar—!" Burgoyne was looking more and more exasperated.

"Commander . . ."

"Stop calling me 'Commander,' dammit! We may not be lovers anymore . . . it may be you can't even stand to look at me, I don't know. But at the very least, you could call me 'Burgoyne.' 'Burgy' even."

She began again. "Commander . . ."

"Oh gods . . ."

"Xy . . . is unique. He absorbs knowledge faster than any living, breathing creature on two legs. He absorbed the curriculum of Starfleet Academy in eight months. His medical degree took a year, and that was only to give the slightest nod to proper form, since he'd really learned all he needed to learn in half that time, rather than the required six years."

"I know all this, Selar. What's your point?"

"The point is that he has given up, Commander. The most incredible mind of his generation . . . possibly any generation . . . has given up."

"He hasn't 'given up,' Selar," Burgoyne said desperately. "He's simply come to terms with the fact that his brilliance comes with a heavy price. It takes him months to cover physical and mental development that others require years for. That's . . . that's miraculous. But, like most miracles, it's destined to be short-lived . . . as is he. We can't know for sure how short a time it will be. Average Hermat life span is forty years . . . Vulcans live over two hundred. It could be longer, shorter . . ."

"You know it will be shorter, Commander," said Selar, her voice alone dropping the temperature in the sickbay down by two degrees. "His hyperfast development was in evidence almost from the day he was born. He has vast potential, and that is being cut short by some sort of . . . bizarre anomaly of our two genetic codes. His contribution toward solving that anomaly could be invaluable. It could make all the difference. He refuses to do so. That, Commander, is illogical. So if it is all the same to you, I shall persist in my course to endeavor to find a cure for him. Unless, of course, you intend to ask me not to do so, and court-martial me should I refuse to comply."

"No. All I intend to ask you to do is be a mother to our son while he's here."

"As mother to our son, my job is to ensure that he will be here for longer than his biology will allow. Particularly since he refuses to do the job and you are incapable of it. Does that conclude our business, Commander? Because, if so, I have a sickbay that very much needs to be repopulated with doctors."

"Just tell me one thing . . ."

"Does it involve you performing an action that is physiologically impossible upon yourself?"

"Do you see him as a failed project?"

It was all she could do to maintain her Vulcan mask of indifference. "No."

"Then what? How do you see him? When you look at him, do you see our son? Do you see someone you love? Do you see—?"

"A freak."

Once spoken, the words hung there between Selar and Burgoyne, objects of great weight.

"He . . . is a freak," Selar repeated, and all the pain and all the rage she felt were smothered and buried deep inside her, deeper than they had ever been. "Of course, I . . . mean that in the strictest medical sense, as an organism created through unusual or strange circumstances. . . ."

"The hell you did," Burgoyne shot back. "A freak is a monster. You think of him as some sort of monster. . . ."

"But he's my monster! My freak! And I have to—"

The outburst was so unexpected that Selar's eyes widened in genuine shock. She put her hand to her mouth as if she could not believe she had said it. Burgoyne looked dazed.

With Herculean effort, Selar pulled herself together. She squared her shoulders, smoothed down her uniform coat, and tilted her chin slightly. "Upon . . . further consideration," she said, her voice so soft that Burgoyne had to strain to hear her, "you may be correct in your . . . concern over the amount of sleep I have been getting as of late. I will . . . take your opinions in that regard under advisement."

"Thank you," Burgoyne said, hir voice hollow.

"Is there anything else, Commander?"

"No, that should . . . that's fine for now."

Burgoyne walked out of the sickbay, looking considerably shaken. Moments later, the technicians and the ensign getting a checkup filed back in. They looked to Selar, question marks in their faces.

She was already back to work, and only a medical scanner would have tipped the fact that her heart was pounding with triphammer force.

The Lyla

i.

Deep down, Kalinda had been concerned that Xyon was trying to trick her. That as soon as she ate something, he would turn around and continue to try and get her out of Thallonian space.

Such was not the case, as it turned out. She filled her belly, slaked her thirst, and Xyon kept the course steady for New Thallon.

She was relieved. For all the icy and imperious demeanor she'd been displaying, the fact was that she'd been so ravenous it was all she could do not to break down in tears. But a show of weakness like that one would hardly have helped her situation.

At the same time, though, she had to admit to herself that she felt a bit . . . saddened. For in acquiescing to her demands—in realizing the error of his actions—something seemed to have been extinguished in Xyon.

You crushed his heart. What did you expect? That was what one part of her mind demanded. This, of course, was quickly replied to by the other part of her mind, which demanded, *He took you against his will and treated*

you as if you had no rights at all. What did he expect?
There was absolutely no way she should feel any guilt
over Xyon's feelings. No way.

And yet . . .

*No "and yet"! Don't let yourself even begin to think in
that direction!*

She had to admit that, for his part, Xyon wasn't
doing a thing to try and heap some sort of guilt upon
her. The decision having been made to return her, he
was all business. Not angrily so or arrogantly so. He
operated his ship with brisk efficiency, as if Kalinda
were simply a young woman who had booked passage
aboard his vessel. He asked after her concerns, he did
his best to make her comfortable. He even engaged in
harmless small talk.

Still, she felt that there was a faint air of melancholy
hanging over him. But certainly that was completely
his problem, not hers. And he wasn't trying to foist it
upon her or make it her problem, so she made the conscious decision to ignore it.

Except . . . he was so damned sad . . .

"No!" she said firmly. "You're not going to do it."

Xyon had been keeping a wary eye on the console,
but now he turned and looked at her in bemusement.
"Do what?" he asked.

"Sit there and make me feel guilty."

He appeared to consider that. "All right," he said,
saying each word individually and carefully as if he
were dealing with a dangerously deranged person. "So
you wish me to . . . what? Stand? Sit somewhere else? I
don't . . ."

"Don't be cute."

"It's a curse," he admitted sadly. "I've learned to live with it."

"Xyon . . . !"

"What do you want from me, Kalinda?" He shook his head, looking rather hopeless. "I realize I was wrong to take you. I'm bringing you back. And I'm being careful about it. . . ."

"Why 'careful'?"

"Because," he told her matter-of-factly, "there are still ships out there in sizable numbers looking for me. If I run afoul of them and they haul us in, my saying to them 'Oh, but wait, I was returning her to New Thallon anyway' is hardly going to weigh in my favor. Chances are they'd push me out an airlock and take bets as to how many seconds I'd last in the vacuum."

"Not necessarily. I could let them know you're telling the truth."

"Really." He swiveled his chair so he was facing her. "Here's a thought: They won't care."

"Of course they would—"

"Kalinda, now you're just being naïve. They care about getting you back. They care about punishing me. And if someone finds you, they'll fall all over themselves to be the first ones able to tell your brother that I'm a shriveled corpse floating inside an asteroid belt somewhere. For that matter," he continued, giving the subject further consideration, "the fact that Si Cwan and your beloved spread the word about your disappearance may do you as much harm as good."

"I have no idea what you're talking about."

"Well, work it out," he urged her. "The general populace of the great New Thallonian Protectorate knows that the sister of the great Lord Si Cwan is in the hands of . . . of whatever epithets they use to describe me. I'm sure I'm not considered someone of good repute. I very much doubt that Si Cwan will publicize that I've taken you because I'm madly in love with you and would sooner cut off my right arm than harm you or allow you to be harmed in any way. So they've doubtless attributed some sort of nefarious reasons for my vile deed or, at the very least, allowed others to conjure up their own suspicions of my evil ends. That leaves a significant downside."

"I still don't see what you . . ." Then her eyes widened.

He gestured grandly. "And the dawn arises."

"They'll assume I was taken to be ransomed."

"Yes."

"Which means that if some . . . some . . ."

"Villain?"

"Yes," she nodded, "some villain gets his hands on me . . ."

"Go ahead," he urged, "you're almost there."

Kalinda made an irritated face at him, not appreciating the condescending tone he'd adopted . . . although she had to admit that it really should have been self-evident. ". . . then said villain will simply pick up where he believes that you've left off, or where he left you off."

"Yes. And there's every chance he won't treat you as well as I have."

"I'd hardly be patting myself on the back if I were you when it comes to your treatment of me," she told him archly.

Xyon seemed unimpressed. "Believe me, there are people out there who would treat you far worse than—"

That was when every warning device in the ship went off at once, up to and including Lyla abruptly appearing out of thin air. Considering her normal expression was one of infinite calm, the tremendous concern she was displaying now was more than enough to underscore the severity of the situation. "Xyon!" she called out over the alarms. "Long- and short-range sensors have picked up an incoming vessel."

"Long- *and* short-range? How—?"

"Because it's moving so quickly that by the time the long-range scanners picked it up, it was practically right on top of—"

"I *get* it! Cloak us now! *Now!* Shut off everything except the cloak, minimal life-support, and the viewscreen! And bring us to full stop!" He pointed at Kalinda. "I don't know any ship that can move that fast, and if it's unknown, I want to make damned sure it doesn't notice us. So don't talk! Don't even breathe!"

"But—"

"*Shut up, I said!*"

Kalinda slammed her mouth shut automatically. Instantly all the lights went out. She had become so accustomed to the steady hum of assorted instrumentation that it was startling to her when it suddenly ceased. She leaned forward in her chair. It squeaked. Immediately she went to the floor, crouching, waiting, staring fixedly at the viewscreen.

Space shimmered a short distance away, and a vessel dropped out of warp space. It was unlike any that Kalinda had ever seen. The design made no sense whatsoever. Just about every vessel Kalinda had ever seen had some degree of symmetry. Not this one. It was almost as if the various parts of it had been stuck together haphazardly, a series of tubes (or maybe tunnels) affixed to pulsing globes. It looked like nothing so much as a gigantic molecule. There was no sense of design to it, although certainly it made sense to whatever entity or entities had crafted it.

Kalinda had no idea how big the thing was, since she had nothing to compare it to, but she had the uneasy feeling that it was gargantuan compared with the *Lyla*. She couldn't even determine where its method of propulsion lay. Kalinda glanced nervously in Xyon's direction, but he seemed just as bewildered as she. She started to inhale in preparation for asking a question, but he fired her a furious look that seemed to scream "Speak so much as a syllable and I knock you cold." Perhaps he hadn't been thinking that, but whatever he was thinking, she suspected she wouldn't like it. So she kept her mouth closed.

The vessel slowly pivoted in space. Although she had no way of proving it, Kalinda was getting the uneasy feeling that the thing . . . whatever it was . . . was looking for them. For her.

Everything that Xyon had said to her about someone far worse than he getting their hands on her came back to her, and suddenly Kalinda had never wanted to be so far from a particular place in her life.

And then the molecule-shaped vessel stopped turning. She prayed that was because it was about to head off in some other direction. Hell, perhaps it wasn't looking for her in the first place. Perhaps its presence here was pure coincidence.

Then it started toward them, slowly but with enough certainty that Xyon muttered, "*Grozit*. Lyla, engines back on line, now."

Quickly he backed the ship up, pacing the far larger vessel, going exactly the same speed but in reverse.

"Can they see us?" she whispered.

"No, the cloak's still in place. But I don't know their . . . maybe they can . . ." His mind was racing so fast he wasn't taking time to finish thoughts. "It's possible they see us. It's also possible they don't really know we're here. But I can't afford to just sit and take the chance. I'm changing our direction. If I move out of their way, maybe they can't track us. . . ."

And then the bigger ship began to speed up . . . and altered the angle of its approach so that it was heading right toward Xyon's ship.

"Then again, maybe they can. Hold on to something. I'm getting us the hell out of here."

"Xyon," Lyla said, reappearing. "The approaching vessel appears to be far faster than we are."

Xyon ignored her. Instead he whipped the ship around 180 degrees and hurtled off into space. He prayed it would be enough, that somehow, miraculously, this was all coincidence and this monstrous new ship would be left behind.

"It's after us," said Lyla.

"I know!"

"It's gaining."

"I know!"

"It's still gaining and I believe it's actually toying with us."

"*Shut up, Lyla!*"

"Who *are* they?!" demanded Kalinda.

"Well, hell, Kalinda, and here I thought they were friends of yours." He scanned them even as he drove the ship in retreat. "I think they've got weapons systems, but it's not anything I'm familiar with. I'm not taking any chances. Lyla, drop the cloak and give me full power to shields."

"If you drop the cloak, they'll see us!" Kalinda cried out.

He pointed angrily at the screen. "I'm not sure if you've noticed, but they seem to have no problem following us. Which means the cloak is doing us zero good. They might have an even more advanced version of a tachyon detection grid than Starfleet does. So if they start shooting at us, I want to have at least some chance of withstanding an attack."

"How do you know their weapons won't easily destroy the shields?"

"I don't," he said pointedly. "You want to jump out here and take your chances?"

Kalinda clambered back up into her seat and

watched with mounting concern as the vastly larger ship bore down on them. "Do you . . . have a plan?"

"Yeah, I have a plan," he shot back. "Since I'm not skulking around, we hope that some of the other ships looking for you—hopefully the ones captained by men of principle—detect our movements and come running. They fight our new friends, we escape in the melee, and I bring you back to get a reward."

"A reward! You *kidnapped* me!"

"I don't have time to dwell on details."

"Obviously! You're not even dwelling on the little detail," and she pointed at the ship on the screen, "that maybe they're not hostile! Maybe you're just worried about saving your own skin."

"I'm definitely worried about that," he assured her. "But it's your skin I'm worried about, too. They're hostile."

"You don't know that."

"I do," Xyon said, and there was no trace of doubt. "I just . . . I sense it. You would too, if you opened your mind to it. I mean, you're the one who's had truck with the dead. What do you get off our new best friends?"

In response to the challenge in his voice, she turned and focused on their pursuer. She tried to see it in some sort of . . . of new way. She wasn't exactly sure what way that was, or how to look at it, especially considering she wasn't actually looking at it, but instead an image of it on a screen. All she could think to do was just clear her mind, to open herself to general impressions from it. Allow it to . . .

. . . to . . .

. . . and then it began to crawl into her.

Blackness, and flashes, just quick flashes, of something gelatinous, and there were tentacles reaching out toward her, and there was screaming of such deep-seated terror, and . . .

"*Kalinda!*"

She blinked and looked up, terrified. Xyon had somehow crossed the cabin and was standing right in front of her, shaking her with rough urgency. "What happened? You . . . you blacked out or something, I—"

"Get us away," she whispered, and then much louder, "*Get us away!*"

Without hesitation, Xyon leaped over to helm. "Lyla, everything we've got in terms of speed!"

"You have it, Xyon," said Lyla, her holograph form materializing next to him. "But it's matching our speed."

"Is there anything around here we can lose them in."

"There's the Singfer Nebula at—"

"I don't care where! How long to get there?"

"Nine minutes at current speed."

"Lay in the course—!"

Instantly the coordinates were in the navigational system, and Xyon changed the ship's direction. The pursuing vessel course corrected to keep up.

"What did you see?" Xyon asked tersely.

"I . . . I don't . . ." Kalinda gulped. "Just keep me away from it."

"But I need to know—"

"No, you don't. Trust me, you don't. All you need to know is to stay away."

"I'm trying!" He looked in frustration at the ship, never slowing. "I don't get it. Why aren't they firing at us? Or overtaking us?"

"Maybe they don't have weapons. Maybe they're just waiting for us to run out of power or something. Maybe they think we'll surrender."

"Then they don't know me very well."

Lyla spoke up. "I don't think they know you at all."

"I know they don't."

"Then why did you say . . . ?"

"Not now, Lyla."

Lyla promptly vanished.

The long minutes ticked down. Everyone in the cabin stopped talking. The small vessel hurtled through space, the vast pursuer right after them, never slowing, never speeding up, just constantly and invariably there.

When Lyla suddenly reappeared, Xyon jumped slightly in surprise and Kalinda gasped. "Two minutes to nebula border."

"What happens when we get into the nebula?" Kalinda asked.

"Well," Xyon said, his thoughts racing furiously, "there's no guarantees, but it should interfere with our new friend's sensory devices and their visuals. So we may be able to give it the—"

That was when Lyla screamed.

The entire vessel began to shake as if something

had seized hold of it, and the first thought that howled through Xyon's mind was *Tractor beam!* But they weren't slowing or being pulled in the other direction.

And Lyla was there with her arms thrown back, her head tilted back, her mouth wide open, the initial sound of the scream having vanished immediately. And then her hard light form split apart, almost particle by particle, flying explosively in all directions at once with a flash that was nearly blinding.

Xyon shielded his face against them; they passed through him harmlessly. But there were spots hanging in front of him since he'd been looking right at Lyla when it happened. He could barely make out Kalinda or anything else . . .

"*Xyon!*"

He looked toward where Kalinda's voice came from, and although his vision was still blurred, he was able to make out what was happening. He just didn't understand it or believe it.

Some sort of light grid had appeared atop Kalinda as if someone had drawn carefully detailed squares all over her body. Frantically she shoved at them, as if she could push them off herself. She twisted and turned and they followed her. "*Xyon!*" she cried out again, and suddenly she began to disappear. But it wasn't with the explosive force that had blown Lyla apart. Instead it was eerily similar to the effects of a transporter. There was no sound, though. All of it was transpiring in eerie silence broken only by her plaintive pleas for help.

"It's not possible!" he shouted even as he lunged toward her. "Transporter beams can't go through shields!" At that moment, he didn't consider the fact that he couldn't stop whatever was being instigated from the other end. All he knew was that, if Kalinda was being taken away, he was going to go with her.

That, as it turned out, was not an option. The instant he came in contact with the energy field that had enveloped Kalinda and was stealing her away, he was blasted back with a jolt more violent than anything he'd ever felt. He hurtled backward and slammed into the far wall of the main cabin with sickening force. He heard a distant crunch and realized it was the sound of his own skull striking the hard surface. Then the floor was under him and he didn't even remember sliding down to it.

He lay there helpless, frantically commanding his body to get up, to do something. Instead his arms and legs were immobile. He had no more chance of convincing them to do anything than if they'd belonged to someone else. Kalinda, terror etched on her face, reached for him across what seemed a vast distance and then, in a shower of particles, she was gone.

Get up! Get up! Do something! Xyon's mind screamed at him. It was useless. He wasn't budging. Distantly he became aware that his ship was no longer moving. The other ship passed over him. He couldn't see it, but he could sense it, like a great black angel of death, and he even fancied that in the distance recesses of his mind, Kalinda was still shrieking his name.

Then the darkness reached out toward him, and he did nothing to resist it.

ii.

The first thing Xyon became aware of was pain.

He realized in a detached manner that someone was hitting him in the face. And they were shouting something at him, but his mind was so scrambled that he couldn't quite make out what it was. He also realized that there was some sort of pressure on his chest, but didn't know at first what was causing it.

As the world swam back into existence around him, he realized that it was someone's knee. Someone had their knee on his chest and was leaning over him, slapping him fiercely.

He managed to open his eyes and regain enough command of his senses to say "I'm awake!" just before another blow took him. It snapped his face to one side, and with a grunt, he tried to force his way up to sitting. But he had only partial command of his body back, and suddenly he was choking. He realized why almost immediately: He'd swallowed some of his own blood. The side of his face was already swelling and his lips were bleeding, presumably from cuts thanks to the fact that his assailant was wearing heavy metal gloves with serrated edges.

The face glaring down at him was not a pleasant one. At first Xyon thought it was Tiraud, but then realized that it was likely another member of Tiraud's race. Nelkarites . . . that was it. He was a Nelkarite. So the good thing was that it wasn't Tiraud himself. The bad thing was that it probably wasn't going to make that much difference. There were several other Nelkarites visible behind him. Obviously they had invaded his ship. Equally obviously, he was in deep trouble.

"Where is she?" snarled the Nelkarite. That was actually an impressive feat, considering the general singsong melodiousness of the typical Nelkarite. "Where's the Lady Kalinda?"

"They took her," Xyon managed to get out.

"Who did?"

"I don't know. But we have to go after them."

The Nelkarite looked at one of his associates, who shook his head grimly. "Sensor sweeps indicate the presence of no other vessel in this area."

"That's impossible. Lyla!" Xyon called out. "Replay visual record of the ship that was after us."

Lyla did not materialize, but her voice said calmly, "What visual record of what ship, Xyon?"

"The visual record! Of the ship! The huge one!"

"I have no record of any such pursuit, Xyon."

Xyon was thunderstruck. "It . . . they must have erased your memory somehow, Lyla. That's the only answer, Lyla."

"Actually, there's a far simpler one: You're lying!" the Nelkarite inquisitor informed him, and smashed him across the face again.

"Okay," Xyon said abruptly, trying to stop the

world from spinning around him. "I'm lying. But I'll only tell the truth to Si Cwan."

"You are in no position to bargain, you bastard! If you don't tell me what we want to know, I'll . . ."

"Kill me?" Xyon's voice sounded thick to him between the blood trickling into his lungs and the swelling of his mouth. "Then no one will ever know."

The Nelkarite considered that a moment, and then the pressure of his knee was gone from Xyon's chest. Instead he was being hauled to his feet by other Nelkarites, gripping him firmly by the arms and keeping him immobilized. "All right," the Nelkarite said to him, his face mere inches from Xyon's own. "You seem just stupid enough to refuse to cooperate. We'll bring you back to New Thallon. And you will tell everything you know there or by the gods, you'll regret the day you were born."

"Not a day goes by when I don't," Xyon said.

U.S.S. Excalibur

i.

Moke, the adopted son of Mackenzie Calhoun, sauntered through the corridors of the *Excalibur*. At approximately fourteen years of age, he had developed into an impressive, strapping young lad. On occasion Calhoun would introduce him to newcomers simply as "my son," and it amused Moke tremendously when people would invariably say, "Oh, yes! He looks just like you!"

At that moment he was walking back to his quarters from his day's worth of lessons. His teacher was quite pleased with him, and had told him he would be getting high marks on just about all his subjects. This was a relief, since his studies had taken a downturn the previous month, and Mac had been all over him about buckling down and getting the job done. He was having dinner that evening with Calhoun and was looking forward to imparting some good news about his academics for a change.

As he rounded a corner, someone moving very quickly in the other direction nearly slammed into him. The impact was avoided at the last second by a quick, graceful movement on the part of the other person.

Nevertheless Moke was irritated by the closeness of the collision and started to snap off an annoyed comment.

It died in his throat as he looked up and saw who it was that had nearly collided with him.

"Moke!" said Xy, looking genuinely pleased to see him.

"Oh. Hi," Moke said.

"It's . . . been a while."

"Yeah." Moke suddenly found the tops of his shoes to be of great interest. "Well . . . it's a big ship."

"Not that big." Xy paused, studying Moke thoughtfully. "Have you been avoiding me?"

"No, not at all."

"Well, look," said Xy, pointing in front of him, "I was just heading down to the team room. I thought maybe . . ."

"Can't."

"We could catch up . . ."

"Later," Moke said, and was heading off down the hall, calling over his shoulder, "Now is really a lousy time. Later. We'll make it later."

"All right," Xy called after him softly.

ii.

Mackenzie Calhoun did not have psychic powers . . . at least, not in the traditional sense.

He did have an instinct for danger that bordered on the psychic, if not the supernatural. He preferred to ascribe it to a long and proud tradition of being able to pick up on danger signals that others might have noticed but didn't.

Nevertheless, as he sat at the dining table opposite Moke, he considered the fact that it didn't require supernatural powers of any sort to realize that something was bothering the teen. Granted, the fact alone that he was a teenager was more than enough to warrant a desultory manner. But Calhoun had happened to run into Moke's teacher, who had spoken expansively and enthusiastically of the lad's work in recent days, and also mentioned that he'd praised Moke that very day.

So he'd expected something akin to jubilance from his adopted son this evening. Instead Moke had been cordial but distant. Calhoun even gave him the opportunity by saying, "So how have your studies been going lately?" Moke's response: an indifferent "Fine," and that had been that.

"Is the steak not to your taste?" Calhoun asked after a bit.

"It's fine. Why?"

"Because you've hardly eaten it."

"Hmm?" He looked down at the sizable remains on his plate. "Oh. Okay, sorry." He proceeded to make more of an effort to down the portion.

Then Calhoun reached over with his knife and laid it atop Moke's. Moke looked up at him with mild confusion. "Is this, you know . . . some sort of Xenexian challenge to a duel?"

"No. It's my challenge to you to tell me what's on your mind."

Moke shrugged. Calhoun moaned softly. "Are we back to shrugging?"

"Back to—?"

"When you were younger, I'd have entire conversations with you that consisted of me asking questions and you shrugging. I was hoping those days were long gone. I would have liked to think that you'd hoped that as well."

Reflexively, Moke began to shrug, but stopped himself. As a result it looked like he had just smothered a cough. This prompted Calhoun to smile slightly, but he managed to hide it. "Seriously, Moke . . ."

"Seriously, there's nothing . . ." He took a deep breath. "It's not important. It's stupid."

"Never, ever consider your feelings about anything to be stupid. I don't want to hear that word in connection with you ever again. Do you hear?" Calhoun said firmly.

"Yes, sir."

"I didn't quite hear that."

"*Yes, sir,*" Moke repeated, not mumbling it this time.

"Good. So . . . what happened?"

"I bumped into Xy in the hallway and sort of just ignored him."

Calhoun "harrumphed." "Well . . . that was stupid." "*Mac!*"

"An action can be stupid without the person being stupid."

"You're a big help."

"Why did you just ignore him?"

"What else am I supposed to do?"

"Have you considered *not* just ignoring him?"

Moke had been twiddling with his fork all during that time. Finally he put the fork down. "Nobody needs me," he said in exasperation.

Calhoun leaned back in his chair. "Now what kind of self-pitying—?"

"It's not self-pitying. It's the truth! I mean . . . Xy used to be this . . ." He held his hand about a foot or so off the floor. "I used to carry him around, for God's sake! On my shoulders! And he looked up to me and smiled! Now he looks down on me and . . . and smirks! I mean, I have to struggle and work so hard to pull my studies up to a level you're satisfied with, and Xy . . ."

"Has already graduated medical school."

"Right! I feel like an idiot compared to him!"

"Compared to him, just about everyone on this ship is an idiot," Calhoun reminded him. "You can't beat yourself up just because of that."

"Yeah, I guess so. But . . ."

"But what?"

"But how am I supposed to . . . I don't know . . . relate to him? I feel like it was practically yesterday that he was a baby."

"Practically yesterday, he was a baby. And practically tomorrow . . ."

Calhoun hesitated, and Moke fixed a level gaze on him. "Practically tomorrow he'll be dead? Is that what you were going to say?"

"More or less."

"And . . . and how am I supposed to feel about that?"

Calhoun smiled sadly. "I can't tell you how to feel, Moke. It's not right that I should dictate to you what your feelings are. Still . . . for all your frustration that you're feeling right now . . . your embarrassment that Xy has developed beyond anything that you're capable of keeping pace with . . . I think it's wise to remember that he's paying a terrible price for that. He could probably use every friend he can get . . . even the ones who used to be taller than him and are now shorter."

"I guess."

"You guess?"

"It's just . . ." He was clearly trying to find the best way to say it, and Calhoun quietly waited, letting the lad take his time. "It's just . . . it probably will sound stupid and selfish and self-centered and completely un-reasonable . . . but I feel like everyone leaves me be-hind. That's what I mean when I say that nobody needs me."

"Leaves you behind? Who's left you behind?"

"My father. My mother. Now Xy . . ."

"Oh, Moke. That's just . . ."

"I said it was stupid."

"It's not stupid," Calhoun told him, "but it is . . . I'd say 'unreasonable.' Your father, he was . . . well, he was what he was. And your mother passed away, Moke. You think she didn't want to stay with you? You think she wouldn't have given everything she had to be with you? To watch you grow up, to grow strong and healthy? And Xy didn't ask for the cards that fate dealt him."

"I know there's reasons. Good reasons. Reasons

that it would be just . . . just ridiculous to think that . . . but . . ." All the thoughts tumbled about and he felt strangled trying to express himself. "All the reasons, as good as they are, as . . . as reasonable as they are, 'cause I know my mom and Xy didn't ask for what happened . . . but after all the reasons are given, it still comes down to that I'm left behind. That they . . . moved on."

"And have I left you behind? Hmm?" demanded Calhoun. "Have I done anything to make you feel as if you're no longer of consequence to me? That you're not a part of my life?"

"No, sir."

"Because it hasn't been easy, Moke. Don't think it has. It hasn't been easy to balance the demands of being a starship captain with my loyalty to you and wanting to be there for you. Not easy at all."

"I'm sorry, Mac," Moke said honestly. "I didn't mean to make you feel guilty."

"Don't worry, you haven't. My conscience is clear," Mackenzie Calhoun told him with utter confidence. "Moke . . . I think maybe you want to spend some time with the ship's counselor."

"Whyyy?" Moke moaned.

"Because you have some serious emotional and abandonment issues, and I think it would help you to speak directly to someone more experienced in such matters than I am. The one thing I can do," and he raised his voice slightly to get over Moke's continued moaning, "is assure you that I will never 'abandon' you. I will always give you my attention—as much as is possible in any given circumstance—and make sure that no one can . . ."

His combadge suddenly beeped. He tapped it with obvious reluctance. "Calhoun, go."

"Bridge here, Captain," came Burgoyne's voice. "We're receiving a transmission from Thallonian space."

"Thallonian space?" He looked up at that, his attention suddenly engaged. "Point of origin?"

"It's a live uplink from New Thallon. Lieutenant Commander Robin Lefler. She stated it was of the utmost urgency."

"Robin! All right," he said after a brief hesitation, "send it down here."

"Aye, Captain."

Seconds later, the screen wavered out to be replaced by the grim expression of Robin Lefler.

"Greetings, Lieutenant Commander Lefler," Calhoun greeted her. "You're looking well."

"I appreciate that, Captain, but I can't say I'm feeling well," Robin said. "At least you're close enough that I could get a real-time message to you."

"If you're contacting me to tell me about Xyon . . . I already know."

"Oh really. What do you know?"

"Well, that he apparently absconded with Kalinda, and that everyone and their brother is out looking for him. We're on our way . . ."

"Yes, well, I suggest that whatever means you might be able to utilize to speed up 'your way,' you employ them."

He was immediately all business. "What happened? Tell me everything. Leave nothing out."

Robin told him, beginning with what had happened when Xyon had been brought before Si Cwan. Half an hour later the heartsick Calhoun, in absorbing everything that Xyon had gone through, looked around and realized that Moke had walked out of the room without saying a word . . . and Calhoun hadn't even noticed that he had left.

Calhoun tapped his combadge. "Calhoun to Moke." No response came. "Morgan, Moke's location, please?"

Morgan's voice replied readily over the combadge, "Moke is in his room."

Calhoun got up and headed over to Moke's quarters, where the first several pushes of the door chime were ignored. "Moke," he said in annoyance. "Open up."

"I'm sleeping. I can't hear you," Moke replied.

"Moke . . ."

Several crewmen walked past, glancing at the odd sight of their captain standing in a corridor and having to beg repeatedly for someone to obey a direct order. He forced a half-smile and waited until they were gone, at which point the smile faded. "Moke," he said, with something very nasty lurking about in the lower reaches of his voice, "let me in, or I will instruct Morgan to release the door lock, I'll come in anyway, and you will come to regret every single second you left me standing in this hallway."

"Come," Moke said immediately, and the door slid open.

Nice to know I still have what it takes to browbeat a teenager into submission, he thought grimly as he walked in.

Moke was seated on the edge of his bed, his hands folded on his knees. "Listen, Moke," began Calhoun.

"I'll go to the ship's counselor," Moke said.

"That's not the point. . . ."

"Respectfully, sir, I disagree." Moke's eyes were wide and unblinking. "You said I have things to work out. I think you're right. If it's all the same to you, I'd rather work them out with the ship's counselor. I would hope that's acceptable."

"Moke . . ."

"If you want, I'll make an appointment right now. If you don't trust me to do so on my own, I mean."

This kid should play chess, Calhoun thought, before he remembered that not only had he taught Moke chess, but Moke in fact had beaten Calhoun rather handily on several occasions.

"I trust you to do so, Moke," Calhoun sighed. "All right. See it done, then."

Calhoun turned, headed for the door, realized that he should really say something like that he loved him, didn't feel comfortable with it, half-nodded vaguely in Moke's direction, and walked out.

As soon as the doors slid shut so that Calhoun couldn't hear him, Moke said, "Yeah. I love you, too."

New Thallon

Ankar, Si Cwan's full-time (and Robin Lefler's part-time) aide, walked into Robin's office and said briskly, "The kidnapper is being brought in now. The Prime Minister assumed you'd want to be there." Not waiting for a response, he went out just as fast as he'd come in.

Robin sighed, put aside some correspondence that she was in the middle of, and headed out after Si Cwan. Si Cwan's manner with her had been stiff and formal ever since the altercation with Fhermus and Tiraud after Kalinda's abduction, and having this news relayed by an aide was just another example of that. She reasoned that she shouldn't be too upset with Cwan. That, indeed, if anyone was going to be understanding with him, it should be her. Not only was she his wife and therefore obliged to try and be supportive whenever she could (or whenever he wasn't being a total ass), but she was Starfleet liaison to New Thallon, and obliged to try and help things to run smoothly whenever possible. Furthermore, purely in terms of human compassion, she knew that he was under a formidable amount of strain as a worried brother.

Still, she was relieved to have heard back from Admiral Jellico so quickly. It was only a four-word message, but they were the words she needed to hear: "I'll alert Calhoun personally." She noticed that Jellico didn't specifically say he was going to send Calhoun into Thallonian space. That did not surprise her. These were delicate times in Sector 221-G, and discretion had to be observed whenever possible. Nevertheless, she was positive that Calhoun would be showing up as soon as humanly—or Xenexianly—possible.

Even though she hadn't been specifically told, she still knew where Xyon would be brought: to the main reception hall, where all the major affairs of state were tended to. It was there that new ambassadors or dignitaries were greeted, and where reception revelries were held. Xyon, of course, fitted into none of those categories, adding a skewed perversity to the proceedings.

For all that the main reception hall was supposed to be part of the traditions of the New Thallonian Protectorate, it still evoked an imperial throne room as far as Robin was concerned, right down to the large chair at one end that faced out onto the room. The hall itself was decorated with flags, banners, or symbols of all fifty-seven members of the Protectorate, giving the entire place a busy and festive air.

There was nothing festive about the atmosphere of the place now. Instead various Protectorate representatives were there, grouped in a vague semicircle, facing the "throne" upon which Si Cwan was seated. He was not leaning back in his typical relaxed pose, but instead was perched on the edge, looking like a tiger ready to spring and only barely managing to hold himself back.

Fhermus was standing just to Si Cwan's right. *His right-hand man*, Robin thought grimly. She had grown accustomed to the elaborate acrimony between the two of them and had even accepted that it was a necessary evil in terms of keeping the Protectorate functioning. The fact that the two of them were now clearly of one mind should have pleased her. Instead it caused a chill in the base of her spine.

Next to Fhermus was Tiraud. It had always seemed to her that Tiraud didn't seem all that much like his father. Certainly the fact that he'd fallen in love with Kalinda indicated that he was far less rooted in the enmities of olden days than was his father. Now, though, in mien and attitude, he seemed indistinguishable from Fhermus. Robin definitely didn't like the looks of that.

There was sustained muttering from the other ambassadors and representatives, and then the doors at the far end of the room thudded open. All eyes went to it as, moments later, Xyon was shoved into view. His hands were bound behind his back and, for extra security, there were manacles at his ankles linked together by two feet of chain. It impeded his ability to walk, forcing him to sort of shuffle forward. Several Nelkarites came into view behind him, the foremost shoving Xyon yet again, as if his slow progress were somehow his fault.

Inwardly, Robin let out a sigh of relief. She'd been worried that the Nelkarites might have worked Xyon over, and he had a bruise or two on his face. But it didn't appear to be anything serious, and she was sure he had sustained far worse in his lifetime.

Part of her still couldn't believe it. Like everyone else, she had thought him dead, so seeing him here, now, risen from beyond the grave, as it were . . . well, it was quite a bit to handle.

Si Cwan's brow furrowed, which was the only way in which his severe expression altered. Tiraud, for his part, looked as if he wanted to spring forward and knock Xyon on his ass. Robin supposed she couldn't blame him, but hoped that Si Cwan would have the intelligence and forbearance to realize that violence was not the answer to anything.

Still, what it came down to was this: They'd found Xyon, but there'd been no sign of Kalinda. This was as disturbing to Robin as it was to anyone else. The question was: How was Si Cwan going to handle it?

Xyon made his way toward the throne, but when he was about halfway there, Si Cwan raised a hand pre-emptively. "Stop right there," he snapped.

Responding instantly to the order, Xyon halted. He smiled wanly, inclining his head toward his bonds. "Worried I'm going to attack you with these on?" he asked.

"Even if you were unshackled, I wouldn't be concerned about your attacking me," Si Cwan informed him. "Your bonds are not to protect us from you. They're to protect you from us."

"Oh? How so?"

It was Fhermus who spoke up. "It would be in violation of Thallonian tradition for any member of a noble house to take the life of a bound prisoner. As long as your hands and feet are immobilized . . ."

"We won't give in to the temptation to kill you where you stand," Tiraud said.

Xyon nodded in mock respect toward him. "Your unbridled concern for my welfare is much appreciated. Where the hell is my ship?"

"You don't get to ask questions of us!" Tiraud started toward him, but Si Cwan put up a hand and shook his head. Tiraud looked to his father, who nodded, indicating that he should attend to Si Cwan, at least for the time being. Reluctantly, Tiraud stepped back to where he'd been standing before.

"Your ship is on my private landing field just outside this building," Si Cwan told him, "under heavy guard. It's being scanned very carefully. So if you're hoping that you can somehow slip out of here, get to your ship, and thus effect an escape . . . I assure you, the moment your life signs are detected on that vessel, it will be blown to scrap." He stepped down off the throne and approached Xyon. "You see? That is how reasonable individuals operate. You ask them a question, they answer it. So I am certainly hoping that we can all count on one another to behave as reasonable individuals as matters progress. For instance, I expect that you will answer all questions given to you without impertinence."

"No impertinence. Got it." He thought a moment and then asked, "Can I be a bit saucy? How about that? Would that be out of line?"

Si Cwan's fist moved so fast that Robin barely had

time to register it was in motion. He drove it deep into Xyon's stomach, doubling him over, driving all the air out of him and leaving him with only a strangled grunt. There were nods of approval from all around. Robin gasped, but managed to keep it to herself.

"Go right ahead," said Si Cwan. "Be as 'saucy' as you wish."

"Thanks . . . maybe later," Xyon gasped. He tried to stand up straight and managed only to get to about halfway. From the onlookers, there came appreciative chuckles.

"Now then," Si Cwan said, circling Xyon, who looked like he was having trouble staying on his feet, "the only reason you're alive is because you said you would tell me, and only me, where my sister is."

"Really. That's the only reason I'm alive?"

"That's right."

"Well, that's not much incentive for me to tell you, is it? Because once I've told you, then you can kill me."

"Not until we have her back safely," Tiraud said. Si Cwan glanced at him and nodded. Fhermus patted his son on the back.

"I see. And once you have her back safely . . . ?"

"We may kill you or may not," Si Cwan said. "That will depend entirely upon how cooperative you're prepared to be. End this travesty here and now and tell us where she is, and you may indeed get out of here with your life. I cannot guarantee all your limbs will still be in working order . . . or even attached. Most likely one, maybe more, will be gone. But you will still have your miserable life. If you fail to cooperate, well," and he shrugged indifferently, "I cannot be held responsible for the outcome."

"How lucky for you," Xyon said.

Again Si Cwan's hand flew, this time a savage backhand that took Xyon across the face, knocking him off his feet. Xyon thudded to the floor, landing badly on his elbow. He moaned from the impact which no doubt sent fierce shooting pains up his arm.

Robin wanted to shout, *Si Cwan, that's enough!*, but she kept quiet. She knew that Si Cwan was in a difficult situation, with the young Xyon openly defying him in front of the entirety of the Protectorate. He didn't need a Starfleet representative—and his wife, to boot—trying to hold him back. Still, it took everything she had not to at least try to step in.

Xyon tried to roll himself to standing, but Si Cwan didn't wait. "Problems? Allow me," and he reached down and hauled Xyon to his feet as if the young Xenexian weighed nothing. "Well, Xyon? More smart remarks? More attitude? More quips in the face of danger you'd care to share with us? Or perhaps you would simply like to tell us where Kalinda is now."

"I . . ." Xyon's eyes were bleary for a moment and then they refocused. "I . . . don't know. That's the truth."

"You don't know."

"Not a clue."

Si Cwan pivoted and threw Xyon down to the floor. Xyon barely had time to cry out before Si Cwan was crouched over him upon the floor, his hand at Xyon's throat.

"You must be in love with pain," Si Cwan snarled down at him, his control beginning to slip.

"No. Just with your sister. But . . . they're becoming . . . synonymous," Xyon managed to gasp out.

"Where is she?"

"I don't know."

He tightened his grip on Xyon's throat. Xyon gasped, trying to draw in air, not succeeding.

"Where is she?"

"Gods as my witness, I don't know!"

"That's ridiculous. How can you not know?"

"She was taken," Xyon told him. "Another ship . . . came out of nowhere. I tried to run. They grabbed her away . . . some sort of transporter beam, like I've never seen. A ship like I've never seen."

Si Cwan stared down at him for a moment, then looked back at the Nelkarites who had captured Xyon. "What is this ship he speaks of?" he demanded. "Did he tell you of it? Why did you not tell me before?"

The Nelkarite who appeared to be the most high ranking stepped forward, bowed respectfully, and then said, "He told us of it, yes, milord, but we said nothing since it was not worth informing you about. It was simply a pathetic lie to try and save his own neck."

"How do you know that?"

"There was no sign of any ship in the area save his and ours, milord. No tachyon or ion signatures. No trace of warp coil emissions. No sign of any disturbances, and I assure you, we swept the area twice, very thoroughly. Furthermore, we checked his ship's visual log. There was no record of any such vessel or its having pursued his own. He claims a ship absconded with Kalinda, but the facts do not support him."

"I see." He glared down at Xyon. "Then again, the facts supported the notion that he was dead, and yet here he is. Master of lies and duplicity. Perhaps, as far as your status is concerned, we should take pains to have the reality match the myth, eh?"

"Oh, don't go to trouble on my account," Xyon, still on the floor, said, and then he groaned as Si Cwan kicked him in the side.

"You are trying my patience, Xenexian!"

"And you . . . mine. But we . . . endure . . ."

He kicked him a second time, and a third, and this time Robin Lefler could contain herself no longer. "Si Cwan, wait!" she cried out.

"Oh . . . Miss Lefler," Xyon managed to get out. "Good day . . . didn't see you there . . . standing as you were . . . in Si Cwan's long shadow . . ."

Si Cwan did not even bother to look Robin's way. "Where is she?" he demanded, grabbing Xyon and hauling him to his feet. The only thing that was preventing Xyon from collapsing was Si Cwan's grip on him. "Where?"

And suddenly Fhermus was at his side, and with a snarl of "You're being too soft on him!" plunged a dagger directly into Xyon's thigh.

Xyon let out a shriek of pain as, from all around, there was a sudden surge of cheers from the onlookers. Robin was horrified at the bloodlust. It was like pulling back a curtain in time and watching ancient Romans bellowing for blood in the Coliseum.

Si Cwan continued to hold Xyon aloft as Fhermus twisted the blade that was lodged in Xyon's leg. *"Gods' truth, I don't know!"* Xyon cried out, and there was a strangled sob in his voice. "I know what they said! I know the ship left no trace! But it was there! It was this . . . this great thing that looked like . . . like a floating molecule! And it took her away from me, and I want to find her as much as you do."

"You lying dog!" Fhermus snarled. "You insult the House of Fhermus! You steal my son's fiancée. And now you cravenly try to avoid facing the responsibility of your heinous actions!"

"All right, Fhermus," Si Cwan said firmly, "you've made your point . . . literally, I might add. Remove your dagger."

"He—"

"Remove it."

With a reluctant growl, Fhermus yanked the blade out with such force that Robin could practically feel it from across the room. Blood was welling up from the wound. Si Cwan released Xyon at that moment. The prisoner made an effort to support his own weight, but between the pounding he'd sustained and the stab wound, it was simply impossible. Xyon collapsed in a heap, moaning softly.

Si Cwan started to draw back his foot to kick Xyon once more, and suddenly Robin was crossing the room, calling out "Ask me for help!" as she was doing so.

Not understanding why, but clearly in no shape to question, Xyon said, "Help . . ."

"Prime Minister," Robin Lefler said, coming in between the startled Si Cwan and his target. "The prisoner has requested help of the United Federation of Planets. As the UFP's duly deputized representative to the Thallonian Protectorate, I am honoring that request and taking him into my custody, pending—"

"What are you talking about?" demanded Si Cwan. "You can't take him into custody. He's a prisoner of the Protectorate."

"He is also a citizen of the United Federation of Planets. As such, he has the right to request aid and shelter from a UFP rep. That would be me, and I am honoring that request. . . ."

"You pay attention to this woman," one of the Boragi representatives called out, "only because she is your mate."

"Perhaps you would prefer," Robin shot back, "that he simply ignore me because he is my mate . . . as is the case, so I'm told, with how your mate views you."

There was a raucous chorus of laughter in response to that, and the Boragi's skin paled furiously.

Si Cwan was studying her as if she were some new type of bacteria. Finally he said, "Lieutenant Commander, I do not recognize your authority in this matter."

"I suggest you do so, then," Robin warned him, "unless you're really interested in initiating an interstellar incident with the United Federation of Planets."

"Bring them on!" shouted a Shubbite from the back of the room, and others chorused the challenge.

"I very much doubt," Si Cwan said skeptically, "that the Federation is going to be willing to go to war over the fate of a lying, kidnapping freebooter. . . ."

"Even if he's the son of a Starfleet captain?"

"Even if."

"And if the Starfleet captain chooses to go to war with you on his own?"

That brought Si Cwan up short.

"Why should we give a damn!" called out the Shubbite again. "Why, who's he the son of?"

"Mackenzie Calhoun," Robin informed them.

This brought a satisfying, deathly quiet to the room. The representatives looked around one at the other, and there was some uncomfortable clearing of throats.

"Calhoun the God?" one person asked.

"That is how he's known on some worlds, yes," Robin said.

There was more muttering this time, this time with far less enthusiasm than before.

"He is no god, I assure you," Si Cwan said, but then admitted, "He is, however . . . formidable."

"And you will allow yourself to be intimidated by him?" demanded Fhermus. Robin could see veins standing out on his throat.

"Most assuredly not." Si Cwan looked thoughtfully at Xyon, who was lying on the floor and looking helplessly at the stab wound in his leg. The bleeding was slowing, but it still needed to be tended to.

"I need bandages for this man," Robin called out.

"No, you don't," Si Cwan said quickly. "Ankar!"

Ankar came forward, bowing slightly.

"This is Ankar," Si Cwan said in a conversational tone to Xyon, who was still on the floor. "Ankar has served my family for quite some time. Ankar, tell the young gentleman your current duties."

"I am your senior aide, milord. I am responsible for maintaining of appointments, of assuring the smooth flow of—"

"And would you mind telling the gentleman," Si Cwan interrupted him, "what you did for my family when you first came into our service?"

Ankar smiled in a wistful, nostalgic manner. "Interrogation, Lord Cwan."

"Were you skilled at it?"

"Very skilled, milord."

"And have you kept your . . . tools . . . finely honed even after all this time?"

"Yes, milord," Ankar assured him.

"Si Cwan, you can't!" Robin said.

"Lieutenant Commander . . . I very much can." He turned back to Ankar. "Bring him down to one of the storage facilities in the lower chambers. Take whomever you need with you to get the job done."

"The job being to learn the whereabouts of your sister?"

"And my fiancée!" Tiraud called out.

Ankar gave him a withering look. "Well, since they're both the same individual, that should cut my workload in half." He then snapped his fingers and several of Si Cwan's personal guard came forward and hauled Xyon to his feet. Unable to stand, he hung on either side of them, clutching on like an energetic slab of meat.

"Thanks for the help," Xyon muttered to Robin. She saw blood trickling between his lips and began to fear that serious internal injury had been done him.

"Xyon, he's telling the truth," Robin said.

"How do you know that?"

"I can sense it."

"Tragically," Si Cwan replied, "I can sense that he's lying. Stalemate, it seems. Take him away, Ankar, until he's prepared to tell the truth. . . ."

"You want the truth, Cwan?" Xyon's voice was raspy. It was clearly an effort for him to speak at all. "You really want it?"

"Yes," Si Cwan said impatiently. "I really want it."

"All right. The truth is . . ."

"Is what?"

"The truth is," and he forced a smile, revealing blood between his teeth. "The truth is . . . after all this time, you still punch like a girl."

"Get him out of here!" Ankar shouted.

"A little girl!" Xyon called behind him as he was escorted out of the room by Ankar and the guards. "Not even a big girl! You punch like a little, little girl! You call that a punch!? I've been served harder punches out of punch bowls!" With his taunting still echoing in the room behind him, the doors slammed shut even as Xyon's voice continued to echo in the room.

"He'll talk," Si Cwan predicted calmly. "He'll talk . . . and we will learn where he's hiding Kalinda."

"And if he's telling the truth?" asked Robin.

"He's not telling the truth. He must know where she is."

"But if he is?"

"He. Is. Not." Si Cwan's voice could not have been any more confident. "There are indisputably two people in this galaxy who know where Kalinda is right now. We have one of them now, and once we elicit the information from him, we will have the other . . . namely, Kalinda."

Captivity

Kalinda had absolutely no clue where she was.

She knew that she had been transported into a dark and lonely place, an area so inky black that she literally could not see her hand in front of her face. If it was designed to be evocative of the grave, then it was succeeding beyond the wildest expectations that any designer could have had for it.

But the grave held little fear for Kalinda. She had learned long ago that what led others to fear death was the uncertainty of what lay beyond. Kalinda did not claim to have absolute knowledge of those mysteries, but what she did know beyond a certainty was that death was not the end of anything at all. Instead it was simply the next step in existence after life. She wasn't enamored of death particularly, nor was she reckless in the way she lived. But the prospect of passing didn't concern her the way it did others.

So she took comfort in the fact that, if her captors were endeavoring to demoralize her by putting her in fear of her life, they were going to fail utterly.

She was so focused on the possibilities of psychological gamesmanship that it didn't occur to her for long minutes that there might be something hiding in the dark preparing to leap at her, take her down, and kill her on the spot. As soon as she did realize it, she held her breath and listened attentively to see if, indeed, she was alone. The longer she didn't breathe, the louder the pounding of her own heart became to her. All that time, she heard absolutely nothing, and finally expelled her breath in a rush. She felt a bit silly that she had been so paranoid until she concluded that when unknown pursuers have whisked you out of a ship and into a pitch-dark prison, it no longer qualified as paranoia. Someone truly was out to get her.

At one point she called out, "If you return me to New Thallon immediately, and unharmed, not only will you not be punished, but I'm reasonably sure you'll receive some sort of reward." She didn't actually expect a reply, but she wanted to allow her voice to bounce around the room a bit so she could get an idea of just how big it was. Trying to pace it out would have been a waste of time: She would have had no idea whether she was going in a straight line or not. Furthermore, for all she knew, there was some horrific drop waiting for her at the edge. At least where she was, it was more likely that nothing was going to happen to her.

She had no clue how much time passed. All she knew was that she remained exactly where she was until she could stand no longer. Then she sat, and then she slumped over, exhausted from all that she had endured and also lulled into sleep through sheer sensory deprivation in the darkness.

When she awoke, she was somewhere else.

It was still darkness all around. That much had not changed. But something else had. Something seemed very different. At first she couldn't put her finger on what that might be, but then she realized that it was two things. The first was that there was total silence. Before, there had been a very faint but steady humming of power, undoubtedly from whatever unseen engines powered the bizarre vessel. She'd barely been aware of them while she'd been aboard the ship, but now that they had been silenced, she realized they were missing. That meant that either the ship had gone completely dead in space or she herself had been relocated.

She came to the conclusion that it was the latter, because something smelled different as well. The air in her previous place of containment had been oddly sterile. The atmosphere she was in now smelled like . . . well, like an atmosphere. Instead of the meticulously filtered air of a space vessel, she was inhaling genuine, regular planet air. She hadn't even realized there was a substantial difference. Now, though, with only her nose and her hearing being of any use to her, those senses were far more attuned to her new reality.

She was also feeling hungry, but she wasn't about to inform her captors of that. If she was willing to let herself starve to death while in Xyon's captivity, she certainly felt no different about the subject now.

For a brief time, she wondered if somehow this was some sort of elaborate subterfuge that Xyon was engaging in. That he had masterminded this entire involved affair, either to beat her down, or so that he could come sweeping in, rescue her, and thus try to win her love once more. She came to the conclusion that this was not the case. If there was anything Xyon had proven—indeed, if there was one great personality flaw he had (among the many he had thus far displayed)—it was that he was an inveterate juvenile who acted purely on impulse in all things. Complex planning and involved schemes were simply not his strength. No, she was inclined to believe this was exactly what it appeared to be. She'd been kidnapped and, while being returned by one kidnapper, had been grabbed by another.

"I know you moved me," she called out. "You're not fooling anyone . . . least of all my brother. He's going to find me, and I promise you, it will go badly for you. So if you have any desire to keep your heads on your shoulders, you'll open up whatever serves as a door in this place and let me out."

Suddenly she heard a grinding of metal and, some feet away, what appeared to be a large circular door was rolling away from an opening.

"That was easier than I could have thought," she muttered. "I should have said something ages ago."

Suspecting a trap, she still made no move toward the exit. She heard some sort of shuffling and, long moments later, a figure appeared in the doorway. She tried to make him out. It wasn't easy, because he was severely backlit by the light in the hallway. Nor were matters helped by the fact that she'd been in pitch blackness for who-knew-how-long. So she was having vast difficulties adjusting to the sudden flow of light to her eyes. Tears were running down the side of her face, she was squinting so hard.

"Who are you?" she demanded.

"Come here, child," replied her captor, and he gestured in what appeared to be a gentle manner. His tone did not sound especially rough either. "Do not be afraid."

"I'm not afraid."

"You're not?" He sounded vaguely disappointed. "Snatched away from those you know and love? Thrust into an unknown situation? You're far braver than I. I'd be terrified about now."

"Well . . . I'm not. . . ."

"Why . . . I think my knees would be trembling beyond my ability to control," he continued in that same mild tone. "My hands would be shaking . . . my breath racing . . . my heart pounding so hard against my chest that it would feel as if it were trying to break out and skitter away across the floor."

Kalinda was sure that she felt her heart endeavoring to do just that. "Why don't you just shut up," she said.

"All right," he said calmly. "Just making conversation."

Her eyes were beginning to adjust to the new light source, and she took several tentative steps toward the being who was standing there. Slowly she started to be able to make him out. "Wait a minute," she said finally. "You're . . . you're a Priatian."

"Yes."

"Why is a Priatian here?"

"Well," he replied, "we're not all that uncommon

on Priatia. In fact, you see us more or less wherever you go."

"What the hell am I doing on Priatia?" demanded Kalinda.

"Talking to me."

"I mean . . . you know what I mean!"

"Yes, I do. You'll have to forgive me. This is a new and different situation for me, so I'm feeling a bit uncomfortable."

"First of all," Kalinda informed him, "I don't have to forgive you for anything. In fact, I tend to be disinclined to forgive you for a single damned thing. And second, this is a new and different situation for me, too, so why should I care about any discomfiture you might be feeling."

"Is it really?"

"Yes!"

"Odd," said the Priatian. "I'd been given to understand that you've been kidnapped a number of times before. I should think you were quite experienced at it."

She paused and then said grudgingly, "All right . . . all right, I'll give you that. I have been, well, kidnapped more times than most people would consider . . . I don't know . . . sane. Then again, I am a Thallonian noble, so that makes me a valuable prize to many, including, I suspect, you. I mean, that is what this is about. Right, whoever you are? This is about seeing what sort of bargaining value you can get from having me in your possession."

"I can see how it would seem that way."

"What other way should it seem? And speaking of whoever you are, who are you?"

"Oh. My pardon. I am known as Keesala," he said. "Can I get you anything? Something to drink, perhaps?"

"You can get me out of here, Keesala."

"Anything except that." He tilted his head, studying her intently. "You have much of your brother's general bearing."

"You know my brother?"

"Yes."

"Then you know," she said, her voice harsh, "that he will kill you for keeping me imprisoned in this way."

"Would you prefer to be imprisoned in a completely different way?"

"That's not what I mean and you know it."

He nodded. "Yes," he said sadly, "I do." But then something in his manner changed, and his face darkened. "If, however, you are looking for someone to blame for the situation in which you presently find yourself . . . or, for that matter, someone to blame for what's going to happen to you . . . then you really need look no further than your beloved brother. It is his fault that this has happened."

"His fault." She was walking back and forth, studying him with a contemptuous air. "Is that what it comes down to, then? My abductor is so lacking in conviction that he has to blame the brother of his victim in order to excuse his own vile actions?"

Keesala did not move from the spot where he was standing, being content to watch her pacing with unwavering gaze. "Just to clarify: I did not kidnap you. Others did that. My brethren and I are simply holding you here against your will."

"Oh, I see." She was dripping with sarcasm. "Merely the fact that there was no transportation of my person is sufficient to lessen your guilt."

"I am just trying to be accurate. And as for guilt . . . I feel none. None whatsoever. And before you ask me why I don't," he cut her off before she could speak, "the question should be . . . why don't you?"

"Over the loss of your worlds?" She sniffed disdainfully. "I have heard these arguments many times in the past. You refuse to deal with the truth of the matter: My ancestors fought your ancestors. Yours lost, mine won. Now we reap the benefits of that win, and you suffer the consequences of your loss. Asking now for us to willingly turn over that which our ancestors fought and died for is simply too ridiculous to be contemplated."

"And who is that speaking, I wonder?" he asked. "Is that your own voice? Or your brother speaking for you."

"My mind is my own. My words are my own."

"And yet your future is not your own. Rejoice in your small victories, little noblewoman, for the small ones are all you have left to you." He advanced on her and she stood her ground. "To think that I felt some sympathy for you."

"Feel sympathy for yourself. My brother will find me. You will pay for your actions. You will all pay."

"You see?"

It was another voice, from behind Keesala. A second Priatian had been standing there, who knew for how long. "You see, Keesala?" he said again. "Are you satisfied? She's no different than the others."

"Yes, I see, Pembark," Keesala said tightly. "I see very well."

"So there will be no whining from you over what is demanded of—"

"*Quiet!*" He whirled to face the Priatian called Pembark, and his body was trembling with suppressed anger. "Do what must be done. I set aside my objections. But never again address me in such a disrespectful manner. Is that understood?"

"Perfectly," replied Pembark easily. He moved toward Kalinda and grabbed her roughly by the wrist. "Come with me, girl. Don't make this harder on yourself than—"

Kalinda didn't hesitate. Rather than trying to pull away, as Pembark had no doubt expected, instead she shoved toward him. With a fast twist of her wrist, she broke his grip, and then drove the heel of her hand into his face. She was satisfied to hear something break upon contact. He fell like a sack of rocks, moaning and clutching the general area where she had broken something. Immediately she whirled to face Keesala, anticipating an attack.

Instead he just stared, and there even seemed to be a hint of sadness in the way he looked at her.

"Such fervor," he said. "That comes from your pure Thallonian blood, no doubt."

"No doubt." She tried to move around him, but he

took a step to match hers and remained blocking her path. Pembark was still groaning in his pain. Both Keesala and Kalinda ignored him. Kalinda cocked a fist, ready to knock over Keesala. "Don't keep blocking my way."

"It needed to be pure, you see," he said. He was speaking to her in a distant manner, as if she weren't there and he was talking to himself. "It's what they require, in order to accomplish what must be accomplished."

"They? They who?"

"The Wanderers. Those who came before. They who gave us the Many Worlds . . . the Many Worlds that we foolishly allowed to slip away."

"How nice for you. Now step aside. I won't warn you ag—"

"No need for more warnings," he assured her. He moved to one side and swept his tentacle in a broad gesture to indicate that she should feel free to walk past him.

She did so without hesitation. She had no notion what she was going to do once she got out of the room. At that moment, though, all that was important to her was making a clear statement that she would accept nothing less than complete and total freedom, and a return to her home. She stopped at the threshold, turned and said archly to Keesala, "If you hold these 'Wanderers' in such high esteem, then why don't you turn to them to help you in your cause? Oh, I forgot. You cannot do so, because they've abandoned you. Perhaps, Keesala, that should tell you something."

"Oh, it did," he replied. "On the other hand, think of what it told us . . . now that they've returned."

"Returned?"

She hadn't the time to process the word before something wrapped itself around her waist. Instinctively she tried to push it off, and instantly her hands were covered in some sort of viscous ooze.

Kalinda looked down and saw to her horror that a huge tentacle—much larger than a Priatian tentacle—had wrapped itself around her waist. She shrieked, all of her poise and confidence gone, and she tried to shove it away from her. Then a second wrapped itself around her torso, and a third snagged her legs, and then they were all over her. Her cries were muffled by yet another tentacle that wrapped around her mouth, and then she was lifted off her feet, helpless as an infant.

She heard Keesala's voice with that same apologetic air. "I would very much like to tell you that what's going to happen to you now isn't going to hurt. But I try to be honest in all things."

Kalinda screamed, but no one was able to hear it.

U.S.S. Excalibur

Moke shifted uncomfortably in his chair as the ship's counselor leaned forward in his, the two chairs facing each other.

"Left behind?" asked the counselor. "That's most intriguing that you would feel that way."

"Thanks," Moke said uncertainly.

"It wasn't intended as a compliment *per se*. Merely an observation." The counselor tapped his note padd thoughtfully. "Is that what you truly believe? That all these people in your life have left you 'behind' somehow?"

"It's not as if I'm imagining it," Moke said. "I mean, they really did leave."

"So you would perceive it to be. But I'm not entirely sure that's truly what you mean."

Moke shook his head. "I don't understand."

"Moke . . . do you really mean that you're upset because people leave you behind? Or is it that you feel that somehow you become . . . well . . . less important to them?"

"Less important?" Moke echoed.

"Take your mother. Once upon a time, you were the center of her world. But then she developed other interests, including a romantic one in Captain Calhoun himself, as I recall. And, in a way, that interest wound up costing her her life."

"I don't blame Mac for what happened to my mom!"

"Don't you?" asked the counselor gently.

"No." He paused. "Well . . . not that much, I guess."

"If I'm not mistaken, that's the sound of rapidly wilting conviction," the counselor said. "And then there's Xy. I know you took him under your wing when he was small. That was very decent, very generous of you."

"Yeah," Moke said ruefully, "and look where it got me. I bet he's got girlfriends and everything. I don't. I got nothing."

"Other things took priority."

"And it's happening again!"

"How so?"

"Mac's son!" Moke pointed out. "His real son. The one he thought was dead. Now it turns out he's back, and he's in trouble, and that's what Mac's worried about. Not me. Not in the least. Leaving me behind, like I said. I don't get how that's any different from what you were saying, about priorities changing and stuff."

"The difference is this, Moke: When looking at matters in the way that you do, you take it personally. You see it as a failure of some sort on your part. You figure that if you were only better or smarter, more clever or more lovable . . . that the status quo wouldn't change. But life isn't like that, Moke. Life is change. There's always something new and different going on somewhere. You may not always like it. You may often-times wish that it was not the case. But it is, and there's nothing you can do about it."

"Well, thanks," Moke said sarcastically. "You're making me feel lots better now."

"I'm not out to make you 'feel lots better,' Moke."

"Good thing, too."

"I'm out to be honest with you. To get you to view the world outside of the prism of your own concerns, and instead realize that things happen to people that they weren't expecting, and they have to deal with it. When they do so, it's not a referendum on you or your worth as a person. It's just all a part of change. Things can change very, very dramatically, and you can make yourself insane if you try to control them. Instead you simply have to be willing to go with those changes. Have you ever been to a beach? Gone swimming in an ocean?"

Moke shook his head. "I grew up on a desert planet. Mac once tried to take me to a re-created beach on the holodeck, but I couldn't swim. He said he used to have the same problem but overcame it. I didn't want to overcome it. I just wanted to avoid drowning. Anyway, no, I didn't go in the ocean. It was too loud and it made me nervous."

"Putting aside that you never could have drowned inside a holodeck re-creation . . . if you'd allow yourself to do it, you would have found that the waves, as they washed over you, would have lifted you up. If you'd fought this lift, you would likely have gone under and gotten a chestful of water for your trouble. If, on the other hand, you went loose and allowed the water to carry you, you would have had a very enjoyable ride, and it would have deposited you somewhere else without doing you the slightest harm. Life," and the counselor rested a hand very, very carefully on Moke's shoulder, taking care not to crush it, "is very much like that. Fight like mad and you can go under. Allow yourself to experience it, to see where it takes you, and you can have some pleasant surprises."

"That's all well and good, but . . ."

At that moment, the counselor's combadge beeped. He tapped it. "Go ahead," he said.

"The captain wants you to report immediately to transporter room one," came the voice of Burgoyne. "We're in orbit around New Thallon. Time for you to do your other job around here."

"Transporter room one, aye. I'll be right there."

The counselor stood up from his chair and, as was usually the case with him, seemed to go on and on forever in the standing. "You're going to have to excuse me, Moke. And I certainly hope that not for an instant will you take this departure as yet another example of someone walking out on you. The truth is, I would much prefer to remain here, discussing the delicate aspects of relationships and interpersonal dynamics. Tragically, I'm afraid I have to accompany your father and, quite possibly, smash a few heads in the process."

"That's okay, Zak. I think I talked about this as much as I wanted to today, anyway. Although . . ."

Moke remembered when he first met Zak Kebron. The massive Kebron, member of a race called the Brikar, was the single most intimidating individual Moke had ever encountered, both physically and in his brusque, monosyllabic manner.

"Although what?" Kebron prompted. "Finish the thought, Moke."

"Well, I was just wondering . . . when you were talking about change, were you talking about yourself?" Moke asked him.

The Brikar stared down at him. His thick, nigh-impenetrable hide had become a darker hue of bronze since he had undergone the developmental process that had caused him to shed his skin like a heavy-gravity snake several years earlier. Not only had his physical appearance changed, but even more striking was the alteration in his very nature. Si Cwan had once remarked that Kebron had gone overnight from a typically surly teenager to a feelings-obsessed adult. Moke hadn't been thrilled with the characterization of teenagers as typically surly, but had been too annoyed and crabby to take issue with it.

"Myself?" Kebron said thoughtfully. "I hadn't consciously been thinking about it, but, you know, I might well have been thinking about it unconsciously. I shall have to ponder that further. In the meantime, be of good cheer."

"I'll try."

"Try?"

"I'll do it."

Kebron pointed one of his three huge, thick fingers at him. "That's the boy." And he walked out of the room, looking as always like a surging land mass.

And Moke, his lower lip sticking out, sank back in his chair and muttered, "Knew he'd leave. Mac's real son is involved, so that's much more important than me."

New Thallon

i.

Si Cwan wasn't unaccustomed to having Robin mad at him about something or other. She was an opinionated woman. Indeed, that was one of the things that attracted him to her in the first place. So he had anticipated that the recent business with Xyon was going to result in some very unpleasant consequences insofar as his relationship with Robin was concerned.

But her reaction had been unlike any that he'd previously encountered. He'd expected a barrage of arguments, of condemnation, of scolding, for he'd seen the way she'd been reacting to his actions and he knew she hadn't been pleased.

Instead she said nothing. Nothing at all. She said nothing to him. And it wasn't as if she were giving him "the silent treatment," smoldering in mute indignation. Instead, if she looked at him, it was with a sort of vague sadness, as if he had monumentally disappointed her somehow.

He had tried not to respond to it. He'd kept waiting for her to say something. Instead the silence from her side of the bed was deafening, and if he did try to engage her in conversation about anything at all, the only replies he got were monosyllabic and disinterested.

It was the middle of the afternoon when he went to her office himself to inform her that the *Excalibur* was in orbit and Calhoun would be down shortly. To his surprise, she wasn't there. Lately she'd practically been living in the place. He turned around and saw that she was coming down the corridor behind him. "I was looking for you."

"Yes?" she said.

"I came here to tell you that Captain Calhoun is on his way."

"You came to tell me this yourself." She smiled ever so slightly. "How generous. I'd have thought you would send your aide . . . oh. Wait. That's right. He's otherwise engaged."

It was the most she had said to him since Xyon had been dragged away. "We need to talk, Robin."

"I actually knew he was coming, Cwan," she informed him. "Word is out. I believe the representatives are gathering in the main reception hall. Again. Perhaps we should just roll out cots or sleeping bags."

"I did what I had to do, Robin."

The smile now became a passionless, fixed thing on her face. "Yes, and you certainly enjoyed doing it, didn't you."

"No, I didn't."

"Then you disguised your true feelings admirably."

"Don't you see that I may have saved his life, and also the Protectorate?"

"All from beating up a single bound prisoner." She tapped a finger on his chest. "Tough guy. Hope you're proud."

She turned and started to walk away from him, but he grabbed her by the upper arm and swung her back around. "Let go of me!" she said angrily, dropping her air of detachment.

"I had to be strong!" he told her, not releasing her. She tried to pull her arm away from him. Not only did his grip never slacken, but she didn't even manage to budge his arm. "You have to understand that. I had to take a definitive stand, and that stand was that he was not telling the truth. I could not allow for any gray areas, or even the slightest whiff of uncertainty. It would have made me look weak in the eyes of the members of the Protectorate. They will only follow someone who is strong."

She eased her struggling for a moment to say angrily, "And if he had been telling the truth? What then? What if you'd chosen to take the firm and unrelenting stand that he was speaking truly and had no idea at all where Kalinda was?"

Si Cwan yanked her toward him so they were practically nose to nose. "*Let go, Cwan!*" she practically shouted.

In a voice so low that she was the only one who could possibly have heard him, Si Cwan said, "If he was telling the truth, then he was dead. When I say I saved his life, I wasn't joking. He was dead. You understand why." Abruptly he released his hold on her, but she did not back away. "Tell me you understand why."

"Because . . . of Fhermus," she said slowly.

"Damned right, because of Fhermus. In case you've overlooked it, Xyon assaulted the heir of the House of Fhermus. Nelkarite law has special considerations for those in higher authority . . . which should not be all that surprising considering those in higher authority write the laws in the first place. An assault on a noble leader of a house, or his immediate family, is punishable by death. Frankly, it's an attitude with which I can sympathize, because if I could get my hands on whoever has Kalinda right now, I'd want their heads in a bag. So Fhermus would have a superb excuse to take charge of Xyon, what with him being the offended party, and execute him. And I would be in no position, nor have any excuse, to stop him.

"But Fhermus and Tiraud think that Xyon knows where Kalinda is. They believe he's lying. All that's keeping him alive is that belief."

"So . . . this was all a trick," Robin said slowly.

"I had to be convincing."

"And what about sending him down to be tortured. That was all part of trying to be convincing?"

"Of course it was."

"And you're . . . not really having him tortured?"

"Oh, no," Si Cwan said, shaking his head, "he's really being tortured. The little bastard tried to treat me with disrespect in front of the entirety of the Protectorate. Actions must have consequences."

Her lips pursed, Robin turned on her heel and walked stiffly away from him.

Si Cwan threw his arms up and allowed them to slap loosely on the sides of his body in exasperation. "Women," he sighed.

ii.

It hadn't seemed possible that the main reception hall would, or even could, be more crowded than before, but such was apparently the case. Robin had certainly been right when she'd said that word about Calhoun's arrival had gotten around. Apparently everyone who was part of the New Thallonian Protectorate was anxious to catch a glimpse of he whom some did indeed refer to as Calhoun the God.

Si Cwan had just taken his place in the main hall when he heard the familiar humming of activated transporter beams. Moments later, two even more familiar forms shimmered into existence ten feet away from him.

Mackenzie Calhoun and Zak Kebron stood in the middle of the hall and looked around. Calhoun appeared to take great interest in the arched ceilings, while Kebron was fascinated by the various works of art. It was Kebron, interestingly enough, who spoke first: "I love what you've done with the place."

It was all Si Cwan could do to suppress a chuckle. The old Kebron had openly and actively despised Si Cwan. The new Kebron was a very different animal.

"Thank you, Kebron," Si Cwan said with forced politeness. "I take that as a great compliment, since the high quality of your taste is legendary."

Kebron bowed slightly in response, or at least as much of a bow as his inflexible body joints allowed him. Once upon a time, Si Cwan would have seen it as a mocking gesture. Now, though, he knew it was performed in all sincerity.

"And Captain Calhoun," Si Cwan turned his attention to the *Excalibur*'s commander. "You look well. I'm pleased to see your shoulders are square."

Calhoun raised a quizzical eyebrow. "Pardon?"

"Well, I would have thought your wife's promotion over you would have weighed heavily upon you."

If he was hoping to unsettle Calhoun with the jibe, the plan was a major bust. Instead all Calhoun did was chuckle. "Of all the things that weigh upon me, Lord Cwan, my wife's rank does not even register." Then the chuckle evaporated, as did any approximation of humor in Calhoun's expression. "The situation involving my son, on the other hand . . ."

"Ah yes," said Si Cwan. "Tragic, that."

"Indeed. I sympathize with your difficulties and the sense of loss you must be enduring, Lord Cwan . . ."

"Difficulties and loss that had its genesis in your son's actions."

"That is a point well taken. However . . ."

"There is no 'however,' Captain," Si Cwan told him politely but firmly. "You must understand, Calhoun . . . he did bring it upon himself."

Calhoun's expression and tone of voice never wavered. Si Cwan had the feeling that if he measured Calhoun's heartbeat and respiration right about then, there would be no change. He was just that cool in the clutch. "What I understand, Cwan, is that you're having your people torture him. Is that correct?"

"That also, Captain, he brings upon himself. Were he to cooperate, tell us of Kalinda's whereabouts, things would be very different."

"How would they be different? What if he knew of Kalinda's whereabouts, and even told you where she was and how to go and get her right back?" asked Calhoun.

At this, Fhermus spoke up. He took several steps forward and said defiantly, "Then we would execute him for the crimes against my House."

Si Cwan fired a glance toward Robin that said *See?* She wasn't looking at him, though. She was gazing at Calhoun with what appeared to be fond nostalgia. *All that she gave up for you, and look how you're repaying her,* he thought, but said nothing aloud.

"A bit of a no-win scenario you have him in there, Cwan," Calhoun observed.

Si Cwan considered a moment, tapping his fingers on the edge of his chair. The entirety of the hall was silent, waiting for what he was to say next. He liked it that way, that all were waiting. He felt that was how it should be.

"Perhaps something could be arranged," he said after due consideration.

This prompted an annoyed look from Fhermus. "What 'something' would that be, Prime Minister?"

"We must be willing to negotiate these matters, Lord Fhermus."

"Oh, must we? The insult and assaults that his son," and he stabbed a finger at Calhoun, who gave him only the blandest of looks, "inflicted upon me and mine—"

"Are secondary, I should think, to the concern of recovering your son's true love, wouldn't you say?"

Tiraud was about to respond to that, but Fhermus didn't provide him the opportunity. "My son's true love wouldn't be in this fix if not for Calhoun's spawn."

"That's as may be . . . and we could go round and round about how we came to this state. But that will accomplish nothing, whereas some form of compromise might." Just as Fhermus didn't allow his son to respond, so now did Cwan angle the conversation away from Fhermus so that he too could not offer rebuttal. "Tell you what, Calhoun. If you can appeal to Xyon's, dare I say it, better nature, I might be able to steer my way clear to releasing him into your custody." He fired a preemptive, silencing look in Fhermus's direction that, fortunately enough, worked. At least temporarily.

"And how would you define his 'better nature'?" asked Calhoun.

"Why, obviously, by convincing him that it's in his best interest to cooperate."

"Obviously. All right: Take me to him."

"Ah," and he sounded regretful, "I'm afraid that's not advisable at this time. Tragically, there are some here who do not trust you, Captain. So any discussions you have with Xyon would have to be subject to public scrutiny. Do not be concerned, however. You see, the moment Xyon came into our possession, I suspected you would be along." He cast a sidelong glance at Robin, who still wasn't looking at him. "So I took steps to prepare for your arrival. Kindly turn your attention toward the far wall."

Dozens of heads turned in the direction that Si Cwan had indicated. A large painting of Si Cwan's father was hanging there, and then it slid aside with noiseless precision to reveal a large viewscreen.

"I hope you like it," said Si Cwan. "My people worked extremely hard to have it in place in time. Viewscreen, activate please."

The viewscreen flared to life, and the sight upon it prompted audible gasps from some and satisfied growls from others.

Xyon was there, strapped to a table that was angled at forty-five degrees so that he was visible to all. He had been stripped naked and was held to the table via various clamps. Save for his leg where he'd been stabbed, there were no cuts anywhere on his body. It was, however, covered with bruises. He was a mass of swellings, almost from head to toe. His eyes were little more than large gray and black puffiness. His breathing wasn't steady, but instead ragged and raspy.

Si Cwan was hoping that the sight would provoke a reaction from Calhoun. Some sort of outcry, which would certainly be seen as a sign of weakness. But there was nothing. Calhoun might as well have been carved from teak. Kebron, however, was heard to murmur, "Oh my God."

"Xyon," Calhoun said. His voice was flat, unemotional. A Vulcan would have displayed more reaction.

Xyon tried to lift his head and look around, unaware of where the voice was coming from. "Who's that?" he croaked out.

"M'k'n'zy of Calhoun," said the Starfleet captain, using his Xenexian name.

"Oh." Xyon stopped trying to look around, allowing his head to slump back. "Hi. Look . . . you caught me at a bad time." He sounded as if he were gargling gravel.

"In a bit of a fix, are you, son?"

"It's under control."

"Is it."

"No problem. Father . . . sorry about pretending to be dead. Fortunately . . . at this rate . . . I'll be making up for the 'pretending' part."

"I'll get you out of there, Xyon."

Xyon made a small movement of his head that was clearly an endeavor to shake it. "They won't let me go . . . till I tell them where Kalinda is."

"Then tell them, Xyon. There's no point in keeping it to yourself. If you love her . . ."

"The fact that I do love her . . . is what's killing me . . . killing me way more than they can. Because I should be out finding her . . . but they've got me locked up down here." And then his voice began to rise as he found desperate strength bubbling up within him. "Find her, Dad. You . . . gotta find her . . . save her. Only you . . ."

"That will do for now," Si Cwan said mildly. The screen shut off. Si Cwan tried to see Robin's reaction to all that, but his attention was pulled away by Calhoun before he could spot her.

Because Calhoun was walking toward him with calm but determined stride. "Turn him over to me, Si Cwan."

"What, just like that?"

"Just like that."

"I'm afraid it's not that easy, Calhoun. You see, clearly he's still not ready to cooperate. I was hoping that seeing you would jog loose his stubbornness. . . ."

"He doesn't know where she is."

Before Si Cwan could stop him, Fhermus stepped in between Si Cwan and Calhoun. "We have only his word for that, and he is a liar and deceiver of the highest order."

"We have devices on the *Excalibur* that would be able to determine the veracity of what he's saying. There would be no margin for error."

"Oh, and we are to trust you, are we? You, who have everything to gain from so-called infallible machines, except it would benefit you when they allegedly verify your son's ignorance of the girl's whereabouts."

Calhoun looked slightly exasperated. "Who are you again?"

"Fhermus of the House of Fhermus. The one who has suffered at your son's hands."

"It seems to me that Xyon is the one doing the suffering."

"Indeed. And I assure you that, if I had my preferences, I would have contributed far more to it than I did."

"Meaning . . . ?"

"Meaning when I stabbed him in the leg to urge him to speak."

Si Cwan saw the scar on the side of Calhoun's face flush crimson. "Fhermus . . ." called out Cwan.

"That was your doing?" Calhoun growled.

"Handiwork of which I'm quite proud, actually."

"Fhermus," Si Cwan tried to warn him, "I really wouldn't . . ."

"They brought your arrogant whelp in here, all trussed up, and I showed him," said Fhermus proudly, "I showed him the cost of—"

There was the sound of a loud crack, and it took the assemblage a few moments to realize that Calhoun had just broken Fhermus's jaw.

Calhoun was standing there with fist cocked, his knuckles skinned. Fhermus was staggering, trying to maintain his footing, his knees buckling. His jaw was at an odd angle to the rest of his face. Tiraud was paralyzed, staring in shock at his father's condition.

Fhermus swung a flaccid punch that missed Calhoun by two feet, and Calhoun took a quick step forward, his arm moving like a piston. His fist slammed squarely into Fhermus's face, and that was it for the Nelkarite. He toppled backward like a tree and crashed to the ground, arms flung out to either side.

"Well, *that* was inevitable," sighed Zak Kebron.

Tiraud was immediately at his father's side, trying to revive him, and the hall erupted into shouting that only died down after Cwan, on his feet, spread his hands wide and repeatedly bellowed for quiet. When he finally got it, he stared gravely at Calhoun. "I cannot believe what I just saw."

"Nor can I," admitted Calhoun, sounding concerned. "Did you see that? It took two punches to put him down. I must be getting old."

"This isn't funny, Calhoun!"

"Notice my absence of laughter, Si Cwan."

Tiraud was on his feet and he was bellowing, "This is an outrage! *An outrage!*"

"Your father stabbed a helpless prisoner," Calhoun said calmly, never coming close to raising his voice. "I can think of no greater outrage than that."

Tiraud whirled to face Si Cwan. "I am demanding that this man be taken into custody, and if you don't do it, then I will call upon my personal guard to see it done."

"Is there anything around here to eat?" asked Zak Kebron.

The question was so completely out of left field that Si Cwan gaped openly at him. "What?"

"Well, I was figuring if there was, we could have dinner *and* a show."

It was at that moment that a cry of *"Prime Minister!"* rang through the great hall, and Si Cwan frowned in confusion. "Ankar?"

It was indeed the voice of his personal aide and occasional torturer. Ankar sprinted into the room, looking out of breath, as if he'd run the whole way from wherever he'd been off tormenting the helpless Xyon. "He's gone, Prime Minister!"

"He? He wh—?" It was so unthinkable to Si Cwan

that at first it didn't register on him who Ankar could possibly be referring to. But then the truth dawned upon him. "You can't be serious."

"I was standing right there! Right there! My back was turned, and suddenly I heard a loud buzzing noise, and when I looked back, he was gone!"

Instantly there was an uproar from the onlookers. Everyone was talking at once, and the words "Outrage!" and "How dare he!" were the loudest being bandied about.

It was everything that Si Cwan could do to make himself heard over it, and what he did shout was *"Calhoun!"* But as it turned out, he failed utterly, because the voices were rising and his angered outcry blended in with all the rest.

And then the walls and floor shook, and the paintings swung to one side, and several of the busts trembled on their pedestals and one nearly fell over, and it all happened as a result of one single word bellowed at ear-splitting, unconsciousness-inducing, wall-shaking volume.

"QUIIIIIIIIIETTTTTTT."

The bellow was so thundering that it brought everything crashing to a halt. Si Cwan had found it necessary to grab hold of his chair lest he fall over, and he stared with outright incredulity at the source.

The only one in the room who hadn't been staggered by the unleashed sound was Calhoun, which was impressive considering he'd been closest to the source. Not that he'd been totally unaffected; he'd put his hands to his ears to provide some degree of shielding.

When the bellow had run its course, he looked up at Zak Kebron and said, "That was impressive. I didn't know you could do that."

"I don't like to. It hurts my throat. Still, that's nothing. You should hear the Brikar Light Opera Company," Kebron told him modestly.

"Actually, I don't think I should."

"Calhoun!" Si Cwan finally managed to get out.

"Yes?"

"You helped Xyon escape! Don't deny it!"

"All right. I don't deny it."

"Then you *admit* it!"

"No. I don't admit it."

"But you didn't deny it!"

Calhoun shrugged. "You told me not to deny it. I was just trying to be accommodating."

"*Calhoun—!*"

"I didn't take him, Si Cwan," Calhoun said, his voice changing and becoming less laconic and more forceful. "You saw me. I was standing right here. I issued no order, gave no command to my ship."

"He was beamed out! This is no different than when you helped Janos to escape from custody years ago—!"

"There is one minor difference, in that this time around I had nothing to do with it. Other than that, the two occasions are completely identical."

"You . . . you won't get away with this!" Tiraud cried out. He had dragged his father to a nearby chair. Fhermus, half-slumped in it, was just starting to come around. "Do you hear me? You won't get away with this!"

Calhoun gave him a look that seemed as if he was judging whether Tiraud was worth his time to reply to. Apparently deciding to err on the side of whatever shreds of diplomacy might be left to the situation, he said coolly, "I'm not trying to get away with anything. I have as much invested in this as do you. In point of fact, I have no intention of going anywhere until this matter is sorted out. My son is missing, and this time I'm not going to presume him dead unless I see it for myself."

"You're offering your continued presence here as assurance of Xyon's return?" Si Cwan said carefully, clearly wanting to leave Calhoun no room for political maneuvering.

"Since I wasn't responsible for his vanishing just now, I'm not in a position to assure anything about his return," Calhoun replied. "The only thing I can assure you is that I'm not leaving until this matter is re-solved."

"Then you will remain in the custody of the House of Fhermus!" snapped Tiraud. Si Cwan heard the thun-dering of feet and saw ten or so of Tiraud's personal guards massing.

Calhoun looked them up and down. "That won't be happening," he said quietly.

Si Cwan's gaze flickered from Calhoun to Kebron to Tiraud. "Tiraud . . . I respect the House of Fhermus, and in that sense of respect, I suggest you stand down your intentions here. For one thing, you don't have enough men."

"Oh, I think my fighting force here is up to the

task, Prime Minister," Tiraud said, brimming with confidence. "However, I always have more men in service to the House of Fhermus if need be."

"I was actually *referring* to the total number of men you have in service," Si Cwan replied. "Candidly, I doubt we have enough men on the *planet* to get the job done, if arresting Mackenzie Calhoun . . . particularly with Kebron standing here . . . is your intention."

"And I respect your concerns, Prime Minister" was Tiraud's taut reply, "but I am going to take this man into custody and throw him into the most dank, repulsive accommodations that the House of Fhermus has to offer."

"And they say chivalry is dead," rumbled Kebron. "Captain . . . with your permission . . . ?"

Calhoun shrugged. "Be my guest."

"Young Nelkarite," Kebron said, folding his arms across his massive chest, "believe it or not, I comprehend your outrage. You feel humiliated and are planning a show of force to balance that. Understandable. Very understandable. Believe me when I tell you, however, that it will not go well for you if you embark upon this course of action you intend. Right now, with all that's happened, I very much feel your pain. However, if you launch this assault, I will cease to feel your pain. You, on the other hand, will continue feeling your pain, for about as long as you're capable of feeling anything. The same for those under your command. So I implore you . . . do not do what you're contemplating do—"

"Get them!" shouted Tiraud, and his guardsmen

surged forward with a collective shout of fealty to the House of Fhermus.

Kebron sighed and glanced at Calhoun. "That never works," he admitted.

"I know," said Calhoun, poised on the balls of his feet, a grim smile of confidence on his lips. "But I never get tired of watching you try."

The guardsmen started to reach for their disruptor weapons hanging at their sides, but Si Cwan immediately shouted, "No! There will be no shooting in here! Bystanders will be injured! If you want them, take them without weapons . . . if you can."

"You doubt us!" Tiraud cried out, sounding outraged.

"No. But I don't doubt them, either," said Si Cwan, nodding toward Calhoun and Kebron. Kebron tossed a slightly mocking salute in Cwan's direction.

The guardsmen of the House of Fhermus holstered their weapons and, as one, charged.

Kebron stepped in between the onrush of attackers, his arms spread wide. They tried to move around him, determined to get at the higher-ranking officer, who, as it happened, also looked to be far less formidable than Kebron. Several of them, however, assaulted Kebron, swarming over him like so many Lilliputians attacking Gulliver. Their success in that endeavor was similarly transitory.

With a dull roar, Kebron began flinging them aside. All the while he kept grumbling "Sorry about this" and "You really shouldn't be doing this" and "I wish there was another way." He didn't bother with various fight-

ing techniques; the sheer brute strength of his arms was
more than enough to send guardsmen crashing into
one another, their unconscious or moaning bodies pil-
ing up like logs stored for winter.

Several of them, including Tiraud, managed to
maneuver in behind Kebron, and it was these that
came at Mackenzie Calhoun. At first it seemed as if
Calhoun didn't notice them coming, because his back
remained to them as he watched Kebron flipping attackers about as if they were poker chips. But when
Tiraud drew to within two feet of Calhoun, he
learned something with brutal certainty that others
could have told him: Mackenzie Calhoun practically
had eyes in the back of his head. How else to explain
the booted foot that shot backward like an uncoiling
spring, catching Tiraud squarely in the gut. It
knocked all the breath out of him and he fell backward, clutching his stomach.

The others advanced on Calhoun and then they
hesitated as they saw in his eyes an almost feral excite-
ment. It was enough of a delay that they were caught
flat-footed as Calhoun came at them. A backhand
punch in the face to one sent him staggering while, at
the same time, Calhoun spun and smashed his foot
into the kneecap of the man nearest him. The man let
out a yelp and crumpled, clutching his leg, as Calhoun
ducked under a missed roundhouse from a third man.
He punched the attacker solidly in the solar plexus,
and there was the sound of a rib cracking from the
impact.

The rest of the room was in chaos as Zak Kebron

continued to shot-put around the guards who were foolish enough to attack him. The only person in the room who seemed to have no vested interest in the proceedings was Si Cwan himself. Once the pandemonium had begun, Si Cwan had chosen simply to lean back in his large chair, prop his chin up with one hand, and watch the festivities with the air of a bored spectator at a tennis match.

Tiraud had yanked his dagger from its sheath and—even though he was in pain from the shot he'd taken moments before—swung the dagger in a long, sweeping arc. Calhoun saw it coming at the last second and twisted around, barely getting his stomach out of the way. A quarter inch closer and his digestive system would have been spilling out onto the floor through the newly created slice in his belly.

Calhoun turned full circle and came up on Tiraud's side. He locked one hand immovably onto Tiraud's wrist, rendering it helpless, and his face was inches away from Tiraud, who was suddenly pale with fright.

"Just a twist," snarled Calhoun, applying the slightest pressure onto the knife which was now pointed at Tiraud's belly, thanks to the manner in which Calhoun was holding it. "Just one twist and I sheathe this in your own body. You have no idea what you're up against."

With that, he brought his other arm up and across and slammed Tiraud in the face. Blood spurted from the young man's broken nose as Calhoun pushed him down. The Xenexian held up the blade, staring at it from several angles. "Nice craftsmanship," he observed, and suddenly his arm was up, the point of the knife aimed straight at Tiraud.

"No!" screamed the closest guardsmen, and they skidded to a halt. Everyone froze. Si Cwan sat up slightly, looking mildly interested.

Calhoun brought the blade slamming down right toward Tiraud's crotch. Tiraud let out an earsplitting scream as the blade thunked home . . . harmlessly striking the floor in between his legs, missing his family pride by no more than the width of an eyelash.

Tiraud stared down, gasping for breath. Standing up, Calhoun flipped the blade to Tiraud so it landed with the flat of the blade across his chest.

"You can forget trying to capture Mackenzie Calhoun and Zak Kebron," Calhoun warned him, "unless you're prepared to come at us with a lot more than that. And I really wouldn't advise—"

At that moment there was a stampede of feet and a score of guardsmen came charging in, howling for blood.

Calhoun and Kebron exchanged glances. "That never works," Calhoun grunted.

"I know," Kebron replied, "but I never get tired of watching you try."

U.S.S. Excalibur/New Thallon

i.

Morgan Primus, aka Lefler, was at peace.

She knew that there had been a time when that was not so, when she was never at peace. In those days she'd had a mortal body . . . except it was not really mortal as such. Instead year after year had rolled over into century after century, and it had reached a point where she was desperate to find some way to terminate her endless, dreary existence . . . even if it meant leaving behind the daughter she believed she loved.

But that was before the freak accident that had destroyed that supposedly indestructible body and transferred her neural patterns, her mind—who knew, perhaps even her soul, if such a thing truly existed—into the computer banks of the *Starship Excalibur.* Suddenly the woman who felt that she had seen it all, known it all, couldn't be surprised by anything and felt enveloped by boredom and ennui . . . suddenly that woman effectively had a starship for a body. Furthermore, her mind could reach out, interface with other computers. None of them naturally had a hope in hell of approaching what she possessed when it came to the ability purely to think, to feel, to reason. All those aspects of her humanity had come along with her into her new "residence." But the automatic gathering of knowledge, the abilities that were hers, had taken that tragically dull life of hers and transformed it into something that was an ever-continuing voyage of discovery. And with the holotechnology of the *Excalibur* at her command, she could reconstitute a simulation of a body whenever she felt so inclined.

She missed smell, however.

She hadn't needed to replicate sight and hearing, of course. Those were hardwired into holographic software. Touch had been slightly tricky, but not all that difficult. Creating skin that was sensitive to extremes of hot and cold, sharp and dull. She had not yet endeavored to take a lover as a hologram because she wasn't one hundred percent sure that her epidermal simulation was sufficient to match the subtleties and ecstasies of sex. Granted, there were individuals who created holograms specifically for that purpose, but the holograms were simply programmed to simulate the proper reactions. They didn't actually feel what was transpiring. Morgan wanted to get it to the point where the sensations of sex matched her recollections exactly. Either that or have it be long enough since her last sensual encounter that she didn't much remember any of it, and thus would have no basis for comparison.

She had also managed to replicate taste to some degree. She knew precisely which taste buds triggered salty, sweet, etc. Encoding them into her tongue, she had been able to rig her holographic taste buds to respond to particular stimuli the way they were supposed to in life, although there had been a bit of fine-tuning required to get such nuances as "sour" correct.

But she hadn't cracked the sense of smell.

Not only had this been an impediment to taste, since the full impact of taste required an accurate sense of smell, but it had been a particular disappointment for Morgan, since smell was such a potent trigger of memories. She missed the smell of everything from flowers to fresh-baked bread, and all the joyous recollections that such smells prompted. Of course, it wasn't as if the *Excalibur* was overrun with flowers and bread, but it was the principle of the thing. Morgan took pride in her work, and her inability to provide an olfactory sense for herself irritated her.

So deep within the recesses of the computer, Morgan was contemplating new programs for a sense of smell when she received a direct alert from Robin.

Morgan's many other duties around the ship didn't cease when she was "withdrawn" as she was now. Being part of a computer, she was able to replicate herself easily enough. At that moment, Morgan Primus was seated at her station at navigation, keeping the ship in perfect geosynch orbit around New Thallon. She was having a pleasant, if not particularly intellectually stimulating, conversation with Tania Tobias at ops.

As always, Morgan was—unknown to Tania—meticulously monitoring her vital signs. During her time on the *Excalibur,* Tania had never once shown the slightest sign of having one of her . . . fits. But Calhoun was always wary, and asked Morgan to keep an extremely close computer eye upon Tania at all times. If Tania displayed even the slightest aberrant behavior, Morgan was instructed to alert Calhoun instantly.

While this was happening, Morgan was also being called on by Dr. Selar on a consult, researching information. She was also aiding Selar's son, Dr. Xy, who had been made the *Excalibur* science officer upon his return. It was considered a bit of an unlucky position, considering what had happened to Soleta, and the even more depressing fate of her successor, Lieutenant Candido, whom nobody liked to talk about since it prompted such staggeringly depressing memories. Candido's name had once come up at Si Cwan and Robin's engagement party, and Kebron had waxed Shakespearean to say, "Who would have thought the old man to have had so much blood in him?" That more or less put an end to *that* party.

But Xy had taken on the assignment with a morbidly cheerful attitude of "What's the worst that could happen? My tragically premature death is even more tragically premature?"

And while Morgan was engaged in face-to-face discussions with various of the ship's personnel, her subroutines were engaged in thousands of other matters, big and small. She handled them all with facility, and even felt as if this was turning out to be a fairly light day.

During this time, her core personality—that which

she regarded as the "real" her, if such a thing still existed—hovered in a sort of computerized womb, contemplating all manner of abstract concepts that might enable her to create a sense of smell. But she put all that aside instantly when Robin's call came through. There was exactly one person in all the galaxy who had the private binary code that linked directly to Morgan's core, and Robin was it. It was a sort of gift that Morgan had given her, feeling that after everything she had put her daughter through, the very least she could do was provide her with something that was unique and personal. Robin tended not to use it all that often. In fact, Morgan had begun to wonder if Robin even remembered that Morgan had provided it to her. When the call came in, though, any vestiges of concern that Morgan might have had were swept aside.

"Robin!" Morgan said, her voice echoing within her own mind. Naturally in her cocooned state, such human notions as bodies were irrelevant. "Darling, how nice to hear from you. Of course, since we're in the neighborhood, I was hoping to—"

"Mother." Robin's voice sounded concerned. Only her voice was coming through on the link; she wasn't utilizing any sort of viewer. That naturally made Morgan wonder what was going on. "I need to talk to you, down here, face-to-face."

"Well, that could be a bit of a challenge, sweetheart, especially since you're not near a viewscreen. You're using your combadge. Can you locate a—"

"A viewscreen won't do it. Mother, can you lock on to my whereabouts?"

"Yes. Why? Do you need me to beam you up here?"

"No," Robin said firmly. "If you did that, if you brought us up, that would just undermine Captain Calhoun's position. I can't allow that."

"Undermine his . . . I don't understand. 'Us'? What us? Are you and Si Cwan . . . ?"

"Never mind that now. Mother, if you lock on to my current location, you'll find that—"

"A holosuite," Morgan said promptly. "You're in a holosuite."

Robin sounded slightly surprised. "How did you know that?"

"I was picking up some localized computer chatter over your link and managed to identify it as a holosuite."

There was a pause. "Computer chatter?"

"Yes."

"The computer in the holosuite was talking to someone?"

"No. It was talking to itself," Morgan told her. "All computers do that as part of diagnostic subroutines. Normally it's not something that's detectable, but to me, it's as if they're shouting."

"All right," Robin said briskly, "can you use the holosuite? Use it to create a body for yourself and come down here?"

"Of course. Do you need me to . . . ?"

"Yes, please."

Although she sounded quite calm, Morgan could sense a sort of controlled urgency in her voice. Summoning her core consciousness, she sent it down into the holosuite where Robin was awaiting her. Bits of hard light swirled around as she collected and sorted through them, choosing all the correct bits to create a body for herself. It seemed to Morgan subjectively that it was taking her an age to do so, because she wanted to make sure she looked just right for visiting with her daughter. She considered all the ways she could make herself look better than she ever had in life, starting with making her backside trimmer, removing the wrinkles around her eyes. Her face, as with all humans, wasn't really perfectly symmetrical, so perhaps she could do something about that. But after considering the matter for some time, she decided that Robin really wouldn't appreciate such endeavors on her part. That Robin just wanted to see her mom the way she remembered her, not as some artificial construct that bore only a passing resemblance to the reality of her.

All this pondering of how she should look took her exactly one-half of one second, and so it was that Robin's voice barely had time to fade before her mother's holographic form swirled into existence in Robin Lefler's private holosuite.

She took one look at who was next to Robin and gasped out, "Oh my God."

Robin was doing everything she could to keep Xyon on his feet, but she was only barely succeeding. Morgan wasn't even sure that Xyon knew where he was. His head was tilting from one side to the other as if it were being held to his shoulders by a length of string instead of his neck.

"Help him," Robin said desperately.

"We need to get him up to *Excalibur*!"

"We can't, Mother. It's like I told you. I can't undermine the captain's position. As long as he's here, Calhoun can maintain plausible deniability. But if he's brought up to the ship . . ."

"All right, yes, I understand. I don't necessarily agree, but I understand."

"Can you help him?"

Instantly Morgan took complete command of the holosuite. She didn't have to utter any commands; anything that she could envision simply snapped into existence. Robin looked around in surprise as she found herself surrounded by an approximation of sickbay.

"How did you get him in here?" asked Morgan as she and Robin eased Xyon onto the examination table. He seemed confused, disoriented, looking around in bewilderment.

"I sent a message to his ship. It's got an onboard AI that calls itself Lyla. It's about the most advanced AI I've seen. . . ."

"Short of me, you mean."

"You're not artificial, Mother."

"Funny. We once had an argument when you said I was the most artificial—"

"Mother, could we not do this now!"

"Sorry," said Morgan as she helped Xyon lie back. She reached over and swung a large metal enclosure over him that clicked into place on the pad. It covered him from just under his neck to just above his knees. "So you contacted this Lyla. . . ."

"Right. So his ship has an emergency transporter device aboard. Short-range only, but that's all I needed."

"You had her beam him out of captivity and into here? Why not just aboard his own ship and he gets the hell out of here?"

"Because his ship's being closely watched. A brief energy surge with no apparent result may leave them wondering, but it won't set off any alarms. But if Xyon materialized aboard the ship, they'd detect his presence and there wouldn't be enough left to scrape into a small bag."

"Yes, yes, that makes sense," Morgan admitted. She was studying Xyon's vitals. "I didn't think anyone could sustain this many subdural hematomas and still live."

"My host was . . . very expert," Xyon managed to grunt. Then, remarkably, he half-smiled. "But . . . you know what? It's not hurting so much. . . ."

"That's the bioregenerative field," she said, tapping the cocoonlike device that enveloped him. "It's easing the pain from the damage you sustained and is regenerating the cells."

"A hologram of a medical unit can do that?" asked Robin, a bit surprised.

Morgan looked at her with quiet confidence. "Mine can," she said. Then she admitted, "Things would go faster, though, if I could give him medication to speed the process. Re-creating machinery is one thing, but I don't have the raw materials at my disposal to produce medication. Still, this will do for now."

"Yes, and for as long as it doesn't occur to Si Cwan

to come bursting into here, looking for his missing suspect." She came around the table so she was closer to Xyon's face. "Xyon? Can you hear me?"

"Only if you talk," he said.

She and her mother exchanged glances. "Who would have thought that being a smart-ass was genetic?" said Morgan with grim amusement.

"Xyon . . . you know I want to help you. I need you to tell me . . . more to the point, tell my mother here . . . everything you can about the ship that took Kalinda."

"You . . . believe me, then?" he asked.

"Xyon, you strike me as many things," Robin told him. "But I don't think you're stupid. I suppose it's possible that you dropped Kalinda off somewhere, have her in hiding, and are assuming that you'll be able to go back to her and pick up where you left off."

"I wish I had. I wish I could." He sighed and there was the sound of something ugly rattling around inside his chest. She cast a worried glance at her mother, but Morgan just shook her head to indicate that either it wasn't anything to worry about, or that the bioregenerative field was in the process of attending to it. "But I was bringing her back. I was."

"Why? Because you thought better of it?" asked Robin.

"No. It was probably the single dumbest thing I've ever done, and I still haven't thought better of it," he replied. "I was bringing her back to make her happy. Because she wanted to be with . . . him," and he inclined his head in a vague direction that he probably thought indicated, in some manner, Tiraud's where-abouts.

"She told you that?"

"I figured she'd think better of it once away from his influence. But . . . she didn't. So . . . to hell with her."

"You really feel that way?"

"No, but I'm hoping that if I tell myself that enough, I'll believe it," he sighed.

"You think he's telling the truth?" asked Morgan.

Robin considered it a moment. "Yeah . . . yeah, I'm thinking he is. I've seen enough men in my time to recognize that genuine kicked-puppy-dog look they acquire when they're moping after a girl. I think he's being honest."

"Could you not talk about me as if I weren't here?" asked Xyon.

"Oh, believe me, I'm very glad you're here," Robin assured him. "Because you're going to tell me everything you can about the ship that you say took Kalinda."

As quickly as he could, Xyon did so. Robin frowned. "Well, he's consistent, I'll give him that. That's more or less how he described it when he was first captured."

"Still here and still not appreciating being discussed as if I were elsewhere."

Robin ignored him. "Mother," she said, "does it sound at all familiar to you? Because it doesn't sound like any ship I've ever heard of. But you've got access to far more sources of information than I do."

"That's true. Hold on." It took Morgan long moments to scan all ships in the Federation registry, and then she shook her head. "Nothing. It doesn't match any known race in all the . . . wait."

"What?"

"Wait." Morgan tilted her head slightly as if she were listening to something that someone was saying from very far away. "Okay . . . wait. I've got something. It's very old, though."

"Old?"

"From a Federation research party that came to Thallonian space back before the Thallonians were being very aggressive about keeping outsiders away. It was a scientific expedition investigating alien cultures. Interesting."

"What's interesting about it?"

"It was the *Excalibur.*"

Robin was obviously surprised. "Calhoun's ship?"

"No. This research party was in the year 2267, under the command of Captain Anton Harris. It was one of the last missions the ship undertook before most of its crew was killed the following year by an out-of-control computer during war games."

"Okay, Mother, but that was over a century ago. What could they have discovered then that would be remotely pertinent?"

Morgan looked at her sadly. "Patience was never your strong suit, was it, dear."

"Mother!"

"On a planet called Priatia," Morgan said, "there were drawings. Drawings in texts, paintings hanging upon walls of some of the residents. The science team at the time made visual records of them."

"Let me guess," said Robin with grim certainty. "The drawings were of spacegoing vessels that match what Xyon said he saw."

"Absolutely right."

"Those little *bastards!*" Robin snapped, and she was so angry that she slammed a fist down on the metal shielding atop Xyon. Although the impact didn't hurt him, he started slightly. "I should have known! I don't have the slightest idea how I should have known, but I should have."

"Should have known what, Robin?"

"They showed up," Robin told her mother. "Here."

"Here in the holosuite?"

"No, here in my office. They wanted to see Si Cwan. They were complaining about wanting their territory back. I should have known. I should have put it together and realized that they must have kidnapped her in order to apply pressure to Si Cwan."

"There's two problems with that theory, dear," Morgan said. "First, they haven't actually contacted Si Cwan . . . or anyone. Somewhat difficult to apply pressure and get what you want if you don't actually tell the person you're theoretically trying to put pressure on. And second, that pictured vessel . . . it's not something the Priatians actually had in their possession or at their disposal. It was a rendering of an ancient vessel. Very ancient."

"Let me take yet another guess," said Robin. "A vessel belonging to the Wanderers?"

"Exactly right."

"So obviously what this means is that they found a way to create a replica of one of the Wanderers' ships, and use it to rally support and strike fear into any who see it."

"Sure scared the crap out of me," admitted Xyon.

"See there?" Robin said, pointing at Xyon. "It scared the crap out of him."

"Considering how monumentally full of crap he is, that's quite an achievement," said Morgan.

"Thank you very mu—hey!" said Xyon.

Morgan ignored him. "I'm not sure you're right, Robin. The complexity of the vessel, particularly if it's constructed as Xyon described . . . I don't know that it would be within the capabilities of the Priatians as they currently are. Or, for that matter, our own capabilities. Granted, we're not slouches when it comes to designing spacegoing vessels, but this ship—in both its size and mysterious means of propulsion—is unlike anything we currently have active or in development."

"So what are you suggesting, Mother? That their progenitors, their 'Wanderers,' have wandered back?"

"It's possible. Don't you think it's possible?"

"No. Well . . . maybe. Okay, yes, it's possible. But I don't think it's likely."

"In terms of likelihood, I think it ranks far above the notion that the Priatians have become the most advanced builders of ships known to the Federation, short of the Borg."

Robin opened her mouth but then closed it.

"Okay," she admitted, "there's something to be said for that. Still, no matter how you look at it . . ."

"There's a case to be made for pointing the finger of suspicion somewhere other than at Xyon? Yes, I'd have to agree with that."

"Of course you agree with that. You practically shoved the notion down my throat."

"Yes, well, Mother knows best."

"That being the case, Mother," said Robin, "what would you suggest be our next move?"

"I think we should find a way to inform Si Cwan and his associates of our discoveries and dispatch a ship as soon as possible to Priatia to investigate."

"Yes . . . yes, that makes sense." Robin considered it a moment, then said, "Mother . . . here's what I'd like you to do."

ii.

Burgoyne wasn't exactly sure what to expect when s/he, backed up by a dozen security-team members, beamed down to the main reception hall of Si Cwan's residence. What s/he saw upon arrival stunned hir . . . for about two seconds. Then all s/he could think was *Well, yes, that figures.*

The room was a madhouse.

People who appeared to be some sort of soldiers were charging in from all directions, and it was clear their targets were Mackenzie Calhoun and Zak Kebron. Burgoyne wasn't sure what Calhoun could possibly have done to antagonize people to this degree, but it must have been something of stupendous magnitude.

There were unconscious bodies strewn about, and Calhoun and Kebron were mowing through all comers. Burgoyne had seen Calhoun in action any number of times, and was always impressed how Calhoun's facial expression never wavered. Once, out of curiosity, Burgoyne had used a medical tricorder to scan Calhoun during a brawl (an ill-advised drinking contest on Bravo Station had gotten a bit out of hand) and was astounded to discover that Calhoun's heart rate barely accelerated the entire time.

S/he suspected that, were that study being conducted right now, the results would be precisely the same.

Calhoun, moving with the smooth efficiency of a machine, was effortlessly weaving through his various attackers. Taking the opportunity to observe, Burgoyne saw that there was a clear and consistent pattern: Whenever someone thought they had a bead on Calhoun, he was somewhere else. As a result, either they would expend energy swinging at empty air while leaving themselves vulnerable to attack, or else they would so badly miscalculate that they would strike one of their own fellows. Either way, no one was managing to lay so much as a finger on Calhoun.

Kebron needed neither grace nor artistry. He simply tossed his assailants around as if he were a towering windmill and they so many pint-sized Don Quixotes.

The only person in the place who wasn't either trying to beat up Calhoun and Kebron or, at the very least, shouting encouragement, was Si Cwan. He was eating some sort of snack food out of a bowl on a small table nearby him. One of his long legs was draped over the chair's armrest. He looked like someone who had clearly settled in for an evening's entertainment.

"Commander?" asked Ensign Burton, a lieutenant in the security squad. "Shouldn't we . . . ?"

"Right, of course," said Burgoyne, shaking hirself out from under the relentless violence's spell. "Let's get their attention, shall we?" With that, s/he pointed hir phaser straight up and fired a single shot.

The shot struck the ceiling, blowing out a chunk. Some debris tumbled and, before anyone could move, struck Ensign Burton on the head. He went down, arms splayed, out cold.

The volume of the phaser shot startled everyone in the place. Everyone froze, gaping at the sight of Burgoyne standing there with hir arm still upraised while looking down in total chagrin at the unconscious security guard.

Calhoun didn't hesitate, shoving away someone who had been grabbing at his arm but was now just standing there in bewilderment. "And that," Calhoun called out loudly, "is what we're capable of doing to our *own* people! So just think about what we could do to *you* if we decided to."

Insanely, the pronouncement appeared to do the job. Everyone began to back off, staring with extreme concern in Burgoyne's direction.

"Make sure Burton's okay," Burgoyne said under hir breath. Then s/he quickly walked over to Calhoun, with most of the guards following hir while one remained to tend to Burton.

"Greetings, Burgoyne," Si Cwan called, waggling his fingers as if it were a chance encounter on a seashore. "It's been a while. You're looking well."

"Thank you," replied Burgoyne, still evidently puzzled and allowing hir voice to reflect that bewilderment. S/he turned to Calhoun. "Were we having a problem down here, Captain? Mr. Kebron?"

"Strangest thing," Kebron said. "We were minding our own business, having a perfectly civilized discussion, and suddenly we were attacked for no reason."

By that point, however, Fhermus had recovered most of his consciousness and was being supported by his son. His lower jaw was one massive bruise and his eyes were beginning to swell up as well. "Eee ode ahfaze!" Fhermus cried out.

Burgoyne tapped the side of hir head, concerned that the universal translator had malfunctioned. "What?"

"Eee!" Fhermus practically howled, wincing in pain as he did so, and he pointed angrily at Calhoun. "Eee ode! Ahfaze!"

Helplessly, Burgoyne looked at Calhoun. "What is he . . . ?"

"He's saying," Si Cwan spoke up, seemingly amused, "that the good captain here broke his face."

"Not the whole face," Calhoun demurred. "Just the lower half."

Burgoyne wasn't entirely sure what to say to that. Somehow "It figures" or "Terrific" didn't seem the supportive spirit one expected from a second in command. "I'm sure you had good reason to, Captain," s/he said judiciously.

Fhermus tried to speak again, but Tiraud silenced him with a sharp "shush" noise. Fhermus glared at his son but fell quiet, keenly aware of just how ridiculous he sounded when trying to speak. "So this is how the great Federation and its Starfleet operates, eh, Captain?" Tiraud called out. "You abscond with a prisoner of the Protectorate, giving tacit approval for his kidnapping of a high noblewoman. Then you deny knowledge of his whereabouts while resisting proper arrest. . . ."

"I do not acknowledge your right to arrest me in any manner, proper or not," shot back Calhoun. "And even though we have no idea where my son is . . ."

Burgoyne muttered in Calhoun's ear, "In point of fact, we do have an idea of where he is."

Without blinking, Calhoun said, "And even though we have only a vague idea of where my son may be . . ."

"Actually," Burgoyne continued, "we know exactly where he is."

This time Calhoun blinked as he turned and stared at Burgoyne. "Exactly?" he whispered.

"Yes, sir."

"We know *exactly* where he is?"

"Yes, sir."

"And you're just telling me this now?"

"In fairness, Captain, I just got here."

"Where is he?"

"I don't know."

"*Burgy!*"

"Well," Burgoyne amended, "the thing is, Morgan knows exactly where he is. And since Morgan is part of 'we' in a very literal sense, if 'we' is taken to mean the ship, then we do know where he is."

"Problem, Captain?" Si Cwan called out.

"Just getting an update," Calhoun replied before turning back to Burgoyne. "Is he on the ship?"

"No."

"Are you sure?"

"No."

Calhoun closed his eyes. "You're killing me, Burgy. You really are."

Clearly realizing that something was afoot, Si Cwan now stood. "Captain," he said slowly, "do you know where your son is?"

Calhoun gave it a moment's thought. "It depends, I suppose, on what your definition of 'is' is."

"*What?*"

"I believe what the captain is saying," Kebron spoke up, "is that we have a specific area in which we may or may not believe that Xyon is situated at this moment in time, and he may or may not still be there." He looked hopefully at Calhoun.

"Okay," said Calhoun.

There was now growing grumbling from the onlookers. Worse, some of the guardsmen who were down were recovering consciousness. Burgoyne had no desire to transform the interior of the chamber into a free-fire zone. "Captain, if I may . . ."

He considered Burgoyne warily, but then gave a resigned shrug. "Go ahead."

"We have had the chance," Burgoyne said, "to speak to Xyon."

"*I knew it!*" shouted Tiraud.

Over the rising, angry cries of protest, Burgoyne called out, "In fairness, you have no grounds upon which to lodge a grievance, for you yourselves have had ample time to speak with him. So why should we—who have as vested an interest as you in maintaining the peace and restoring Kalinda to her home—not have the same opportunity?" This comment quieted them some, but not much. "However," Burgoyne continued, "unlike you, we did not dismiss his story out of hand. We investigated it, and have uncovered some interesting results."

"What sort of results?" demanded Tiraud.

"There's some difficulty in my telling you . . ."

"What difficulty?!"

"The difficulty is that *people keep interrupting me!*"

Tiraud took a step back at the obvious rebuke and glared at Burgoyne. Calhoun put a hand over his mouth in a casual manner to hide the smile.

"The ship that Xyon described," continued Burgoyne, "fits exactly an ancient style of vessel that is part of the planetary history of the Priatians. Supposedly their founding race, the Wanderers, piloted such ships."

There was a stunned moment of silence, followed by a cacophony of reactions that ranged from outright disbelief to calls for the heads of every single living Priatian.

It was then that Si Cwan took the first active hand in the proceedings since the insanity had broken out. He said nothing. Apparently he didn't need to. Instead, he almost seemed to grow taller, as if his normal posture were a bit of a slump and he was now straightening his spine. He put his arms up to either side. Had an old Earth football game been in progress, he would have looked as if he were signaling a field goal.

It seemed to Burgoyne that Si Cwan was somehow imposing his will upon the assemblage. He wasn't doing it through any sort of mystical means. Just the sheer force of his personality was enough to, gradually but inevitably, bring the room into some semblance of order. It took long seconds, but soon all eyes were on Si Cwan as the assemblage waited for him to speak.

"The Priatians," he said. Burgoyne nodded. Then Si Cwan called out, "Lieutenant Commander Lefler!"

No response came. Si Cwan looked around, appearing both concerned and suspicious. "Robin!"

"Right here."

She was standing a few feet away. She appeared to Burgoyne to be slightly out of breath.

Si Cwan's eyes narrowed. He looked as if he desired to say something to her, but then changed his mind and went in a different direction. "A Priatian delegation came to us not long ago, did they not?"

"Yes. They came to present their case for wanting their worlds back. You dismissed them out of hand."

"A possible motive," Zak Kebron noted. "What better way to get your attention?"

"What better way," a Boragi spoke up, "to ensure the destruction of their entire race!"

"Or what better way," said Tiraud, "for these Starfleet officers to throw us off the trail of the man responsible for Xyon's escape? The only reason we're even having this conversation is because they," and he pointed angrily at Calhoun, "clearly have Xyon in their possession, and are trying to muddy the waters . . . !"

"Truth is often muddying," Calhoun said. "Facts are dirty, confusing things that get in the way of a rush to judgment."

But Tiraud wasn't having any of it. "We should bring in the fleet of the House of Fhermus! Surround the *Excalibur*! Force you to turn Xyon over to us!"

"By all means," replied Calhoun. "Bring on the fleet. My people haven't had target practice in a week."

"Captain," Si Cwan said reprovingly.

Calhoun ignored the rebuke. "Si Cwan . . . we're wasting time when we have a concrete lead. We've nothing to lose by heading to Priatia and seeing if Kalinda is there. They can't hide her from us."

"They can't hide her from us, either!" said Tiraud.

"Oh really?" Burgoyne spoke up. "Our ship's sensors are sophisticated enough to be able to detect a single Thallonian life-form hidden amongst billions of Priatians. How's your technology on that score?"

Tiraud scowled. Burgoyne wasn't surprised. S/he knew the tech level of just about every ship in the

Federation data banks, and the capabilities of ships in Thallonian space were no exception to hir knowledge.

The same Boragi said, "So the House of Fhermus is expected to simply stand here and allow the *Excalibur* to depart . . . with quite possibly the only lead to this fiasco on board?"

"We don't have to go anywhere," said Calhoun, tapping his combadge. "Calhoun to *Excalibur*."

"*Excalibur*, Tobias here."

"Tania, I need you to raise a channel to the *Trident* and patch me through."

"Aye, sir."

Tiraud, clearly impatient, demanded, "How long will all that take?"

Apparently Tania had no trouble hearing him over the link. "Little less than a minute," she said.

Fifty-four seconds passed. It was quite possibly the fifty-four longest seconds of Burgoyne's life. Everyone in the place was glaring at hir (except for Si Cwan, who continued to appear faintly detached from the proceedings). Not a word was spoken by anyone. That didn't especially bother Burgoyne. In this environment, it seemed the moment anyone said anything, it led to an extended brawl.

On the fifty-fifth second, a familiar voice came over the combadge. "This is the *Trident*. Mueller speaking."

"Captain Mueller, this is Captain Calhoun."

"You sound a bit out of breath, Captain. Is everything all right?"

Calhoun glanced around the room. "Just finished

an extended exercise program. Captain, are you aware that Kalinda of New Thallon—"

"—has been kidnapped? Yes, Captain, I received a communiqué to that effect."

"We have reason to believe she's being held on a planet called Priatia." There was a pause. "Kat . . . are you still there—?"

"Say again, Captain? Priatia?"

"Yes, that's right."

"*Scheisse!*"

Burgoyne and Calhoun extended confused looks. "I didn't quite copy that, Captain," Calhoun said cautiously.

"Captain, we were sent into Thallonian space on a science survey by the Federation in order to investigate unusual particle readings. They were characteristic of a transwarp conduit."

"Yes, I was informed of that by Admiral Jellico, Captain. Stand by a moment," said Calhoun. He tapped the combadge once to suspend the communication and turned to Si Cwan. "Cwan, you have to tell me right now: Have the Borg been through here?"

"The Borg!" echoed Si Cwan, and this prompted an immediate chatter of worried comments from the onlookers. Si Cwan quieted them with a sharp gesture and continued, "Why would you think that?"

"Because a transwarp conduit is the typical means of transport for the Borg."

"I think I would have noticed if a giant cube had been passing anywhere nearby. Anyone?" He looked to the spectators. "Has anyone in this room had any encounter with the Borg?" There was a collective shaking of heads. "I thought not. And frankly, Captain, I'm surprised at you. What purpose would we have in keeping such information secret from you? If the Borg turned up here, don't you think the Federation would be the first ones we would alert? Ask for help?"

"I don't make that assumption at all," Calhoun responded. "My first thought was that you'd believe you could, and should, handle the matter yourselves."

"Why would we think that?"

"Because the collective pride and ego in this room could, if harnessed as an energy source, power the entirety of Starfleet for ten years."

Si Cwan considered that a moment, and then nodded ruefully. "All right. That's true."

Calhoun tapped the combadge once more. "Captain Mueller? Still there?"

"Absolutely, Captain Calhoun, because I have nothing else to do except sit here and wait for you to get around to talking to me."

"Sorry about th—"

"My point," she interrupted, "which you stopped me from making before, was that we traced the origins of the transwarp conduit to within range of the planet Priatia."

"Are you sure?"

"There was a sinkhole a few hundred thousand kliks away from them. There's no mistaking that."

"Did you send an away team down?"

"That's what I'm kicking myself over," Mueller said with clear anger directed at herself. "The profile we had on them was that they weren't remotely capable of the sort of technology required to generate a transwarp conduit. So we ascribed it to coincidence. But if Priatia's coming up in connection with Kalinda's kidnapping, that's too much to dismiss as happenstance. What makes you think Priatia's involved?"

"Because the ship believed to have taken her is one connected with Priatia's ancient history as belonging to their supposedly founding race, the Wanderers."

"And if such a vessel had returned now, they might indeed be utilizing such technology. It's possible. Are we going to rendezvous at Priatia, Captain?"

"Actually," Calhoun said slowly, his gaze not leaving Si Cwan, "I need you to investigate this for me. We're somewhat tied up on another matter."

"Another matter? Let me guess: It has something to do with that ass Si Cwan, and his assemblage of howler monkeys."

There were stunned gasps mixed with laughter from nearby and Si Cwan's face became slightly redder than it typically was. "Captain Mueller," Si Cwan called out, "you should know that Captain Calhoun is standing not ten feet away from both myself and the assemblage."

There was a pause. "Oh. You heard that?"

"Every word."

"Good," Mueller's voice came back. "I was hoping you were within earshot, you ass."

Si Cwan looked with some chagrin at the dumbfounded onlookers. "We . . . had a relationship once," he said by way of explanation.

"Relationship? Don't flatter yourself, Si Cwan, it was just sex—"

"Yes, all right, Kat, we get the picture," Calhoun quickly cut her off.

All business, Mueller said, "Very well, Captain. Do you want us to go to Priatia and retrieve Kalinda?"

"I want you to go there and determine whether she's on Priatia or not. But I don't want you to risk her or yourselves. If you detect any sign of that vessel, get the hell out of there, because we don't know what we're dealing with yet."

"Understood. I'll keep you apprised. *Trident* out."

"It appears, Captain Calhoun," Kebron remarked, "that your penchant for tact rubbed off on Captain Mueller back in her days as the *Excalibur* executive officer."

"So now what?" demanded Tiraud.

"Now?" replied Calhoun. "Now . . . we wait."

"Very well." Si Cwan walked over to Calhoun and Kebron. "Gentlemen . . . I see no reason for Burgoyne or your squadron of security guards to remain here."

"Really? Because I do," replied Burgoyne.

"I give you my word that no harm shall come to either Captain Calhoun or Mr. Kebron here as long as they are guests in my home."

"I can see why we should believe that, of course," said Kebron, "since you've done such a terrific job of extending courtesy to guests thus far."

"Had I thought anyone here capable of hurting you, I never would have allowed it to occur," Si Cwan

said coolly. "In any event, I pledge no continued hostilities . . . provided I have your word that you will
remain here on New Thallon until we have heard a
report back from the *Trident*?"

"Absolutely," said Calhoun.

"Captain," began Burgoyne.

But Calhoun shook his head. "It'll be fine, Burgy.
Your intervention was most timely, but I think matters
here are under control . . . at least for now."

"All right," said Si Cwan, "in that case—"

"It is not 'all right'!" Tiraud declared. "They—"

But Si Cwan cut him off. "Mackenzie Calhoun has
given me his word, Tiraud. That is enough for me . . .
and if it's not enough for you, too damned bad. Lieutenant Commander Lefler . . . if I might impose upon
you to bring the captain and Mr. Kebron to guest quarters where they can relax until the *Trident* accomplishes
its mission?"

"I still don't trust him," grumbled Tiraud.

"That, Tiraud, is your problem, not mine. Right
now I suggest you have your father tended to."

Tiraud was about to respond, but a low moan from
his father prompted him to think better of it.

"And I will ask all of you now to depart," Si Cwan
continued. "Once this potential connection to Priatia
has been investigated, we shall reconvene in the council chamber—the more appropriate environment for
such discussions—and decide on our next course of action. That is all."

If any of the assemblage had any problems with Si
Cwan's declarations, they wisely kept it to themselves.

Within a few minutes, the entire main hall had cleared out of both the Thallonian Protectorate and all Starfleet personnel, leaving a thoughtful Si Cwan to himself.

iii.

Robin Lefler stood outside the holosuite with Calhoun, and she rested a hand on his arm. "I have to caution you . . . he looks pretty bad, but it's not as bad as it looks."

"All right," said Calhoun.

The door slid open and Calhoun and Robin entered. The imagery in the holosuite was just as they'd left it, with Xyon lying on the sickbay bed. Morgan was monitoring the functions and she looked up in mild surprise as Calhoun entered.

"*Grozit*," Calhoun said, going straight to Xyon's bedside. Xyon's eyes were closed, his chest rising and falling steadily. He looked up at Morgan and there was more vulnerability in his face at that moment than Robin Lefler had ever seen in all the years she'd known him. "Is he in pain?"

"No," Morgan assured him. "Right now he's sound asleep, which is the best thing for him. The bioregenerative field is healing him. It'll take some time, but the important thing is, he's on the mend."

"Mother's known what to do every step of the way," Robin said proudly.

"You should have been a doctor," Calhoun told her. "Or at the very least, a nurse."

"Don't get me started," said Morgan.

He continued to stare down at Xyon. Even though he knew Xyon couldn't hear him, Calhoun said softly, "I never believed you were dead, you know. I learned to accept it . . . but I never believed it."

Robin Lefler suddenly felt uncomfortable, as if she were intruding on an aspect of Mackenzie Calhoun that she should not have any part of. "Uhm . . . I have other, uhm . . . I'll wait outside."

Calhoun didn't say anything to her. He might not even have heard her. Quickly Robin backed out of the room, the doors opening behind her. She stepped out, turned, and almost shrieked.

Si Cwan was standing right there, arms draped behind his back.

"Oh," she said, which was the only thing that occurred to her at that moment.

"When were you planning to tell me?" he asked, his voice cold and controlled.

"Tell you . . . ?"

"Don't be coy with me, Robin. I know that Xyon is in there," and he nodded in the direction of the holo-suite. "I give you a gift at no small expense, and this is how you repay me? By using it to throw a match upon an already incendiary situation?"

"No," she said, her anger starting to grow. "By using it to save our marriage."

He stared at her blankly. "Come again?"

Her voice dropping to a hoarse whisper, she said,

"You tortured him, Si Cwan. You sent him down to be tortured. It was the most cold-blooded, the . . . I can't . . ." She was so seized with emotion she couldn't find words. "I . . . I watched you do this thing, and I thought, 'No, that can't be my husband. He's a great man. A great man would never do such things.' "

"It's more complicated than that. . . ."

"No, it's exactly as uncomplicated as that!" Robin shot back. "We don't do such things—"

"We?" demanded Si Cwan. "What 'we' would that be? 'We' the Federation? I assure you there are member races who do far worse than anything I've done. 'We' Starfleet? The head of Starfleet isn't trying to hold an uneasy alliance together with his bare hands and not show the slightest sign of weakness. 'We' the human race? Don't make me laugh, Robin. Despise torture? Your people perfected it. We learned lessons from you."

"We meaning you and me, Cwan!" she said in her soaring wrath. "Us! We're better than that! We have to stand for something, to symbolize something greater than either of us could ever hope to achieve! If you truly believe that torture isn't the way even when others do, then you have to be the leader who stands firm and says, 'No! We will not descend to that, no matter what others may do or might have done! We're going to learn from our mistakes and we're going to be better!' "

He towered over her. "Don't you dare lecture me," he said.

"Little late for that, isn't it. If I were in your position—"

"In my position? Do you want to know what I should do, in my position?" His fists were clenching and unclenching. She had never seen him so angry. "As Prime Minister of the Protectorate? I should have you either thrown in prison or banished from this world! I should have you brought up on charges! I should have you dragged in front of the council so they can decide your fate! I should turn you over to the House of Fhermus because, in your actions, you've become an accomplice to the crimes Xyon committed, which remain indisputable, whether you believe his story about alien vessels or not! All this and more is what I should be doing if I am to remain true to my oath and my word to those who depend upon me for leadership!"

"Then why don't you?" she demanded.

"You know why. It is because you are my wife, and you were counting on that bond to save you when you knew that your actions, if taken by any other individual, would result in condemnation, imprisonment and possibly death. If anyone has acted in a manner that's unworthy of them, it's you. You've put me in an untenable position without caring about the ramifications, and counting on my love for you to save you. And that is cheap manipulation, Robin. I expected better of you."

She stared at him for a long moment and then, very softly, she said, "You expected better of me than my counting on your love?"

"Prime Minister?"

Slowly Robin turned and saw Ankar standing there, staring at them quizzically. "Prime Minister," he said again, "several delegates are waiting in your office, wishing to speak with you. Is there some sort of problem here?"

For Robin, it was as if she were hiding in shadows, trying not to be spotted by some pursuing enemy. She could hear the breath heavy in her lungs, sense the pounding of her heart, the pulse in her temple. The very noises of her body's presence threatening to give her away. She was paralyzed, afraid to make the slightest movement lest her sudden gnawing fear give her away.

As for Si Cwan, carved from marble, he replied coolly, "No, Ankar. No problem at all. I'm right behind you."

Ankar turned and walked away, and Si Cwan followed him without so much as a backward glance. Moments later, Mackenzie Calhoun stepped out of the holosuite, looking with concern at Robin. "Do we have a problem?" he asked.

"I think we have a big problem, yes," she sighed. "But I don't think it's a 'we' that you need concern yourself with at the moment, Captain."

U.S.S. Trident

i.

There was an air of tension on the bridge of the *Trident* that wasn't there in their previous mission to Priatia. It did nothing to interfere with the smooth and efficient running of the ship, but Mueller noticed a distinct dropoff in the banter and back-and-forth that characterized her bridge crew. They had adopted a very businesslike attitude, and Mueller, for one, wasn't upset by that.

It wasn't simply that they didn't know what they were going to be dealing with, or that they were worried some sort of supercolossal killer star vessel could drop out of space practically on top of them and cut through their defenses like a knife through cheese. The additional pressure being faced by the crew of the *Trident* was that the potential well-being of Mackenzie Calhoun was hanging in the balance of what they did next. They all knew, liked, and respected Calhoun, and they wanted to do right by him.

"Priatia, dead ahead, Captain," Gold announced.

"Bring us into geosynch orbit, Mr. Gold," Mueller said.

"Geosynch orbit, aye," and Gold brought the starship into standard orbit with the planetary body below.

"Arex . . . I want full tactical focus on that sinkhole. You got that?"

"Aye, Captain," Arex assured her. "If a tachyon so much as twitches, you'll be the first to know."

Mueller took some comfort in that, but not much. She couldn't help but feel that the sinkhole was like a giant cannon pointed squarely at their backs that could go off at any time. She felt as if the ship had its flank exposed for as long as they were in the vicinity, but there was nothing she could do about it.

"All right," Mueller said thoughtfully. "M'Ress . . . sensor scan on the planet's surface. Full strength. See if there's a Thallonian down there."

"Aye, Captain," said M'Ress, and she began the sweep.

Desma sidled over to Mueller and said in a low voice, "Captain . . . you are aware of the amount of time such an endeavor will consume. Unless we're extremely lucky . . ."

"We could be here for a day or so," Mueller acknowledged. Desma didn't look happy about it, and Mueller could understand it. She wasn't exactly tickled about it herself. "There's no way around it."

"Actually . . . there may be."

Mueller had been staring at the screen, but now she turned and focused on Desma. "What are you suggesting, Commander?"

"A more . . . aggressive stance, perhaps?"

"Are you suggesting," Mueller said slowly, "that we confront the Priatians? Tell them we believe that Kalinda is down there and we want her back?"

"Not exactly. I'm suggesting we inform the Priatians that we *know* Kalinda is down there, and if they don't turn her over to us, we will rain destruction down upon them like the right hand of God."

Mueller's eyebrows rose so high that they appeared to be bumping up against her hairline. "Really."

"Well . . . maybe not that exact phrasing . . ."

"I should hope not. Still . . ." and Mueller tapped her fingers thoughtfully on the arm of her chair. "They must have some sort of planetary system that's informing them we're here. One assumes they're not stupid. They'll know this isn't a social call. If our presence here is going to prompt them to take a violent action against Kalinda in a panic . . ."

"Then the sooner we head that off, the better."

"Of course, it's taking a chance. Contacting them and letting them know we know she's there could prompt them to . . . oh, I don't know . . . kill her? After all, we can't detect life signs if she's dead." She looked at Desma questioningly, even a bit challengingly.

Desma inclined her head slightly, acknowledging the point. Her antennae bobbed up and down in reaction to the motion. "There's one upside to your following your own instincts on this decision."

"And that would be?"

"You'll take the heat for them, not me."

Mueller kept a straight face, but inside she laughed slightly. For her part, Desma's expression was purely deadpan. "Mr. Takahashi," she called out, "see if you can raise me up a government official."

"Aye, Captain."

It wasn't the easiest endeavor in the world. The initial contact from the *Trident* was shifted around from one office to the next in what turned out to be an impressive little bureaucracy. Eventually, though, a calm, rather detached individual who called himself "Keesala" appeared on the screen. He appeared to be some sort of spokesman for whomever the planetary head or governing board was. "We are honored," he said. "My understanding is that it has been many, many years since a Federation starship visited our world. The last time, as I recall, was some sort of scientific endeavor, yes?"

"That's correct," said Mueller.

"And is this another such?"

"No. Actually, it has to do with a matter of some urgency. A matter . . . do you have a title?"

"A what? Oh. No, no. 'Keesala' will do." He smiled thinly. "We tend to be informal hereabouts."

"It is a matter, Keesala, the nature of which—to be blunt—we believe you already suspect."

"Indeed!" His voice indicated that he was most perturbed at the notion. "Perhaps it would be best if you brought me to your vessel with one of those marvelous matter-transportation devices I understand you're equipped with."

Mueller glanced at Desma, who shrugged. "All right," Mueller said cautiously. "If that's your wish. Stay where you are, and we'll beam you aboard. Bridge to transporter room."

"Transporter room, aye," came a brisk female voice.

"Lock on to the signal we're currently receiving and bring the individual on the other end aboard. I'll be right down. Arex, with me," Mueller said briskly. "Hash, take over watch on the sinkhole. Desma, you have the conn."

Hash moved to the tactical station as Arex headed for the turbolift. Before she walked away, however, Mueller leaned in toward Desma and said, "Good strategy there, Commander."

"Thank you, Captain," said Desma, positively beaming as Mueller headed into the turbolift.

ii.

Mueller hadn't been certain quite what to expect when Keesala beamed aboard the *Trident*, but it certainly wasn't remotely close to what she got.

The moment he materialized on the transporter pad, all the soft-spoken, overly polite air vanished, and Keesala came remarkably close to being a complete gibbering wreck.

He practically stumbled as he came off the transporter platform and approached Mueller so quickly that Arex got in between them lest it turn out to be some sort of attack. It quickly became clear that assaulting the captain was about the farthest thing from the visitor's mind as could possibly be.

"Thank the gods!" Keesala cried out as Arex kept

him from getting too close. It wasn't all that difficult, for Keesala wasn't exceptionally strong, and Arex's multiple arms were more than up to the task. "Thank the gods you people arrived! It's not too late for her!"

"For her," Mueller echoed. "You mean for—"

"Kalinda, yes. The Thallonian girl."

"Arex," and Mueller indicated with a movement of her head that he should stand aside. Arex did so, but he watched Keesala intently lest he make some sort of hostile move. Mueller stepped in close and said, "You admit you have her."

"Admit it? I would do anything to get rid of her! Her presence courts disaster! You have no idea what it's like to be the one sane voice in a sea of madmen!"

Believing that extended discussion of a matter this delicate wasn't appropriate to the middle of the transporter room, Mueller promptly hustled Keesala away to the nearest conference lounge. She settled him into a chair in hopes of taming, to some degree, his extremely jumpy nature. "First things first," she said. "Is Kalinda unharmed?"

"Completely. At least, she is for the moment. But we're dealing with exceptionally volatile personalities," he said. "People who do not take kindly to anyone who tries to gainsay them."

"And you're one of those people?"

"Of course! They've forced me to . . . to say things. Do things." He shook his head, looking despondent.

"If you consider them to be so oppressive," Arex said thoughtfully in his high-pitched, whispery voice, "it's strange that they would be willing to let you depart your world and have a private conference with us."

"Do you think me a complete fool?" demanded Keesala, bristling at the implication. "Do you think that I have at all let on to them what my true feelings are? My life would be forfeit! No, no . . . they think me entirely on their side. They have no clue where my true loyalties lie, and that is precisely the way I wish matters to remain."

"Who are 'they'?"

"A faction. A crazed faction of my people who believe that they are not mere Priatians, but instead the second coming of the Wanderers. They have lost their minds, suffering from wildly inflated egos."

"But why did they kidnap Kalinda? What was their plan?"

"There was no plan!" Keesala said. "Their encountering her and the man who absconded her was purest happenstance. They saw an opportunity and they seized it. And I . . . I should have stopped it," he admitted sadly. "But I did not do so, for I am one and they are many. And a number of them hold far higher rank in the government than I. So I smiled and cooperated as thoroughly as I possibly could. Participated in bizarre mind games and stunts they performed on the girl in order to keep her off balance. Make her think she was seeing . . ."

"Seeing what?"

"Monsters," he told Mueller. "Creatures of abomination. All designed to confuse her. To keep her from focusing on escape, or on anything that was potentially inconvenient to us. But even as I aided in these twisted endeavors, I felt my heart sinking on behalf of my people.

"But you're here now! You can end this!"

"Can you tell us where she is?" Arex demanded.

"Absolutely," Keesala assured them. "I can provide you with planetary coordinates so that you will be able to pinpoint her location."

"As soon as we do that," Arex commented to Mueller, "we can use sensors to lock on to her. Sensor sweeps take no time at all if we know exactly where to look."

"Thank you for doing such a superb job of apprising me of that which I already know," Mueller told Arex, who did a remarkable job of covering his chagrin over the gentle rebuke. "And what of you?" she continued. "What will they do to you upon learning that the girl is gone."

"I will tell them you tortured it out of me," Keesala assured them.

"We don't torture captives!" Mueller protested. "For that matter, you're not even a captive."

"Yes, but my people do not know that. What, are you concerned over the reputation of your precious Starfleet, Captain?" He sounded amused. "Of what possible consequence is that when compared to recovering a helpless young woman?" Then his tone darkened. "You cannot begin to comprehend what they've already done to her."

"You said she was unharmed."

"Physically, yes, but I've already described to you

some of the mental pressures they've brought to bear on the girl. In some regards she is already not herself. If you wish to retrieve a young woman who bears at least a resemblance to the one who was taken, then you will allow me to cooperate with you. Frankly, I cannot believe I even have to speak that sentence. Allow *me* to cooperate with *you*."

For a long moment, Mueller studied him. "Mr. Arex, a moment of your time, please. Keesala, please make yourself comfortable." As Keesala watched them with what was clearly wide-eyed astonishment, the two Starfleet officers stepped out of the conference lounge and into the corridor. They spoke in low voices and every so often, Mueller would nod in acknowledgment as a crew member passed and greeted her. Her attention, however, never wavered from the discussion.

"My instinct," she said, "is not in love with this."

"I know what you mean, Captain. I mean, it could be just as he says. He's appalled by something his fellow Priatians are doing or have done and he wants to set it right."

"True. All it takes for evil men to succeed is for good men to stand by and do nothing. And perhaps he is simply a good man. On the other hand . . ."

"What were the odds that we managed to get in touch with exactly the man we needed?"

Slowly she nodded. "Which would indicate that we were steered toward him."

"But why?"

She leaned back against the wall, her arms folded

across her chest. Her mind was racing, but one could never have told from her calm demeanor. "Possibly it's some sort of trap. But if we don't go down there . . . if he provides coordinates and we just beam her up . . . how devastating a trap can it be?"

"They could have done something to her. Placed a deadly virus within her. Standard transporter and virus scans would detect any sort of explosive device upon her and any obvious illness, but it could be something unknown."

She nodded. "So we would need to bring her up directly into quarantine. Have her checked out thoroughly."

"There's another possibility," suggested Arex. "Perhaps we simply got here before they had fully in place whatever their plan was in relation to kidnapping Kalinda. Perhaps they weren't expecting we'd catch on to them so soon."

"And now they're endeavoring to cut their losses? And sending Keesala as the scapegoat to claim that it was simply a small faction of his people rather than a government plan?" She pursed her lips. "That could be."

"Either way, as long as we get her back and she's safe, does the why of it make a difference?"

"It does, actually . . . in the long term. Right now, though, the long term isn't our concern."

With that, she walked back into the conference lounge, Arex skittering behind her.

Keesala stood, looking up at them expectantly.

"Can you pinpoint exactly on your planet where she

is?" asked Mueller. When he nodded, she said, "All right. Come with me."

They headed down the corridor, Keesala looking around with great interest at all he saw. "You seem impressed with our technology," Mueller observed.

"Oh yes. Very much so. You're most advanced."

"So would you mind telling me how you developed that gargantuan space vessel that is unlike anything we currently have at our disposal?"

He stopped, stared at her blankly for a moment, and then understood. "Oh. The ship of our ancestors." He chuckled low in his throat, as if about to relate an amusing anecdote. "That was a standard-sized vessel. Nothing extraordinary about it at all. Your own ship would doubtless have been able to destroy it in a matter of seconds. But my people do have their clever moments. It was a . . . what would be the phrase you would use? A . . . magic trick?"

"A magic trick?"

"Yes, Captain. A light field—not even a hard light field—projected around the ship, in a manner not all that different from the way defensive screens are erected. The field created the image of a vast and formidable space vessel around the far more unassuming one. That was what the young fellow who originally absconded with the girl saw. But it was simply an illusion. There is no such ship currently stalking the spaceways . . . or, if there is, I assure you we had, and have, nothing to do with it."

They entered the transporter room and Mueller said, "Ensign. Give me a view of Priatia."

Ensign Patience Halliwell (twin sister to a transporter operator over on the *Excalibur*) brought the image of Priatia up on her console screen, then stepped aside as Keesala stared at it. As he did so, Arex said, "Transporter room to M'Ress."

"Bridge, M'Ress here. Go ahead, Arex."

"Prepare to coordinate sensor scan with transporter room A. Lock into the transporter console so you can scan the area of the planet that you're about to have specified for you."

"Got it."

Mueller nodded in approval. Arex and M'Ress, both time-tossed castaways into an era that wasn't theirs. Even though there had been some serious bumps and bruises along the way, they had adapted well to their new environment and always worked extremely smoothly together. She couldn't help but think that they might have made an interesting couple were it not for the fact that they were completely incompatible physically.

"How do I indicate . . . ?" Keesala asked tentatively.

"Just touch the screen itself," Halliwell told him. "The computer will do the rest."

"All right," he said, watching his homeworld turning on the screen. "All right . . . she's being held on the continent of Nemosia . . . the capital city of Cheng . . . which would put her right about . . . here," and he tapped the screen with his finger. Then he let out a surprised "Oh!" as two lines, perpendicular to each other, intersected on the screen and targeted the area he'd just touched.

"M'Ress?" prompted Arex.

"Have the data. Scanning now . . ."

There was a long pause, perhaps as long as thirty seconds, and then M'Ress's voice came back triumphantly. "Got a lock! Found an individual with Thallonian bioreadings, no question."

"Do we know for sure it's her?"

"Not for sure, no, but it's a hell of a coincidence if it's not. Sending coordinates back to you."

"Captain to sickbay," Mueller said to the air.

"Sickbay, go," came back the voice of Doc Villers in her customary brusque manner.

"Ready the quarantine lab. We're having someone beamed in there in a moment."

"Thanks for the lengthy heads-up, Captain," grunted Villers. "We'll be ready. Sickbay out."

Mueller turned to Halliwell. "Ensign . . . ?"

"I have the coordinates, Captain."

"Beam her directly into quarantine."

"Aye, Captain." Halliwell nodded as she proceeded to manipulate the controls.

The transporter beams began to glow. The platform lit up and Mueller watched intently as a slender female form began to coalesce. Before it could do so, however, it dissolved once more and, moments later, the familiar whine of the transporter beams ceased.

"Sickbay, this is the cap—" Mueller began to say.

But Villers's voice overlapped her own. "Captain, this is Villers. We've got her."

"How does she look?"

"Like a confused Thallonian female. Were you expecting anything else?"

"No. I'll be right down. Mueller out."

"What about me, Captain?" asked Keesala politely.

"You," she said, "are going to stay right here with him for the moment," and she indicated Arex.

"Very well." He didn't sound especially perturbed about it . . . which naturally bothered Mueller all the more.

iii.

By the time Mueller got down to sickbay, Kalinda had apparently gotten over her confusion and was now instead flooded with relief. "Kat!" she called out the moment she saw Mueller, and then promptly restrained herself and corrected, "I mean . . . Captain Mueller. An honor, as always."

She didn't appear any the worse for wear. She was clad in a simple gray jumpsuit rather than her normal Thallonian attire. But she had no marks upon her, didn't appear thinner or ill in any way. She reached up and tapped the clear wall that stood between her and the rest of sickbay. "May I ask . . . what the purpose of this is . . . ?"

"Quarantine," Mueller said. "It's so . . ."

"So you can make sure I'm not some sort of carrier of germ warfare," Kalinda immediately said.

Mueller nodded. "You catch on quickly."

"Someone in my position has to learn to do that."

Changing gears, she said, "Xyon. Is he all right? Where is he?"

"Back on New Thallon. And from my understanding, not doing particularly well."

Her hand fluttered to her mouth. "Of course. Because he told them that I was taken away, and they didn't believe him. Are you taking me straight back?"

"Yes. Doc Villers here can check you over en route and give you a clean bill of health." She looked at Kalinda askance. "Aren't you at all curious as to how we found you?"

"Honestly? No. That you found me at all is all I care about. That, and getting as far away from this godsforsaken world as possible."

"All right," said Mueller. "We'll talk later, then."

"Yes, I'd like that," and Kalinda smiled a genuinely warm smile.

Mueller returned to the transporter room, lost in thought. When she got there, Keesala looked at her expectantly. "Well?"

"She appears to be in good health. We'll be checking her over, of course."

"Oh, of course." He let out a heavy sigh. "Please understand, Captain . . . these actions were taken by a group of radicals. They did not think what they were doing, and they pose no threat to the Thallonian Protectorate. I shall find a way to make certain they are dealt with . . . if, in no other way, by stressing what a close call my people had just now. If you were so inclined, your weaponry could lay waste to my world. I will stress that, and make sure their power is broken. It may take time, but it will happen, I assure you. And now if you would just be so good as to return me to my world . . ."

Mueller stepped in close to him, looking him up and down, making no effort to hide her suspicion. "Understand something, Keesala. We have a record of your molecular pattern now, since we beamed you up. If something turns out to be wrong with Kalinda . . . if this is a double cross in any way . . . we will return here and we will find you and then, sir, you will severely regret the consequences."

"You know, Captain," Keesala replied mildly, "in envisioning what you would say before sending me back home, I somehow imagined it would be more along the lines of 'Thank you.' "

"Thank you," she said icily.

"You're welcome."

With that, he stepped over to the transporter platform and up onto it.

"Energize," said Mueller, and in a shower of light, Keesala was gone. "Captain to bridge."

"Bridge, Desma here."

"Take us out of orbit, Executive Officer. Have Gold set course for New Thallon."

Desma didn't reply immediately, and for an instant Mueller wondered why. Then she realized: It was the first time she'd felt comfortable enough with Desma to address her by the title—Executive Officer—that she, Mueller, had once held.

"New Thallon, aye, Captain," Desma said, and then added with indisputable pride in her voice, "Executive Officer out."

"Mission accomplished, Captain?" asked Arex.

She stroked her chin thoughtfully. "I never like to say that, Lieutenant," she said warily. "It always seems that, when you believe a mission has been accomplished, you're just begging for unexpected casualties."

New Thallon

i.

Mackenzie Calhoun strode into the council chamber and was all too aware of every angry eye upon him. It certainly wasn't the first time in his life that he'd been surrounded by hostility, nor did he ever feel intimidated by such circumstances. Instead it was almost energizing for him.

Behind Calhoun came Zak Kebron. He remained, however, toward the back of the room as Calhoun continued forward. The message was clear: Kebron had Calhoun's back, but Calhoun wasn't afraid to face the opposition more or less on his own.

Calhoun strolled down to the middle of the chamber, where the table was set up that had Si Cwan and Fhermus in physical opposition to each other. Fhermus's jaw was looking a bit swollen, but it had been set back into place. If looks could kill, Calhoun would have been dead the moment he entered the chamber. Calhoun winked at Fhermus, which caused Fhermus to tremble silently with rage. Si Cwan's gaze flickered from one to the other, taking in the reaction, but he said nothing.

Calhoun stepped down to table level, taking up a point at the far end from Si Cwan and Fhermus. Then he announced, "Kalinda has been found."

There were sharp intakes of breath from all around him, and Si Cwan leaned forward. "Alive?"

"Alive. Well. Unharmed. She's aboard the *Trident* and on her way back here even as we speak. My guess is that they're traveling at maximum warp speed, so she should be here shortly."

All those breaths were exhaled simultaneously in relief and Si Cwan actually extended a hand to Calhoun. "That is superb news, Captain. Well done. Well done indeed," and he shook Calhoun's hand firmly.

"Yes, well done," grumbled Fhermus, who made no endeavor to extend the hand of friendship to Calhoun. "The father has mended the sins of the son."

"I would not dispute that," Calhoun said.

"Where was she?"

"She was on Priatia, Prime Minister."

Immediately there was an uproar from within the council chamber, fists slamming on the round tables, representatives trying to bellow above one another to make themselves heard. Although the specific words were different from the representatives, the sentiment was consistent, and that was that the entire planet of Priatia should be reduced to free-floating chunks.

It was with great effort that Calhoun managed to shout the assemblage down, and then it was only with the aid of another one of Kebron's earsplitting bellows that everyone shut up. As they rubbed their ears in pain, Calhoun said calmly, "My understanding is that the theft of Kalinda was a stunt undertaken by a radical fringe group who saw an opportunity and seized it. Upon the *Trident* showing up, a government official volunteered her whereabouts with no prompting and aided Captain Mueller in extracting Kalinda from the planet. The vast majority of the people of Priatia knew nothing of this, and those in charge seized the very first opportunity given them to make it right. Take my opinion for what it's worth, but I see little point exacting revenge upon the population of a world that is almost entirely blameless. The Priatian government is seeing to the renegades who undertook this endeavor, and I suggest you allow them to handle it internally."

"I see your point, Captain," Si Cwan said thoughtfully. "Punishment and revenge is of far less interest to me than the safe return of my sister. I should think you feel the same in regards to your future daughter-in-law, do you not, Lord Fhermus?"

Slowly, Fhermus nodded. "The Priatians are of little interest to me. They are a relic of a time long past, and their incessant bleating over wrongs that are—at best—ancient history, is tedious to me. I would just as soon not give them new excuses to complain that they were ill used. However," and he raised his voice slightly, "that does not address the matter of your son, Calhoun. The Priatians may have seized an opportunity, but it was Xyon who provided it to them. There must be punishment."

"There *must* . . . be *punishment?*" There was a strong hint of danger in Calhoun's tone. "He was extensively tortured for information after providing all he knew. I would think that qualifies as punishment, don't you."

"Not enough. Not nearly enough."

"You stabbed my son, Lord Fhermus," Calhoun reminded him. "If you were interested in having a personal hand in retribution, you've done so."

"And he stabbed the honor of my House to its heart!"

From the back of the room, Kebron called, "Captain . . . permission to offer extended critique on the excessive melodrama inherent in that pronouncement."

Desperately missing the old, taciturn Kebron, Calhoun said, "Denied," before continuing, "I have found, Lord Fhermus, that clinging to vengeance is much like riding a horse that chases nothing but its own tail. It doesn't take much of a wise rider to know when to dismount."

"So you say," snarled Fhermus, "and yet you cannot deny that you struck me in order to gain revenge upon me for my having stabbed your son!"

"I cannot deny that, no."

"*Well, then—?!*"

Calhoun shrugged. "I'm an enigma."

Fhermus began to sputter, particularly when—to his obvious annoyance—several members of the council snickered in response to Calhoun. Before he could say anything else, however, Si Cwan interceded.

"What would you suggest, Captain?" he asked in measured tone. "That Xyon be turned over to you and you leave Thallonian space with him?"

Fhermus's eyes widened upon hearing that, and he turned toward Si Cwan. "You know where he is! You could not speak of turning him over if you didn't have him! You know where he is!"

"It may have come to my attention," Si Cwan said.

"Where is he? The offense against my House—!"

"Is secondary to the offense against mine," interrupted Si Cwan, towering over Fhermus. "Granted, your son was ill used. But it was my sister who was kidnapped and exposed to all manner of danger. If anyone is in a position to take umbrage and hold the fate of Xyon in his hand, I am. And if, in my opinion, it will best serve all concerned to put an end to this affair with minimal acrimony, then that's what will be done."

"You do not have that right!"

Si Cwan drew himself up to his full height, gaining what seemed another six inches on Fhermus. "I am Lord Si Cwan of the House of Cwan, Prime Minister of the New Thallonian Protectorate, and I have every right to do what can and should be done."

"Prime Minister," Calhoun said, weighing every word carefully, "allow me to take my son and depart. I give you my personal assurance that he will not return to Thallonian space."

"And if he does?" demanded Fhermus.

"He will not," Calhoun said with assurance, "but if he should, you have my full permission to kill him."

"I do not need your permission to kill that criminal!" Fhermus retorted.

There was a pause and then Calhoun leaned toward

him and said, "Right now . . . at this moment . . . you very much do." Fhermus bristled, but said nothing.

Quiet hung over the chamber like a shroud.

"I see no point in having this be a protracted affair," Si Cwan said at last. "The criminal Xyon will be turned over to Captain Calhoun," and when voices of the council members began to rise in protest, Si Cwan spoke over them with little effort, "if for no other reason than that—thanks to Calhoun's actions, and those of his fellow captain—Kalinda is being restored to her people and her fiancé. That is all that matters to me. We may place a burden of blame upon Xyon, but Xyon's father has balanced the scales. For that, I am indebted, and in that, I am content. This is not a decision for the council to make, but for me. And if any here have a problem with that," and he swept the chamber with a fierce glare, "I challenge them to bring it to me and we shall settle it in the traditional and brutal manner of my family. Are there any takers?"

The members looked at one another, each silently prompting someone else to make the first move. No one did, which was very likely exactly what Si Cwan expected.

"Lord Fhermus," said Si Cwan, after it became apparent that no one was going to take him up on his offer. "I believe we have a wedding to plan . . . ?"

"So it would seem," Fhermus said, still looking none too pleased, but clearly ready to let the matter drop.

"Then we are adjourned," said Si Cwan.

Calhoun let out a low whistle of relief as the assemblage began to rise from their seats. "Well . . . that was fairly painless," he said.

"Not everything is settled with a fistfight, Calhoun," Si Cwan told him.

"Yes, I know," sighed Calhoun. "Then again, no one ever said we live in a perfect world."

ii.

"I don't want to leave."

Xyon's pronouncement didn't exactly startle Calhoun, but it was still the last thing he needed to hear. They were standing in the holosuite, just the two of them. It was still in the image of a sickbay, but Morgan had made herself scarce. Much of the healing had already been performed upon Xyon's battered frame, but there were still some bruises that would take longer to disappear than others. He had stepped down from the diagnostic bed and was pulling on his shirt.

"You don't have a choice in that, Xyon," Calhoun told him. "The only choice you get is this: Either I instruct the *Excalibur* to beam you up right now, or else I walk you out to your ship, you take off, and park yourself in our shuttle bay. And don't even think about trying to run for it, because I've taken the liberty of having your cloak disabled and I assure you that your engines, on their best day, won't be able to shake off our tractor beams."

"You sabotaged my ship!" Xyon exclaimed. "Where do you get off—?"

"Where do *I* get off?" Calhoun was incredulous. "Xyon, do you have the slightest clue of the magnitude of the break you've received? Of the luck you've had?"

"Luck! The girl I love is marrying someone else, and I was tortured!"

"You won't be the first man to lose his woman, and I daresay not the last. And as for torture," Calhoun continued, his voice dripping with sarcasm, "what you suffered physically is the slightest taste of what I and everyone who cared for you suffered mentally when you chose to hide your status from us. We thought you were dead, Xyon, and you left it that way."

"I did what I thought best."

"You did what you thought convenient, and don't pretend it was anything else."

"Spare me, Father. As if you really gave a damn whether I lived or died—"

And Calhoun took two quick steps forward, grabbed Xyon by the front of his shirt, and slammed him up against the wall so hard it shook. Xyon was frozen in shock and fear at the pure fury he saw in his father's eyes. "Don't you ever," said Calhoun, his voice trembling with rage, "question my love for you."

Xyon looked down at the grip his father had on him. "You have a funny way of showing it."

Barely managing to rein in his anger, Calhoun

said, "I'm a funny guy." Then he stepped back, releasing Xyon, who stumbled slightly before regaining his footing.

They regarded each other with suspicion for a moment, and it was Xyon who dropped his gaze first. "Just . . . so you don't get the wrong idea . . . I appreciate whatever it was you did to get me out of here, and to find Kalinda. I guess . . . that is the most important thing."

"You 'guess'?"

"All right, it *is* the most important thing, okay?"

"Good. As long as you realize that."

There was another long pause, and then Xyon said, "You know . . . I kind of missed you, even if you are an ass."

"I'll try to keep my ego from swelling over such effusive praise. So . . . transporter or your ship?"

"My ship, provided you don't think we'll be ambushed along the way by—oh, I don't know—Kally's irate fiancé."

"I doubt that will happen."

They walked out of the holosuite and Robin Lefler was waiting for them. "You're looking much improved," she said.

"You saved my life," Xyon said simply.

"I don't think that's the case," she replied. "But if you want to tell me I made it a little less uncomfortable, I'll accept that."

"What did this cost you, Robin?" asked Calhoun.

"Pardon? Cost me, Captain?"

"Cost you. With Si Cwan. You can't fool me, Robin. You did this behind his back. But he obviously figured it out; he's not stupid."

"Yes, so I discovered," she admitted.

"So what was the cost? How angry was he? Did it hurt your marriage?"

"Captain," Robin sighed, "with all respect . . . that's none of your business."

"I tend to think it is."

"Well, the nice thing is, you're no longer my CO, which means I get to tell you when I think you're wrong," she said.

He smiled slightly. "Odd. I've had any number of people who were, and are, under my command and never have any trouble telling me they think I'm wrong."

"Funny how that works."

"Hilarious." He put a hand on her shoulder. "Do you want me to talk to Si Cwan about—"

"That," she told him, patting his hand with hers, "is just about the worst thing you could possibly do. It'll work out. These things always do. My best advice right now is that you take your son and go."

"All right. I'm going to break protocol now."

"What—?"

He reached around and gave her a quick, non-Starfleet hug. "Take care, Robin."

"You too, sir."

"Thank you again," said Xyon. Calhoun noticed he was walking with a bit of a limp. He hoped it would smooth out in time.

"Stay out of trouble."

"That's part of my plan."

"Come . . . I'll walk you to the landing port where your ship is."

"Why?" asked Xyon.

"To help you stay out of trouble," Robin told him. "That's part of *my* plan."

New Thallon/U.S.S. Trident

i.

As Robin escorted them to the field, she couldn't help but wonder what, indeed, this entire business had cost her. She hoped the price, whatever it was, wouldn't be too high . . . and couldn't help but worry that it would be.

She wasn't at all surprised that Zak Kebron fell into step beside them shortly after departing the holosuite. Clearly Calhoun wasn't about to take any chances, and if one was looking for someone to run interference against potential enemies, Kebron was the walking brick wall to do it.

"You've changed, Kebron," Xyon observed as they walked through the halls, heading for the exit that would take them to the private landing field. "Your color looks different, and you seem more . . . I don't know . . . relaxed, maybe?"

"I was never what you would call 'tense,' " Kebron replied. "I am, however, far more at peace with my essence."

"You also talk more. And stranger."

"I have no idea how to react to that. Fortunately for

both of us, I don't care all that much, either." He glanced around warily. It was always easy to tell when Kebron was looking around. Since he had no neck to speak of, his entire torso would swivel. "I wonder if Si Cwan is going to see us off."

"I suppose anything is possible," Calhoun said.

"He will." Xyon sounded exceedingly ominous in making that prediction.

Robin regarded him warily. "I very much doubt my husband is going to try and cause trouble at this late date," she said.

"You're probably right. But somehow I think the House of Fhermus isn't quite done with me, and I can't help but surmise that Si Cwan will be part of it."

Robin wasn't sure what to make of that. She could only hope that Xyon would be completely wrong in his assessment.

As it turned out, he was entirely right.

This realization caught up with Robin when they were approaching the landing field and saw a small group walking toward them with the kind of determination that said this was to be no chance encounter. Naturally she recognized Si Cwan among the group almost immediately. And, sure enough, there was Fhermus. And Tiraud. And several guards.

And Kalinda.

Obviously the *Trident* had more than done its job, getting her back to New Thallon in impressive time. The ship's ability in that regard was not at all surprising to Robin Lefler.

What was surprising was the way that Xyon stared

at the oncoming entourage, tilted his head slightly, and said, "Who's that with Tiraud?"

"What?" Calhoun glanced at his son. "What do you mean?"

"The girl? Who's that . . . ?" Then he stopped and stared. "Is that . . . Kalinda?"

"Of course it is," Robin spoke up, wondering what in the world Xyon was playing at. "Of course it is. Who else would she be?"

"I . . . don't know," Xyon said, sounding utterly confused. "I just . . . I thought she . . ." He shook his head. "I . . . didn't recognize her at first. . . ."

"Not surprising," said Kebron. "It undoubtedly has to do with the torture you endured. Since Kalinda was the impetus for it, it's natural that you would come to associate her with—even blame her for—what you were subjected to. So encountering her now, you reject her because of the negative connotations her very presence creates for you."

"You really think so?"

"That's one possibility."

"What's another?"

"That I don't know what I'm talking about."

The two groups came to the inevitable face-to-face encounter. They stopped several feet away from each other, and Robin noticed that Tiraud was keeping one arm draped prominently around Kalinda. Robin couldn't say that she was entirely impressed by his be- havior. It was as if he were showing Kalinda off as some sort of trophy, or prize that he had snatched away from Xyon that he was now dangling in front of him. Nor did Kalinda seem to mind, as she snuggled against Tiraud and regarded Xyon with open suspicion. Xyon's attitude was pure stoicism, however. He was obviously studying Kalinda closely, not deigning to give Tiraud even the slightest glance.

"Satisfied, offworlder?" demanded Tiraud. "She is with me now, not you. Not you. As you can see."

"Yes, I can see, and yet you feel the need to tell me anyway," said Xyon. He continued to stare at Kalinda. "Are you all right?" he asked her.

"I'm . . . fine, Xyon." She had been meeting his gaze, but something in it clearly disturbed her and she looked down instead. "It's . . . it's all over. I think it's time we both moved on."

"Yes. Yes, you would think that," Xyon said, sounding somewhat distant.

He took several steps toward her, and suddenly Tiraud had his knife out and pointed threateningly. "No closer," he warned.

"Put that away!" Calhoun said sharply, and continued, "Xyon, back off. I mean it."

"Oh no, Calhoun, let him come," Fhermus challenged. "Let the boys have at it. It'll do them both good, don't you think?"

"Sheathe it, Tiraud," Si Cwan warned him. "Right now. I'll have none of this. He's seen you with Kalinda. He sees she's happy. That's the end of it."

Xyon was shaking his head, still staring at Kalinda.

"Apparently he disagrees!" Fhermus said, trying to stir things up.

"I don't disagr—" Xyon sounded genuinely bewildered, and Robin was starting to wonder whether he had taken some severe blows to the head that they were only just now learning about. "I just . . . Kalinda? Are you sure it's . . . ?"

"Enough of this!" declared Fhermus. "Come. Let us adjourn to the main dining hall and speak of more pleasant things than this fellow here."

With that pronouncement, Fhermus and his entourage headed away. Hanging back for a moment was Si Cwan, who exchanged an inscrutable look with Robin before heading off after Fhermus.

"You shouldn't have let him do that to you, you know," Calhoun told Xyon.

Xyon looked as if Calhoun's words hadn't registered on him. "Do that? Do what?"

"Get to you. Confuse you."

"He didn't get to me, Father, and he didn't confuse me. She did. Something's wrong with her. I don't think that's Kalinda."

"*What?*"

"I don't! Something seemed—I don't know—off about her. The way she walked, maybe, or carried herself."

"And you think you would notice such a thing when her brother himself didn't?"

"Maybe," Xyon protested. "A lover knows better than a brother about things, like the way a woman moves her body. It just . . . it didn't seem like her. I think something's wrong. I'm going after her. . . ."

He got only two steps before Kebron was standing in front of him, blocking him, while Calhoun stood behind him and gripped him by the wrist.

"That's enough, Xyon," Calhoun said sharply. "Enough lies. Enough attempts to gain sympathy and play others."

"But I wasn't! She—"

"*Xyon!* After everything you've put all of us through, it's time to stop! Do you hear me? It's *time to stop!*"

Xyon made a noise that sounded like a frustrated choking, but then, looking small and defeated, he nodded. "Yeah. Yeah, okay. I swear, Father, I wasn't trying to fool you . . . but . . . I guess maybe I was trying to fool myself."

"You mean telling yourself that the only way she could possibly have no interest in you is if she was, in fact, not herself?" suggested Kebron.

"That's right." He laughed softly to himself. "Guess that's a pretty stupid way for me to react to her, huh?"

Understandingly, Calhoun patted him on the back. "You've been through a lot, Xyon. You need to get yourself centered. You need some rest, and you need to be among friends."

"I thought you and the entire crew hated my guts for letting you think I was dead."

"We do," Calhoun assured him. "But for now, we're the closest thing to friends you've got."

ii.

The Ten-Forward of the *Trident* was empty save for two people, both of them captains.

Mueller glanced with pleasure around the popular rest and recreation hangout. "I love this time," she said to Mackenzie Calhoun. "There's a time just between shifts, at night . . . just now . . . when this place is usually empty. I'm not quite sure how it happens that way, but it does. Always the same time, no matter which ship I'm on. I noticed it back in my night-shift days and it's remained one of the few constants in my life. This is the time when I hit the bar."

Calhoun was nursing the synthehol in his glass. "You know," he observed, "some would say there's a certain perversity to frequenting a place designed for socializing only when you know there's no one there to socialize with."

"Perversity and I are old friends," replied Mueller, taking a shot from the schnapps she kept hidden away for such occasions.

Calhoun laughed softly at that, then leaned forward, his attitude changing from convivial to businesslike. "So the Priatians didn't give you any difficulties?"

"Not really, no. I'll tell you, I exercised every caution in the book, and it was as if I'd wasted my time. Everything was strictly aboveboard. We retrieved her without so much as a shot being fired. Doc Villers checked her out head to toe and gave her a clean bill of health. In retrospect, it was the single dullest rescue mission I've ever undertaken. It's almost as if it was too easy."

That caught Calhoun's attention. "What are you saying?"

"That I'm too suspicious. That sometimes you and I, who are so accustomed to the vessels we command, forget exactly how intimidating it can be to have one of these monsters orbiting your planet. The sight of us alone, with enough firepower to level half a planet, can be daunting to anyone with a guilty conscience."

"But we'd never use our firepower to level half a planet."

Kat shrugged. "They don't have to know that."

"Except it wouldn't matter to them if they really did have that gigantic spaceship that Xyon says he saw."

She shook her head. "They swear they don't. That it was just an illusion. A mirage."

"And you believe them?"

Once more she shrugged. "Pretty much. It makes more sense than anything else."

"I suppose." He took another sip, wished that there were something more potent within reach, and then said, "In any event . . . thank you for attending to our little problem. You did well. So what's your next port of call?"

"Elias sector. Observing a developing world. You?"

"Border patrol around the Selelvian territory. There's rumors of terrorists trying to cross over, and we're to look for suspicious vessels."

"Dangerous times we live in."

"When aren't they?" he said without humor. He got up from the table and she did as well. "Thanks for everything, Kat."

"My pleasure," she replied, coming around the side so that she was standing close to him, facing him. Calhoun was very aware of her, of the nearness of her, of her scent as his nostrils flared slightly.

Suddenly she draped her arms around him, drew him to her, and kissed him with barely repressed urgency. Calhoun was startled by the raw need that she was displaying, and he had a feeling it was catching her off guard as well.

For a heartbeat he felt as if he were swimming in her, and then he pulled away exactly the same time as she did.

They gazed at each other, and Calhoun's breath felt heavy in his chest.

"Tell me, Calhoun," Mueller said, "do you ever think about . . . you know . . . picking up where we . . . ?"

"No."

"Me neither."

She cleared her throat as she stepped back and smoothed her hair, but she did not seem the least bit sorry. She smiled and repeated, "Me neither," as if to convince herself.

"Good-bye, Captain," Calhoun said to her with a smile. "Give my love to Elizabeth."

"I intend to," she assured him. "In fact, I was so determined to do your love justice, that I was just engaging in a—"

"Refresher course?"

She nodded. "Exactly."

"I hope it was enough to jog your memory."

"Consider it jogged."

iii.

Mueller waited until the transporter room sent word that Mackenzie Calhoun had returned to the *Excalibur,* and then ordered the *Trident* to be taken out of orbit and set course for the Elias sector, at warp six.

She couldn't help but notice that, as the *Excalibur* dropped out of orbit about the same time her ship did, Calhoun's vessel adopted a cruising speed of warp 1.5. She wondered why the hell he was dragging his heels. He had no more love of Thallonian space than she. So why wasn't he moving as fast as he could to put the area behind him?

It was almost as if Calhoun thought there might be some sort of trouble that he hadn't foreseen, and was taking his sweet time lest he was needed.

U.S.S. Excalibur

i.

There was something wrong with her. . . .

As much as Xyon wanted to believe what his father had said . . . as much as he wanted to embrace that explanation since it was the simplest one . . . he still couldn't help but feel that something was deeply wrong.

They had left New Thallon far behind. To the best of Xyon's knowledge, the wedding had already been held. He had no doubt it was a lavish affair. Lying on his bed in his guest quarters, staring up vacantly at the ceiling, he could see the entire thing playing out in his head. The solemn ceremony followed by the music, the dancing, the sheer joy over the uniting of the House of Cwan and the House of Fhermus. And he could practically hear Tiraud boasting to his friends, talking about that young idiot "space pirate" who thought that he could somehow interfere with what was obviously a destined match. Yes, yes. They would characterize him as a fool, a gnat at best. Someone who wasn't worth the brain cells required to remember his name.

He wondered if Kalinda was going to be joining in the laughter.

With a moan, he yanked his pillow out from under his head and held it over his face.

"Are you trying to smother yourself?"

The voice caught Xyon completely unawares and he snapped upright, clutching the pillow to his chest in the darkness. "Who's there?" he demanded. "How did you get in?"

"Morgan let me in," said the newcomer from the dark. "She does that sometimes when I need her to. We have a relationship, y'see."

"Morgan? You mean . . . Robin's mother? What does she have to do with . . . where are you?" His eyes were beginning to adjust to the darkness. He wasn't anxious to bring the lights to full. It would both hurt his eyes and make him an easier target, just in case the intruder's intention was to start shooting at him.

"Morgan's the computer now."

"The . . . computer . . . ? I don't . . . who the hell are you?"

"Lights to half."

The lights obediently partly illuminated the interior of the cabin, and there was a young fellow there who appeared to be in his early teens. He was staring intently at Xyon.

"Who are you?" Xyon demanded again.

"My name's Moke. I'm . . . well . . . I'm sort of Captain Calhoun's son."

Xyon didn't know what to make of that. Calhoun hadn't given him all that much of an update as to what was what aboard the *Excalibur*. Nor had Xyon provided an opportunity, for as soon as he had docked the *Lyla* in the shuttlebay and had emerged, he had pled total exhaustion. And that hadn't been a lie. Despite the healing process he had undergone, he had felt so mentally and physically battered that it was a wonder he could even stand up. After ascertaining Xyon's basic medical fitness, he had provided his son with guest quarters and sent him packing off to bed.

Since then, Xyon had lost track of the hours. He could have asked the computer what time it was, but at the moment he was more caught up with the intruder purporting to be his brother.

"You're sort of his son?"

"Yes."

"How did that come about?"

"He adopted me. Well . . . sort of adopted me. Because my mother was killed."

"Okay," said Xyon. "So . . . where's your real father?"

"Oh, he's a god."

That one took Xyon a bit longer to process. "Okay," he said again.

"People call him Woden. And sometimes Santa Claus."

A longer pause. A longer "Ooookay."

Xyon couldn't help but feel that the boy was practically dissecting him with his eyes. "Look . . . Mook . . . ?"

"Moke."

"Right. Moke. Look, Moke . . . is there some reason you're here, in the middle of the . . . of whatever time this is?"

"Yes."

"There's a reason?"

"Yes."

"You want to share it with me?"

Moke contemplated this notion. "I was going to," he announced, "but I've decided not to."

"Outstanding. Lock up when you leave." Xyon flopped back onto the bed and could already sense sleep overtaking him once more, when Moke abruptly spoke up again.

"Are you going to replace me?"

Slowly he forced himself to sitting once more, staring in bleary-eyed confusion through the dimness of the light. "Replace you? I'm not even sure what your current function is. . . ."

"I told you: I'm Captain Calhoun's son."

"Yeah. Okay. Well . . . I am, too, and I guess the universe is big enough for two of us. All right? Now go to sleep."

And suddenly Moke was seized with an almost thunderous rage as he advanced on a stunned Xyon. "Oh, sure. That's what you say now. That the universe is big enough for the two of us. But I can just see it. I know what's going to happen. Mac is going to spend more and more time focusing on you and worrying about you and telling everyone proudly about everything that you've accomplished—"

"My recent accomplishments weren't exactly grounds for paternal boasting," Xyon said.

It didn't seem as if Moke even heard him. "And he'll spend even less time with me than he does right now, and he won't care at all. But if I complain about it, he'll just send me to other people to talk to about it, and probably he'll just pack me off to some school or something on Earthside to make way for you in his life—"

"I didn't want to be in his life! I've got my own life, thanks."

"And why couldn't you have stayed dead?!"

Xyon gaped at him and then said, "Well, excuse the hell out of me for living."

And there was something of consummate menace in the boy's voice as he replied, "You know . . . I don't think I will." With that, he turned on his heel and stormed out. As he did so, Xyon wondered if he'd imagined that the very air around him seemed to crackle.

Then, just as the doors almost shut, they slid open once more and someone else walked in. Xyon stared at the newest arrival, tall and elegant, with Vulcan-like tapered ears, but an air of amusement about him that belied any Vulcan heritage.

"Hello," he said. "I was passing by and would have let you sleep, but I heard shouting and figured you might be awake."

"Okay," said Xyon. "And you are . . . ?"

"Xy."

"Okay. Interesting name. Similar to mine."

"Actually, it *is* yours. My name is Xyon."

"Really. You have a Xenexian name?"

"Well, technically, I suppose I do." Xy smiled. "The fact is, I have *your* name."

"Okay. You do realize I'm still using it, right?"

Xy strolled across the room and carelessly sat on the edge of the bed. Xyon backed up, making sure to keep the sheets around him, watching Xy suspiciously. He was starting to wonder if Xy was making overtures to him. "You don't understand. I was named after you."

"You were . . . ?"

"Named after you, yes."

"Okay. Just for the record, before I was just mildly bemused. *Now* I don't understand."

"What don't you understand?"

"The part about being named after me. You're as old as me . . . maybe even a little older."

"Oh! Of course," and Xy laughed softly. "Everyone here is so used to my personal situation, I tend to forget when encountering someone new. I actually look much older than I am."

"Okay. Because, you know, you don't look *bad* or anything, just . . ."

"Actually, chronologically, I'm four years, eight months, nine days old."

This time the silence was more extended than any that had preceded it.

"Four years?"

"Eight months. Nine days."

"Well, then I take it back. You look terrible."

Xy laughed again. "Thank you. I appreciate your candor." He tilted his head and looked in confusion at Xyon, who was now leaning back and thumping his skull against the wall. "You know, you really shouldn't be doing that. A concussion could result."

"Oh, you're a doctor now?"

"Yes, actually."

That stopped Xyon. He stared at Xy and said, "So you're a doctor named after me who's actually four and a half years old. And just before this I was visited by an envious adopted brother whose father is a god. Have I got that right?"

"More or less. Anyway, I just wanted to meet my namesake and get to know you better. See how the stories I've heard compare to the actuality."

"The stories never compare well to anyone's actuality. Could you go away now?"

"All right," said Xy, never losing his air of calm. He got up, headed for the door, paused, and said, "If there's any way I can be of service . . ."

"No, thanks," Xyon said quickly. "I don't need you to service me . . . I mean, I don't need any service . . . of any kind."

"All right," Xy said again, and he walked out of the room.

Xyon sat there in the half-darkness for some time. Then he muttered, "I wish they'd left me in the damned torture chamber," flopped down, pulled his pillow over his head, and fell into a very fitful sleep, filled with terrifying dreams that all involved Kalinda.

New Thallon

i.

Robin Lefler stood there for a long time in her nightgown as she watched Si Cwan in bed, his back rising and falling steadily in what was a clear simulation of sleep. "The wedding went well, don't you think?" she ventured. "Everyone seemed to have a good time." No response. "I've never seen Fhermus drink that much. For that matter, I've never seen anyone drink that much." Still no response. "I don't think Kalinda's ever looked more radiant. The vows they spoke . . . they were very touching. It's nice that they're spending their wedding night here at the manor tonight. So tell me more about this 'vacation world' they'll be leaving for tomorrow."

Still nothing.

Finally she said, "You're not fooling me. I know you're awake."

He paused and then said, "How could you tell?"

"Because you snore."

"That's a lie."

"No, it's really not."

Si Cwan sighed heavily and rolled over in the bed to look up at her. "Actually, I thought you might wind up spending the night in the holosuite."

"Would you prefer I did?"

He turned away once more so that his back was to her. "Do whatever you wish, Robin. It's evident that's what you do anyway."

"Ohhhh no," she said, angrily pointing at him even though he didn't see it. "Don't you start that. Don't you act as if you're the injured party."

"You're in a position of trust here. You violated that trust, both as my wife and as a representative of the United Federation of Planets and Starfleet."

"How do you figure that?"

"As my wife, you operated behind my back, knowing that I would object if I found out, knowing that it could seriously undermine my authority. As a representative, well, I seem to recall there being something about a noninterference directive."

"The Prime Directive doesn't apply in cases when it . . . it . . ."

"When it what?" He twisted around to look at her once more. "When doesn't it apply?"

"When it's . . . you know . . . really irritating," she finished in a less-than-convincing manner.

Which of course explained why Si Cwan looked less than convinced. "I see. Well, you should remember that explanation. I'm sure that Starfleet would be dazzled by that logic." And again he looked away.

Robin came around the bed to the other side, forcing herself into his view. "I'm not worried about Starfleet right now."

"Oh? And what are you worried about?"

"You. What you did to Xyon."

"I did what I had to do."

"Torture is never an answer, Cwan!"

"Neither is kidnapping," Si Cwan retorted, propping himself up on an elbow. "But one foul deed begets another. Maybe it would have benefited Xyon to consider that before he committed the act, and maybe it would benefit you to consider that I shouldn't be blamed simply because Xyon suffered the consequences of his actions."

"But you tortured him! And you were proud of it!"

"I wasn't proud of it! I was simply open and honest about it, which is a hell of a lot more than you were in your actions!"

Anyone stepping into the glare emanating from between the two of them would have been incinerated on the spot. Such hostility could sustain itself only so long, however, and in short order they both lowered their eyes as if in mutual shame. Neither would admit it, of course.

She sat on the edge of the bed, turned away from him. "Are we going to make it through this?" she asked.

"I don't know," he said honestly.

Robin sighed. "It's just . . . I felt I saw a side of you that was . . . there's no other way to say it . . ."

"Barbaric?"

She nodded.

"You did. What I did was barbaric, and cruel, and unfortunately it was what needed to be done."

"And did you enjoy it?"

He didn't answer immediately. She looked at him, and he seemed thoughtful.

"Cwan . . . ?"

"My immediate impulse," he said slowly, "was to say no. The more I think on it, though . . . and if this costs me your love, then so be it, but I wish to be honest with you . . . some part of me did."

"Oh really," and her voice was cold. "And what part of you was that?"

"The part that would have wanted to please my father, even though he's long gone. He would have loved it. I could almost sense him smiling down upon me. He was a bit of a monster, my father was."

"And is that what you want? To be like him?"

"Before the entire business with Xyon, I would have thought not."

"And now?"

"Now," he told her with a tinge of regret, "I still wouldn't want to be like him. But for all the times he claimed I was weak, I would have liked to hold up the entire Xyon business as a way of telling him that I could have been just like him . . . but simply chose not to."

"What difference do you think that would have made to him?"

"Probably none," he admitted.

"So . . . where does that leave us?"

Before he could answer, that was when they heard the screams.

ii.

Tiraud, gazing at his reflection in the mirror, was vacillating over whether he should be waiting for Kalinda stark naked when she emerged from the changing room, or instead sporting some minimal sort of clothing. He settled for wearing a dressing gown that ended at about midthigh. He was quite proud of his legs and didn't mind showing them off, particularly on such a night as this.

He had draped his clothes, dagger, and belt on a nearby chair, and he called in his most musical of tones, "Kalinda? Are you going to be much longer?"

A door hissed open behind him and Kalinda was standing there, smiling enticingly. She was wearing a sheer gown that left nothing to the imagination.

"Not much longer at all," she purred.

He couldn't take his eyes off her. It was as if the room, the rest of the world, was just falling away, and there was only she and he together.

She drew close to him, draped her arms around his neck, and her lips sought his. He kissed her eagerly, hungrily. Then she lifted her mouth up to his ear and whispered, "Hurt me."

He drew back, looking at her in confusion. "W-What?"

"Hurt me." Her eyes were alight with eagerness.

"I . . . I don't understand. . . ."

"It will excite me . . . arouse me. You want me aroused, don't you?"

"Y-Yes. Of course." His face was a portrait of bewilderment. "But . . . it just seems . . ."

"It's what I want. Come on." She nibbled on his throat. "I'll beg if you want to."

"All . . . all right." He reached behind her and slapped her on the rump. "How is that? Is that—?"

"Oh, come on!" She sounded disappointed. "Push me! Hit me! Be brutal!" She started shoving at him, not gently. "What are you, afraid? The heir of the House of Fhermus? Wait until I tell everyone that you couldn't satisfy your wife on your wedding night!"

Until that moment, Tiraud had been overwhelmed by mounting bafflement over Kalinda's behavior. But when he heard her threats, a mounting haze of anger began to hover behind his eyes.

"You wouldn't!"

"You bet I would—"

"*Why?*"

"*Why not?* Or is the truth something so repulsive that—"

"*All right, fine! You win!*" Even as he spoke, he drew back a hand and hit her across the face.

Kalinda stumbled backward, her head snapping around from the impact, and she fell against the chair.

And at that moment, as instant regret lurched into Tiraud's mind, so too did a horrific realization occur to him. "*Of course!*" he cried out. He moved toward her as she looked up at him, blood seeping from the side of her mouth, her lip already swelling. "They did something to you! Those bastards who had you! They did something to your mind!"

He reached for her, pulling her toward him, and that was when he felt some sort of stinging and odd pressure in his chest.

"Close," whispered Kalinda. "Very, very close."

Tiraud looked down, uncomprehending, staring at the hilt of his ceremonial dagger against his chest. He was so disconnected from the moment that he was wondering where in the world the blade itself could possibly have gotten to. Then, as the blood began to coalesce and thicken around the entry wound, he thought dully, *Oh. There it is.*

He dropped to his knees and stared up at Kalinda. Her face was remote, passionless. "Understand," she said. "There's nothing personal in this. You're simply a pawn in a much greater game. Unfortunately, pawns oftentimes have to be removed from the board."

"My chest hurts," Tiraud said, and then slumped to the side, dead before he struck the ground.

She prodded him with her toe for a moment. He didn't respond in the slightest. Then she took several deep breaths until the air in her lungs had a ragged quality, and let out a series of screams. They were high-pitched and piteous and filled with fear and despair.

There was the sound of running feet and pounding at the door. Voices were calling, "Lady Kalinda! What's wrong? What's happening?" She reasoned that it was servants or guards who were shouting, because no one had yet entered even though she had taken care to leave the door unlocked. None of common birth, after all, would dare to enter the marriage chamber of Kalinda, sister of Si Cwan, and Tiraud of the House of Fhermus.

Then there came an authoritative pounding and an unmistakable voice. "Kalinda! What's happened!"

"C-Cwan," she managed to choke out.

The door slid open and Kalinda stumbled toward Robin, holding out her arms. Si Cwan looked in clear horror at the marks on Kalinda's face and then saw Tiraud lying on the floor. Not fully realizing what had happened yet, he shouted angrily at Tiraud, "Are you insane? Why did you do this? Why would you strike Kalinda?"

Robin had gone over to Tiraud, and she gasped in shock. "Cwan, he's dead!"

"Dead? What do you . . . dead?" He looked from Robin to Kalinda and back again. "Why is he dead? Did he fall badly somehow? Strike his head . . . ? But . . . that's ridiculous! He can't be dead!"

For answer, she rolled him over so that the protruding dagger was clearly visible. There were shocked murmurs from the house staff who were peering in through the door.

Seeing the knife, Cwan said, "All right, he *can* be dead. But why?" He gaped at Kalinda. "Why?"

"Oh gods . . . Cwan," she sobbed into his chest, "he wanted to do such . . . such bestial things to me. Such awful, awful things. I never . . . he never gave any indication . . . I didn't know. How could I know? Now that we're married, he'd changed so completely! He was like . . . like a different person! An animal! And . . . and when I wouldn't submit . . . he . . . he threatened me . . . struck . . ." She touched her swollen lip gingerly. "He was raving! Coming at me! I . . . I swear, I thought he was going to kill me! And I . . . I . . ."

"You killed him first," noted Cwan, and he held her tightly. "You did what you had to do. You defended yourself. I understand. Anyone would understand."

"Why do I have a feeling," said Robin with obvious concern, "that Fhermus is not going to understand?"

iii.

"I . . . don't understand," Fhermus said.

The main hall was deserted, save for Si Cwan and Lord Fhermus. Fhermus was looking bleary-eyed, the effects of all the alcohol he'd imbibed clearly not coming close to having worn off. Nor had it helped matters that Si Cwan had summoned him from his home in the middle of the night with no explanation whatsoever aside from that it was "of the utmost importance."

And now Si Cwan had said something about Tiraud? About a "problem"?

"What type of problem?" Fhermus rubbed his eyes, trying to shove his vision back into place. He lowered his hands and squinted and the two Si Cwans standing in front of him settled into one Si Cwan . . . who merely looked twice as concerned as he had been.

"The problem is that . . . Fhermus, there's no delicate way to put this. . . ."

"Then settle for an indelicate manner so that I can go back to sleep. . . ."

"There was an . . . incident . . . with Tiraud and Kalinda."

"An . . . incident?" Fhermus tried with only minimal success to process the word. "What sort of incident? Not a traveling accident . . . they were spending the night here, weren't they . . . ?"

"A fight. They had a fight."

Fhermus took this in, and then laughed with a sense of incredulity. "You summoned me in the middle of the night for a damned lovers' quarrel? Granted, the timing is poor, what with this being the night of their bonding, but certainly we can leave it to the youngsters to—"

"A bad fight. Very. Bad."

The subtext of Si Cwan's words began to trickle in through Fhermus's consciousness. Suddenly the fog on Fhermus's brain was burned away and a sense of dread permeated his being. "Si Cwan . . . where is Tiraud? I want to see my son. I want to see him now."

"Fhermus . . . I have to tell you—"

"*Where is he?*"

"He's dead."

Fhermus shook his head as if the subject had just been abruptly changed. "Who's dead?"

"Your son. Tiraud. Your son is dead."

"No, he's not!" Fhermus said dismissively, the very notion clearly ridiculous. "They had a fight . . . it's . . . there's nothing to . . ." And then, very slowly, his still-reeling mind began to piece together just what was being said. His face grew ashen and his knees trembled, but he remained upright. He started to speak but nothing emerged.

"Fhermus . . ."

His words were barely over a whisper. "Take me to him."

"We haven't moved his body yet . . . I think it best if . . ."

Now there was no whisper. Now there was a thunderous roar. *"Take me to him!"*

Apparently realizing there was no point in discussing it further, Si Cwan called out, "Ankar!"

His aide showed up almost immediately in that amazing manner he had. "Ankar," Si Cwan said softly, "Lord Fhermus wishes to be brought to his son."

Ankar nodded once and gestured for Fhermus to follow him. Fhermus did so, even though he could not feel the blood in his legs, could not sense that they were moving or that he was actually trailing after Ankar. He was unaware of the time passing, didn't focus on the corridors they walked through or the various servants or guards who looked upon him, or away from him, with sadness. All he knew was that one moment he was in the main hall, and the next, he was standing in the doorway of a room where his son was lying on the floor. Tiraud was wearing a bathrobe, and the dagger he'd given his son for his tenth birthday was sticking out of his chest. There was blood all over him and on the floor.

Kalinda was there, with a blanket draped over her that was covering her gown-clad body. She was seated in a chair at the far end of the room, staring fixedly at Tiraud. Robin Lefler was next to her, her hands resting gently on Kalinda's shoulders.

Tiraud, get up at once! This is a foolish prank and you're scaring people. That was what Fhermus wanted to say, but the words died in his throat before being uttered. Slowly he walked over to his son's body, stared down at him. He sensed his brain beginning to shut down, but he knew that if he passed out now, he would never live it down. He forced himself to remain conscious as he said, as if speaking from very far away, "How . . . did this happen . . . ?"

"It appears that—" began Si Cwan.

But Fhermus said harshly, "No. Not from you," and he pointed at Kalinda. "From her. She was here. You were not. Only her words matter."

In a slow, halting manner, Kalinda said, "He . . . wanted to do things to me. Awful, perverse, violent things. He said it was the only way he could be . . . excited. When I refused . . . he did this," and she touched her swollen lip. "And he was prepared to do more. And worse. I thought . . . I think he was going to kill me. He left the knife within reach. He attacked me. I . . . I wasn't trying to kill him . . . just stop him . . . I . . . am sorry."

For a long time, no one spoke.

Finally, Fhermus did. His voice was dripping with anger and contempt, and he said, "What nonsense is this? What . . . pathetic, vomitous tale are you putting forward?"

"Lord Fhermus," and there was an edge of warning to Si Cwan's voice.

Fhermus ignored him. "Violence? Perversity? This is . . . this is idiocy! That was not my son! My son would have desired no such . . . he was . . . my son was a gentle soul! Too gentle for the murdering likes of you!"

He started toward Kalinda, who shrank back, and suddenly Si Cwan had interposed himself between Fhermus and Kalinda. "Lord Fhermus, I, as do you, grieve for your loss. But—"

"*You grieve as I do? Have you lost a son this night!?*" Fhermus turned away from Si Cwan, dropped to the floor at Tiraud's side, and let out a scream of such misery, such hopelessness, such utter and total surrender to grief, that it seared itself into the minds and souls of all those who heard it. He choked back the sobs that begged to issue from him, and instead scooped up his son's body into his arms. He cradled him as if Tiraud were a newborn, and then growled, "Your sister will accompany me. She will be tried, condemned, and executed for her crime."

"Her *crime?*" Si Cwan sounded stunned. "Her crime is that she fought for her life against the brutal attack. . . ."

"*Lies! Lies!*"

"Are you calling my sister a liar?"

"Why stop there?" His voice was giddy with anguish. "I call *you* a liar, Si Cwan. You, your sister, your damned House, your damned Protectorate! Any who support you or ally with you are my enemy! So unless you care to strike me down so I can join my son, I suggest you step aside and prepare to reap the harvest that your murdering bitch sister has sown!"

Si Cwan looked as if he were about to take Fhermus up on his offer. His fists trembled slightly, as if he were intending to smash Fhermus in the face, crush his skull. Finally, barely restraining himself, Si Cwan stepped aside. Holding the limp body of his son tightly against him, uncaring of the blood that was getting all over the front of his clothing, Fhermus strode out of the room.

All eyes were upon him as he left.

All eyes except two pairs.

Those were the eyes of Ankar and of Kalinda . . . who exchanged a long, significant look, and then a slight nod, as if congratulations were being extended on a job well done.

U.S.S. Excalibur

i.

"*War?*"

In his ready room, Calhoun was staring at the image of Robin Lefler gazing out at him from the computer screen. She was nodding, looking miserable, as if she had just lost her best friend.

If Calhoun was amazed at what he'd been hearing, no less so was Xyon. He had come up to the captain's ready room to discuss the strange nocturnal altercation he'd had with Moke, but the interruption by Lelfer's transmission had completely reoriented their priorities.

As she'd informed them of the recent developments, Xyon had at first looked utterly shocked. But as the litany of disaster had continued, his amazement had given way to what seemed, to Calhoun, like suspicion. He said nothing to Xyon, however, preferring to let Lefler finishing telling him all that had transpired.

"Yes, war," she said grimly. "After Fhermus stormed out of the manor, it was this . . . this mad race between the two of them. Si Cwan and Fhermus, both trying to shore up support from those they felt to be their closest allies."

"Let me guess," said Calhoun. "Those who were already close to Si Cwan believe that Tiraud assaulted Kalinda and she was acting in self-defense."

Robin nodded. "Exactly. And those who are long-time allies of Fhermus naturally believe that she brutally stabbed him to death for no other reason than that . . . I don't know. That she's Thallonian nobility. For all that the daily business of the Protectorate manages to suppress it, there's a good deal of ancient hostility bubbling just below the surface."

"And how is it shaking out?"

"Too soon to say . . . except that it's ugly and getting uglier."

"How's Si Cwan holding up?"

"He looks like a walking ghost."

Calhoun took a deep breath. "Robin . . . try and keep it together there. We're going to fix this."

Lefler blinked in surprise. "Fix this . . . ? Captain, I wasn't looking for a solution. I was simply keeping you apprised. This . . . this horror show isn't your fault. . . ."

"Yes. Yes, of course. You're right. Foolish of me to think so. Thank you for keeping me up to date, Robin. We should do this more often. *Excalibur* out." Her confused face disappeared from the screen before she could reply.

Mackenzie Calhoun stood up, turned away from Xyon and, with an uncharacteristic roar of pure fury, slammed his fist into the wall. "*Grozit!*" he shouted in frustration as he did so. "How could I have been so

damned blind!" He faced Xyon. "How could I have ignored you? I should have trusted you. Yes, you de-
ceived me for years about the fact that you were alive,
but still—!"

"Father . . . ?"

Calhoun spoke right over him. "All the times I've
relied on my instincts and been right . . . I should have
known that your instincts wouldn't have led you
astray."

"Are you saying—?"

"Don't be coy, Xyon," Calhoun admonished. "I can
see it in your face. You're thinking the same thing I
am."

"That it's not Kalinda."

"Exactly."

Xyon let out a sigh of relief and sagged back in his
chair. "You'd almost convinced me . . . hell, I'd almost
convinced myself. You know, that I was simply jealous.
Or that I didn't want to let her go."

"I think you sensed something. Something that
even Si Cwan didn't see. . . ."

"Why should he have?" asked Xyon. "After all, he
was anxious to believe that she'd come back. I was anxious not to let her go. So naturally . . ."

"You each saw what you wanted, except you happened to see more accurately." He was staring at his
reflection in the sword hanging on the wall . . . the
sword that he'd taken off the man who had, years earlier, given him the vicious scar that still adorned the
side of Calhoun's face. "When Mueller described to
me her mission at Priatia, she told me she couldn't be-

lieve how easily it had gone. Her instincts were right on the money as well. The only one who missed the mark completely was me." He rubbed the bridge of his nose. "I must be losing my edge."

"So what do we do?"

Calhoun shot him a glance. "You know, if you'd said I *wasn't* losing my edge, I wouldn't have resented it." Then, before Xyon could respond, he walked out of the ready room. Xyon immediately followed him as Calhoun stepped onto the bridge.

"Morgan!" he called out. "Set course for Priatia. Best possible speed."

"Priatia, aye, sir."

Burgoyne, from hir chair, looked up in surprise. "Priatia, Captain? Is there a problem?"

"Yes," Calhoun said briskly. "The problem is Priatia. And once we get there, I intend to see it no longer poses a problem . . . for anyone."

ii.

"Target all major cities and fire!"

Every head on the bridge of the *Excalibur* turned and stared at the Xenexian who had just issued the startling order.

"Xyon," Calhoun said slowly, "you don't get to blow up cities."

Xyon regarded his father with disappointment. Below them, the planet Priatia continued steadily and unmolested in its orbit. "I was just trying to save you time and energy, Father. I knew you'd give the order sooner or later and I figured . . ."

"Why not sooner?" Calhoun smiled thinly and with no air of amusement. "Xyon, try to give another order on this bridge, and I will fire upon the planet's surface . . ."

"Excellent!"

". . . with you as ammo."

Xyon winced. "That would hurt."

"I daresay," Morgan piped up.

"Therefore," continued Calhoun, "I will remind you that you are a guest on this bridge . . . surrounded by people who still aren't especially happy that you had them mourning your passing not all that long ago."

"The captain was most eloquent in his eulogy for you," Zak Kebron said.

"Not now, Kebron. Xy," he called to his science officer. "Begin scanning the planet's surface. If it was good enough for the *Trident*, it's good enough for us."

"Scanning, Captain."

Burgoyne leaned over in hir chair and said softly, "Do you really think we're going to find Kalinda down there? That the Kalinda the *Trident* brought back to New Thallon was some sort of impostor? Is that possible?"

"Yes, it's possible. A clone, perhaps. . . ."

"Grown to the same age that quickly? It seems unlikely. And, by all reports, she had all Kalinda's memories, and personality. . . ."

"I don't have all the answers, Burgy," admitted Calhoun. "That's why it's called a 'mystery.' We . . ."

"Captain! Receiving a transmission from the planet's surface," Kebron announced.

"I'm not entirely surprised. Put them on screen, Mr. Kebron."

Moments later, the image of a Priatian appeared on their viewscreen. He did not appear to be especially concerned over the fact that a Federation starship was circling at spitting distance from his world. "I am Keesala," he said without preamble. "And I would very much suggest that you depart this area immediately. It will turn out badly for you if you do not."

"This is Mackenzie Calhoun, captain of the Federation starship *Excalibur*. Your concern for our welfare would be far more touching to me if it weren't inextricably linked with your self-interest. You know why we're here."

"Yes. You want the Thallonian girl, Kalinda."

Calhoun was beginning to get the same sense of "It can't be this easy" that Mueller had expressed. "That is correct."

"You are aware that the one who left here with your other vessel was not the original."

"It came to our attention when she stabbed her husband to death, yes."

Xyon was standing directly behind Calhoun, and he could no longer contain himself. "Give her back to us, you bastard!" he practically shouted.

"That, I'm afraid, is not going to be happening," Keesala said apologetically as Calhoun glared at his son.

In a harsh whisper, Calhoun said *"Shut! Up!"* to Xyon before turning his attention back to Keesala. "That, sir, is exactly what is going to be happening. If you think for one moment that we're going to be leaving without her . . ."

"That is, to be honest, exactly what is about to happen."

It was at that moment that Tania Tobias, seated at ops, suddenly pitched back in her chair and started to scream.

"Tania!" Kebron called out, and started toward her.

"Stay at your post!" Calhoun ordered. As Kebron froze where he was, Calhoun was at Tania's side. *She's having a fit, now of all times. I should have known. I never should have given her this opportunity.* "Tobias!" he called to her. "Snap out of it!"

"It's coming! It's coming!" she gasped. She seemed as if she were looking somewhere else, her eyes wide and wild.

And that was when the hairs on the back of Calhoun's neck began to rise. She was right. Hysterical, but right. Something was coming. Something extraordinarily dangerous.

"Captain!" Kebron shouted. "Sensor readings indicate massive tachyon surge directly to starboard!"

"On screen!"

The apologetic face of Keesala vanished, to be replaced by a clear view of something gargantuan swirling in space, like a massive whirlpool of energy. Energy crackled as if the very ether itself had come to life, and then it spat out a huge vessel the likes of which Calhoun had never seen.

"*That's it!*" Xyon shouted, pointing at the screen. "That's the ship that came after me! The one that took Kalinda!"

"Doesn't look like any mirage to me," said Calhoun. "Red alert! Morgan, shields up! Kebron, full phaser batteries online!"

The new arrival swatted them.

That was what it felt like, at least. Something, some sort of energy barrage, slammed into them just as their shields came up. The shields withstood the impact, preventing the *Excalibur* from being shredded, but they weren't sufficient to stop the ship from spiraling out of control, as if the far vaster ship had simply reached through space and knocked them aside.

Throughout the ship, crew members were hurled this way and that, slammed into walls, ceilings. No one knew which way was up or down.

The whirlpool of energy coruscated on the screen directly in front of them, and Tania Tobias was shrieking, and Morgan was calling out "We're out of control!" as if that needed to be said, and Xyon was shouting Kalinda's name, and that was when a tumbling Calhoun struck his head on a railing. The world began to spiral into blackness from the impact, and the last thing he heard before blackness claimed him was the apologetic voice of Keesala saying over the still active com link, "Please understand that we have nothing but the highest regard for you. Unfortunately, it appears you've gotten in the way." And then came another voice, at the last possible moment, also filtered, shouting his name, and it sounded like Soleta of all people, but she was gone, long gone, another failure of which this new incident was only Calhoun's latest and possibly his last. . . .

And then the world went dark and he was gone.

Seconds later, so was the *Excalibur*. . . .

TO BE CONTINUED . . .

The adventure continues in
February 2006 with
the eagerly-anticipated new hardcover

STAR TREK
NEWFRONTIER®

MISSING IN ACTION

by *New York Times* bestselling author
Peter David

Turn the page for an electrifying preview
of *Missing in Action*. . . .

Soleta was on the bridge of the *Spectre* when they drew within range of the *Excalibur*. The starship had fallen into orbit around Priatia. Her gaze riveted to the viewscreen, she felt a curious tugging at her heart that was not remotely in keeping with the sort of attitude she felt she should have toward her former vessel. The bridge of the *Spectre* was remarkably cramped in comparison to a Federation starship bridge. Instead of the commander chair being in the center of it, Soleta's chair was on a raised structure in the back, enabling her to look down upon the entire bridge in one sweeping view.

"Keep your distance, Centurion," she told her helmsman, an extremely capable young pilot named Aquila who possessed a brashness Soleta found surprisingly refreshing.

"I hope you're not concerned about detection, Commander," said Praefect Vitus from the tactical station. Gruff and aggressive, he was all for throwing the *Spectre* into any manner of challenges, confident in the ability of his ship to prevail. "The stealth capability of this ship is second to none in the galaxy."

"That's as may be, Vitus," replied Soleta. "But I can tell you from personal experience that Mackenzie Calhoun has almost a sixth sense for danger that borders on the supernatural. I have absolutely no interest in doing anything that could possibly trigger it." She turned to the comm officer. "Maurus . . . are they talking to the planet surface?"

"Yes, Commander," said Centurion Maurus. "But it's scrambled. It'll take me a few minutes to punch through and tap in to the frequency."

"Keep at it," she said. "I want to know what they're saying."

"You used to be the science officer on that vessel, Commander," pointed out Lucius. "Perhaps you have some insight that can expedite the process . . ."

Soleta shook her head. "The frequencies are stacked on a random oscillation variable," she told him. "Makes it harder to listen in. And since it's random, your guess is, quite frankly, as good as mine. It'll be as much luck as anything else if Maurus is able to listen in."

"I don't need luck, Commander," Maurus said confidently. "My skill will suffice."

"Your confidence is appreciated, Centurion," she replied. "Make certain to—"

"Commander!" It was Vitus who had called out to her. He was far too veteran an officer to show fear or even be disconcerted. But the concern in his voice was obvious. "I'm detecting a tachyon spike . . ."

Soleta was immediately out of her seat and at Vitus's side. She had too much of the old science officer instincts in her to just sit about while someone else did the analysis. If it irritated Vitus, he gave no indication. She studied the readings, feeling—not for the first time—that Starfleet equipment was superior to what the Romulans had to offer. Still, this was sufficient.

"Something's forming out there," she said after a few moments. She looked up at the screen. "Something big. Helm, bring us back another five thousand kliks. Maurus, forget about trying to eavesdrop. Open up a direct channel to the *Excalibur*."

It was a frozen moment on the bridge as all eyes turned to Soleta. "Commander," said Lucius slowly, "are you suggesting we drop stealth . . . ?"

"I am suggesting nothing, Tribune. I am *ordering* a direct channel to the *Excalibur*. Centurion Maurus, why don't I have it yet?"

"Hailing the *Excalibur*, Commander," Maurus said stiffly.

Soleta turned and was surprised to see that Lucius was standing right there, barely half a foot away from her. In a low tone that suggested burning anger and suspicion, he said, "With all respect, Commander, this is a breach of proto—"

She cut him off. "If something happens to the *Excalibur*, I want to find out who the hell they were talking to. I want to know what's going on, and if that means—"

That was when the sounds of chaos came over the comm unit. Maurus made no attempt to hide his surprised reaction as the sounds of barely controlled pandemonium filtered through the *Spectre*.

She heard a woman screaming, and shouted reports coming from all over the bridge. Voices that she knew, although it was as if she were recognizing them from a lifetime ago. Before she could focus on it, try to discern what everyone was saying, Praefect Vitus was calling out with a measure of alarm that matched what was happening on the *Excalibur* bridge. "Commander, tachyon readings off the scale! Something's forming in front of us . . . something huge. It's . . . a vessel, Commander!"

"On screen!" called out Soleta, but it was already appearing on the monitor even as she ordered it. Her eyes widened as she said, "It's too big. Reduce image size so I can see it more clearly!"

"That *is* with image size reduced," Vitus said. At helm, Aquila audibly gulped.

"Back us up another five thousand kliks, Aquila," Soleta said evenly.

The *Spectre* promptly moved even farther away from the debacle that was unfolding before it, and Soleta was finally able to get a clearer view of what they were dealing with.

The design was completely asymmetrical, which made it look like no other vessel Soleta had ever seen. It was almost as if the various parts of it had been stuck together haphazardly, a series of tubes affixed to pulsing globes. It resembled the model of a gigantic molecule.

It loomed before the *Excalibur*, looking ten times as big. Energy was crackling around it, and suddenly something huge, swirling rippled into existence in front of the embattled starship. They were clearly trying to hold their position, but some sort of monstrous forces were exerting themselves upon the ship, dragging it forward despite its best efforts.

"*Calhoun!*" Soleta shouted, the name bursting from her almost against her volition. The outburst prompted glances from her bridge crew, and she could see the suspicion in Vitus's eyes, but she ignored them.

It was hard for her to discern whether what she was seeing was genuine, or some bizarre trick of light, a distortion unrelated to reality. But it seemed to her that the *Excalibur* was actually twisting back upon itself, bending around as if it were made from rubber. Unimaginable energies had taken hold of it, swirling around the ship like some sort of cosmic sinkhole. It bore a resemblance to transwarp conduits such as she had seen the Borg use, but it was different, and the energy readings she saw on Vitus's board didn't match up precisely either. This was something different, with molecular contortion capabilities that were unlike anything she'd seen.

It was no doubt a trick of perspective, but the *Excalibur* appeared to get smaller, smaller. It seemed to take an excruciatingly long time instead of the seconds it truly required, and then the energy wheel—for such did it look like to Soleta—spun in and upon itself and vanished. She thought she saw a brief little burst of energy that might have been the *Excalibur* right before it disappeared, but she couldn't say for sure.

And then it was gone.

"What in the name of the Praetor is that thing?" whispered Aquila.

"I don't know," said Soleta. "But I'd very much appreciate, Vitus, some hard information so we can answer Aquila's very reasonable question."

"It's not there," said Vitus.

"*What?*" She turned to him, her face a question. "Are you saying it's a mirage?"

"I'm saying that whatever's there, our sensors aren't picking it up," Vitus told her. "All I've got is the residue of the tachyon emissions, but that was likely generated by whatever that rip in space was. I'm telling you,

Commander, that thing . . . it's almost as if it's fake. An illusion."

"Care to bet our lives on it?" asked Soleta.

He met her gaze without wavering. "Absolutely."

"All right. Arm weapons. Drop cloak. Prepare to fire."